Born in 1949, Sue was brought up by her grandmother, and educated at private school, where she was not outstanding. After studying business, she joined the Police, and served in many roles for 28 years. On retiring she went to agricultural college and now farms on the Yorkshire Dales. She keeps sheep, several cows, a variety of fowl, and has three dogs, Bentley, Froyle and Rosie, and four cats. She enjoys caving, wool craft and the outdoor life.

She has also worked as a railway station master, barmaid, chambermaid and shepherd since moving to Yorkshire.

THE
CELLAR PETS

Sue Woodcock

The Cellar Pets

Vanguard Press

A CIP catalogue record for this title is
available from the British Library
ISBN 1 843861 94 1

*Vanguard Press is an imprint of
Pegasus Elliot MacKenzie Publishers Ltd.*
www.pegasuspublishers.com

First Published in 2005

**Vanguard Press
Sheraton House Castle Park
Cambridge England**

Printed & Bound in Great Britain

Dedication

This book is dedicated to many friends, especially Wayne and Sue, who encouraged me, and to Miss Lambourne, my English Teacher at St. Swithun's School, Winchester, who not only taught me to love English, but to write it.

The Swallow Family

Mother   Mrs Esther Swallow. Neé Gough

Her children are:

Peter Swallow Married to Jane	Ingrid Heldman Married to Francis	Caleb (d)	Clive Swallow Married to Judith	Ruth Swallow

Children: **Children:**
Sharon   Alison
Alistair   Anthony
Alexander   Arthur

Great Aunt Susan (Holt) was a distant cousin. Jack Gough is brother of Esther and is the father of Anne who is married to Eric.

Mike Price – married to Marion and is a friend of Clive and Caleb.

The Porthwaite Estate

Jim Morpeth	farmer
Mary Morpeth	farmers wife – cook
Nora Morpeth	mother of Jim – Housekeeper
Sally Morpeth	Jim's daughter
Chris Morpeth	Jim's son, twin to
Tim Morpeth	Jim's son
Stuart Lloyd	head gardener
June Lloyd	his wife
Julian Lloyd	their son
Charlotte Lloyd	their daughter.
Bill	gardener
Liam	his nephew – gardener
Sam Armthwaite	handyman
Lucy Armthwaite	his wife – seamstress/nanny
Betty Nuttley	cleaner
Haley	her daughter – cleaner
Dot	cleaner, married to
Derek	farm worker
Wesley Carpenter	PA/Manager
Karen Cooper	secretary/farm secretary
Reg Hall	cowman
Brian Hall	his son
Maggie Hall	Reg's wife
The Rev. Arthur Pike	The local vicar at St Mary's.
Dr Patrick Tippett	GP
Mr Gregory McDuff	Legal friend
Tom Barker	Solicitor
Celia Johnson	his secretary
John Boyle	Tom Baker's junior partner

Albert Wynn	All partners of
Gerald Cummings	Wynn, Cummings and Porter -
Simon Porter	Land Agents

Nancy	Post lady
Erica Kitson	Local Police Commander
John Arrowsmith	Local Police Office
Jake Falls	Policeman

Mr Aaron Sandell	Shopkeeper – village store
Rachel Sandell	his daughter – assistant cook

Tanya Harbottle	Art expert

Other police officers:

Superintendent Dennis Carlton	
Dawn	
Geoff	
Mr Elgar	Chief Constable

'Toby' Jugg	Landlord of The Gargoyle Inn
Delilah Jugg	Landlady of The Gargoyle Inn

Garr Guardians:

Judith	Zood
Susan	Zan
Elsie	Zless
Agatha	Zagath
Charles	Narles

The Garr:

Goy	Gatherer Garr
Gleete	Gatherer Garr
Grreth	Warrior Garr
Glot	Digger Garr
Glyff	Maker Garr

Young Garr:

Glave
Galak
Glire
Gan
Gode
Glant

Animals:

Tiddles – a small tabby and white cat owned by Lucy.
Zan – an Irish Water Spaniel

Preface

Judith watched idly as the traffic whizzed by on the motorway. Clive was driving at a steady fifty miles an hour as they moved with a car full of luggage towards their new home. She felt rather excited, and longed for the journey to end. If someone had told her a year before that she would be starting a new life, in Yorkshire, in a rambling old mansion, with a husband she had met and married within six months, she would have laughed at them. Now she was married and was moving with him to the house left them by an eccentric old great aunt.

As they drove along, the hum of the traffic on the motorway made her drowsy and her mind drifted back to their wedding, some ten months before, where Great Aunt Susan had been talking to her. She had liked the old lady and had found her to have a sharp wit and a great sense of humour. They had talked about music, the family, and books, and most of all, about the Dales. At the time, Judith had felt that she was being 'vetted' for Clive, whom Great Aunt Susan obviously considered to be her favourite nephew. Judith was invited to stay with the old lady, which was a rare honour, if Clive's sister, Ingrid, was to be believed. Judith had promised to stay and while their affairs were being put in order, she had written often to her, promising to visit as soon as they could. The replies were scripted in a beautiful hand and were very witty and conversational. There were no indications in these letters that Great Aunt Susan was anything but alert and happy. She had written about having many friends, but had never named them.

Then Clive had received a telephone call to say the old lady had died in her sleep, aged ninety–three. Judith felt very guilty when she heard this, as she had wanted to visit and know the old lady better. Soon after, they had been notified by a solicitor that Great Aunt Susan had left everything to her and Clive.

Clive had nearly fallen off his chair when they had been told that they had been left the house, described as a mansion, and estate (not a car, as Judith had first thought), two large farms, and a great deal of money, stocks, shares, works of art; in fact everything. The whole inheritance amounted to a vast fortune.

Clive, who had farmed (amongst other things), abroad, decided to take up farming again and Judith decided to take on the role of a farmer's wife. She had sold her home in urban Hampshire, and finally, probate having been granted, they had come to the day of the move. What little furniture and effects they possessed had gone ahead with a removal firm the previous week and after a wonderful week in London, visiting friends, shows, shops, and museums, they had loaded up the car, and set off.

Judith could not remember being so happy. After her first marriage had broken up she had been used to living and coping alone. Her job had been her life for years and it was on a caving holiday abroad that she had met and fallen in love with Clive.

Chapter One

"Oh God!" gasped Clive. "There's going to be a crash!"

Judith watched in horror as a large articulated lorry in the centre lane on the other side of the motorway seemed to jackknife in slow motion, slewing across the flow of traffic, with the sound of screeching brakes. A loud crash was followed by the sound of others, and the lorry rolled over and over, with bits flying everywhere, heading straight for them. Clive reacted quickly, slamming on the 'crash flash' and braking steadily whilst heading for the hard shoulder, to get out of the way. The trailer of the lorry rolled towards them, sweeping up the red Mercedes in its path. Judith saw the Mercedes split open and as they came to a standstill at the side of the road, the trailer came at them from the front and right. With a ghastly bang her world went black.

Judith woke slowly and painfully, aware of much sound and many strange voices around her. There was an urgency in these voices. She couldn't move, except for her head and her left arm. A voice beside her said, "Don't move, please. Can you hear me?"

Judith thought about this and muttered, "Yes."

She tried to remember what had happened. Then something came back to her, and she was confused, because she could hear the sound of metal being cut. She looked to her right, slowly, and saw Clive, unmoving, and covered in blood, beside her, and she knew, instantly, horribly, that he was dead. She couldn't move and the pain was nauseating! There were people moving around her and she saw the mangled remains of their car. She could smell hot metal and there was a lot of dust and debris around. She saw a policeman walking in front of the car, and in his arms was the unconscious body of one of the children from the Mercedes. She could hear the annoying tick of the 'crash flash' still working in the car. She tried to reach out to touch Clive, but darkness and nausea swallowed her up.

The journey in the ambulance was a collection of people talking at her, and the sound of two–tone horns, as they sped along. She stayed still, not by choice, but of necessity. On the other side of the ambulance was the unconscious child. The paramedic was working on him, while the policeman was talking to her. She felt helpless, and very sick.

When they reached the hospital, a team of medics rushed to the ambulance and took the child away. Then it was her turn. Reassuring voices mixed with sounds from the next cubicle, which she knew meant that the child was in trouble. She still felt sick, and said so, and then, as she retched, everything went black again.

When she woke up, she was in a bed, obviously in hospital. A nurse smiled at her and said,

"Hello, at last, you've woken up, I'll get the charge nurse."

Judith stared at the ceiling and the curtains around the bed, and soon a young male nurse came in. He asked a lot of questions, and explained that she had a broken arm, broken leg, cracked ribs and concussion and cuts and bruises, and other injuries. He was just starting to say she would be all right, when she suddenly felt angry, not at him, but with the whole situation.

"Wait," she said, "I know, I must know, my husband's dead isn't he?"

The young man sighed, drew in his breath, and said, "We were not going to tell you just yet, but it is obviously vital for you to know. I'm sorry, yes, he died at the scene of the accident. I am so sorry."

"But it wasn't just him, was it? Did the little boy make it, the one from the other car, in the same ambulance with me?"

"I don't think you need to worry about that, do you? Not just now."

Judith felt really angry, and pleaded, "Please don't patronise me, I want to know everything. I need to know. It isn't just my life that's ruined, there must be other people involved. It is no good saying I will be all right, physically, maybe, but I hurt. I saw it happen, and could do nothing to stop it. Don't treat me like a child. Who can tell me? I might make sense of it, if I know."

She was getting panicky, and knew it could be heard in her voice. She stared at the young man, not trusting herself to say any more. She didn't want to be labelled as an 'emotional female'.

"OK," he said, "I'll get someone to come and talk to you as soon as I can. Do you mind telling the police what happened? "

"No," Judith said, and promptly burst into tears. The first nurse came back and sat with her for a while. When the first bout of tears was over, Judith asked where she was, and when they established that she knew she was in hospital, but wanted to know where the hospital was, the nurse laughed and explained that she was in Birmingham.

When she was calmer, Judith was able to sit up, have a wash, brush her hair and compose herself further. The policeman came in, sat down, and after he had taken full details of her and Clive, she was able to explain that she had herself been a police officer, so she knew what to expect. She asked, and was told, what she needed to know. The accident had caused the death of seven people, and the injury of three more, herself included. The family in the Mercedes had all died, as had the lorry driver and, later, in hospital, another driver who had been on the south–bound carriageway, plus Clive. She made her statement, managed to sign it, and the policeman left, promising to keep in touch.

Over the next few days Judith saw doctors, the police, and several other people who were concerned with her. Her worst interview was with Clive's mother, when they both broke down and cried. The inquests were opened and adjourned, and Judith was released from hospital to attend Clive's funeral. This was like a strange dream. He was buried next to his father, in the family grave in Somerset. The family were there in force, Ingrid and her stockbroker husband, with their three nauseous brats, squabbling and whingeing to get attention from their parents, Clive's younger sister, Ruth, and his older brother Peter, with his family of two good–looking boys, one at Sandhurst, in the army, and the other still doing 'A' levels at Winchester. Their sister was a stunning looking model, who had flown in that morning from Milan. Judith quite liked Peter's wife, a quiet, competent blonde called Jane, who stood no nonsense and didn't ask silly questions like "How are you feeling?"

Also present was Clive's Uncle Jack. He was a semi-retired solicitor, who dealt with all the family affairs, and always had done. Judith knew him from dealings they had had over the wedding, and he had drawn up, and arranged for them to make, their wills at that time. There had been a few bequests that Clive had made, but everything else went to her. Judith stayed at the family home on the Mendips for some time after the funeral. Uncle Jack lived nearby, and she visited him to sort out the legal matters. He had invited her for lunch, and instead of having it at his home, he took her to the local pub. He didn't, he explained, **do** cooking, and so they sat in a corner of The Ring of Bells, and over an excellent lunch, she learned that she was indeed a wealthy woman. All Great Aunt Susan's estate came, in its entirety, to her, plus Clive's own money. Jack put away the papers and looked directly at Judith. He said,

"Now that is the official paperwork out of the way. I need to talk to you about more important matters. I feel I should warn you about a few things, which you may not know. I don't know what Clive told you, but you have some enemies. I do not wish to alarm you, or seem disloyal, but there are rifts within the family, and you should be very careful of several of them. Would you like a brandy?"

Judith stared at him, and felt intense curiosity. "I think I might need one, thank you!"

She watched as he walked stiffly over to the bar, returning after speaking to the bar manager.

"They are bringing them over, but this is why I brought you here. Ruth and Peter often visit me, and I do not want them privy to what I need to say. I hate to admit it, but you have married into one hell of a family! How much do you know of Clive's younger years?"

"Not a lot, he said it was better forgotten, and I never pressed it, I thought he would tell me when he was ready. I know he adored his mother, but I feel he had little love for any of his siblings. He loathed Ingrid, I think, but he wouldn't say why."

"You're wrong there, he did love one of his siblings, his twin brother, Caleb. Caleb and Clive were inseparable for years. They went from Winchester to Cambridge together. They both joined the army, and Caleb was killed in the Falklands. He left everything to Clive, but the others tried to contest the will. Caleb had made his will just before going into action. Ingrid, or more accurately, her husband, tried to claim that they were owed a lot of money by Caleb. I never believed it, but the end result was that Clive, who didn't believe it either, said if that was how they felt, the rest of the family could go to hell and take Caleb's estate with them. Their father tried to intervene and ended up taking Ingrid's side. Clive never forgave him. That is why, when he left the army, he went abroad. It broke my sister's heart. Clive's mother is a fine woman and she missed him very much. She kept in touch with him and eventually he agreed to re-join the family. But I digress, I need to talk to you about now. Another brandy?"

Judith gratefully sipped the next brandy, and as soon as the bar man had gone out of earshot, she said,

"I never even knew he had a twin, were they identical?"

"No. They were very alike, but Caleb, who was the eldest, was taller and had fairer hair. I have never heard Clive speak of him since he left the army. I have photographs at home, I'll look them out for you. You have been left a lot of money and there is no doubt that the rest of the family want their share. They probably feel that you, as an outsider, are not entitled to it. I know Ingrid's husband tried to contest Susan's will, on the grounds that she was potty. I drew up that will, so I made sure it was bomb proof."

"Yes, everyone tells me she was potty, but I didn't get that impression. She seemed to be quite on the ball to me, I really liked her. She adored Clive. Why do they think she was potty?"

"She was not potty. She was an astute, canny old lady, who disliked the rest of the family as much as Clive did. Yes, she was pretty eccentric, and often talked to imaginary people, so it's said. I never heard her, and she only did it in her own home, but my dear brother-in-law, tried to have her committed. She never forgave him."

"Did she like you?"

"Yes, and I liked her, but I was too close to the rest of the family. She offered me a considerable sum when she made her last will, but I did not want it. I have enough for my needs, and she knew I would never move now. Anyway, I have a dicky heart, and won't be around long enough to do justice to seriously putting all that money to good use. I have had notice to quit, and have a couple of years at the most, so I am telling you all this now, as you need to know. I will not be around long enough to protect you, but I'll do what I can, and can put you in touch with a good man in Yorkshire, and I suggest you use him, trust no one else, especially from this family."

He paused to sip his glass of brandy. Judith looked into her brandy glass, as she thought all this through. She looked up to find him looking at her intently from under his white bushy eyebrows.

"Can I trust you?"

"Yes. I try to keep in with all the family, but I will not see any more damage done. I will do nothing to hurt you. I cannot live long enough, and I do not have the strength, either physically or mentally, to deal with family business much longer. My son-in-law, Eric, is taking over my practice, and I want to enjoy my retirement. He will do the family work. I suggest you have this man in Yorkshire, he's the son of an old school chum. I think you will like him."

Judith picked up the mint that came with some coffee, nibbled it, and shuffled back in her chair. Progress was slow with two plaster casts, sore ribs, and a crutch that kept escaping no matter how carefully she propped it up. She said,

"What can I expect the family to do then? Will it help if I make a settlement on each of them? From what you say, they will expect it. I don't want to seem mean."

Jack sipped his coffee, and then replied,

"That is up to you. I cannot see why you should, and whatever you give them, they will want more. What are you going to do, anyway, have you thought about it? You could sell up, move on to new life, there are no strings attached."

Judith shook her head,

"No, I've thought about that. Great Aunt Susan wanted us to live in the house, and I feel that is why she left it to us. I would like to honour her wishes. She loved the house. I see no reason why I cannot start my new life there. I've got to do something, have something to work towards, a goal. From what she said the place had got pretty run down, and needs some investment. I'll need a lot of help, but I've always loved the Dales, and nothing, especially after what you've said, holds me down here. She said she had a good farm manager, I'll try to work with him. Is it feasible?"

Jack nodded. "You have more guts than I thought. You'll have a fight on your hands if you do, but if that's what you want, I'll do what I can. I can see why Clive married you, and he would have approved. Are you really planning to live in that huge house on your own?"

"Why not? She managed it in her nineties, so I reckon I can. I need time to heal, mentally and physically, and somewhere to grieve on my own. At least I can try."

"True, but you know it is in a terrible state, parts have been shut up for a long time. She never managed to get any staff to live in, and had cleaners from the village. Good luck to you, it will be very lonely, very isolated. There is a farm close by, but not much before the village. Are you scared of being on your own?"

"I think I am more scared of not being on my own. I want to try and I'm going to give it my best. You will come and stay?"

Jack looked quite startled, and said, "Yes, I'd love to, at least I can escape this odious family for a while, but keep this to yourself"

She laughed and said, "Of course, and thank you for your kindness and your candid advice. You can come and visit whenever you like."

Jack helped her gather her bits together and hovered while she hobbled out to a waiting taxi.

"Come to the office later this week, we'll sort out the paperwork. Think what you want to do, say if you need money, and I'll get you an advance."

As he handed her crutch in to her in the back of the car he leaned in and said, "One other thing, I don't want to scare you, but it is a very strange house, odd things happen there. Don't expect it to be normal, it is a special place, but I cannot explain why. She loved it, others haven't!"

As Judith drove away she watched him heading back into the pub, looking as if he needed another drink. She was sure she did. She asked the driver,

"Are you in a hurry? I need to go somewhere quiet to think some things over, can you suggest somewhere?"

"Sure I can, Mrs Swallow, I know just the place. Clive loved it there, we used to play there as boys, me and Clive and Caleb, that is. We started caving there. I'm ever so sorry about Mr Clive, he was a good man, and a good mate. We'll go to Burrington Coombe, if you like. Sit by the Rock of Ages, it always helped him to think there."

Judith said, "You must be Mike, he spoke fondly of you, and you'd better call me Judith. You are just the man I need to talk to, I want to know all about Clive and Caleb, and about when you were boys together. You can probably help me with some other information too."

They drove off to chat at the cafe in Burrington Coombe, and then Mike helped her to buy some lovely plants as presents at the garden centre. When she returned to the house, Clive's mother was delighted with the gifts for the garden. If she thought that Judith had been away a long time, she never said so. Judith, grateful for her silence, went to her room to 'rest'. She had a lot of serious thinking to do.

By that evening, Judith had begun to formulate a plan. It was almost a relief to have something positive to think about. She knew she needed to be very careful, and probably rather clever. Well-meaning as Uncle Jack had been, she had to find out for herself. Mike had told her a lot of interesting things, and had tended to back up what she had been told. Her meeting with him had been fortuitous, as she could now introduce the subject of Caleb into the conversation. 'All in good time, don't rush things,' she told herself.

At dinner, where the whole family, except Jack, were round the huge dining–room table, she sat next to Eric, Jack's son-in-law. Conversation with him was hard going, and he was obviously friendly with Peter, and Ingrid's husband, Francis. She felt very much the outsider, everyone was being so polite to her. Jane chatted amiably about gardens and cookery. Ingrid looked, as usual, as though she had just been kitted out at a top fashion house. Ruth was chatting about horses, dressage and the costs of keeping several three–day eventers. Peter's boys said little, but did discuss computers and rugby. The model, Sharon, ate almost nothing, and said less. The three younger children were noisy. Judith sat listening to a family world, in which she felt a total stranger. After the dessert, she turned to Ingrid, and said,

"I wonder if I could ask a terrific favour of you? As you are probably aware, most of my clothes and bits and pieces were either sent up to Yorkshire, or lost in the crash. Would you have time to come with me to Bath and help me buy a suitable set of new clothes? You always look so chic, you must know all the best places"

Ingrid lit up. She turned towards Judith, and said,

"Oh, what a super idea, I'd love to. When shall we go?"

Judith tried to speak with the same enthusiasm,

"Well, whenever is convenient to you. At the moment I have no commitments. I'm a bit awkward, and I'll never have your figure, but I don't want to go on my own and my needs are rather pressing."

Ingrid snorted (in a lady like fashion) and simpered, "I had sort of noticed, but I didn't like to say. Let's go tomorrow, but how far can you walk? Parking is a problem."

"Actually, I hoped Mike could chauffeur us, and we could do lunch somewhere. Jane, are you free to join us as well? I could use your advice on some new stuff for a kitchen."

"I'd love to, it could be a fun day. Mum, can the kids stay here with you for the day?"

"Of course, dear, I'd love it. What a good idea, Judith. Bath is a good shopping centre."

"But we want to come too." Alison, Ingrid's daughter, piped up.

"Why can't we come?"

"Because," said Judith, before anyone else could join in, "I thought you wanted to go pony trekking at the local stables. You can all go if you want to. It would be really boring watching me trying to struggle into clothes. I take so long with these plaster casts."

"Great, we'd love to," gasped Anthony, "when do we leave?"

"You are booked in for 9.30, anyone who wants to go, that is."

Judith smiled at the assembled group. "Mum, can I get anything for you in town?"

Clive's mother said, "Yes, actually you can. Mike knows where to go. I've ordered something from the jewellers, which needs picking up."

Alison, hardly able to contain her excitement, turned to her brothers, Anthony and Arthur, and said,

"I'm so glad we've got a rich relative now, isn't life going to be fun!"

The silence that followed was quite imposing. The only person who was not embarrassed was Judith. Everybody began talking at once, some trying to apologise for Alison's gaff, others hissing covert threats to the child to apologise.

Judith said not to worry, and could she help with the washing up? She was, however, excused this on the grounds that she would probably break most of the china, due to her plaster cast.

The children were packed off to bed shortly after supper, the others adjourned to the living room, where the talk was mainly of clothes. Judith pleaded tiredness, and adjourned to her room.

Her plan was taking shape!

The following morning the young people were packed off to the stables, and Ruth elected to go with them to supervise. Judith managed to get into the front of Mike's car, and they drove into Bath. The first thing they did was to pick up the package from the jeweller, and then they hit the shops. Great fun was had on the escalator in one of the department stores, until a kind member of staff helped Judith with a trip in the lift. Judith bought all sorts of clothes on Ingrid's advice, thinking it highly unlikely she would ever wear them. Ingrid spotted a very expensive and stylish silk blouse. Judith saw her opportunity, and suggested that it would suit Ingrid much better. They agreed on this, but Ingrid said it was too expensive. Judith said it was the least she could do, and bought it, and a suit to go with it, and a lot of other clothes for her and Jane. The staff at all the shops were very helpful, not surprisingly, considering what Judith was spending. The assorted items, including some very expensive saucepans, a set of china, and numerous other items, were packed off for delivery.

Judith took the opportunity of asking for advice from her two companions about presents for everyone. This caused much discussion, but whatever was suggested was purchased to prevent any argument. Ingrid, having lost her inhibitions, wanted the most expensive things for her children, Jane was more reserved. They compiled a list over a cappuccino, and all the items were packed off. Judith bought Uncle Jack a case of the best malt whiskey she could find, knowing he would appreciate it. Eric needed a lawn mower, so that was acquired. Eric's wife, Ann, posed a problem for a while, but eventually a suitable gift was found. Nobody was forgotten, but Ingrid was quite shocked that Judith suggested a present for Mike.

"He isn't even a member of the family," she complained. "Why give him anything at all?"

"Oh, Ingrid, he was a good friend to Clive and Caleb," said Jane, obviously trying to placate her. "If Judith wants to, I think it is a good idea."

"I think it is a waste of good money, but if you want to." Ingrid was gazing at an expensive but quite stunning dress. Judith pretended not to see, and suggested lunch.

The restaurant was very expensive, very exclusive, and served minute portions of highly decorated food. Jane confided in Judith that she would rather have a decent meal, and they agreed to raid the cream teas later. Judith rather liked Jane, and after ordering, asked,

"Tell me about Caleb. He was Clive's twin wasn't he? What was he like?"

"Arrogant, very arrogant. He never had any time for anyone but Clive. I always suspected he was potentially gay. He was totally irresponsible with money. Francis said he couldn't understand how he had so much by the time he was killed. That was awful. Clive wouldn't listen to anyone, and went off in a huff. When they were little, they would never play with us girls and we never got a look in. I know you liked him, Jane, but even though he was my brother, I didn't. Yes, you can look daggers at me, but she did ask. Look, Judith, I'm sorry if this upsets you, but I'm not going to lie. Mum adored the twins, but Daddy understood. Caleb reminded me of Beau Geste."

Jane said, "He wasn't gay, I can assure you. Let's talk about something else."

Lunch was completed while they discussed their purchases. Over coffee, Jane said,

"What do you intend to do, Judith, have you thought about it at all?"

Ingrid turned excitedly, and commented, "Well, you certainly can't live with Mum, can you?"

Judith decided to lay (some) of her cards on the table,

"No, and I don't intend to. You have all been very kind. As soon as I am fit enough, I shall be moving up to Yorkshire, where Clive and I intended to live. I shall be out of your hair soon, and I want to run the estate up there."

"You cannot be serious, you will never be able to live there, anyway, of course you must sell that old mausoleum. It should fetch a lot of money. You could buy quite a nice place near here. You could get to know all of us better."

"I could, but I am not going to. I will be going to Yorkshire, and I will see how things work out when I get there. You can always come and stay with me. I gather the house is plenty big enough."

Jane stirred some sugar into her coffee and said,

"I think Ingrid had hoped that she and Francis would have that house. She remembers it fondly from a time they went to stay there as children. I've never been there so I shall take up your offer and visit. It sounds a fascinating place. Peter says the house has driven everybody who lived there slightly mad. Are you sure you want to take it on?"

Judith laughed, "I shall be quite at home there then, and yes, I think I do. It could be a super place for summer holidays, I should imagine. Nothing is set in stone yet, and I'll have to get a lot of things sorted before I move in. Now, let's spend some more of my money, and see just how much we can get into the car on the way home."

With much manoeuvring and dropping of shopping bags they sallied forth, to totally astonish yet more shop assistants.

Mike picked them up as the shops closed. He looked vaguely startled at the volume of shopping they had with them, but they arrived home in time for supper. A splendid day had been had, and pleading truthfully this time, near exhaustion, Judith went up to bed.

The next day she went to see Uncle Jack and arranged for some generous settlements on everyone. He told her she was being too generous, but took the details, and arranged for the paperwork to be completed. Jack handed her a large envelope with some photographs in it. They pored over these while he explained who was in them. He apologised that the best one of Clive was missing. Clive's mother had asked for it, and he had no other copy. After another pub lunch, she kissed him fondly and rang Mike on his mobile, to pick her up.

When she got back to the house, the presents had been delivered, and were distributed to squeals of excitement from the children and a fashion show from Ingrid. Everyone seemed delighted and then Clive's mother gave Judith a present. It was the parcel from the jewellers, which turned out to be a lovely, plain, but classy, silver photo frame, containing the missing picture from Uncle Jack's set. Judith burst into tears to see Clive's face looking out at her. Her present to Clive's mother had been on similar lines, a photo album, and in it she had included a photo of the twins in their army uniform. This set them both off and they had to have several cups of tea to recover.

Clive's mother, alone with Judith, put her hand on Judith's arm, and said, "Please, dear, don't let the others influence you. Do what you want to do. My son loved you very much, and he told me of his plans for your life together. He would have wanted you to be happy, to go your own way. You can stay here as long as you want, but have you considered what you really want?"

"Yes, Mum, I think I have, and it is for me as much as for Clive, you, and even Great Aunt Susan. I am going to take on the house in Yorkshire. I have the money to restore it, and I need to build a new life now, to have a purpose in life, do you understand?"

"Of course, and I wish you luck. The others are not very happy about the idea, and I think some of them are jealous. You are richer than I ever thought possible, and while the others are quite comfortable, as I am, they see your wealth, and want it. I am ashamed sometimes, but we have had enough of rifts in the family."

"I'll try not to cause any more rifts, and I will get out of your way soon. If I can help, you will ask, won't you?"

"Thank you, dear, I will. Just be happy, for me, and for Clive."

They sat and talked, mainly about Clive and Caleb as children. Then there was supper to prepare, and the evening wore on. Judith retired quite late, and slept fitfully.

The next day she needed to attend hospital in Bristol and returned in the late afternoon. She sat in the sunshine in the garden, writing letters.

Francis came to talk to her. He tried to tell her she was being foolish to take on the Yorkshire house, and offered her advice on how to sell it. He had, it seemed, a friend who was an estate agent, and could get a good price for her. He also offered to invest any money for her, to see she was comfortable. She thanked him sweetly, and said she would think about it. He got up, and she imagined she saw him slithering off towards the back door.

Halfway through the next letter, Peter came to talk to her. He was similarly full of good advice, which mainly seemed to consist of encouraging her to sell everything, and he offered to help her do so. There was a nice house for sale in their village, quite close to them, that he considered would be ideal for her. Jane liked her, he confided, and she could help her get to know the local people. Visions of Jam and Jerusalem flitted through Judith's mind, as she listened to the seemingly well–meant homily Peter was expounding.

Having said his say, he walked off towards the kitchen.

She was just finishing the next letter, when Ruth came out with a pot of tea. As they sat in the sunshine, she blurted out,

"Judith, would you help me? I really am in trouble, I basically cannot afford the mortgage on my house, I've had so many expenses recently, and I dare not tell Mummy. I am sure I am going to get promoted soon, in the publishing firm where I work, but I am at my wit's end. I know it is a cheek, but you have so much money, could you lend me enough to tide me over?"

Judith was rather taken aback. She knew Ruth kept several horses, and had quite a decent job. She also knew Ruth had a 'boy friend' who was a gambler. At least she was honest enough to ask straight out. What did alarm Judith was the way Ruth burst into tears. They hardly knew each other. Was this how it was going to be? A constant string of cadging? She needed to be very careful.

"Ruth, I'll have to think about it. Things are not settled yet. I don't even know exactly how I stand," she lied glibly, "Can you leave this with me and I'll let you know within a few days? How much do you need?"

Ruth immediately took this as a 'Yes', and said, "Five thousand should see me right, but six would sort out one or two other bills as well. Thank you so much!" She bounced off like a rabbit with St Vitus' Dance, round to the front of the house.

Judith finished her tea, and just as she resumed her letter writing, Sharon came out of the back door. She sat down by Judith, very elegantly, and said,

"Are you OK?"

"I'm not sure, why?"

"It's all right, I am not on the cadge! I just want your advice. I hate this modelling. It is so artificial. I cannot eat anything I like, I'm always tired, hungry, and it is very difficult to stay away from the drug scene. I want to get out but Mummy is so proud of me, so is Daddy. How can I tell them I want to do something else?"

"What do you want to do, Sharon?"

"You will think I'm crackers, I want to be a police officer. You were one, were you not?"

"Yes, and I do think you need to think carefully. How can I help?"

"Tell me what it is really like."

During the next hour Judith found Sharon to be an intelligent, sincere girl, who was direct, and a refreshing change. Not once did she ask for money, and Judith really liked her. Nor did Sharon say anything bad about any of the rest of the family. She advised Sharon as best she could, and determined to help her if she could. Sharon gracefully thanked her, and offered to post any letters before she went out for the evening.

To her great surprise, it was Eric who turned up next. He only, he assured her, wanted to guide her away from any hasty decisions. He did not believe she understood the implications of taking on a large estate, and she could safely trust him, or even Francis, to handle her money. With such a large amount of money, it would be best if she invested the capital, and had an allowance, to make life easier for her. Of course, she would want to buy a house nearby, he knew of a suitable one. It was obvious that Jack had not confided in him. Judith was furious, and could hardly hold back her temper. She smiled sweetly at him, thanked him, and said she would think about it. As soon as the patronising jerk had retreated to the house for a sherry, she gave up the idea of letter writing and reached for her mobile and made a couple of telephone calls.

Ingrid turned up next, and with a sugary smile, suggested that Judith should give her the Yorkshire house, and intimated that she would be doing Judith a big favour by taking it off her hands. Judith, with an equally sickly smile, said she did not think the suggestion was a proper one, and that she hadn't made her mind up.

Armed with a gin and tonic, Ingrid pretended the whole thing was a joke, and went into the sitting room.

Judith went to bed.

The next day was the penultimate one before the inquest in Birmingham. She had arranged for Mike to drive her up to Birmingham early next morning. She packed her few clothes and belongings, and by midmorning was with Uncle Jack, signing up the bequests. She made a few amendments, and set a few enquiries in action. By the end of the morning she felt that she had 'done the right thing' by her in-laws, and asked Jack to tell the family the following day, when she wasn't there, what she had done. He was delighted with the whiskey, and told her off for her generosity. Mike turned up for her at lunch time, and she asked if he could take her somewhere quiet for lunch. She wanted to talk to him, too, and he said he knew just the place.

To her total bewilderment, they drew up outside a house on a council estate in Radstock. He helped her out of the car, and inside, where he introduced her to his wife. The children, he explained, were at school. His wife, Marion, was a cheerful, welcoming, practical woman, and laid on a simple but good pasta dish, followed by a cheese cake. Judith reached into her bag and pulled out a small package. She handed it to Mike, and said,

"I really did not know what to get you. I wanted you to have something of Clive's, and this was the only thing I thought you might like. It is a bit dented, but it was always with him."

Mike slowly unwrapped the package. Inside was a beautiful old Hunter pocket watch. It was engraved C. S. Swallow, with a date in the early 60s. Mike gasped when he saw a further engraving, 'M.T. Price - a faithful friend', with the year engraved below.

He almost whispered, "But this was Caleb's, then, when he was killed, Clive never let it out of his sight. It was the most precious thing he had."

Judith said, "I hope you are not offended, I thought it should come to you."

"No, Judith, I am not offended, I shall treasure it. Thank you."

They began chatting on more mundane matters. She was told that Marion and Mike had always wanted to run a pub, and Mike said it had been his dream to own a Free House.

Judith came back to the house about three o'clock, and went to see Clive's mother. She explained that she would not be returning after the inquest, and thanked her for her kindness. She said that she would be returning to hospital and then staying with friends in Hampshire for a couple of weeks, and handed over the telephone number and address of where she could be contacted.

She extended an invitation to Clive's mother to visit her whenever she wanted, and to call on her, if she could help.

Mike was ready to pick her up early the next morning. She said her goodbyes to Clive's mother, and to Sharon, who were the only ones who were up, and thankfully began to relax as they drove away.

Judith promised herself she would never stay there again. She chuckled to herself, when she realised she didn't have to. She wondered how they would react when Jack told them what she had done. Now she had to concentrate on getting the inquest over, getting well, and then, in front of her was this amazing challenge. One she almost relished, and one she was determined to master!

Chapter Two

Wisteria House,
Hinton Mendip,
Nr. Bristol

My dear Judith,

I hope the inquest went smoothly. I understand the verdict was, as expected, death by misadventure. I hope you were not too distressed by it. I enclose some documents and copies for you, and your new will, which you should get signed as soon as you can. The details of my friend, the solicitor Tom Barker, are enclosed.

I hope also that your stay in Hampshire did you good. Are you out of plaster yet? How are your injuries healing? The insurance company shouldn't take too long to settle now the verdict is in.

When are you moving up to Yorkshire? I need to know, so I can keep in touch, and send you any more documents. I will also keep you informed about developments here.

I have written to the Morpeths (the farm manager and his family). They should have a few days' notice, as they want to get the house at least partially habitable for you. Mrs Morpeth is a lovely lady. I used to stay with them sometimes. Let me know and I'll pave the way for you.

My word, did you stir up a hornet's nest? I have not enjoyed myself so much for a long time! I took the easy way out, and let them all believe that this was all your idea, and I was only acting on your instructions!

The day you left, I got everyone to come and see me at the office. Mike too.

They just fitted in the conference room. I even wasted some of that good whiskey, while they all assembled. Francis likes whiskey and hit it rather hard, and that was before we got started!

To make life easier, I had prepared it all in a written document, which I enclose, and told the lot of them to shut up, until I had read it.

When I had finished there was a stunned silence, and

then Peter and Francis began stuttering, and spluttering, Ingrid had some quite spectacular hysterics, Jane began to laugh, her boys were dumb struck. Sharon (you are right about her, she's the best of the bunch) cried with relief and Eric and Ann were really quiet. I was sure they had expected nothing. My sister was quite composed and I think not too surprised. Mike liked his gift very much, and he and Marion asked me to say they will be writing as soon as you are settled up north.

They have all agreed to your conditions, of course, because they are mostly too greedy to let anything go. Ingrid is now spitting tin tacks, and Ruth is none to pleased that you didn't fall for her little scam. She cannot complain, however, as you have been very generous with everyone. Francis is cross that you will not be using his stockbroking services, and assures me that you are heading for a fall. I neglected to tell him, however, that you have some background in business management, which I hope you will find enough to get you through!

I enclose various letters of thanks, appreciation, sickly insincere good wishes, etc. etc. which will probably amuse you. I know you well enough to see that you will read between the lines.

Sharon wants to talk to you, she wouldn't say why. Can you ring her soon?

As I said, keep in touch, and I will fix things this end if I can. The Ring of Bells has happy hour soon, so I must close now.

With fondest regards to my fellow conspirator,

Jack Gough.

==========

Document prepared on instruction of Judith Swallow, formerly Bates, nee Murphy.

Following the death of Clive Stanley Swallow, and upon the settlement of his estate the following are offered as gifts to members of his family, and friends. These gifts are offered on the understanding that if they are accepted, then the recipients will enter into a contract which will be legally binding, and that they will make no further claim on the estate of Clive Swallow, Susan Holt, or Judith Swallow. Neither will they seek any further gifts or settlements unless invited to do so.

Following conversations with Mrs Judith Swallow, you will all be aware, at least in part, of the reasons for these gifts. Mrs Swallow is aware that most of you were disappointed when you were not included in bequests from Clive Swallow, and from Susan Holt. Judith Swallow also wishes it to be known that there are no bequests to anyone named, in her current will.

It is partly in appreciation of kindness shown to her and her husband, that she is making settlements at this time. It is also in appreciation of previous friendships to Clive and Caleb Swallow.

This may be considered as a final and permanent settlement. Mrs Swallow expresses a wish to keep in touch with anyone wishing to do so, but will not impose herself again on the generosity of her mother-in-law, Mrs Esther Swallow, to whom she is profoundly indebted.

To Mrs. Esther Swallow improvements	£10,000 for garden
For a cruise or holiday.	£15,000
To Mrs Ingrid Heldman	£50,000
To Francis Heldman	£5,000

To Alison Rachel Heldman}
To Anthony Saul Heldman}
To Arthur Karl Heldman}   £5,000
each, for an educational trip, or adventure or outdoor holiday, which shall be taken before the age of 21 is reached, and shall be approved by Jack Gough or his appointed trustee. These monies are to be used for no other purpose. If not used, the monies shall be donated to the NSPCC.

To Peter Swallow   £10,000

To Jane Swallow   £20,000

To Sharon Swallow   £85,000
to be gifted to her, with interest, for the purchase of, or
deposit on, a residential property, in Britain, of her choosing,
providing she is in regular employment in one of the following
professions: Police, Armed Forces, Fire Brigade, Nursing or
Medicine, Ambulance, Legal profession or as shall be agreed
between Mrs Judith Swallow and Jack Gough or his appointed
successor).

To Alexander Swallow   £10,000

To Alistair Swallow   £10,000

To Eric Stanley   £2,500

To Anne Stanley   £2,500

To Ruth Swallow   £22,457
on the express condition that it is used for the full settlement
of her outstanding mortgage loan, and she agrees not to re-
mortgage the property.

To Jack Gough
Sufficient funds to cover expenses and professional fees for the
administration of such trusts.

To Michael Price
The vintage Rolls Royce, previously owned by Clive Swallow,
and £30,000, for the setting up of a quality limousine hire
company, or for such use as he feels appropriate.

****

The Laurels,
Midsummer Upton,
Somerset.

My dear Judith,

Thank you so much for your generous gifts. I hope to have a
new kitchen fitted with my bit. The boys are still undecided
between a sports car each, or some foreign trip. Hawaii was
the last destination, but they will probably listen to Peter and
save it for something special.

I was totally confused and bewildered about your gift to
Sharon. I just did not comprehend it. I asked Jack to explain,
and was quite offended when he suggested I talk to her. I did.
I had no idea she had felt so pressured, I honestly believed she
liked modelling! Peter is furious that she wants to do
something more mundane. Thank you for listening to Sharon.
She is still set on the police, much to Peter's disgust, but she
has yet to get in. If that is what she wants to do, I will support
her. She tells me that she believes the money is for a house, so
she can work in any area she chooses. I see your reasoning. I
was upset at your interference at first, but I now see it as a
blessing. Can I still come and stay sometime?

Let me know how you are, and keep in touch.

Your affectionate sister,

Jane Swallow.

****

The Old Stables,
Nr. Glastonbury.

Dear Judith,

I don't quite know how you found out what my mortgage
settlement figure was, but I should thank you for your
generosity. I don't feel very grateful though, because it means
you caught me out in a bit of a fib. I'm sorry about that. It
wasn't to pay my mortgage that I asked you for money, it was
to pay off another couple of debts. Please do not tell anyone
what I did. I can pay them back now, in instalments, as I do

not have to pay the mortgage every month. Were you trying to humiliate me, making sure I couldn't use the house to raise more money? I suppose I asked for it.

I hope you are happy with all your money. I could have had some lovely horses with some of it. I could even have given up work.

Thanks for the gifts, I hope they don't make you feel guilty.

Yours,
Ruth.

****

Country Health Club,
Malvern

Dear Uncle Jack,

Thank you for your wonderful letter, and for all the sterling work you have done, and are continuing to do. I hope I haven't asked too much of you, and your heart is holding up.

I have signed the will and had it witnessed here in Malvern, and I enclose a copy for you. If anyone wants to see it by all means show it to them, but let me know who does see it.

Yes, the inquest was pretty awful, but much as I expected. After it, I spent some time with a good friend in Hampshire. I went back to Birmingham, and to the hospital, where I had two operations on the leg, and then the plaster finally came off, and I am now at a convalescent centre, suffering physiotherapy, counselling, and sympathy for another month or so. The ribs seem OK now, and the arm is stiff and painful, but working and on the mend. It seems that I will always have a bad limp, which may get less pronounced as the leg strengthens. I will be able to do most things, but long distance running, and ice skating or skiing seem to be inadvisable, at least for a year or two!

They have offered me corrective surgery on the facial scars, but at my age, I think I can live with them. I never was much of a beauty! My hair has really started going grey, something triggered by trauma, apparently. I see the specialist next week, for the insurance claim.

I had a very interesting chat with the specialist at the hospital. I didn't tell anyone, but I lost the baby Clive and I were expecting, in the crash. This was harder than anything. The insurance chap says it will make a lot of difference. Suddenly everyone seems to be thrusting money at me! Like I need it now! Please keep the bit about the baby to yourself. It would have been a boy, but I wasn't that far into the pregnancy, so at my age, nothing was certain. Clive had wanted to call it either Jack (after you) or Susan. It looks like I'll never have children now.

Enough despondency, and I need to think positively. My plans are a bit vague, but go something like this:-

I am buying a cheap car, for the moment. I'll hang on here for two weeks, then I will need a month, probably with a great friend down near Fishguard. On the way back, I'll spend some time with some friends in Libanus, near Brecon, and after that, I shall be heading up to Yorkshire. I will ring Mrs Morpeth two or three days before, so she can get in some fresh food for me.

Thanks for sorting the banks out for me, and for forwarding the cheque books etc.

I have sent a load of stuff up to the Morpeths already, to store until I get there. They sound really nice people.

I rang Sharon, and we had a long chat. She will want to talk to you, let me know what she decides.

Looking at the whole case of documents you sent, am I right in thinking I actually own a pub in Applebeck, which I think is the local village to the house? I gather a manager is in it now. Can you forward anything more you have on it? At some time in the future, I might have a plan for it.

I was a bit startled to see all those mining shares that Clive had. I had no idea he had anything but a passing interest, but it seems I was wrong. He did talk about managing a mine, I didn't realise it was his own mine!

I enclose details of where I will be, you can always reach me on the mobile.

Keep fit and happy,

Love,

Judith.

****

Judith,

Thank you for the money. You can spare it, I suppose. I had hoped you were going to come and live down here, and you could have made a good investment in Francis' business. He could do with a bit of help at the moment.

I will give you due warning, you won't be happy in Yorkshire. I expect you think that Clive's luck will rub off on you. For you, I hope it does. That house is weird, don't let it get to you.

I hope the clothes are suitable, you know, you should really stick to 'cool' colours if you can. Try and get plastic surgery on those scars on your face. It will make you feel a lot better.

The children are delighted with the trips. Alison wants to go skiing, Anthony wants to start scuba diving, and Arthur has his heart set on an Outdoor Adventure holiday or, later, an Outward Bound Course.

I hope I don't sound too ungrateful, everything has been a bit stressful recently. I know you mean to help. Thank you. Do let us know how things progress. Francis says his offer is still open. Ingrid.

****

Country Health Club
Malvern

Dear Mr Cummings,

As you are aware, my proposed occupation of Porthwaite Hall has had to be delayed after the death of my husband, Clive Swallow. The accident in which he was killed has left me with injuries that will take some time to heal, and matters that need to be sorted out. It is my intention to take up residence there as soon as I can.

I am unable to find amongst Clive's papers any accounts for the Porthwaite Estate, which I know your firm has been running since Miss Holt's death. I know he spoke to you about the estate, and you kindly advised him of the current situation, but I would be most grateful if you could arrange for a summary of the financial state to be sent to me here, where I will be for at least two weeks.

I would also be grateful for a full description of all the land and buildings on the estate. I have copies of the wills, but these do not really give me a full picture of what to expect.

Could you also arrange, please, for the utilities to be reconnected to all the properties, if they have been disconnected. Although it is summer, I do not want the houses getting damp or cold, and would like everything in working order when I arrive. I am sure I will have enough to do, without anything like that.

Yours faithfully,

Judith Swallow

****

Wynn, Cummings & Porter
Land Agents.
The Chambers,
Clipping Court
Harrogate.

Dear Mrs Swallow,

Thank you for your letter. I am so sorry about your husband's death. This must be a difficult time for you, and I would advise you not to burden yourself with too much at the moment. I did suggest to Mr Swallow that the Porthwaite Estate was far too much to take on, and that he should consider selling all or part of it, as most of it is very run down, and the farms are not very profitable. There is some income from parts of the estate, but I can, if you so direct, seek a buyer.

The house itself has a bad reputation, and is a huge old house, not suitable for a single person's occupation, as I tried to tell Miss Holt. She was not, in her latter years, really able to comprehend the complexities of running such a large estate, and I was able to assist her by taking on the day to day matters.

I have arranged for the caretaker, Mrs Morpeth, to check the house and the other buildings, and she will arrange for the premises to be checked for damp as you requested.

If you do decide to visit the house, I am sure you will find that you will not want to live there. I will be delighted to meet you there, and I will bring you all the books and documentation, which is quite considerable, and far too bulky to post, when you arrive.

As you are a recently widowed woman, I would strongly advocate you to reconsider your plans, and not to entomb yourself in a house that can be most depressing and will require considerable investment, beyond most peoples' means, to bring up to standard.

I look forward to meeting you, and remain your humble servant,

Gerald Cummings.

****

Country Health Club,
Malvern.

Dear Mr Cummings,

Thank you for your letter, and for your obvious concern for my welfare. I will consider your kind advice, but I do plan to live at Porthwaite Hall. If the documentation is so weighty as to be impracticable to post, could you arrange to have it delivered to the house, so I can look at it upon my arrival. My instructions for the time being are :-

Nothing is to be sold or disposed of, and the houses and buildings are to be maintained in good condition.

The two farms should be maintained, and all staff kept on until I can decide what to do about them.

Please do what you can to maintain the gardens and grounds in a neat condition. Employ contractors, if necessary.

Keep me informed of any actions taken. I will let you know when I intend to take up residence, and I would ask for a set of keys to the house to be forwarded to me as soon as you can, as I may arrive late, and do not wish to upset the Morpeths by knocking them up late at night.

Please inform any employees of the situation, and assure them that I will discuss anything involving them, with them before coming to any decision.

Yours faithfully,

Judith Swallow.

Chapter Three

The car tyres made a scrunching noise as Judith pulled up outside the house. She looked at her watch, and saw it was just after five o'clock. 'Good timing,' she muttered to herself, as she climbed stiffly from the car and stretched. She reached into the glove compartment, and took out the huge old key she had been sent. She limped to the front door, but wasn't surprised to find the door unlocked. She had been expected, as she had rung the night before and asked if someone could light a fire and get in a few essentials. The door creaked stiffly as she pushed it open, and she went inside into the gloomy panelled hall. A deep crimson carpet on the stone–flagged hall floor looked warm, if a little shabby. There were fresh flowers in a hideous vase on the trolley in the hall. The room was sombre, but warm enough. It was a huge hall. Judith called out,

"Hello, anybody about?"

Somewhere upstairs there was a loud bang. Children ran across the landing above her as they came charging to greet her. They came down the stairs two, or was it three? at a time and skidded to a halt on the rug. They grinned a little sheepishly and took stock of Judith. From above, a more measured step could be heard.

Judith looked at the two children in front of her. She saw boys of about eight years old, twins apparently, wearing jumpers and jeans and with trainers on their feet. The laces were undone, and one boy had his toe sticking through the left shoe. His socks were lime green. The boys were different, she decided, one was a little taller and the shorter one had curly hair. They were both redheads, freckled, with brilliant blue eyes. They were looking her up and down and she was amused that they looked quite crestfallen.

"I'm Judith Swallow," she said, "and you must be Mr Morpeth's sons. Nice to meet you."

She held out her hand to shake hands. As if a spell had been broken, the taller boy stepped forward, shook the proffered hand and stepped back, saying,

"I'm Tim Morpeth, and this is my brother Chris."

Chris stepped forward and shook hands and retreated beside his brother. Chris said,

"Mum's coming down, she's getting a room sorted for you, you're early."

"Yes," said Judith, "I know. The roads were quite quiet."

Chris went to the door and peered out, came back and whispered to Tim.

"Is there a problem?" enquired Judith.

"Sorry about that," said Tim. "It's just we were expecting you to have a BMW, at least, you are rich aren't you?"

Chris said, "Is that all you have, a tatty old Astra?"

Judith laughed, "At the moment, yes, our other car was written off in the accident."

As she spoke a pang of grief grasped her like a steel band round her throat, and she knew that tears had sprung to her eyes, and she fought back the inclination to cry. The feeling seemed to echo around her in a silent scream. Depression, tiredness, and pain hit her like a knock–out punch. She felt herself sag. She was aware then of a wave of sympathy sweeping towards her from somewhere. She looked around. The two boys were looking at her rather awkwardly. The sympathy did not seem to come from them. Tim shuffled his feet, and cleared his throat. Judith took a deep breath and managed a wry smile,

"Sorry, the other car was a Granada."

Chris came closer to her and looked up at her. "You'll need more than an Astra for round here, you know. Dad says you must have a four–wheel drive for around a farm, and for our winters."

"Will I? Well, you had better come with me to choose one, if you like?"

The boys faces lit up, "Really? Can we? Dad will have to come too, 'cos he knows about these things."

"I'm sure we can fix that fairly soon."

Judith smiled again and she and the boys moved to the foot of the stairs, where a woman in her thirties was standing on the second step up. She was wearing a track suit and was holding a box of cleaning items.

"Mrs Swallow, welcome. How was your journey? I'm Mary Morpeth, Jim's wife. You are earlier than we expected."

"My journey was uneventful, if a bit tedious, but I am here now. Thank you so much for what you have done."

They shook hands.

"Please, call me Judith."

Tim spluttered, "She's going to let us come with her to get a car, Mum!"

Chris, with a very winning smile, added, "You couldn't get a Ferrari as well, could you?"

"I take it the twins have introduced themselves," laughed Mary and put the box down on a table. "Do you want a cup of tea first, or get your things in? When all the other things came, some months ago, we didn't like to unpack anything, so we stored it in a couple of rooms. You'll need a hand with it all." It almost sounded like a question.

"Let's get the car cleared first, then have a cuppa," Judith decided. She turned and limped towards the door, and Mary saw her walking stick for the first time. She gasped, and said,

"Oh, I'm so sorry, I didn't realise you were still suffering. Boys, you go and unload the car, and put it all in the hall here. You bring it in, I'll move it from here, and don't break anything, please!"

Judith tossed the car keys to Tim and the boys disappeared. Mary said,

"You must be exhausted, you sit down and I'll move it."

"I've been sat down for ages, I'm just a bit stiff, that's all."

Bit by bit the car was emptied, and the pile on the floor grew. When the car had been locked, Judith said,

"Show me the kitchen, and let's have that cuppa."

"We've a proper tea ready at our house, down the path. Would you eat with us? Then you can talk to Jim, and we'll all come back and help. You can stop the night at our place tonight, if you'd rather, and begin here in daylight."

She stopped speaking abruptly, as if she had just been about to say something awful.

Judith turned to Mary and said,

"I'd love the tea and to meet you all, but I won't impose myself on you for the night, I'll come back later, kip down, and start in the morning."

"But I haven't made a bed up yet, I only managed to air the room, and put a bit of heating on. There are blankets to air yet."

"It's all right, I've got a sleeping bag with me, I'll use that for a night or two, I'm fairly used to roughing it. I didn't expect even a bed, so no need to worry. How far is your place?"

"Not too far, if you can manage the path, it's about five minutes."

"I'll take a little longer I expect, I still need the stick. Bear with me, I'll get there."

Mary called to the boys,

"Come on lads, back home for tea. It's scones, jam and a cooked tea, go on ahead and warn the others, and call your Dad in from the top field. It'll be dark soon anyway. Tell Sally to get the tea mashed, and tell Gran we're coming. Mrs Swallow cannot hurry."

"Judith, please. Do I need to lock the door? I doubt it."

"No, not round here, no one would dream of coming in here uninvited, not if they're from round here, anyway, and we don't get strangers."

"Why, is it haunted, or something? Does Great Aunt Susan stalk the house, repelling boarders with ghostly moans and clanking chains? That I would like to see. I would quite like to be haunted by her, we got on very well!"

"No, not exactly, I mean, of course not, but no one will come in, I can promise you!"

Judith looked sharply at Mary, but was met with a direct stare, which told her nothing.

The boys scampered down the gravel drive and ran off up a side path. Judith walked slowly and rather painfully after the boys, Mary at her side. She stopped to rest by the side path and turned to look back at the house.

"It is much larger than I thought, I think I'll get lost in there without a map. Thank you for the lovely flowers, are they from your garden?"

"No," laughed Mary, "they are from yours! You have a huge garden, mostly overgrown, but there are still some good bits in it. I hope you like gardening."

"I had never even thought about the garden, I must admit. I suppose the grass is nine foot high, and there are brambles everywhere, and the place is overrun with foxes or worse. Maybe you could put me in touch with a couple of gardeners?"

"I am sure Jim will know of someone. We turn right here, how good are you on steps? There are a few down to the farm garth. Look, would it be easier if I fetched the car?"

"Actually, I need the exercise. I'm getting stronger, and I must keep going. Just say where to go. If I fall flat on my face, and I probably will, you can help pick me up. I hate being lame, but I am assured it will get better. When I am accused of being drunk, at least I'll have an excuse! Now, are these the steps?"

"Well, some of them. Did this happen in the accident? I am so sorry about Mr Clive. We all are. You'll let us know if we can help, please?"

"Yes, thank you, indeed I will. I think I need to do this bit on my bum, could you take the stick?"

Halfway down the steps, Judith got the giggles, which soon spread to Mary, and by the time they reached the farmhouse door, they were laughing heartily, and any reserve between them had gone, along with any dignity on Judith's part.

They entered the porch together, and Judith looked at the collection of wellington boots, dog leads, coats, the odd bucket and bailer twine. There was a skateboard, and a single roller skate in the corner. The door led into a large kitchen. It was warm, bright, and cheerful. An older woman was removing something from an Aga oven, and a pretty, redheaded girl of teenage years was by the sink. The boys were laying the table with abnormal care. The kitchen smelled of new baking and was spotlessly clean.

An old dresser was by one wall, with a Coleport dinner service displayed. Mary introduced her mother-in-law, Mrs Nora Morpeth, a wiry, middle-aged lady, with hard-worked hands, and a charisma that shone out. She had black hair, going a little grey, in a very long plait, and pale grey eyes, with smile lines, and a fantastic complexion. She wiped her hands on her pinafore, and came over and shook hands.

"Welcome to Caulders Farm, Mrs Swallow. May I take your stick? Do sit down. I'm glad you have finally come."

Judith was not sorry to sit down, and relinquished her stick. She pushed her chair round, and smiled at the girl, who came to her and said,

"I'm Sally, and how should I address you?"

"I would like everyone to call me Judith. Could I wash my hands? I fell over in the mud just now, and Mary kindly helped me up, but I managed to put my hands in something, I'm not sure I want to know what it was, but it looks a bit cowish."

The boys sniggered.

She was helped to the sink, and washed her hands and face, and was handed a towel. She sat down again in the chair, while huge piles of food appeared in front of her. The boys were banished to the bathroom to wash, and Judith asked if she could do anything to help.

"Not at the moment, thank you, you are a guest. Jim will be in soon and we can get started."

Nora paused after putting a laden plate on the table, and Judith asked,

"How old are the boys, about eight?"

Sally interrupted,

"They were eight last week, but the way they go on, you wouldn't think so sometimes."

Nora snorted with exasperation, "It's not so long since you were as bad, Miss High and Mighty!"

Sally smiled,

"I'm almost twice their age, I've grown up a lot."

"She's fifteen on Christmas Day, and starting to be quite useful around the place now," said Mary.

They all paused as the door opened and a tall thin man entered, and hung up his coat by the door. He took his boots off, and padded in hand-knitted socks across the floor to the sink, where he washed his hands and face. He dried them on the towel and strode across to Judith, holding out his hand. She stood up and grasped his hand.

"Welcome to Yorkshire. Welcome to this house, Mrs Swallow, may I call you Judith?"

His handshake was firm, and his manner reserved. She looked up into bright blue eyes, set in a long face covered in freckles and topped with short ginger hair. He had worry lines in his weathered face and there was the residue of a slight frown.

"Judith is going to buy a four–wheel drive, and we can help her chose it!"

Tim was jumping up and down and Chris was tugging hard at his father's jumper. With a sigh of reservation, Jim Morpeth turned and quietly spoke.

"All right, calm down, let's eat, and talk about it after tea."

Judith sat next to Nora, and when they were seated, Jim turned, and asked,

"We always say grace before a meal in this house. Judith, would you care to thank the Lord for us?"

Judith was not surprised. Jack had told her that the Morpeths were upstanding folk, strong in the local church. She nodded, waited for silence, and calmly said,

"For the gift of food and friendship, we thank you Lord, please guide us in the future, and care for all we love. Amen."

This seemed to meet with approval, and soon the food was dished out and the meal was underway. Several times the twins were told not to talk with their mouths full, and when the eating was done, the dishes were cleared from the table and loaded into the rather old dishwasher.

Sally went out to the barn and the boys were sent off to do chores. The four adults sat round the table with a pot of tea. After politely asking after Judith's health and the journey, Jim got up and left the room, returning with a number of ledgers, which he placed on the table within Judith's reach.

"You'll be wanting to look at the books, I expect. It's been a middling year. No doubt you will be wanting to make some improvements when you take over. There has not been a lot of money for them of late." He sounded tired, and as he sat down he seemed to slump.

Judith was horrified. She sat back in her chair, and looked at him. She knew she would have to tackle farm accounts at sometime, but hadn't expected it this soon, or so directly. She also knew that the Morpeths were totally honest, hard workers, who had been on the farm for years. She wondered what they had been told, and by whom.

Suddenly, she realised they were frightened of her, and of losing their home. Someone had been making mischief, and she vowed to find out who and why.

"I think there has been a misunderstanding. I don't know what you have been told, but I don't want to take over the farm at all. I wouldn't know what to do! I had hoped you were happy as manager and would agree to stay on. Yes, I'd like to be involved, but I was hoping to be involved in a less directorial sort of way. Please, you are willing to stay, aren't you?"

There was real desperation in her voice.

The others were exchanging glances, and Nora had a 'I told you so' look on her face. Mary sat staring at a point about a metre above the window, and Jim looked confused. The atmosphere was very tense.

"Oh," sighed Mary, "We thought we were going to have to leave when you came. We understood you would be getting a new manager and putting the two farms together. We thought you would be getting rid of us. Is that not the case?"

Jim got up and stared out of the window. His knuckles were white as he gripped the edge of the sink. The silence was very awkward. Judith was puzzled and tried to explain.

"You were manager for Aunt Susan, were you not? She was happy with you and trusted you. Why on earth would I want to change that? I know things have got very run down in the latter years, and she was very old, but I had hoped we could sort things out. Please, don't tell me you have had a better offer."

Jim turned back to the table. His piercing stare did not leave her face for more than three minutes. He seemed to be searching her very soul. At last he sat down and the tension eased.

"Yes, I managed for your aunt, and my father before me, God rest their souls. No, I have not had a better offer. I dreaded your coming, because I thought you would ask us to leave the only home I have ever known. Please, please, be honest with us. Don't string us along until you find some fancy chap who will take over the farms. Do you really mean what you say? Are we safe here, is my job safe? I've lived with this worry for months now, we all have. We were told you would come for a while, and then sell up, the whole estate, and we would be out on our ear."

Judith stared him out, and as he looked away, she said,

"Listen to me. I do not know who told you that, and I mean to find out. What I will tell you is that I mean to stay here. You are, and will be, in charge of both farms, and you and your family have a home here for as long as you want it. I'll make a legal document saying all that, if you want me to. Until I can sort it, you'll have to accept my word. I need you to help me get this whole place back the way it should be. I need all of you, Please, say something!"

Nora started to cry, a whimpering snuffle, and Mary kept saying, "Thank God". Jim got up again and walked slowly around the room several times.

He sat down, got up, had another tour of the room, fiddled with a tin opener, and came back and sat down. He held his hand out to Judith, and for the first time, smiled at her and spoke at last.

"I want no legal document, your word is good enough for me. I believe you, and I am sorry for doubting you. Mr Clive would never have married someone who wasn't straight, and the old lady liked you. I should have known, and trusted them. You'll do. You have brought us great happiness tonight, and I thank you. You are truly welcome here."

"Oh, give over, Jim, let her take her breath, and give her hand back. She don't want her arm pumped like that, she's not long out of hospital, put her down!" Nora was pulling at her son's jumper, as he hugged Judith.

Mary joined in and dragged Jim away and then hugged him herself. Nora put her head between her hands, shook her head, and then rushed into an adjoining room, where she could be heard clinking bottles.

Judith sat down and watched their joy. Nora returned with glasses and bottles, and to Judith's relief, a couple of ash trays. She offered a cigarette to Judith and one to Mary. Jim took a baccy pouch out and lit his pipe. They all sat down, and smiled, and grinned, and smiled. They all looked rather ridiculous, and no one was able to finish a sentence for several minutes.

Nora got up and picked up a needlework bag from the sideboard. She looked at Judith, and asked,

"Do you mind if I knit, I'm trying to finish a jumper for Sally. I always knit to calm me down, silly, isn't it?"

"Go ahead, I knit too, when I can. Look, maybe I should go. I think you need time for yourselves. Maybe we can discuss things in the morning?"

"Oh no, you don't, you stay and celebrate with us. You are, after all, the reason for our celebration. God has been very good to us today. I always said Miss Susan would know. Mr Gough said you were sound too. Look, pet, don't talk about all this now, we can sort out the nuts and bolts tomorrow, you are tired, and you've had a long drive."

Jim, now rather more composed, reached for a glass and asked,

"We seldom drink alcohol in this house, and all we can offer is whiskey or ale. We are not very sophisticated, I'm afraid, probably not what you are used to. Will you take a drink with us?"

Judith smiled at him and confided,

"I would love an ale, thank you, please. I'm no sophisticate! I don't enjoy a posh life style, and would rather have beer than champagne, and be in the company of honest folk."

She accepted the beer, and Jim poured himself one, and Nora and

Mary a whiskey each. As they raised their glasses, Sally came into the room. She stared in astonishment at her father, and said,

"Are we celebrating? Can I have one? Great, I'll have a double whiskey."

Jim laughed, wagged his finger, and commented,

"You know better than that, no, or the twins will want one. Try beer or lemonade."

Sally opted for beer. A little later Chris came in, and then Tim. They were allowed a very weak shandy each. Soon after, Judith asked Nora where the loo was and Nora showed her to a downstairs toilet. When she emerged, Nora was waiting for her. She was ushered into a small sitting room, and Nora peered into Judith's face and confided,

"There is much you do not, and could not know, about this place. You may not find it suits you, and no one would blame you, if you change your mind. Now is not the time to talk. Stop with us tonight, and we will go up to the big house tomorrow, when it's light. Don't go there and sleep alone in the house, it has been empty some time, such a big place. Jim can fetch anything you want. I've a bed here."

"You are kind, thank you, but I would really prefer to be in the house. I'm not worried by strange houses, and I am used to roughing it a bit. I need to be on my own sometimes, you know, so I can have a good cry, without embarrassing myself, or anyone else. I shan't take much rocking. It has been a long day. I need to make some phone calls, and have some food to put away."

Judith thought she had dealt with that rather well. She liked these people, but she wanted to do some thinking, and she remembered a good bottle of Bordeaux in her bag. She was also longing to have a quick look round and get an early night. It seemed she had a lot of sorting out to do the next day. Her leg was aching and she wanted to be on her own.

Nora patted her hand. "I understand, I think. I knew Miss Susan real well. She liked her own space too. She liked you, and that counts with me. We'll get together after milking tomorrow, we'll come up to the house. I'll show you round, you'll get lost on your own. If you change your mind, drive round, the door won't be locked. Old houses have strange ways, funny noises you know. It's just an old house."

Judith grinned, and commented, "I doubt if even the ghosts could bother me tonight, but thank you for the offer."

Nora made a sort of "Hrump" noise, and they went back into the kitchen. Judith had her glass refilled and sat for a while, not saying much, but watching the others enjoying their rare celebration. Jim suddenly remembered he had to feed the dogs and left the room. When he returned, Judith asked if someone could walk with her back to the house, as she had no torch, and needed to be shown where the kitchen, bathroom and a bedroom were.

This prompted an animated debate, while everyone discussed how she could get back without knowing the path and being lame. Judith, by this time having got to the door, spotted a quad bike parked outside.

"Can you give me a lift on the quad, it might solve the problem? How far is it round by the drives?"

Jim seemed a little shocked, and looked at the muddy condition of the quad, and then at Judith. "If you don't mind, but it don't seem none too fitting, though! It's not far, and it is no problem to get the car."

"I would love it, the quad will suit me fine. I really don't do posh, and it would be quicker."

The boys offered lots of advice, as she climbed onto the back of the quad, and Mary handed her her stick and shoulder bag.

"I'll meet you up there," she cried, as the engine roared into life, and Jim carefully rode off. Judith rather enjoyed the short ride and as the quad drew up by the front door, Mary could be seen, with her torch, coming round the corner. Mary opened the front door and put on the hall light, while Jim helped Judith off the bike. Armed with her stick and bag, they went inside, and Mary moved off to the back of the hall to open a door and put on more lights. Jim saw a bag of shopping, picked it up, and headed after her, while Judith sorted a sleeping bag, an overnight case and a few other smaller bags, into a pile at the bottom of the impressively wide stairs.

Fitted to the stairs was an electric chair lift, which she was examining, when Jim came back. He came over and showed her how it worked, and then asked what else needed to go into the kitchen. Looking at the pile, Judith decided there was quite a lot, and she picked up a bag, and he grabbed several, and she followed him down a long corridor to the back of the house. They passed several large oak doors, on both sides of the corridor, and went into a huge old–fashioned kitchen, with a large central table, a huge Aga oven, and an electric cooker. It was well lit, and Mary was busy unpacking on the table, putting some perishable items in a huge fridge. They all unpacked for a while and Jim went back into the hall to fetch the last box of food. Mary picked up pasta and rice, and led Judith to a door, which when opened, led to a long shelved larder, with it's own light, and a lot of built–in, old–fashioned meat safes. She opened one of these and put the pasta and rice into it.

"Anything not tinned is best put in these," she explained, "I put tins and jars on the shelves," and proceeded to fetch coffee and tins and put them on the shelf.

Judith stood and looked at the larder. Mary went back to the hall for more bags, while Judith saw the array of goods on the shelves. The arrangements just seemed odd to her. When Mary returned, she found Judith looking under the shelves and meat safes, and said,

"Have you dropped something?"

"No, but I was wondering how whatever it is that gets in here to raid the food, does get in. I am sure I heard a rustle behind the wall. Is there a rat problem, or mice? If there is, then they are bloody big ones. It's like Fort Knox in here."

Mary shrugged her shoulders, and answered,

"Not that I know of, it has been like this for years. I never thought about it, to tell you the truth. The other pantry just has shelves."

She opened another door, on the opposite side of the kitchen, which had another walk–in pantry behind it. This, too, was lined with sturdy shelves, which were laden with dishes, plates, bowls, pots and pans, and from the upper shelves hung ladles and spoons. There was even a large tray of cutlery, and a large knife block with some lethal–looking kitchen knives in it. There was an array of chopping, pastry and cheese boards. On another shelf were patty pans, baking tins, cake tins, and some implements Judith did not recognise. Some looked like they were borrowed from a mediaeval torture chamber. She shivered, and felt as though she was being watched.

Back in the kitchen, she espied an electric kettle, which she filled and switched on. There was instant coffee in a jar, and some cheerful mugs on a mug tree. A drawer revealed some teaspoons. A biscuit barrel had been filled, and as she looked, she found some cheap glasses in a cupboard.

Mary came in with Jim, with the last of the food and kitchen packets.

"Mary, thank you so much for getting so much in for me. I must pay you back, did you keep the receipts?"

"They are in the top drawer over there, but there is no rush."

Jim, sorting through a box, carefully took a tray of eggs, and put them in the fridge.

"You don't need to be buying too many of these, we have plenty of free range, farm laid ones."

"Oh good," confided Judith, "I didn't actually buy them. My friends insisted on giving me half this, because they didn't know what I was coming to. I couldn't offend them by not taking it. I much prefer farm eggs."

"I've taken the liberty of taking your other bags upstairs for you. Mary will show you the bedroom and bathroom that you might like to stay in, at least until you know the house. It's the warmest room on the first floor, and next to the bathroom."

"Thanks Jim, you have all been wonderful. I don't propose to do anything but make a few phone calls, and hit the sack. Do you want a cuppa, or a drink? The kettle has boiled. Where is the phone, and is it connected yet? It should be, I arranged for it to be put on last week."

"Yes. I checked it this morning, it is on. There are several extensions around the house, one in the hall, one in the kitchen, one in your bedroom, and several others. Oh, and I put a TV in the bedroom. It is not a large one, I got it from one of the other guest rooms. Most rooms have an aerial."

Mary paused, and took a deep breath, and then came out with,

"Look, why not come back with us? I hate to think of you all alone in this huge place, not knowing where you are. Are you sure you'll be all right? Our number is by the phone in your room, if you want us for anything."

She almost seemed to be pleading. Certainly she was worried. Judith imagined a flood of large rats flowing from the pantry, in waves up the stairs. She pulled herself up short, and decided she was more tired than she realised.

"Thank you, but no, I've been looking forward to being here. If I'm going to live here, I don't want to start off by sleeping somewhere else the first night. I'll be all right, and **if** I need you, I promise to ring. What time will you be round in the morning? I'll do breakfast. I can at least have coffee ready, and some toast or something. Now, if you show me upstairs, I promise not to go on a midnight prowl and get lost. I couldn't if I wanted to. I am just too tired. I am sure that by the time I've got to bed, I won't even hear the creaking boards, the funny noises old houses produce, or even a chorus of ancient ghosts singing Faust, so stop worrying about me!"

Mary, pouring a cup of coffee, handed her the cup, gave one to Jim, and took one from the side, and they walked to the hall. Judith reluctantly sat in the chair with her cup on her lap, and rode in majestic splendour to the first floor landing. The others joined her and indicated a door on her immediate left. This led into a warm medium–sized room, with a double bed, and a single divan. It was quite modern, and well–carpeted, with a gas coal–effect fire. Judith's things were placed neatly on the double bed. There were flowers in a delicate vase and some fresh towels on a chest of drawers. Mary went to a door at the far end of the room, opened it, and turned the light on in a large bathroom. There was a shower, toilet, and in the centre of the room a huge cast iron bath, standing in isolated splendour on a raised platform. There was lino on the floor, and a howling draught whipping through the room, between the window and the door into the landing.

Judith returned to the bedroom, located the telephone and the hand

53

control set for the television. Mary helped her sort some things into a chest of drawers and disappeared, returning with some blankets, pillows, and pillowcases. Leaving the lights on, they returned downstairs. Jim and Mary seemed reluctant to leave, but finally, having promised to return about nine, they clambered onto the quad, and drove off down the drive.

Judith shut the front door, went to the kitchen, made a sandwich, put it on a plate, found a bottle opener, opened the wine, and with that and a glass, all placed on an elegant tray, took it to the hall. She returned to the kitchen, switched off the lights, and as she closed the door, imagined she heard a distinct rustling from the pantry area. She ignored it, and placing herself regally in the elevating throne, rode upstairs. She decided the chair lift was rather fun!

She took the tray into the bedroom, used the bathroom, but decided to stay dirty for the night. She shut the connecting door, arranged her sleeping bag on the divan with the blankets and pillows, went to the windows, and opened them slightly. She stared out of the window but could see little. There was no light pollution, in fact there was no light. The air was fresh and she felt quite calm. She listened to the noises of the night and decided all was normal. It was just silly to listen, she decided, for noises she could not identify. She drank the coffee and opened the wine and poured a glass out. She telephoned several people and then ate the sandwich. She climbed into her pyjamas, got into the sleeping bag, and took some pills. She switched on the television and watched the news. She sipped the wine, set the alarm clock, became very sleepy, turned the telly off, and fell profoundly, asleep.

The strident bleeping of the alarm woke her and she fought her way out of the sleeping bag and pushed the button down. The light was streaming in through the windows and there were birds singing cheerfully outside the house. She lay listening to their song for a few minutes and then padded into the bathroom. She had an invigorating hot shower, and back in the bedroom, found some casual clothes. In the bottom of the case she saw her photo of Clive, in the silver frame, and put it on the dressing table.

Once dressed, she gathered the bottle of wine, and the dirty crocks, and put them on the tray, and got downstairs with everything still intact. The house seemed much lighter and more cheerful in full daylight. She did not investigate any doors, and went into the kitchen, and switched on the kettle. She found a cork, with which she resealed the wine, and hunted for a toaster, but had to settle for doing some toast on the Aga. After another mug of coffee, she hunted out an old saucer as an ashtray and went back to the hall and sat on the step outside the

54

front door. The drive was long and rather grand. The garden was very overgrown and there were some fine trees at the back of the jungle of a lawn. The birds were really noisy and she spotted a rookery in the trees.

She had a quiet smoke, and a think, and then returned to the kitchen for another coffee, leaving the front door open. She was delighted to find a dishwasher in the kitchen, and began loading it. She found everything she needed for breakfast and got things started. She fetched some real coffee from the pantry, set a percolator going and contented herself with generally tidying up.

Just after nine she heard a shout, and as she went towards the hall, the Morpeths came down the passage to meet her. They all assembled round the kitchen table and Mary explained that the three children had already left for school. Jim was deciding between chocolate spread or marmalade and Nora was eyeing some croissants with deep suspicion, when Judith said,

"I do hope I'm not taking up your valuable time, when you need to be doing something else. I admit, I desperately need your help. Are the cows milked? Do you have to rush off soon? I don't know how you are fixed. Have you the time to show me round?"

"The farm is quite quiet, at the moment, and I don't have to do anything much until about three o'clock. I have arranged for someone else to sort them today and tomorrow, so my time is yours. Are you aware that Mary has been paid for looking after the house since Miss Susan died, and indeed worked here before then? You are paying us anyway, but even if you were not, we'd still like to help."

Nora added, "Actually, I used to work here at the house, too. When Miss Susan died, they said I wasn't needed, so they laid me off. I was rather hoping you would be wanting a bit of help, a housekeeper or something, and I would like to apply for the job. I know this house, as we all do. Are you looking for some help?"

Judith chuckled, and replied. "Yes, of course I am. I am going to need lots. Would you consider yourselves employed, for as many hours as you want? Look, I have been very good, and I haven't been, or looked, into any other rooms, since you left last night, and the suspense is killing me. Please, please, would you show me round?"

She picked up her stick, and stood up. "Where shall we start, the front door?"

"Fine," said Jim. They went to the front door, and began by coming in from there, and opening a door on the right, leading into a reception room, papered in a Chinese style blue paper, and furnished in exotic eastern fashion. On an ornate chest of drawers were some fine Satsuma pieces. There was a silk wall hanging on one wall, and a huge brass dragon on a circular table. An antique Mah Jong set was on an occasional table, and there were several chairs and a sofa.

She had a quick look at some of the pieces of china and at the condition of the furniture, and looked at the beautiful Chinese carpet on the floor. The windows were large, and had elegant silk curtains held back with ornate silk cords.

"This would be the Chinese Room, then?"

Nora agreed, "It's always been known as the Chinese Drawing Room. There is a bedroom upstairs, also done in the same style. It is a pleasant room, especially for tea, or for reading. I think it used to be used as a reception for guests. Come through to the main drawing room."

She moved on to open a double set of doors on the far side of the room, and they entered a huge, elegant room, with three windows to the front of the house, the centre one of which was a set of French windows, opening onto steps leading to the drive. A huge fireplace was set into the far wall, and the whole room was furnished with comfortable, if solid, old English furniture, sofas, easy chairs, some footstools, and some exquisite tables. The fireplace was surrounded with a flooring of Carrara marble, which extended up to the fireplace itself. The whole room looked like a hotel reception area, and was well decorated. The velvet curtains, in a light grey, had some fading, but were in good condition. Above the fireplace was a large oil painting, of somewhere in the Dales. Judith found it rather odd, slightly disturbing, and, she admitted to herself, badly painted.

The floor was covered with a good Axminster carpet, a little worn in places, but partially covered by some rich rugs. Either side of the fireplace were solid pieces of oak furniture, a sideboard, and a substantial table. There was some excellent Crown Derby displayed, and some blue and white plates on display.

The fire irons were unusual. Large, and obviously rather old, they seemed to have strange monsters on the tops. The creatures portrayed looked like sinuous gargoyles, and each one was slightly different. Judith picked up the poker, and looked at it.

"These are unusual, are they very old?"

Jim picked up the tongs, and looked at the grotesque creature.

"Yes, I believe so. They used to fascinate me, as a child. This got broken once, and the local blacksmith wouldn't touch it. It had to be sent off somewhere else to be repaired. There are several sets around the house, they are very unusual. I've never seen anything like them anywhere else. It seems to be a theme around the house, have a look at this chess set over here."

He went to a table in the corner of the room, and showed her a magnificent chess set with more of the grotesque figures. Strangely, the pawns were people. Judith felt a reluctance to touch them.

The doors at the back of the room were opened into a huge, empty room, with light oak panelling. A wooden, boarded floor was highly polished, and there was a dais half way down. Nora explained,

"This was the ball room. I remember wonderful parties held in here. It hasn't been used for years. There is some furniture somewhere, stored away. I think it is big enough for a badminton court. The fireplace there takes almost a whole tree! It can get very cold in here in the winter. Come through here, there are doors into the conservatory."

She unlocked some doors, and they walked into a long, and large, conservatory, furnished with cane chairs and furniture, where a large vine grew up the glass. There were a number of small trees, some bearing oranges and lemons, along the walls, and some old magazines on a chest. The room stretched to the front of the house, and another set of doors brought them back into the drawing room.

Back in the ball room, they went left, through another door, into an elegant dining–room, with a large, long table and a lot of chairs. Glass fronted cabinets stored a huge dinner service, and the room was lit through windows at the rear of the house. Another fireplace had a set of fire irons like the ones in the drawing room. The mantelpiece held a large Ormolu clock.

Next to the dining room, at the back of the house, was a smaller room, with less expensive furniture, some chairs and a large table. This was piled with boxes and tea chests. Around the room were more boxes and packages. Judith realised her goods were stored in here. Two doors led off, one into a passage leading back to the ballroom, and which connected to a door into the kitchen passage. The other door led to a small room, with a small fire place, an easy chair, and a large wine rack, still rather full. There were no windows in the room, but it was well lit.

"The butler's pantry, I believe." said Jim. "Warm, but rather dismal. Through here leads back to the kitchen corridor."

Back in the hall corridor, two other doors revealed a large cupboard, and a downstairs cloakroom and toilet.

Back in the kitchen, Mary made tea and coffee, and they munched on some biscuits, and a very light sponge cake that Nora had contributed.

Having refreshed themselves, they went back to the hall, and this time went through a door on the left, into an untidy, modern sitting room. A large television was in one corner. The curtains on the window were in a burnt orange shade of a woven wool material, and were falling apart. The carpet, a darker shade of orange, was threadbare.

There was a book shelf, some easy chairs, and a lot of boxes. A large fireplace had modern fire irons, and the whole room looked very run–down, but lived–in. They went into the next room, which was poorly furnished, and contained some more of Judith's boxes. This room had a window, and some French windows onto yet another terrace at the side of the house. They continued towards the back of the house, into another room, again with French windows leading onto the terrace, but this room was very modern. Leather furniture, and a very expensive stereo system with eight speakers, a grand piano, music stands, and cupboards full of sheet music, denoted this as 'The Music Room'. The walls were sound–proofed, and insulated. A cello was propped in the corner, and a flute was in a box on the piano. The pictures were of composers or of musical themes.

The next room, at the back of the house, was a library. It, too, had French windows leading onto the patio. Lined with books, it had stout leather Chesterfield furniture, and a huge writing desk. Several leather–topped tables were placed around, with hard–looking chairs, and each table had its own table lamp. The room was neat but very dusty. The fireplace, again with the same weird irons, was empty. Mary seemed very apologetic

"I am afraid that I couldn't keep everywhere clean, not for the hours they wanted me to work. I haven't had a chance to get in here yet."

"Don't worry, how could you do it all? Just how many hours were you expected to do?"

Mary explained, "Ten hours a week, just to keep the place from falling apart!"

Judith exclaimed, "That is ridiculous. I think you put in a lot more hours than that. I promise that will get sorted very soon."

Behind the library was a junk room. That was the only way to describe it. There was some old furniture, some of Judith's boxes, and a number of built–in cupboards, most of which contained a strange collection of items, ranging from old toys, to some flower pots, seed packets, and old magazines, mixed with old standard and table lamps, and an old trouser press. Seed catalogues cascaded from one cupboard, and a massive collection of paper bags, and Christmas decorations from another. There were four doors, two locked. Jim went to one and said,

"This leads down to the cellars. It is like a basement down there, different rooms right under the house. I doubt if anyone has been down there for years. There must be at least half a century of junk down there."

"Did you ever play there as children?" Mary asked.

"No," he replied, "It was always kept locked. The few times I went down, it was cold and rather spooky. I never felt comfy there. It is dry, well, was when I went down there last. Some guests thought they heard noises and insisted Miss Susan got it checked out. There was no one down there. It was probably a bird or something. Miss Susan said to leave it locked. Do you want to go down there now?"

Mary and Nora both said they would rather not, and Judith remembered she had a lot more to see above ground and decided to leave it until another day. Another door led to a flight of stairs.

It was lunch time, so, at Mary's suggestion, they went into the kitchen, which led off the Lost It Room, as it was known.

Some pizza and salad were found, and the pizza cooked in the microwave. As they sat round, Judith said,

"I know that all the estate affairs are run by a local man, Gerald Cummings. Is it him who has been telling you these fairy tales and cutting your hours? What is this man like?"

Jim, who was chasing a long string of cheese, finished his mouthful, and said,

"It is difficult to say. Yes, he told us you would be selling, and he dealt with all the probate people. I think he thought he was saving you money, and he wanted the whole place closed up. He is really in charge of all the estate, including the farms. He's no farmer certainly, and all the time, he's after saving money. He took over the business about ten years ago, he's not local, comes from south of London somewhere. He's a cold fish, got no sense of humour at all. I asked him for another tractor last year, and he got me, eventually, a second hand eastern block thing, that is about as useful as the old Ford it replaced. He wouldn't pay for a lambing assistant either, said I didn't need one, not even a student, and so the whole family had to help. We saved quite a few, but with a thousand ewes, and the cows, it was hard going. Actually, Sally is getting a bit useful with the sheep now, so it could have been worse, but the mean bugger wouldn't pay us an extra penny, said it was all part of the job. Can't say I care much for him."

Mary added, "Yes, it was him cut my hours, said he'd cleared it with the new owners, and told us we might have to leave when you came. He gave the impression you wouldn't be taking the place on, and it was going to be sold. Said that Mum wasn't needed either, and even though she's worked here, girl and woman, on and off, all her life, he said she didn't qualify for redundancy, neither. Maybe that's why we were a bit stand-offish. He's always been quite proper, you know, civil, but I don't care for him. I suppose he's good at his job. Actually, he gives me the creeps, him and his cronies. They go up the country club a lot, and his wife is a stuck-up bitch. Keeps trying to tell us locals how to live, how to decorate the church, and all that. You know, she even tried to tell old Mrs Thistlethwaite, down in the village, that her diet was all wrong, and she needed to have all these health foods. Mrs Thistlethwaite is eighty two, and grows all her own veg still. Sylvia Cummings will be visiting you the first chance she gets, and will want to know all your business, and then she'll tell all her offcumden cronies. You be careful of her and her chums, Judith. She has too much money and nothing to do with it. Of course, I shouldn't be telling you your business, it's not my place, but you need to know about the likes of them."

Nora, listening carefully, chimed in with her bit, "I cannot say I disagree. I don't like either of them, but I've no reason to say they have ever done anything improper. Come to think of it, she's got some of her fancy horses on the low paddock, at the moment."

"Yes," added Jim, "and churning up the grass. It is well poached, and will need some fixing before it will be good grazing again. They said it wasn't part of the farm, that it belonged to the house, and the grass needed eating down."

"What a pity they didn't want to keep the rest of the grass in the gardens down as well," Judith commented as she gazed at a veritable jungle outside the window. "I need to sort all this mess out. I'll make a few phone calls on Monday, and I think they, or him, can come and see me. I'm not used to having money, but one thing I have found is, when you have it, people jump hoops to get on your side. You have been kind and helpful, and I think we will work well together. I'll tell you my plans, such as they are, for the near future."

She sat at the table and lit a cigarette and offered them around. Jim asked if he could light his pipe, and she told him "Of course, you do not need to ask."

"What I had hoped to do was to get the estate running as it should be. From what you say the farm needs investment, and I certainly need some help here. Jim, do you know of anyone nearby that will be able to take on the gardening, someone full–time, and probably an assistant as well? I have not seen much of it, but what I have seen, needs sorting, now. Find out what they want, either hourly, or monthly, and we'll fix up a meeting. I would like you there. Nora, would you want a housekeeper's post? It wouldn't be just you, do you know anyone from round here that will come in and clean? Think on it, and let me know. Mary, any hours you want to do, you say. I know, with a young family, you may not want to do too much. How many people work on the farms, Jim? Do you need any more help?"

Jim drew slowly on his pipe, "You are talking big money here, have you any idea how much we would need to get things back as they should be?"

"Jim, I think you should know that in addition to Aunt Susan's wealth, which was staggering, Clive was weathier. He owned several mines, just to mention some of it. I have the money to do this. I don't want to waste any, of course, but in my experience, if you are straight and pay a fair wage to the right person, you often get a fair deal back. Aunt Susan spoke well of you, and said she could trust you, so that's good enough for me."

They sat for half an hour, discussing the staffing possibilities. Judith, returning from the downstairs toilet, asked them,

"Do you think we can get the Chinese Drawing Room and the library smart enough for interviews by the middle of next week? I want to see this Mr Cummings, and I have other people to see as well."

Nora considered. "Yes, I think so. I know several people in the village who would be glad of the work, and there is a young couple, he was made redundant recently from a factory in Leeds. He was a handyman, gardener, and is a nice chap, you know, young Sam, Jim, would he be interested, do you think?"

As they discussed what needed doing, they made their way upstairs to the first floor. Judith managed the stairs unaided. There were a lot of rooms, and one with a bathroom en suite, at the front of the house. Judith chose this as her room, and assured Nora there was no hurry to get it sorted, as she was happy where she was for the time being. There was a large landing in the centre of the first floor, with a sunken floor, and the bedrooms all led off raised galleries. Two landing passages led from this area, one through a door onto a flight of back stairs, which connected with the Lost It Room downstairs. There were several bathrooms, some very antiquated, and up the back stairs were a series of small bedrooms and three larger rooms. Most of these were unfurnished. Up the stairs again, were the attic rooms, very dirty and unfurnished. There were some odd items lying around, and in two rooms the floorboards did not look, or feel, safe. At the rear of the house, a metal stairway led from a balcony, down to the ground floor, outside the house. The attic rooms all had access to the roof area, leading to this metal stairway.

At some time, an attempt had been made to turn this area into a roof garden. From the roof, Judith could see several outbuildings. Jim pointed out the stable block, the garages, a Folly, and a summer house. He also mentioned a potting shed, a garden shed, a greenhouse complex, a walled garden and orangery, and spoke of a ha ha. There were kitchen gardens, and several orchards.

Judith had seen two lodges by the main gates, and was told they were unoccupied, but with some work could be habitable.

It began to rain, and they went down the stairs. Nora, who had disappeared a little earlier with Mary, appeared after about twenty minutes, and asked Jim to assist with moving something. Judith, curious, followed, to find all her possessions had been moved into her chosen bedroom and Jim was fixing a television for her. The photo had been placed on the chest of drawers. Mary was lighting a fire, and Nora was carrying towels into the bathroom.

Judith thanked them, and saw the bed had been made up. She asked if they could help her in the next few days, and Nora explained that they could, but someone would have to stay at the farm to look after the children. Judith asked if the children would like to come to the house. Nora suggested they could be found plenty to do. At this, Jim mentioned that the school bus would be dropping them off soon, so Mary walked down the drive to meet them.

Back in the kitchen, a hurried tea was prepared. Nora smiled, and happily sang softly to herself, as she competently moved round the kitchen. Jim chuckled and confided,

"She is happy, she's got her job back! She loves this old house, and was heartbroken when she got laid off. She looked after Miss Susan in latter years, and was hoping to move into one of the lodges, but that man let them out as holiday lets this summer. He did the same with the Folly too, and one of the stable flats. You'll be getting a few callers now, the kids will have told of your arrival, so the curious will be round. I expect the first will be the doctor, then the vicar and his wife, nice folk, all of them, then Mr and Mrs Cummings, and a few of their friends, then, and only if the invitation is made, will the villagers come up. They'll be dying to see you, and hoping for work, but they are mostly too civil to rush you. It'll be a change for the kids to have one up on the others, and I'm sure they made the most of it. You will not have to introduce yourself, everyone will know you!"

"Can you extend that invitation for me, please, Jim? It's Friday today, can I invite you all down to the local pub, for a supper with me, tonight? If we go early, the children won't be too late. It will give the locals something to gawk at."

"What, the Ugly Imp? You probably own that. The food is quite good. Old Toby and his missus. would be real pleased. They have been waiting, like I have, to be put out of their home. It would put his mind at rest if he could know where he stands. They are not far off retirement, she's an excellent cook. Mr Cummings put the rent up last year. Miss Susan would have turned in her grave."

"Is it really called the Ugly Imp?"

"No, its real name is The Gargoyle. It is almost as old as this house."

"I think I prefer The Ugly Imp. It's a very strange name for a pub. Why is its called that?"

"Some old legend of the demons from hell, spawning from the earth in these parts, but no one knows for sure."

The children could be heard running down the drive, and soon burst into the kitchen. The boys were marched off to the sink to wash, and Sally arranged the chairs and laid the table. After politely asking after Judith's health, she managed to sit next to her and quietly requested,

"Judith, Mum says there may be some work going here, and I know I'm a bit young, but I'm really trying to save some money, and would you consider me?"

"What are you saving for, Sally?" asked Judith.

"I want to go on a musical tour of the States next summer with the Youth Orchestra. I play the clarinet, and the oboe, and I want to be a professional musician. I don't like to ask, but I do need to upgrade my clarinet, but I know Mum and Dad haven't a lot of money. They would get one for me if they could, but the boys need things too, so I want to save for that. I need a job, but there isn't much round here, and I can't expect them to ferry me round all the time, and a bike isn't really safe at night."

"Yes, Sally, you can have a job. Nora will be in charge, but you must not neglect your school work, or music practice, for work. Where do you practise, by the way?"

"Mainly in the barn. There isn't a lot of room in the house, and the boys make a lot of noise. Thank you, when can I start?"

"Ask your Gran, and I believe I owe you some money for the work you did at lambing. I'll talk to your father about it. Would you like to practise in the music room here? It might as well be used. If you could catalogue the music for me, and tidy it, and care for the instruments in there, we could make that part of your job."

"Could you ask old Mr Jones to come and tune the piano? It really needs it, Miss Susan couldn't play it for the last few years, because of her arthritis. It is a Bechstein you know. She had a good flute too, and a really good oboe."

Over tea, Judith got to know Sally better. The boys were excited. Mary, having enforced order, asked,

"Do you have any children, have you family?"

Judith answered, "Not really, I lost a baby once, but I have no close family of my own. My grandmother brought me up, and she died a few years ago. I have some good friends, and a couple of cousins, but no one else."

Once again, she felt a wave of sympathy flow towards her, as she remembered the baby who might have been. She glanced round, but no one seemed to be listening, except Mary, who hastily apologised, "Oh

Judith, I am so sorry, I didn't mean to pry. Was it long ago?"

"No, quite recent, actually. I'll tell you later, when the others are doing something else. You are not prying, I'd quite like to talk about it sometime. It still hurts, you see."

Mary put her hand on Judith's arm, and poured another mug of tea. "Sorry," she whispered, "Jim's off to the farm to check the milking went all right. He'll take the boys to change, and he'll ring the pub and book us a table. Right, everyone, Judith has invited us all to dinner at the Ugly Imp. Yes, you too, boys, so you must be on your best behaviour, and I want you clean, no Chris, not just a wipe with a flannel, but a proper bath. You'll have to share the water, because the immersion is up the spout. Clean clothes, and no chewing gum in the pockets this time, Tim. You go back with your father, and you'll have to follow later, Sally."

"Hang on," interjected Judith. "The hot water is plentiful enough here, isn't it? From the number of baths and showers I've seen today, some of them must be operational. You can have a bath or shower each, on my reckoning, and some to spare. Will that help? What is wrong with your immersion?"

"It's a bit dead, and they haven't been to fix it for weeks, like everything else you ask them to do," said Nora. "We'd have got it done ourselves, but they have a contract with this firm from Bradford, and they won't let us use anyone else."

"It is now four thirty, ring anyone you want who can fix it, now, and get them to do it as soon as they can. There is the phone, and I'll pay double time if they can fix it by Sunday. This kind of thing will have to stop. As a responsible landlord, I need you to be happy in the house. I'm going to rattle a few cages next week! Jim, I need a list of things that need doing in your house, as soon as you can, and then, on the farm. It sounds as if they are trying to harass you out, and that will stop."

Jim, muttering about not wanting to cross her, and almost feeling sorry for the culprits, rang a man he knew, and then took the boys and Sally off to the farm. He rang the house from the farm to say that someone would be out in the morning, and wanting to know what clothes to bring up to the house. That having been sorted, tea was cleared away, and when Jim came back with the boys, in his car, he made some phone calls. At Judith's suggestion, he asked all the people wanting to help at the house to meet for a drink in the Ugly Imp. Nora and Mary used the phone too, but had to borrow Judith's mobile, to save time. The baths were run, and Judith retired to her room to shower there. She had been quite impressed with the vast contents of the main airing cupboard and linen room, and huge, old–fashioned bath sheets were used by everyone.

They all met on the first floor landing, and the boys looked longingly at the banister of the stairway. "No, you will **not** slide down that in your good clothes" wailed Mary.

Judith, armed with a mobile phone, a note pad and pen, and a cheque book, waited in the hall for the others to assemble. Jim, who had returned the car to the farm, wanted to know how they were to get to the village. Judith explained that she had ordered a minibus, and it would return everyone home. While they were waiting, Judith asked about the hot water supply to the house. She wanted to know just how large a tank it was, and how it worked. Jim thought it was to do with the central heating.

The minibus arrived, and they got in. Judith locked the front door and hobbled out with her stick and the driver asked if she wanted to pick up anyone else. After consultation with the others, she said no, and soon they were pulling up outside The Gargoyle in the village.

Inside the pub, which seemed very crowded, Jim and his family were warmly welcomed. Judith, being shorter, went nearly unnoticed, until the crowds drew back. The landlord, a genial, rather ugly old man with a large beer gut and a red face, came over to welcome her.

He introduced himself as Richard Jugg, adding that most people called him Toby. Judith introduced herself, and as it was so noisy, they retreated into the snug, while she asked permission to have a meeting in the dining room.

He looked a bit startled, and said, "I don't see you need my permission, you own the place." He was almost hostile. She believed she knew why. She sat in a chair, and propped her stick beside her.

"Mr Jugg, can I explain something? No, please, hear me out. I think you may be under a misapprehension that I want you to leave this pub. I do not. Someone, and I believe I know who, has been going round telling a load of lies about me, and my plans. I have no intention of evicting you. I intend to live up at the house and become a part of this community. I am not intending to sell out to anyone, and I want to make the whole estate work again. Where necessary, I will invest what is needed, and I also want to employ several local people. I also understand that the current manager of the estate has failed to provide good maintenance on my properties. If you wish to stay on here, provide me with a list of things that need doing. Talk to Jim Morpeth as soon as you can. He might put your mind at rest. I insist you charge me for the use of the room tonight and keep a tab in the bar. I will settle up with you at the end of the evening. I need to meet people tonight, and they need to give me the once over."

Toby gave her a startled look, and nodded. He still looked rather wary, and then said,

"So you don't want us to move out?"

"No."

"And we can stay here?"

"Yes."

"For as long as we need?"

"Yes."

"And I am the manager, you don't want to run the place?"

"That's right."

"Can I still have it as a Free House?"

"Yes."

"And keep a percentage of the profits, like before?"

"Yes. What do you mean, before, don't you get one now?"

"Yes, but not as much as Miss Susan let me keep."

"How much was that?"

"Twenty per cent."

"Done, as from Monday."

"I've got another question."

"What?"

"What are you drinking?"

"A pint of Black Goblin please."

Toby grinned. His chubby face wrinkled up, and his body began to wobble as he started a rumbling guffaw. He went behind the bar and peered rather myopically at her.

"Another question."

"Yes?"

"Are you sure you only want a beer? I'd have thought you'd be a wine or cocktail person."

"Why?"

"Well, you being a toff, and that."

"I like beer. I take it it is the local brew?"

"Yes."

"I'm not a toff. I'm as common as muck. Just lucky."

"Oh, Sorry!"

"I've got a question."

"Yes?"

"Am I going to die of thirst, before you pull that pint?"

Toby started to laugh, and when he laughed, he meant it! Laughter consumed him, and anyone nearby caught it. Judith began to laugh, and eventually, after a few spillages, the pint arrived. Judith, aware of close scrutiny, downed it almost in one, and held her glass out for a refill.

"I like you!" Toby bubbled it out, between breaths.

"I like you, too. Can I use the room?"

"Yes."

"Will you do me a favour?"

"If I can. What is it?"

"Everyone in the pub, free drink on me?"

"Expensive."

"I know. I can afford a 'one off' evening."

"You're all right."

"So are you. May I call you Toby?"

"Yes. What do I call you?"

"Thirsty. Call me Judith."

"When do you want the room?"

"Now?"

"When do you want to eat?"

"In about half an hour. Can we order now?"

"Yes. I'll get you, and the Morpeths, a menu."

"Jim is asking all the people I need to see, into the dining room. Could you come in too?"

"Why?"

"I want a message to be put out and you can help, if you know what was said."

"OK!"

"Talk to me later?"

"Sure."

By this time they were both laughing. Judith tried to juggle the pint and her stick and the door of the bar as she made her way to the dining room. Toby bounced to help her, and got her to the dining room. She got up onto a table, and sat on it. Jim led in a group of people, who sat down around some of the tables. They paid little attention to her, as she was at the back of the room. Then Jim came in with some more, and Mary and Nora came in with a group of women. Everyone had a full glass, and after five minutes or so, another four people came in. Jim cleared his throat, and spoke rather awkwardly, thanking them for coming, and saying that he thought they might be interested in an offer of employment. He further added that Miss Susan had left the property to Master Clive and his wife. After Master Clive's tragic death, his widow, Mrs Judith Swallow, was the sole heiress to the estate, and wanted to live and work on the estate. For this, she would need the help of the local community, and he would like to welcome her to the village. He turned and Judith started,

"Ladies and gentlemen, I am Judith Swallow. I have asked you here tonight, so I can explain that I want to live in this community, and I need people to work for me on, and with, the estate. Whatever you have been told, forget it. I am not selling up, and I will be running things

When Judith finally got up to leave, she felt rather the worse for wear. The local brew had had its effect, and she wanted to slip quietly away. Instead, someone raised a cheer, and this was the signal for the piano to be played. She settled up with Toby, and as she got into the minibus, strains of 'Yellow Submarine' wafted after her. Several folk needed a lift, so she saw some of the village before she was dropped off outside her front door. Jim walked her to the door and saw her in, before getting into the van to be taken to the farm.

She made it up to the bedroom without incident. She climbed into the huge bed and set her alarm clock. Then she tried to read a book but the page became fuzzy and she gave in, and went to sleep.

During the night she had a strange dream. She dreamed of goblins climbing out of a yellow submarine and running towards the house, where they climbed the walls and got in through the attics. They then slid down the banisters, and disappeared into the pantry. She woke suddenly, and decided to be a little more careful with the beer. After a visit to the loo, she went back to bed, and slept soundly for the rest of the night.

Chapter Four

Judith woke to a fine day, and having dressed, went downstairs, made a cup of coffee, and, collecting her stick, went out of the front door to walk round the house from the outside. The drive carried on past the front door, and round to the side, past the drawing room and the conservatory. There were some overgrown lawns, and a chaotic shrubbery. Then a high wall ran for some way.

Staying on the drive, she came to a large old barn, open at the front, containing a trailer and an oil drum. She ventured in and realised it was used as a garage. There was plenty of room for a number of cars. In the back of the barn was a small room. This contained a table, two old office chairs, a small electric heater, and a sink and draining board. In the cupboard were mugs, some of which were very dirty, and on the top was an old electric kettle. A door at the back led into a toilet. Round the back was a pile of old tyres, and the remains of some old engines. There were some overgrown shrubs, and behind them the wall appeared again.

She left the barn, and continuing on the drive, she came to a large building. This was the old stables. There were ten good stables, and they led onto a yard at the side. When she went in there were signs of recent equine occupation. As she entered she saw a rat disappear through a hole in the stalls. In another stall there was an open bag of horse nuts and some bales of straw.

She walked round and came to an empty tack room and a hay store. The hay in there was fresh. A pile of black plastic buckets had tipped over, and a mouse ran out of one as she approached. As she came back into the yard, she saw a path that led her to two front doors, side by side, that seemed to have stairs behind them. Looking up she noticed curtained windows, and further round the back of the building, was another front door. She was able to look into a kitchen, and then into a shabbily furnished sitting room. All the doors were locked. At the back were some large kennels in a block, with substantial runs. No one had used them in a while and a few old bowls were stacked up inside one of the kennels. There was a tap and a trough. Returning to the drive, she followed it until she came to a large turning circle. The drive continued, but was obviously little used. She walked down it for some way, until she saw a tall wrought iron gate and the high boundary wall and the road.

The gate was chained and padlocked, so she retraced her steps, and at the turning circle found a path which wove between trees and petered out in a wood of fir trees.

Back by the barn, another path led along the very high wall. It was overgrown and she found it hard going. She persevered, and found an old door, through which she went. Inside the wall were some huge yew trees, and beyond them a sunken garden, with flower borders and overgrown lawns. Many interesting shrubs and trees were interspersed with benches and statues. An old sundial was in the middle of the sunken garden, reached by steps from four directions. On the far side she found a huge ornamental pond. She couldn't see if there were any fish, as it was choked with water lilies, which were in full bloom, and very lovely.

A series of small waterfalls flowed down beside the path and under a sluice. Here she met the wall again, and opened another door, to find another garden. The stream emerged from under the wall. The garden was surrounded with the high wall on three sides, covered with fruit trees, and along the other side were potting sheds, some green houses, and cloches. There were a few raised beds and even some recognisable patches of cabbages, over their best.

Judith decided to explore this at a later time, and walked through another door into another walled garden, but this was so overgrown it just looked like a hay field. The path led down some steps to a series of benches. At some stage, she thought, this was either a tennis court, croquet lawn, or a bowling green. The path went round whatever it was, and through yet another door, under a number of old yew trees, and onto a large lawn, vastly overgrown, stretching down hill. Half way down, the stream reappeared and ran into a lake some distance away.

On the far side of the stream, over an ornamental bridge that reminded her of Willow Pattern, stood the Folly. A tall tower structure, it looked rather out of place. As it was some distance away, she left it for another day. Some statues were scattered around, but she needed to press on. Looking to her left, she saw the rear of the house. She saw she was looking up at the ball room and the iron stairs leading to the roof. There was a wide stone terrace, bordered with a low wall, outside the back of the house. Several seats could be seen, and some huge pots, containing plants. Wide steps led down to the lawn.

At the bottom of these, built into the drop, were doors, half glazed, that led into shelters, and behind them doors that must lead into the basement. Judith continued round, and found a large summer house. This looked as though it had two floors and a splendid veranda, and looked out onto the lawn. It was locked. She followed the overgrown path left, and arrived on the terrace, which stretched round from the back, and saw the music room in front of her.

The back door, which she had forgotten to unlock, could be reached from the terrace and from a set of steps, but she walked on and the path turned into a drive just before the turning off to the farm. She went back to the front door. As she approached the front of the building, she noticed that on the upper part of the house were some grotesque gargoyles. Her eye came down to a coat of arms carved above the front door. She walked closer to look at it. It was another one of those goblin–type creatures. It seemed ferocious, and she could see its teeth were quite prominent. Under its paw was a small figure of a person.

She was gazing at this when she heard the Morpeths approaching and went into the house with them.

Nora commented, "You're up early, have you been for a walk?"

Judith said, "Yes, I've had a quick look round. I need to exercise the leg, and I wanted to clear my head, and get some fresh air."

"It's a big place, did you find anything interesting?"

"I found that there is a lot of work to be done, that's for sure! Who has been keeping horses in the stable?"

"That would be the Cummings'."

"Well, I wish they had cleared up! There are rats there now, and mice in the kennels. We need to get things started."

They walked into the kitchen, and armed with coffee, they waited for Jim to join them. The boys asked if they could explore, and were given permission, on condition they left the china alone and didn't break anything. Shortly afterwards, they could be heard uttering squeals of delight, as they slid down the banister. Mary got up to stop them but Judith said,

"At least we know where they are, and it will keep them occupied for a while. Let's talk about what we need to do. Sally, would you like to start in the music room? Have a tidy up, and then come and find us."

Sally seemed pleased, and went to get dusters and polish. Judith suggested they sat in the Chinese Drawing Room, and once they were settled, she asked,

"Have you thought about taking on the job of housekeeper, Nora?"

"Yes, indeed I have. Since my husband died, and Jim had the family, I have been happy to help around the farm. I had a good job that suited me looking after Miss Susan, and when I was laid off, I couldn't afford to move to a place of my own. I want to stay near, but it is rather crowded. I have been looking for a housekeeping job in the area. To be quite honest, I need the money of a full–time job, then maybe I can rent somewhere nearby."

"I think we can solve that problem. Would you be interested in one of the lodges, if we can do it up to be habitable? You could be near the family but have your own space as well? I would like to offer you the job of housekeeper. We'll have to negotiate pay and a contract and holidays and all that. I have to find a suitable agent, but given that we are both happy, do you want it?"

Nora looked very relieved, and replied,

"Yes, please. Could I have the South Lodge, if there is a choice? Actually, I was born there, and grew up in the lodge. I am sure we can sort out everything else. Can I start right away?" She jumped up, and embraced Judith, and kissed her. "Mary will be thankful, I think, to have her home to herself again."

Mary, looking rather relieved, responded,

"Oh, Mum, you know that's not true. You are always welcome, and you have been such a help, but I know you want your own place. Judith, I, too, have been thinking. Jim and I talked it over last night. Is there a job for me? Obviously, it will have to be in mainly school hours, but I could do cooking, or cleaning, whatever. An extra income would be handy, and we could get more for the kids. There isn't a lot of work round here, unless you have a car, and Jim needs me around to help sometimes, like lambing time."

Judith said,

"Yes, I wondered if you could take on the cooking, and help Nora when she needs it? I was hoping to get others in to do the cleaning, someone from the village, maybe. Most of the time it will be pretty simple, and if we have guests, then we'll get in help, or something. I really need the two of you to run the house, look after things. If you want, the children can come here with you, in holidays and whenever you want them. Maybe we could have a games room, with a computer, TV, and video. I'm sure they will find plenty to occupy them, when they are not outside wrecking the garden. You need to be flexible, I understand that. The other thing is, can both of you drive?"

They looked rather surprised, and confirmed they could.

Judith said, "Right, I propose to have a 'house' car, so it can be used by everyone. At the moment it will have to be the Astra, until we get something more suitable. I'll get you all on the insurance today. Then you can come and go as you need, and of course, if you need to use a car in the evenings, it will be available. Maybe, in time, Sally can learn on it."

"That is a good idea," said Nora. "What would you like for lunch?"

"I don't expect you to work at weekends normally, unless there is something on, and then you would get overtime, or time off in lieu. Are you free for this weekend? Thank you. I like simple food, cannot eat tuna, marzipan, or some shell fish. I love veg, and salad, but I can only stand a small amount of cheese at one time. I love puddings, but I do need to watch the weight, and I hate grapefruit. Otherwise I am happy with whatever is easier. I'll just ring the insurance and get you all put on it."

Nora went to the kitchen, and Judith got on the phone. Then she and Mary went through a list of who they would need to contact, and made lists of things to do. Judith sounded out how she felt about Sally working a few hours, and they went to the music room and spoke to Sally, who was busy sorting music and cleaning out cupboards. She agreed to help her mother in the house and to help in the kitchen when needed.

Mary remarked, "You do realise that there will be a string of visitors over the next few days, and that they will be longing to get to work here? Some, you could take on right away, but you'll have to make your own mind up. Jim will be here soon, he is trying to get someone to play in the cricket match for him this afternoon. What do you want to do first? The Chinese Drawing Room is clean, and you could see people in there, or the drawing room. Some of them would rather talk in the kitchen, I think you'll find."

"Was Jim due to play this afternoon?"

"Yes, but I'm sure someone else can cover for him."

"No, of course he must play, is it at home or away?"

"Away, the next village. Our local pitch isn't up to much, the team was allowed to play here, on the pitch on the lawn by the summerhouse, when Miss Susan was alive. She loved to watch the matches, and always laid on a great tea, usually in the summer house, and they had dances here, years ago. She was such a lovely old lady, I really miss her. Are you sure, could we manage without him this afternoon?"

"Of course. I do not propose to take your lives over. I didn't see a cricket pitch, all I saw was a hay field. I think I would like to invite the club back. Some gardeners must be a priority!"

"May I use the phone? Could I tell him that?"

"Yes, do."

Mary rushed off to make the telephone call. Judith went up to her bedroom, and returned with a briefcase, which she took to the library. She cleared the desk, and set up her paper work on it. She also put the lists beside it. She heard a gong sounding, and went to investigate. Nora emerged from the kitchen, and the boys and Mary from another part of the house, and Sally from the music room. Nora explained that a cup of coffee or tea, and a snack was prepared, and they invaded the kitchen.

Just as they were about to sit down, a large bell on the wall started to ring. It was attached to a cord that was being pulled. Judith looked a bit startled until Nora explained it was the front door bell. Judith went out and opened the front door. On the steps were five people, whom Judith recognised as having been at the Ugly Imp the night before. One rather motherly woman introduced herself as Betty Nuttley, and said could they all talk to her? Judith ushered them in to the drawing room. Nora appeared with a large tray of tea and coffee and biscuits, and introduced the others to Judith.

Betty's daughter, Haley, was a happy, rather straight forward woman, and she sat next to another woman, tall and very shy, whom she called Dot. The other two were an obvious couple, the man, a sandy–haired, fit–looking man in his thirties. His wife was very shy, and a petite woman. He introduced them as Sam and Lucy Arnthwaite, and said,

"You asked us to think if we were interested in a job here. I could be very interested, but can you tell me more? I've not many paper qualifications, but I was working as a caretaker handyman, and mechanic in Leeds until recently. I can produce references. I got made redundant when it closed down. Mr Morpeth knows me."

"Thank you for coming, Mr Arnthwaite. Finish your coffee, you come recommended already. Perhaps you and Mrs Arnthwaite would come and chat in the other room in a few minutes? You may not want what I have to offer. Ladies, are you also seeking work?"

They nodded. They almost moved in unison, and made a strange trio.

Nora interjected, "We have known each other for years, haven't we, Betty? You want to come back here, and have your cleaning job back, I expect. Dot, you too? Are you wanting to come and clean as well, Haley?"

The three women nodded enthusiastically. Judith realised they were shy of her and would talk better to Nora. She suggested that Nora talk to them, find out what they were expecting in terms of hours and pay, and then come and find her. She asked Sam and Lucy to come with her, and took them to the library, where she took some details.

Sam explained that after leaving the army, where he had been trained as an electrician, he had done vehicle maintenance, gardening, and general building work. The factory job had been dull, but had come with a flat, and they had had to move in with Lucy's parents when he was laid off. He explained that they had to find a place to live, and confided that Lucy was pregnant. He was sorry to bother Judith, but until they were settled, he couldn't work for her.

Judith asked some more questions, and then left them sitting down, while she had a talk with Mary in the kitchen. She returned and sat down beside Sam and Lucy.

"I could offer you the job of handyman, and general worker here. It would mean you help maintain all the properties, vehicles, and help in the garden, and maybe do some driving around. There is a two–

75

bedroomed flat in the stable block, which will need doing up, but it is habitable, and it goes with the job. You would not be the head gardener, but you would be the 'fix it man'. Are you interested?"

Lucy, speaking for the first time, asked,

"Would there be any work for me, we have no money at all, and I could work, at least for a while. We would have to get furniture. The last place was furnished, and all our savings are gone."

She burst into tears. Sam, looking rather embarrassed, comforted her, and Judith asked,

"What can you do, or would you do?"

Lucy, still sobbing into her husband's shoulder, muttered something. Sam explained,

"Lucy used to take in seamstress work, and general alterations from a cleaners. You'll clean, sew, and iron, won't you love? She trained as a nanny originally, but most people want a 'live in' nanny, so when we got married, she had to find something else."

Judith asked a more composed Lucy, "Would you like to live in the country? Could you hack it?"

"Yes, I was brought up in the Cheviots. I love the country."

Once again Judith left them talking, and went in search of Nora, and they had a quick conference in the kitchen with Mary, and Judith said,

"Nora, you are the housekeeper, and it is your decision, who we use in the house. Can we use Lucy? I wondered if we needed someone to make curtains, mend linen, and maybe do some of the more delicate jobs? I want to offer Sam the handyman job, and I am offering them the two–bedroomed flat in the stables. What do you think?"

Nora thought, and then said,

"Yes, that might be very handy, I know him, he's sound. He is a hard worker, and as honest as the day is long. Can you afford all these staff? We can use three cleaners, these were the ones I had in mind, they all live in the village, and are honest. Dot and Haley have young children, so, like Mary, might be pushed to do so many hours in the holidays. All the husbands work on farms locally, in fact you already employ Dot's husband, Derek, he is Jim's general farm worker."

Judith looked at her, and asked,

"Nora, do we need all these people to run the place properly? Yes? Well then, we need them. I am not a charity, they will earn their money. I do have enough for this, I really do, from the interest I get, never mind the capital. I expect they would like an hourly rate, with overtime, if they work weekends. I propose to offer something similar to Lucy, a little more for a skilled job, but what do you think about having a creche here in the holidays? Lucy is a qualified nanny, she might be interested.

myself. I am looking for various employees, and would rather recruit them locally, before looking further afield. What I am offering is mostly permanent employment, either full or part–time. I am nobody's fool, and I will expect honesty, discretion, loyalty, and hard work. What I am offering is a fair wage, loyalty, and a pension. I am not, and never will be, a soft touch! During this evening, I hope to talk to you all, and Jim has kindly offered to introduce me. All I am asking tonight is that you listen and consider what I say. I will then ask you to come and see me next week at the house, when we can talk further. You will want to discuss this, and so while you do, Toby has agreed to feed me, and I'll come out into the bar in about half an hour, and anyone who wants to stop can chat to me then. If you are not interested, you can slip away or just ignore me."

Judith got up and limped to the Ladies, where she waited five minutes before returning. The room was empty except for the Morpeths, and she joined them. And as she sat down, she asked, "Well?"

Nora said, "That's got them talking! I'm pretty sure not one will go home. The whole village will be wanting to speak to you now. What have you done to Toby? He is still laughing, and so far as he's concerned, you are wonderful. He's on your side, all in ten minutes. What did you say?"

"Not a lot, he saw my point of view without much chat. I think we will be friends."

The meal was simple, but well cooked, and well presented. Judith stuck to beer, which was very good. The puddings were even better, and the boys had two each. Jim chose cheese and biscuits, and as the meal ended, Toby came in, and introduced his wife, equally chubby, and delighting in the name of Delilah. She was as jolly as her husband.

She shook Judith's hand and extracted a promise to come and talk to them soon. Then she retreated to the kitchen out the back and could be heard singing in a gusty soprano voice along with a radio programme.

Mary suggested that she take the children home, and their driver was found in the kitchen, and they departed. Tim had been sampling glasses, and was almost asleep. Chris said he was full. Sally wanted to get to bed so she could be up early to start work. They slipped away and with an escort of Jim, Nora and Toby, Judith went to the main bar. As she entered, the hum of conversation ceased, and she sat at a hastily vacated table. Tentatively, the conversation resumed, but was rather subdued. Jim and Nora introduced her to a number of people, and explained who they were, and what their skills were. All were invited up to the house for an informal chat over the weekend, Judith offering open house to anyone interested in working for her.

We could make a sort of nursery or school room. You settle it with the three ladies and offer them overtime, if they can give me extra hours for a while. When you have done a deal, come and find me. And I would like to talk to them, and I will ask you to talk to Lucy. She will be under you, and she's pregnant, by the way. She looks a bit delicate, no heavy work. I think the poor thing is terrified of me. We're in the library, but I would like them to start as soon as they can."

Nora asked. "Fine, but Lucy will need maternity leave, won't she?"

Judith said, "Yes, but if we pay piece work, she can choose how much she does. She is entitled to maternity, and we will give it to her."

They split, and Judith went back to Sam and Lucy. She explained what she wanted of Lucy, and asked Sam if they were interested. They negotiated a basic salary for Sam. She explained that they could have a look at the flat, and then let her know.

Nora came in, and they all went into the drawing room. Judith explained that she expected honesty, loyalty and hard work in return for employment, and she would have a contract of employment drawn up for everyone, as soon as she could, which she would ask them to sign. She also explained that there would be a period of 'probation' when anyone not happy could change their minds. She suggested that the hours should start after any children had gone to school, and that Sam, should he accept the job, would fetch them from the village, and return them before children came home from school. She also explained that as soon as she could, she would arrange a safe place for the children during the holidays. She asked for a quick decision, but suggested they talk it over before accepting her offer.

Betty, the obvious leader, said, "Mrs Swallow, I don't need to talk it over. My Bob will be happy if I am, and I accept."

Jim came in as they were talking, and behind him, the boys. He knew Sam and Lucy, and thanked Judith for letting him go to the cricket match. Judith asked if Jim could find the keys to the stable flat, and show Sam and Lucy round. Jim went off to the kitchen, and came back with a huge box of keys and he and the boys walked off to the stables with Sam and Lucy.

Nora took the women on a tour of the house, explaining that they would all help each other whenever needed. Mary began hoovering and dusting the library, and Judith felt a bit lonely as she wandered into the living room at the front of the house. It was a nice room but needed to be redecorated and she decided to make it her personal sitting room, with her own furniture. As she looked at the curtains, she heard a car pull up outside, and several visitors got out and approached the front door.

She met them on the front steps. The first was a good–looking man in his forties, called Stuart. He introduced his wife, June. A gnarled old man, who said his name was Bill, followed. The next was a fresh–faced teenage lad called Liam. Judith invited them into the drawing room.

Bill came straight to the point,

"You said you wanted gardeners. I used to be under gardener here for Miss Holt. I know the gardens here. I would like to work here again, ma'am. I don't want no fancy job, nor to be in charge, but I can get these lawns back, and keep the place tidy. I only grows veg, none of these fancy flowers. I'll turn my hand to most general work. This here is my nephew, Liam. He's not got a lot of school larnin', but he can dig a veg patch proper, I had the teaching of him. He's a hard grafter, and he does as he's told."

Liam nodded enthusiastically, and with a big smile on his face added, "Aye, I can at that, I'll not be no trouble, ma'am."

Judith realised he was a little simple, but he looked strong and seemed willing. He and Bill seemed a little uncomfortable in the drawing room. Liam was looking round the room with a startled, owlish expression. Bill wouldn't sit down, and said it wasn't fitting. Mary arrived, and Liam went and stood beside her. He needed a friendly face, Judith decided. Jim had already mentioned these two, and suggested they would be suitable as gardener, and an outside 'lad'. She suggested they went off to the kitchen and had a cup of tea with Mary, while she spoke to Stuart and June.

Judith invited Stuart and June to sit down. They did and she waited for them to speak.

Stuart also came to the point.

"My visit here is similar. My uncle rang me last night, said you were looking for staff. Are you interviewing for head gardeners? That is what I do. I was head gardener at a famous gardens in Hampshire, but the place was sold, and it wasn't open any more, and they didn't want to do much with the garden, so I left. I am head gardener for the municipal gardens in Bradford at the moment, but we would like to live in the country. I have a young boy and a teenage daughter."

He handed Judith an impressive folder of certificates and references, together with a CV, and full details of his family. It looked very professional. He seemed confident, and when she asked him about work he had done before, he talked knowledgeably, and enthusiastically.

Judith felt she was out of her depth. She was not an expert gardener. She liked him; he seemed well educated, and she looked in his CV. He had a degree in horticulture.

She asked, "Who is your uncle?"

He said, "I think you would know him as Toby Jugg. His sister is my mother."

"What did you think of Bill and Liam?"

Stuart smiled and said, "I've known old Bill for years. He taught me a lot. I used to come up here on my holidays, stayed with Uncle Toby and Aunt Dee, and Bill got me interested in plants. He can be a stubborn old sod sometimes, but he knows his stuff. He is an excellent groundsman, and always wins the prizes at the fete for his veg. You won't get much better. Liam, as you probably gathered, is not over bright, but he's a genuine lad. He will do whatever you ask him, so long as you show him once, and he never gets bored. He will dig all day, and he is very strong and always willing to please. He is easily bullied though, and can get very upset if he has the mickey taken out of him, or thinks he has done wrong. If you don't mind my saying, he is just what you want."

"What are your views on organic horticulture?"

"Did you know I was coming? I would love to run an organic regime, but I did not understand you were interested in that. Is that what you want?"

"As far as practicable, yes. Especially the vegetables and any food. I am not too keen on lots of chemicals or genetically modified things. You obviously know the place and the task you would be taking on. Could you work over Bill and Liam, and would you need any other staff?"

"Yes, I would work with them. Have done in the past. I might need a bit of contracting help, with fencing, or hiring a JCB or turfing, but so long as you don't want it done yesterday, I can get this place better than it was. The gardens were wonderful once, and even open to the public at one time."

Judith asked, "If I take you on, will you terrorise me out of my own garden, or shout at me if I pick a rose?"

June laughed. Stuart looked a bit taken aback. "No, of course not, you would be my employer, and if you wanted a bed of delphiniums mixed with dog roses, you'd get them."

"What are your views on dogs, cats and horses?"

"Dogs, fine, so long as they don't dig up the plants. Cats, I love cats. Horses, great for manure, but not in a garden. They need a field or paddock."

"Would you be prepared you take on the plants in the conservatory, the fruit trees, and the orangery?"

"Yes."

"Would you consult with me, before hiring or firing anyone?"

"Of course."

"Will you be wanting accommodation?"

"Yes, that is the problem. I must have accommodation. Can you offer that?"

"I could offer you the choice of the semi–detached stable house, or the North Lodge. I hope that Sam will be moving into one of the stable flats with his wife, and soon, I hope, a baby. Nora Morpeth is moving into the South Lodge. I have offered Sam the position of handy man, driver and general worker, which would mean he would work with you if you needed an extra pair of arms. Would that be a problem?"

"Who, Sam Arnthwaite? Good chap that, we were at school together. He went into the army, and I went to university. We used to be in the army cadets together. I didn't know he was back here. Yes, that would be all right."

"Would you take on supervision of all the outside staff, Sam included? I imagine you have a few staff at the moment. Sam will be needed inside as well, when Nora Morpeth will be in charge. She has accepted the post of housekeeper, in charge of inside staff. In any argument or dispute, you both refer to me, and I want you to work together, not against each other"

"I think I can manage that. Have you plans to do anything with the house, other than live in it?"

"Yes, I have an idea or two. I do want there to be organic vegetable production, the excess to be sold. You will have to work with Jim, and work with the farms. I expect you can help each other, and can use each other's products. The whole estate needs to work together. I would discuss any plans with the staff, before doing everything."

"Could we see the two houses?"

"Yes. How much were you looking for as salary?"

Stuart named a sum that was fair, if a bit expensive. They discussed it and agreed a figure.

Jim arrived back with the keys and kindly went off again to show Stuart and June the two houses. It wasn't long before they returned, and Stuart asked if they could take the stable house.

Judith asked when he could start. He explained that he was owed over a month's leave, and could start within ten days. Judith hired him, and asked him to go and hire Bill and Liam. He went to the kitchen and did just that. When he was gone, Judith asked Jim where he had put Sam and Lucy. Jim said they were talking the thing over and would be in soon.

Nora came in, and suggested that everyone come and eat a buffet lunch in the kitchen.

June, without her husband, was quiet, but after a little coaxing, became quite chatty and seemed to have an excellent sense of humour. She was a hairdresser, and wanted to be a wife and mother. She didn't want to work unless she had to. She admitted to playing the piano, and to loving music. She met Sally in the kitchen and they went off after lunch to the music room.

Bill thanked Judith, and on the way out of the back door, down the passage from the kitchen, he doffed an imaginary cap, to her dismay. Nora said he was happier like that, and it made him happy and not to stop him.

Liam had obviously been told to do the same. He said his piece, and then confided that his Mum was going to be 'reet pleased' with him, and could he start right away, and not wait till Monday.

Bill dragged him away. Sam and Lucy came in and asked to talk to Judith. They accepted the jobs and joined in the lunch. Jim and Sam left to go to the cricket match. Betty, Dot and Haley agreed to start work on the Monday morning, and Stuart and June went for a look round the grounds.

No sooner had lunch been cleared away, than the front door bell rang again. Judith greeted a total stranger. He introduced himself as the local vicar, the Rev Arthur Pike. He welcomed her to the parish, and gave her a pamphlet with service times on it. He hoped she would be able to come to St Mary's Church, and politely got up and left after a brief chat.

As he drove off down the drive in a Lada, another car pulled up. Toby and Dee got out and asked if Stuart had arrived to talk to her. Toby almost bounced up the steps, and accepted the offer of a coffee. Dee scurried after him and soon they were chatting in the kitchen. Toby sang Stuart's praises, and hoped he hadn't been presumptuous. When he heard that Stuart had accepted the job, he invited Judith to the pub for supper, but understood when she asked if she could make it another day.

Stuart and June returned to the kitchen and he asked if they could move into the house the next week. They asked if Sam could fix some things in the house for them, and Stuart told Judith what he wanted to start with in the garden. He had found a rose garden, much neglected, and wanted to plan improvements. June groaned, and told Judith,

"He's off! You'll never get him to shut up now. He dreams of creating the perfect rose. He won't rest until he's done it."

Judith told him, by all means, but asked if she could have some vegetables as well, and could the cricket pitch be resurrected. Stuart, mumbling about asparagus beds, was pulled away by Toby and June. Dee said Stuart would be up on Monday to get started,

Lucy, meanwhile, asked if she could stop until Sam came back, and was taken on a tour of the house by Mary, who was concerned by the sudden silence from the twins. They were found watching the television in a guest bedroom on the first floor.

Nora talked to Judith about meals and unpacking and decorators. They adjourned to the library and together dusted and polished, between writing down, or looking up, addresses. Judith had just sat down when the bell rang again and she went to the front door.

This time it was a youth, rather overweight, with black hair, and wearing track suit bottoms, and a torn tee shirt, which was dirty. He had a walkman, still playing, and looked her up and down.

"You Mrs Swallow?"

"I am, yes, who are you?"

"Brian Hall."

"What can I do for you, Brian?"

"You got a job for me?"

"I don't know, what can you do?"

"I can drive a tractor, and I can ride a quad, and I am good with engines. I know lots about cars."

Judith wondered if he had any idea of the bad impression he was creating. She asked,

"How old are you?"

"I'm sixteen."

"Still at school?"

"Naw, I got chucked out."

"Really? Why should I employ you?"

"I need some money."

"From what you have told me, Brian, I think, if you want work, it would be better if you asked Mr Morpeth. He's in charge of the farms here. He may have something for you, do you know him?"

"Yer, my dad works with him, me dad is the cowman."

"Why do you really want a job, Brian?"

"Me dad says I've got to do something. Me mum says she's fed up with me hanging round all day. I want ten pounds an hour, mind, and I want me own quad."

Judith felt rather sorry for this inept youth. She wondered if he was trying to be funny.

"Brian, I have no intention of paying you anything at all, unless you are worth it. If you want to work, you should approach Jim Morpeth. Before you ask anyone for a job, clean yourself up, and be a bit more polite. There may be some work, when you are older. Sorry, but not at the moment."

Brian shrugged his shoulders.

"Suit yourself, at least I tried." He turned and slouched down the drive. Judith watched him from the hall where Mary was standing, having listened to the exchange.

When Brian was some way away, he bent, picked up a pebble, and flung it at the living room window. He missed, made an obscene gesture, and kicked a peony flower to bits.

Mary was incensed, and was about to pursue him down the drive, but Judith pulled her back.

"Leave it, Mary, please. Poor boy, when you are as unhappy as he obviously is, it must be hard to be turned down. He doesn't even know what he's done wrong, does he? What are his parents like?"

"His dad is a good cowman, and quite a good fellow. Very quiet, rather withdrawn and he has been on the farm for about ten years. Maggie, she has Reg under her thumb. I shouldn't say this, but she ran off with a double glazing salesman a few years ago, and when that fell through, he took her back. She works in the Golden Lion, in the next village, and never seems to be at home. Reg does most of the cooking, and I don't think anyone does the cleaning. Certainly no one seems to do much washing. Brian has been in so much trouble, he is a bit sticky–fingered, so don't have him in the house!"

"Poor lad, how sad. Has he had help?"

"Oh yes, everyone has tried. When he wants to, he can be quite clever. He just cannot be bothered."

"Mary, that reminds me, I haven't seen a washing machine since I got here, have I missed a room? I need to do some washing, and is there a tumble dryer?"

Mary looked a bit stricken and admitted she had forgotten to show Judith the laundry room. This was off the kitchen, together with a scullery. In the laundry they found Lucy who was looking at the machine. She seemed pleased to see Judith and asked if she could talk to her. Mary discreetly left, and Lucy asked, in a pathetic little voice,

"Mrs Swallow, I know this is a cheek, but could we move in right away? We only have the one room at Sam's mum's, and they need the space, so do I. We'll sleep on the floor if we have to, until we can afford to buy a bed, but could we use the washing machine here, until we can get one? We don't have much to move, a few cases. May we keep a cat? Our little cat is terrified by the dog at the house. I'm sorry to ask, and I expect you will say no, but I have been so worried."

"Lucy, you can keep a cat, and you can move in tomorrow. Have you got a car? No? Then Sam can borrow the Astra tomorrow afternoon. We will find some furniture from here to tide you over, and yes, you can do your washing here. Are you worried about the baby? You needn't be. It will be very welcome, I know, and of course I won't expect you to work, if you are not up to it. Have you no furniture?

Nothing? What about bed linen, blankets, all that?"

Lucy burst into tears and admitted that they had nothing.

"Lucy, listen, borrow what you need from here for a few days."

"Oh, Mrs Swallow, you are kind. We have been so desperate. The baby was such a shock, not that we don't want it, but it couldn't have come at a worse time. His mum thinks we did it deliberate, I'm sure."

They went upstairs to the first floor landing and Judith went to her room, and returned and gave Lucy an envelope, saying, "No, don't open it now. Tell Sam I need you to be fit and healthy, call it a welcome to the estate gift. You can pay me back by good work and loyalty. This is between the two of us. Go to the linen room, borrow what you need, and then go and tell Nora I said you were to have a bed and furniture and some food to see you in. Go and do it now!"

Nora and Lucy were soon scouting the house for what they needed. Nora came to check that it was in order, and then asked to run some things down into the flat in the Astra. They loaded up the car, and came back half an hour later and spent what remained of the afternoon picking out furniture.

Judith went to the kitchen to find Mary putting a meal in the fridge.

"This is for you, this evening. It's been quite a day. You don't hang about, do you? You have been here two days, and done a month's worth of work. I'm sure you are supposed to be taking it easy, and you are limping badly again. Sit down and relax for a while. Have a fag. Here is a coffee."

"I could say the same of you, you must have put your life on hold, you have all been so wonderful. Mary, have I done the right thing? Have I been too hasty? Have we got the right people? Have I made any dreadful mistakes?"

"Judith, calm down! I hardly know Stuart, but he seems to know his stuff. Lucy is a nice woman, and the rest I know anyway. We'll have this place up and running soon, don't you worry. Did I see the vicar call?"

"Yes, and he asked me to a service. I think tomorrow should be a rest day. Where is the church?"

"Would you like us to pick you up? About half nine? We'd love you to come. It's a nice old church. You will certainly put the village tongues wagging, even more than today. Come back and have Sunday lunch with us, and then we can get Sam and Lucy sorted. You are being very kind to them, and to all of us. I was worried you would give Brian a job, but you're no fool, are you?"

Sally appeared in the kitchen, and said,

"Judith, I have a confession to make. I found the oboe in the music room, and I played it. I should have asked. Do you mind?"

Judith looked up at her, and asked, "Is it a good oboe?"

Sally sighed and said, "It is one of the best I've ever played. One day, I'll get myself one like that."

"Well I can't play it, so you play it whenever you are in there, and welcome. I know you will look after it."

The twins came into the kitchen, pleading starvation, and were disgruntled when they were told to wait for their supper. Lucy and Nora returned and they all sat round the kitchen table, chatting. Lucy was very good with the children and had cheered up. Nora and Judith talked about meal arrangements and shopping for the next week. Sally was reading a book on Mozart, which she had borrowed from the music room.

Shortly after seven, Jim and Sam returned and sat down with them. They were happy as they had won the match. Nora wanted to get the boys home and into bed on time. Sally had homework to do, and Mary and Jim made some arrangements for the next day before Mary pointed out that Judith was tired, and Jim ran Lucy and Sam back to the village in his car.

Judith cooked and ate her supper, retrieved the wine, and went upstairs and had a relaxing bath. She got out some respectable clothes for the next morning, and put out the lights downstairs after locking up the doors. She was startled to hear people talking on the first floor, and crept down the corridor and burst into a room to be confronted by a television left on by the boys. She went back to her bedroom and watched the news, took a couple of pain killers, and went to sleep.

She woke later to find the television still on and the bedding on the floor. She picked it up, turned the telly off, visited the bathroom, and got back into bed. She could not get back to sleep at once, so she thought through the events of the day. She switched off the light and was just dropping off, when she thought she heard a faint rustling sound from the corridor. She lay there, straining to hear it again, fearing she would, but when all she could hear was silence, she went to sleep.

She had another strange dream. This time the goblins were swimming in the lake, and then coming onto the lawn and playing cricket. The goblins were mixed in with some imps, and all of them suddenly appeared in the stream, and then they were swimming in the fish pond and eating all the fish. The water lilies were missing, and one small imp stood on the sundial and did a handstand. One of the goblins threw a stone and then a peony flower. There was a goblin playing an oboe and a small cat sitting in the linen cupboard.

She was woken by the dawn chorus outside. Her leg and arm were painful, and she used the chair lift to go down to the kitchen. And she made herself a mug of tea, and returned with it to the bedroom to watch the morning programmes on the telly. She dozed fitfully for a couple of hours until the alarm went off, when she got up.

She went downstairs to the kitchen and went to the pantry, and got out a packet of cereal. She fetched milk from the fridge, plus some orange juice, and made herself breakfast. Sitting down at the table, she hurriedly ate, and then loaded up the dishwasher. She was about to put the cereal away when the telephone rang. She chatted with a friend for some time, and went upstairs to change for church.

She went to the library in search of a prayer book. It took a while to locate one, and she placed it on the hall table beside the flowers, together with her handbag and purse. 'Handkerchief, prayer book, collection money, gloves, she quoted to herself, and went upstairs again to find gloves and a hanky. She didn't need to take a stick as she had a lift, and was sure she would get a lift back from the Morpeths.

As she collected her bag from the hall, they came up the drive, past the front of the house, and returned a couple of minutes later. She had locked the front door, and was waiting while the car stopped, and she got in. It was a bit of a squeeze but they all just fitted in.

The journey took only a few minutes and they pulled up in the church car park. The path to the church was made of old headstones, and was bordered by ancient yew trees, which cut out a lot of light. One of the trees was so old that most of one branch had to be held off the ground with supports. The church was delightful, very old and not too large. The boys and Sally ran ahead, to get changed for the choir. Several people welcomed Judith, and she was given a hymn book by an elderly gentleman. Jim, Mary and Nora were talking to friends, and Judith was ushered to a boxed pew which had a beautifully padded seat and seemed to be quite ornately decorated. It had a door at the aisle end and a special set of footstools.

Mary came up to the pew and explained that it was the 'family' pew and Judith would be expected to sit in it. Judith pleaded with Mary to come and join her, as she did not wish to sit in solitary splendour. Jim and Nora joined them, and whispered that this was an honour for them, as normally the pew was empty, unless the 'family from the manor' was present.

The church began to fill up, and Mary whispered that it was an unusually big turn out. Judith was aware of intense curiosity, and felt a bit like a zoo animal. Mary chuckled and whispered that Judith had shown a suitable respect by turning up at church, and the vicar would be delighted as a fuller church would result, at least for a while. The organ began to play. Judith had problems kneeling, and had to pray sitting down, and hoped no one would think she didn't know how to behave.

The choir came in, and she was delighted to see not only the twins and Sally, but Dot and Bill. The service began by the vicar, with a big smile, welcoming Judith both to the parish and to the church. Judith blushed.

It was a simple and pleasant service and the choir was good. They sang a wonderful anthem, 'I will sing with the spirit' and the sermon was based on the beatitudes. The collection plate came round and Judith put her contribution into it. She realised that she should have put her offering in an envelope, as she knew that everyone was trying to see what she had given, and she added a mental note to purchase some small brown envelopes!

After the service, coffee was served in the church hall, which was a typically shabby building. She met the vicar's wife and family, the churchwardens, one of whom was the elderly gentleman who had ushered her to her seat. He seemed very upset, and came to her, and apologised profusely for not having put a special staff on the pew. Mystified, she asked why he would need to. It was explained by several people that when there was anyone from the 'big house' at the service, it was indicated by this staff. Judith assured everyone that she was not offended, and she was told that the staff had been found in a cupboard in the vestry and would be present next time she visited the church. Judith was about to protest, but realised the tradition was important to these people, and said nothing.

A lot of folk wanted to be introduced. She managed to compliment the choir and organist, and the ladies who had done the flowers, and then Jim rescued her and they drove back to the farm.

Lunch was roast beef, with magnificent Yorkshire puddings and fresh greens from the farm garden. It was followed by apple pie and cream. Mary admitted that the apples were from Judith's orchard, and hoped she didn't mind them having taken the fruit. Judith was allowed to help with the drying up, and declined an invitation to stay for the afternoon. Jim ran her back to the house in the car, and she went into the house and headed for her room to change into more comfortable clothing.

She spent an hour unpacking some of her clothes from boxes, and went to the laundry to do some washing. She put many of her own ornaments in her bedroom, and then Lucy and Sam, with several helpers, turned up. They collected the keys to the flat and Sam went to the farm and returned with Jim, who was driving a tractor and trailer. Furniture was removed from various rooms, and taken to the flat. Judith went to the kitchen to make tea and had put the kettle on, when she remembered she needed to put away the cereal. She went to the table, but the packet had gone. A few stray corn flakes led to the pantry, and although she hunted for the packet, it was nowhere to be found. There was no sugar left in the sugar bowl on the table. The bowl was turned on its side, and very sticky.

She washed the bowl, refilled it from the pantry, and swept up the few cornflakes. The kettle boiled and she prepared some sandwiches. She put the sugar bag back into the pantry, in a meat safe, and racked her brains for an explanation. She was vaguely uneasy, but then Lucy came in and they set out the mugs and sandwiches. Judith remembered a half packet of biscuits and went to the side, but they, too, were gone, together with the packaging. She opened a new packet from the pantry and asked Lucy if she had everything she needed at the flat. The only thing Lucy did not have was an electric kettle, and a hunt in the second pantry located one, which they tested and found to be in good working order.

Sam, Jim and the helpers arrived, and she was introduced to most of the cricket team, who devoured the sandwiches and the biscuits and drank copious cups of tea. Lucy helped clear up, and Judith went out to see the cat in a basket in the car. She extracted a promise from Sam to ask if they needed anything, and they all left. Judith returned to the kitchen and put anything edible away. She did more unpacking, and spent the rest of the evening sorting her effects out. As she moved from room to room, she was aware of being watched, and of a general atmosphere of curiosity. She did not feel threatened and decided to put the whole thing down to a benevolent ghost. The missing food did intrigue her, but, much as she thought about it, she could not reach a satisfactory explanation.

She sorted out her bedroom and watched a good film before going to bed. She slept well, but again had a strange dream, this time where she was being questioned by the goblins, who wanted her to go and meet their leader.

She was up early, and walked down to the stable block to check on Lucy and Sam. They were up and she was invited into the flat for a cup of tea. She had not seen the flat and was shown round. They had worked hard, and the place was almost habitable. The cat was curled up in front of the gas fire and she asked if they needed anything. The whole place was in poor decorative order, and the kitchen furniture was old and shabby.

Over the tea, she suggested that all the flats and houses needed refurbishing, and asked Sam to find a firm of decorators to give a quote. She also suggested they think of colour schemes, and she asked them both if, when they had time, they could check all the houses and suggest what they needed in terms of cookers, fridges, washing machines and furniture. She wanted to carpet where appropriate, and they were delighted to help plan the house. She wanted the living room in the house turned into a private sitting room, and then she talked about refurbishing the attic floor of the house.

Sam was very helpful and together they came up with some good ideas. Lucy suggested that they all return to the big house to start work. Judith asked her to get herself settled in first and Lucy said she would have to go shopping very soon. Judith explained that the Astra would be available and the three of them could go into town later.

Sam walked back to the house with Judith and went to do some measuring in the living room, and then went upstairs to the attics. Judith was in the library when Nora arrived, and went through the day with her. Sam returned and asked if he should fetch the cleaning 'trio'. He went off in the Astra, and before long, Dot, Haley and Betty arrived. Nora went off with them and Judith made a number of telephone calls. Mary arrived with a cup of coffee for her and she asked her to join her. Mary fetched her coffee from the kitchen and Judith explained about the cereal and sugar the previous day and asked if Mary had any idea what it might be. Judith explained that it didn't worry her, as much as intrigue her.

Mary looked faintly embarrassed, and thought carefully before she spoke,

"It's the house. It has always happened here, but only in certain parts of the house. I don't want to scare you, but we have always believed there was a mystery here. Miss Susan used to leave some food out, and it was usually gone in the morning. It isn't rats, or mice, we don't know what it is. Miss Susan knew, I think, but said not to worry about it. Whatever takes the food, never harms anything, and never hurts anyone. There is a sort of legend about this place, that it is protected by something powerful. Some old wives' tales talk of goblins, but no one has ever seen anything they can describe. Some years back, so the story goes, before Miss Susan's time, a burglar broke in, and he was found gibbering in the village that demons were in this house. No one believed him, of course, he was a renowned drunk, but the house don't like intruders, but it is a lucky house for those it likes. Have you seen or heard anything?"

Judith said, "Well, yes and no. I have heard some funny noises, I put them down to the house being old, and the heating having been put on recently. I've had some strange dreams, but put them down to various other factors, after all, I have had a lot of worries recently. The last two years have been pretty traumatic. I met Clive, married him, retired from my job, sold my house, we lived all over the place, then Aunt Susan died, we had to change our plans, then there was the accident, Clive was killed, and the stay with his family was not ideal. I also lost the baby in the accident. I was injured and have been trying to mend, and then coming up here. It has been a terrible shock, all in all, especially coming to terms with being really rich. It is an awful responsibility and it's not surprising if I have some odd dreams. It has been two years of stress, but there were some wonderful times too."

Mary gasped, "I had no idea, I am so sorry. You must have been through hell! Look, this house either likes, or dislikes people. No one it dislikes stays long. I think it likes you. Miss Susan said it would. The house won't hurt you, and we like you. Remember to put food away in the kitchen, and in time you will get used to the noises, which are mostly just an old house."

Judith laughed, "I could do without a hungry ghost, though! I feel welcomed in the house and oddly comforted at times. It seems curious about me, so I'll let it decide if it wishes to divulge its secrets."

"You know, this place used to be called Portal House, as it was believed it held a secret portal to the underground. Now it has been changed to Porthwaite Hall."

Judith suddenly remembered something that she had seen, and said,

"Where does the water enter the fishpond, that then becomes the stream? Is it piped? I know it feeds the lake, but I did wonder where it came from."

Mary thought about it, and said,

"Do you know, I've no idea. I've never thought about it. It never runs dry, that I do know, because the cattle drink from the stream. How strange! Jim might know, or even Mum. The area is riddled with caves, but I've never heard of one under the house. How odd!"

"Never mind, no doubt I shall find out in due course, it's not top of my list of priorities, and getting an accountant is, if you are to get any wages this week. Do you want weekly or monthly pay?"

"Jim gets paid monthly, so that would be fine, thank you."

Judith waited until they had finished their coffee and Mary had gone before resuming her telephone calls. Sam knocked on the door and came in. He asked permission to use the phone to contact the decorators, and asked if he could arrange for them to come and estimate for the work. Judith told him to go ahead and asked if there was a telephone in their flat, and when she was told no, she added another job to her list. Sam made the call and asked if they could have the man up on the following day. Judith agreed, and when he left, she looked up a number and rang it.

"Hello, could I speak to Tom Barker please? It's Judith Swallow, from Porthwaite Hall, could he ring me if he isn't available? Thank you, I'll wait."

She waited patiently, and then when he came on the line, said

"Mr Barker, did Jack Gough speak to you about me? Right, look, I need your help, is there any chance you could come and see me at the house this week? Come to lunch, it could take some time, I need your advice on a lot of matters. Today, yes, are you sure? Come as soon as you can. Yes, by all means bring your secretary."

Money, she decided, had it's advantages.

She went off to find Nora and tell her there would be two more for lunch. They had arranged for everyone working in the house to have lunch there. She found Sam and said she wouldn't be able to go shopping that day, but asked him to pick up a list from her when he took Lucy in, and to see Nora for a list too.

She returned to the library and made a lot more phone calls. Then she compiled a personal shopping list and one for the house. She had a number of lists on the go, and tidied up the paper work. The front door bell went. Someone called that they would go and minutes later, Betty came in and said there was someone waiting to see her in the Chinese Drawing Room. Judith went through to find a neat, rather dapper, balding little man, dressed in a brown coat, waiting nervously by the window. On her approach he cleared his throat, and announced he was Mr Aaron Sandell, and explained he ran the village store and post office.

He welcomed her to the village, and on her invitation sat on a chair, and explained that he had hoped she would use the shop. He could give discount on large orders, he explained, and would, of course, deliver, daily, if necessary, to the house. He looked at her hopefully, and handed her a business card. He explained he had an off–licence, and ran a greengrocery and butchers department. He was also the agent for dry cleaning, and had taken the liberty of bringing an order book with him.

Judith thanked him, and offered him a cup of tea or coffee. He was surprised, but accepted, and she went to find Nora, and while she was organising the drink, asked about Mr Sandall. Nora explained that the shop was good, and that it was struggling to keep its prices down.

"He has seven children, you know, and works long hours to make the place pay. Your order would help him a lot, and he only gets good quality stuff. He is a little expensive, but if you want to get the locals on your side, use him. He can never do enough for his customers and supports all the village events, but he doesn't go to church, as he goes to the synagogue in town. He's well liked and people have accepted him."

"Would you come and talk to him with me? You will be dealing with him more than I will. Will he give me an account, do you think?"

Together they returned to the Chinese Drawing Room. Nora

provided a tray, and over a drink they discussed an account. Judith went and fetched some of her shopping list, and in a meticulously neat hand he wrote out an order. Nora gave him a long list and called Sam in and he added another order. Judith assured him that he could pay back the order from his wages. Mr Sandall was delighted to wait, while Mary added some more, and the trio of ladies were asked if they needed any more cleaning materials.

Judith added two boxes of cereal to the list and some more sugar, and grinned at Mary, who saw her do so.

When Mr Sandell left, he was a happy man. He went out to his neat little van, and promised to have as much as he could delivered that afternoon. He was quite servile to Judith and Nora, and thanked them warmly. As he drove off, Judith got the giggles, and was heading for the library again, when she heard the telephone, and spoke to the telephone company. She asked them to come out and estimate for telephones to be fitted in all the houses, and for an internal system between all the estate properties. She had to hang on to be put through to the business section, but finally extracted a promise from them to come on the Thursday. For the next hour she arranged for tradesmen to call, in their masses.

Another visitor, in a smart blue BMW, drew up. A tall, elegant, well–dressed, man got out, and a middle–aged woman, carrying a lap–top computer, approached.

"Mrs Swallow, I'm Tom Barker, and may I introduce my secretary, Celia Johnson? How are you, are you getting better? Jack told me what the score was. How may I help?"

They followed her to the library, where there was a tray of coffee and tea waiting. Judith explained her problems, and her idea of solutions. Celia kept notes of the meeting. It took some time for Judith to explain her outline plans for the estate and her future. Tom listened and asked a few very relevant questions. Judith asked Celia's opinion, from time to time, and then the gong went for lunch. Celia locked her computer and took it with her into the dining room.

The meal was excellent and consisted of a good lasagne, or roast lamb, and some fresh vegetables. All the inside staff ate in the dining room, and the outside staff ate in the kitchen, at their own request. Lucy had come down for lunch, and helped clear the tables. The pudding was rhubarb crumble and custard. At the beginning of the meal everyone seemed a little shy, but by coffee, there was the general hubbub of friendly chat.

Judith, Celia and Tom went back to the library, and Judith made a telephone call to Mr Cummings' office. She followed a carefully scripted format, and Celia listened in and recorded what was said.

Having established that Mr Cummings was to visit on Wednesday, they moved on to other matters, and Judith asked if they could recommend anyone for the post of personal assistant and secretary, who could handle staff wages, PAYE, and pension contributions. and also keep simple books. Judith also asked for a reputable accountant, and she made enquiries about a farm secretary for the estate.

After another hour, they went with her to inspect the empty stable flat, both lodges and the stable house. They also looked at the stables, and spoke to Jim about some matters regarding the horses in the paddocks.

Back at the house they made plans for the Wednesday and Tom and Celia left. Judith went round the house, trying to find Mary and thank her for the meal. In the kitchen she came across Stuart, much to her surprise. He asked her if he could move in the following week, and some points about the gardens. She suggested a meeting on the Friday afternoon, of all the staff, and after that, a managerial meeting, to plan for the following week. Stuart said he would be there. Judith asked him to get Sam, Bill and Liam to come. She said that wages would be paid, as appropriate, then. She hunted Nora down, told her, and asked her to arrange for Lucy, Betty, Dot and Haley to attend with Mary. Then she found Mary and asked if Jim could spare her five minutes, later.

Judith answered the phone, and made several appointments with salesmen and representatives. She was busy for the afternoon and only left the library to sign the delivery note that came with the grocery order. Mr Sandell had included a basket of fruit, and a lovely stephanotis, as well as a fine bottle of wine, for her. There was also a large fruit basket for Nora and a box of chocolates for Mary.

Mary popped in to say that she was going back to see the kids in from school, and she and Jim would pop over after tea to see her. Sam returned from the shops with Lucy, and unloaded many packages into the butler's pantry. Then he drove Betty, Dot and Haley back to the village.

Bill, with Liam in tow, asked to see her. He wouldn't come any further than the kitchen, so she went in there, and over a (large) mug of tea, he said,

"Mr Stuart, he asked me to ask you, what lawns do you want us to do first, ma'am? We have been overhauling the mowers, but they is in such a shocking state, we was wondering, could you ask Mr Jim if we could borrow his hay cutter? There will be a lot of hay, I reckons he could use it. May we have your permission, ma'am? I haven't never seen the gardens here in such a state, that I haven't. It was nice to see you in church yesterday, and you'll let us know what you want?"

Bill was in full flow, and went on for some time about the grass. He had just started on the state of the kitchen garden, when she was saved by Sam, who was to run them home. She assured Bill that she would sort it with Jim, and let him know the next day. She walked round the side of the house with him and Liam, and Bill began to chat with Sam, so she asked Liam,

"Have you enjoyed your first day, Liam?"

Liam blushed furiously, and was so shocked to be spoken to, it took him a while to reply.

"Oh, yes, ma'am, that I have, we was doing the mowers. I liked me lunch, it was grand, we only have grub like that on Sundays. Do I get a lunch like that everyday? You wait till I tell my mum, she'll be fair chuffed, pudding too. Yummy."

Judith thought she had discovered what motivated Liam.

Back in the house, she wrote some letters, found some stamps in her bag, and with her stick went to the front door where she met Nora who was just heading home. Nora told her there was supper in the fridge, and she would be back in the morning. Judith found out from her that there was a post box at the front gate, and despite Nora's protestations, she insisted on walking down to the post box. Nora walked with her, so far, and Judith had a pleasant stroll down the drive.

At the gates she posted the letters and limped back to the house. Just as she got to the front doors, Sam pulled up in the car and asked where the car was to be kept. Judith told him to take it to the barn, and he drove off.

The house seemed strangely quiet after the busy day. Judith found her room had been cleaned, tidied and the bed re-made. There were some fresh flowers in a vase and her washing had been taken away. Her cases had been put away and she found them in a box room nearby. Several bedrooms had been cleaned and looked much smarter. She explored most of the first floor, and had a good look at the bathrooms, box rooms, linen room, and bedrooms.

She went downstairs, had a cup of tea, and returned to the library, wrote some more letters and paid several bills. She was still there when Mary and Jim came in. She asked them if they could make the Friday meeting and spoke to Jim about the farms and her enquiry for a farm secretary, and gave him Bill's message. She asked him to prepare a report about the state of the farms, staff members, and his needs for the farm.

She thanked them for their hard work, and they talked briefly over the events of the day, and what to expect the following day.

Judith had a headache and left the library. She went out of the back door and sat in the evening sun, overlooking the lawns and the lake. The sunset was quite spectacular, and she watched a heron fly off the lake, and waited for the sun to go down.

She heated the supper, took it to the sitting room and watched some television. She returned to the kitchen and was careful to put anything edible away, and then went to bed.

She did wake once during the night, convinced she heard something rustling, somewhere, above her, in one of the upper rooms. She thought she heard light footsteps up there, but was just too tired to worry about it.

Chapter Five

Judith woke early, showered and dressed quickly, and went for a walk before breakfast. This time she went round the back of the house, down the steps, around the hay fields, and followed the stream, crossing it twice, once on an elegant little footbridge, and once on a substantial bridge, where there was a cinder road. She was glad of her walking stick as the undergrowth was lush and, in places, full of brambles. She got to the edge of the lake, which was bigger than she had first thought. Here too, were waterlilies, and as she followed a faint path round the lakeside, she saw a boat house at the mouth of an inlet. She found the door unlocked, and inside was a skiff, two old–fashioned canoes and a kayak. There was a small dingy and an old rowboat with an outboard engine. None of them looked well kept. Next to the boat house was a long jetty into the lake, and a diving board at the end of the jetty. There was a wooden building, which contained a sauna and some changing cubicles, and a store with patio furniture, duck boards, floats and some life buoys.

A paved area led to steps down into the water. There were signs of fairly recent use.

Continuing round the path, across two bridges over more stream inlets, and past a small garden shed, she came to a well–fenced paddock, containing several horses. They were happy to come and talk to her and seemed in good condition. One mare had a foal. The paddock was large but muddy around the edges. The horses soon lost interest in her when they failed to find any sugar or carrots on her, so she walked on and into a cool coniferous wood, with rhododendrons in a clearing ahead.

She stayed with the lake and came through a gate into a hay meadow. This was a profusion of wild flowers and insects buzzing around them. She carefully took her time negotiating the meadow and nearly tripped several times. From the lake shore, the ground rose up through the meadow to a mixed wood, and above that rose steeply onto the fell, above the tree line. There were sheep grazing on the tops, and she could see a limestone cliff rising steeply just beyond the trees. She made it through the meadow, and after carefully closing the gate, stumbled and fell into a large muddy puddle. She struggled up and rolled most of the mud off on some clean grass. When she stood up, her leg hurt, more than usual. She sat on a grassy knoll, and watched the dragonflies on the lake, flitting like jewels from place to place, and hovering for seconds in rows across the water lilies.

The pain in her leg began to ease, the sunshine was warm, and the noises around her began to relax her. She looked out across the lake, back towards the house. A butterfly rested on a flower beside her, sunning itself. A fish jumping in the lake, brought her out of her contemplation, and she got up and limped on. A stand of trees came down to the water, and the path went between two huge oak trees, and she came to the Folly. At the front of the building the path became the cinder vehicle track, and she walked round the very old, tower–like building. There was a door at the front and one at the rear, and two windows on the ground floor. She looked through the windows but the curtains were drawn and both the doors were locked. The grass around the Folly was neatly cut.

Judith walked slowly along the cinder road and noticed fresh vehicle tracks where there was mud or earth.

The lake, wider by now, was held by an ornamental dam, over which was a stone walkway. The water from the lake cascaded in several small waterfalls into a small river. Judith had to pause by a seat on the walkway, as her leg ached. She sat for a while listening to the waterfalls, and mused on how beautiful the place could be. She felt relaxed and comfortable, and safe. It suddenly struck her that she had not felt like that for a long time, and just how stressed–out she was getting.

She looked at her watch, and saw that it was eight thirty, and she walked on, up the track, hoping to get to the house before everybody arrived. The path led round to the back of the summerhouse, and up to the drive. She turned off and went into the house, and went up to her room, washed and changed, and got to the kitchen as Nora came in.

They had a cup of coffee and then Sam arrived with Betty and the others. Bill and Liam made a brief appearance and went off to meet Jim by the barn. Mary and Lucy came through to the laundry and Judith felt very crowded. Haley came to tell her there were some visitors, so Judith went to the hall.

Waiting for her was a cheerful post woman, who introduced herself as Nancy and asked where she should deliver the sack of mail she had. She went out to the post van, and brought in a small bag of post, and a number of catalogues, and three parcels. Judith explained that some of the properties would soon be occupied, but until then she should deliver to the house, and put the post on the hall table. Judith mentioned that there was coffee in the kitchen and Nancy went through to have a cup with Nora.

Judith watched a car pull up outside, and a short, stocky man got out, and knocked on the door.

"Hello," he said, "I'm Dr Tippett, the local GP. I had a letter from your specialist, to expect you, and I was told you had arrived. No one could talk about much else yesterday! Have you time for a quick chat?"

Judith liked him instantly, and invited him into the sitting room. Dr Tippett talked to her and examined her. She confessed to falling that morning, and was lectured on trying to run before she could walk. He arranged to visit regularly and they chatted about her general health. He promised to give her an exercise plan. Just as she was about to suggest some refreshment, a knock on the door revealed that Mary had put a tray in the Chinese Drawing Room, to which they went. After a short chat, he left and she returned to the hall, and Haley helped her take the post into the library, where she spent some time sorting it. There were several letters she had been expecting and some bills to be paid. The parcels were all items she had ordered, and the catalogues she put aside until later.

Before she could read any personal letters, Betty knocked and entered. She had an outraged look of disapproval on her face, and informed Judith, in shocked tones, that two 'police people' were at the front door to see her. She added that they should have come to the back door, if they knew what was proper. Judith thanked Betty and went to see what they wanted.

An inspector, and a PC were waiting in the hall. The inspector, a woman of about Judith's age, introduced herself as Erica Kitson, the local divisional commander, and the PC as John Arrowsmith, the local community officer.

The officers had come on an introductory visit, and PC Arrowsmith asked her for an upto–date list of keyholders. She told them who was living where, and what her plans were. Inspector Kitson assured her of any help she might need, and gave her the numbers of the local station. Judith explained that she was a retired officer, and took them into the Chinese Drawing room and offered them a drink. Judith asked PC Arrowsmith to call whenever he wanted, and asked about poachers and any local crimes that might affect her. After a quarter of an hour, they had to leave.

Betty cleared the tray, and was almost 'tutt tutting' until Judith told her it was a friendly visit, and she wasn't in any trouble. Betty relaxed a bit after that. Before she could get up, the decorator arrived with Sam, to give an estimate. Nora, Sam, Judith, and the decorator toured the house, and told him what was required. He then went off with Sam, to measure up the other houses.

Back in the library, Judith got to grips with the post and had it in different piles in no time. She made several phone calls and sat down to read a letter from Uncle Jack. It amused her and she put it aside and read another from Mike.

She was just reaching for another letter, from a friend in

Hampshire, when she saw the tractor go past the side of the house and the hay cutter behind it.

It was warm in the library and she opened the French windows, and went out to the patio for a cigarette. She watched the tractor, and walked round to the back of the house to see what was going on. Bill and Liam were scything the grass under the trees, and Jim was mowing the grass below the house.

Mary came out of the kitchen and as they watched the men working, Mary thanked her for getting the hot water fixed at the farm. Judith had forgotten all about it. Judith asked her,

"Have you been down to the lake, to the boat house or sauna recently? Someone has, and I hoped it was you and the family?

Mary shook her head, and said, "Not since the hot spell in the early bit of the summer holidays. I hope you didn't mind"

"Not at all, but someone has been there recently, do you think the boys sneaked down there?"

"No. I never let them go down there without supervision. It's a beautiful spot, but too far for kids to be out of sight. I wouldn't let them use the boats, either, unless one of us was there. I know who it is, or I think I do. Mr Cummings brought some friends up last month, and they went down there. They checked the horses in the paddock. It could have been the people in the holiday let."

"What holiday let?"

"The Folly. It was let right up to last month. Some of his friends had it for a holiday cottage until two weeks ago. They came and bought eggs from us a couple of times. They got their car bogged down, and Jim had to tow them out once. He charged them a tenner, and they didn't like it."

"That would be why the lawns have been cut down there, then?"

"Yes. Cummings tried to get Jim to cut it, but Jim couldn't, as he was haymaking himself. I think Cummings got a contracting firm in. He told me I should go and clean the place at the beginning of the summer, but Jim put a stop to that, as he wasn't prepared to pay me any extra. It was sad, though, one couple had a small dog, a Yorkshire terrier. Bloody nuisance it was, they never kept it under control, it was in the sheep most days, but it got out one night, and we think a fox or badger got it. They found the remains the next morning, by the meadow. Ever so upset they were. Poor little thing, it wasn't its fault, its owners didn't know how to train it."

"That's interesting. Poor dog! It seems as if Mr Cummings has been making very free with the property. He's coming here tomorrow, and I would like you to give me a list of what he has been doing, or how he has been using the estate before he gets here. I would like to know how to sort all this out."

"When did you go down to the lake? It is quite a way round it, did you get round?"

"Yes, and fell in a puddle in the hay meadow. Dr Tippett told me off this morning!"

"I saw him arrive. He was ever so good to Miss Susan. His dad was the doctor here before him. Nice family, all of them. Miss Susan was private, of course, and she only had to ask, and he was up here. You have been doing too much, you know, you look tired. Don't knock yourself up, we are all here to help."

"Bless you, I know! Dr Tippett said the same. By next week, things should be a little more ordered."

Sam reappeared with the decorator, and asked if the farm houses were to be included for re-decorating. Judith said,

"Yes, if the people in them want it. Mary, do you want your house redecorated at all? If so, talk to this gentleman, and arrange for him to come and measure up, and show you some colour charts and sample books."

The gong went for lunch, and they all went to the kitchen. The decorator was told there was food for him too, and he and Nora discussed decorating the lodge, over the meal. Everyone ate in the kitchen, and Liam ate three helpings of chocolate pudding. Judith asked how the grass cutting was coming along, and Bill was delighted to go into great detail, most of which she did not understand. All she could get out of Liam was that he had enjoyed his grub, and could he work Saturdays too?

Judith went back to her letters, having asked Mary if there had been any post delivered for her before she had come. Mary assured her all post had been given to her when she had arrived, but all letters to the estate had been taken by Mr Cummings.

She read the rest of the letters, and looked through the catalogues, and marked out some items she wanted to order, and made a dozen or so calls. The telephone man was the next to arrive. For an hour she resisted the 'ready made' systems, and insisted on what she wanted. He went off with Sam to visit all the premises concerned and came back to see her. She informed him there would need to be an extra extension in the basement, and he asked to return later in the week to finalise matters.

To her surprise Celia entered the room in the mid afternoon. She explained,

"I am sorry to intrude, but I have typed up what we discussed yesterday, and what we covered, and I have added some ideas of my own and a couple Tom came up with. You can look through it and let me know if you want anything added. Tom is very sorry, he's in court tomorrow morning, but will try and get here for the afternoon. He has suggested our new, younger solicitor comes in his place with me. Cummings has never met either of us before."

"That's fine, I don't want to tackle him myself, on my own. His not knowing you might help."

"The other reason I came out today is, I have made some enquiries with a friend of mine, who teaches the farm secretaries at the agricultural college. She knows of about five of her ex-students who are seeking work, and are up to the job, and suggested you ring them. I wondered, would you like me to interview with you? I'm not trying to teach you to suck eggs, but on the secretarial side, I might be able to help. Tom says it is fine with him. I have found someone who can draw up the contracts of employment. He's outside in the car now, do you want to talk to him, tell him what you want? He is semi-retired and used to be a personnel officer with the local generating board. His speciality is employment law."

"Celia, thank you. Yes, please do ask Betty to bring him in, meanwhile, let's get Nora, and find out when she is available. She will have to work with the secretary, as will Jim and Stuart. I'd like them to meet the applicants, and get their input. How are you fixed for Friday? We have a staff meeting in the afternoon I'd like to push this on, because I'm getting bogged down and need someone! I'm not very good at it."

A cadaverous old man, stooping, and walking with a stick, was ushered into the room by Betty. Nora came in and spoke to Judith and then took Celia off. Betty brought in tea and cakes and Judith sat down and had a long talk with the man, Gregory McDuff. His appearance was totally at odds with his personality. He listened carefully to what she wanted, and wrote it down in a spidery scrawl with a fountain pen. Nora appeared and was soon introduced and scurried off to get some details of the staff, and returned with Celia who sat down, obviously prepared to wait. Mr McDuff suggested she go back to town and said he would take a taxi later. She agreed and left, giving Judith a folder and promising to return in the morning. Soon Judith was laughing at a slightly risqué joke, and Gregory, as he insisted she call him, was suggesting some matters to include in the contracts. He also advised her on tax matters, and suggested she set up a company to run the estate. Nora popped in to say the staff were due to go home and she had prepared a couple of meals.

Judith asked if Gregory would like to stay for supper, but he asked instead, if she would honour him with her presence at dinner in town and the taxi could drop her back later. She was, he explained, going to be paying plenty for his services, so he could afford it! Nora agreed that it was an excellent idea, as Judith needed a break, and faced with two determined friends, she agreed. She telephoned all the people on the list Celia had left her, and then for the next two hours she and Gregory thrashed out what she wanted for the estate and for the staff.

She changed her clothes and was ready when the taxi picked them up, and they drove into the town, and drew up outside an old–fashioned hotel. Over drinks, a good meal and a superb bottle of wine, Gregory told Judith of his youthful exploits, and his first visits to Porthwaite Hall. He described some of the parties, balls, and fun he had had at the Hall, and how kind Susan Holt had been to him and his peers. He knew, and she suspected had got drunk with, Uncle Jack, and he admitted to having had a crush on Great Aunt Susan. He described, with an amazing detail, how the estate had been, and told of many happy days there before moving from the area to follow his career.

Most of all, he made Judith laugh. The band struck up and a few couples got up for an elegant foxtrot. He said he would ask her to dance, but they might trip each other up with their sticks! Another bottle of wine appeared, and she accused him of trying to get her drunk and he admitted it. He did draw the line there he said, next she would accuse him of trying to seduce her!

When she mentioned her interview with Mr Cummings the following day, he snorted with annoyance and said the fellow was a rogue and she should sack him. He told her several things of interest about Cummings, and then over a brandy, she said she should be getting back. In the hotel lobby, they waited for the taxi and he confided,

"Judith, my dear, you remind me so much of Susan when she was your age, not physically, but in your ways, and your personality. You will grow to love the house, and it will be good to you. I'll be out on Friday morning with these contracts for the staff you have now, and I'll sort out the other business for you. Can I come and visit you sometimes, you are good company, and you would make an old widower very happy, if we could be friends?"

She explained that they were interviewing on the Friday, and she asked him if he would like to be in on the interviews, and have lunch and spend the day at the Hall, and she would treat him to a meal after that. They both hobbled out to the taxi, got in, and he was taken to his home, then the taxi took her back to the Hall. As they were coming up the drive a large black creature, the size of a Labrador, ran across in front of them, just where the headlights were fading, and the driver braked hard. He swore, and then apologised, and checked she was unhurt. He had not hit the creature, but was shaken up and went very white. As they got to the front door, she offered him a cup of coffee. He declined, but walked her to the door, looking nervously over his shoulder as he did so.

"What was that?" he asked, "I've never seen anything like that before, was it a dog, do you have a black dog, it should be in, this time of night?"

"No," she replied, "It must be the black Labrador from the farm," she assured him, "it's a bit lame, and runs funny. You didn't hit it, so no harm done. Thank you for seeing me to the door." She paid him and gave a generous tip. He almost ran back to the taxi, jumped in and drove off steadily down the drive. She heard him speed up when he reached the road.

She shut and bolted the front door and sat down on the stairs. She was shaken too, mainly because she knew there was no big black dog within miles, and also what she had seen was no dog, but something she could not identify. Dogs didn't run on their hind legs, and this creature had done just that. She tried to work out why she had lied so glibly.

She sat for a while thinking it through, and then took herself up to bed. She was unable to sleep for some time, and left the television on, so she couldn't hear anything else.

She woke during the night and turned the set off. As she tried to sleep, she heard rustling from the corridor, and got out of bed to investigate. She was pretty frightened, but annoyed enough to investigate. She saw nothing in the corridor, and limped down to the landing, where she waited and listened, and convinced she could hear rustling downstairs, quietly went down the stairs to the hall. She crept to the kitchen, and saw, and heard, the pantry door closing softly as she entered the room. By the time she got to the pantry door and opened it and put on the light, there was nothing to be seen, but she could hear the rustling coming from behind a grating under the bottom shelf. She could see nothing unusual, and whatever it was, had gone. She switched out the light, and turned the key in the lock as she left the pantry.

She made a cup of tea in the kitchen, and sat at the table, smoking and trying to summon the courage to go upstairs. After another cup of tea, she tried reasoning with herself. Her nerve went, and she went back upstairs, leaving all the lights on in the corridor and hall and on the landing. She even locked her bedroom door.

She finally drifted off to sleep. If she dreamed, she had no memory of it.

Chapter Six

Instructions of client, Judith Cecily Swallow, at meeting held at Porthwaite Hall.

Persons Present –
Mrs Judith Cecily Swallow
Thomas Algernon Barker
Celia Marie Johnson

Mrs Swallow stated that she had been widowed some months previously, in a Road Traffic Accident, in which she had been injured. She had been the main beneficiary of her late husband's will, and had inherited a considerable fortune of several million pounds from him. Prior to this, she and her husband, Clive Stanley Swallow, had jointly inherited the complete and vast fortune of Susan Adela Holt, including the whole Porthwaite Estate, two farms, a public house, The Gargoyle, in Applebeck, all the buildings on the estate, seventeen houses in the village of Applebeck, an industrial premises in Leeds, and other properties in Leeds, plus considerable bonds, stocks, shares, and land in seven English counties, and in Ireland, Scotland, and the Island State of Jersey, and properties abroad.

Death duties having been paid on both estates, the fortune inherited by Mrs Swallow was still sufficient to leave her a vast fortune, both in shares, land and rents, together with her own income. She employed a land agent, Mr Gerald Cummings, of Wynn, Cummings & Porter, to manage the estate at Porthwaite Hall, as he had done for some years prior to Miss Holt's death, and after that, whilst she and Mr Swallow were waiting to take up residence on the estate.

She had written several times to Mr Cummings (copies attached), immediately after the death of Mr Swallow, and subsequent to that, and had requested details of the management of the estate. Mr Cummings had failed to carry out some of her instructions to her satisfaction, and she felt that he was prevaricating. He also attempted to dissuade her from taking up residence, and advised her to sell the estate.

She has not found the estate or buildings to have been

maintained to an acceptable standard, and the property had been devalued considerably, due to what she suspects to be deliberate neglect. Despite instructing that she be informed of any actions taken, she had heard nothing from Mr Cummings for six months, except to be provided with a single door key to the Hall. No accounts or documentation have been delivered to her, despite a specific request.

She intends to invest in the estate and improve it, so that it can provide employment, and ultimately become self–sufficient. She considered his advice to be poor, or deliberately damaging to her, and patronising towards her.

The following need to be investigated, and have come to her attention:-

The Cummings family have used the facilities of the estate for their own purposes. i.e. they have stabled their horses in the stables at Porthwaite Hall, and there are still six mares and a foal in the lower paddock.

The Folly, and the North and South Lodges have been let to friends of the Cummings', and as holiday lets.

Mr Cummings made Mrs Nora Morpeth redundant, without recompense, and reduced Mrs Mary Morpeth's hours to ten per week, to maintain a twenty–seven bedroomed property.

The farm manager, Mr James Morpeth was refused sufficient staff at lambing time, and he and his family were inadequately recompensed for work done.

Despite specific instructions to maintain the grounds in a tidy condition, the gardens and farm lands have been totally neglected.

The houses within the estate, have, in the most part, not been maintained in safe or satisfactory condition, thus leading to considerable devaluation.

The responsibilities of a landlord have been ignored, an example being the failure to repair or replace an immersion heater in Caulders Farm House.

Mr Cummings has, either directly or indirectly, falsely informed some of Mrs Swallow's tenants that she would be evicting them and selling their homes, thus causing them understandable hostility towards her.

There are many keys missing, for parts of the estate.

All these actions, omissions, or events have taken place

without reference to Mrs Swallow, and some of these are in direct contravention of explicit written instructions.

Mrs Swallow had informed Mr. Cummings of her whereabouts at all times. He has personally removed post from the Hall within the last two weeks. She had instructed his office of her intended date of occupation, and arrived on that date.

Mrs Swallow hopes that Mr Cummings can explain his actions or omissions, but as things stand, she suspects either an ulterior motive for his actions or inactions, or incompetence.

She was surprised he showed a willingness to find a purchaser for the estate. She had already stated her desire that nothing should be sold.

Mrs Swallow has instructed us to employ an investigator to obtain evidence on all of these points, as she suspects that there is the possibility of fraud or malpractice.

There is a possibility that there is a connection between these events and resentment from her late husband's family.

Mr Barker advised that she should request an explanation of some or all of these matters, in the presence of witnesses. He has suggested a specific set of instructions be prepared, and a written copy be served on Mr Cummings, requiring him to surrender immediately all documentation relating to the estate, to Mr Barker.

An accountant is to be employed to assess the documents, and report to Mrs Swallow any findings.

The management of all properties owned by Mrs Swallow may have to be reallocated to another firm.

At 14.02 hours, Mrs Swallow telephoned Mr Cummings. This conversation was recorded as follows:-

JS. "Mr Cummings, this is Judith Swallow, at Porthwaite Hall. I am, as you will know, now in residence. Would you please come to the Hall on Wednesday morning at eleven o'clock, and bring with you all the documentation for the whole estate, as I requested some time ago."

GC. "Mrs Swallow, how nice to hear from you, you are at the hall now, are you? I won't be able to come and see you for at least two weeks, I'm afraid, but you could have an appointment here next week

I'll ask my secretary to fit you in."

JS. "No, Mr Cummings, that is not good enough. I want you here on Wednesday. I am paying you a vast amount of money, and that means you come to me."

GC. "I'll be out of the office on Wednesday, it will have to be next week, at the earliest. What is the hurry?"

JS. "I want to ask the questions, and I don't think I have to explain myself to you. Why can't you make Wednesday, are you in court, or at a funeral, or have an operation booked?"

GC. "No, but I have a previous appointment that day."

JS. "Then cancel it, and be here. I need to see you."

GC. "Look, you can't just order me around. My car has to go to the garage for service, so I have no transport."

JS. "That is all right, Mr Cummings, a car will pick you up at ten o'clock sharp, at your office, or at your home, which do you want?"

GC. "I'm not going to be treated like this."

JS. "Fine, then please be good enough to put me through to the senior partner, Mr. Wynn."

GC. "Why?"

JS. "I want to speak to him."

GC. "Maybe I could make Wednesday. I'll use the wife's car if I must."

JS. "No, Mr Cummings, that won't be necessary. Our car will fetch you. We wouldn't want your wife's car breaking down, would we? Do you wish to be picked up from the office or your home?"

GC. "The office, but you're being very unreasonable."

JS. "I know, put it down to being a recently widowed woman, liable to get depressed, shall we? I've waited long enough for you to contact me, and now you can comply with my wishes for a change, I'll see you on Wednesday."

Call ended by Mrs Swallow.

Following the above conversation, Mr Barker telephoned Mr Albert Wynn, who was personally known to him, and asked to meet him the following day, which Mr Wynn agreed to. Mr Wynn also agreed to attend Porthwaite Hall on Wednesday.

Mrs Swallow has already sent for, and will have, a dual tape recorder to record the interview.

Mrs Swallow asked for advice on employing a PA and farm secretary.

****

57 Tennyson Road,
Radstock,
Somerset.

Dear Judith,

I am sorry I have been so long in writing, but we were so astounded at your generosity to us, that we didn't quite know what to say. We have had a good think about your suggestion, and Mr Gough has been most helpful. The Rolls is fantastic, and we have used it a lot especially for weddings. We have hired a decent garage for that and the other cars, and there is a lot more work coming in, and I have been able to take on two drivers, and the business is doing well. If it goes on like this, and it is early days yet, I might be able to buy our house from the council.

I still get to ferry the Swallow family around. Old Mrs Swallow is really nice, and asks after me and mine, and young Mrs Swallow, she is quite pleasant.

Miss Ruth has a gentleman friend, as you know, but he was arrested last week. I don't know what for, but I will try to find out. I think it was drunk driving, because I had to go to the cop shop and pick him up, and his car was still in the police yard at Frome.

Young Sharon asked me the other day if I had any work for her. She is waiting to join a police force up your way, and is fed up with hanging around, listening to the rest of the family moan, so I got her doing some office work, and valeting the cars. She really didn't mind getting her hands dirty. Her father does not approve. She says she is writing to you.

The other day Mrs Heldman (Ingrid) asked me to post some letters for her, after I took her somewhere. (She was too lazy to walk past a post box.) Of course, I did it right away, but I did notice one of them was addressed to a firm in Harrogate, which is quite close to you I believe, and I remember it was to a Mr Cummings, so I noted the firm, Wynn, Cummings and something. It was written by Mr Heldman, I know his handwriting. I wondered if it would interest you.

In the same post were several other letters from him, and one was to a doctor at a psychiatric hospital. I don't trust him, and I am worried he's after old Mrs Swallow's money, or yours.

I may be imagining things, but be warned, something is being planned. I know you will be discreet.

Do let us know how you are getting on, we worry about you. Are you out of plaster yet, and is the house haunted?

Kind regards,

Mike.

****

Wisteria House,
Hinton Mendip,
Nr. Bristol.

My dear Judith,

Just a few lines to keep you up-to-date with things down here. You asked me to let you know if any of the family wanted to see your will. Three did, Ruth, Francis and my sister.

Ruth wanted a copy, but I refused. She asked if it could be challenged. I told her why it couldn't, and she was a bit miffed. I also told her I wouldn't act for her if she tried. Her partner, Paul, who is going through a divorce with his wife, got his car repossessed the other day, and is facing a drink drive charge. Ruth asked if there was any way she could re-mortgage the house, and I explained the only way she could do so was to sell the house outright, and move to a smaller place. She didn't seem too pleased about that, either. She railed about you, and said you were interfering with her life, and if she asked me, could I get a loan from you. I reminded her of the conditions on which she accepted your gift, and told her to carefully consider bailing her boyfriend out. I hear he owes thousands, and I think he is a bad lot.

Francis looked at the will, and also asked for a copy, but accepted it when I said no. He didn't say much. From something he said the other day, he seems to know you have arrived at the house, but seems convinced you won't stop there. He says the place is unfit to live in, and you will be selling it. Is that true? I wonder how he knows what is going on.

My sister looked at the will, and seemed quite amused. She is getting rather frail now, and was ill last month. She has had to give up the car, so Mike drives her. She loves riding in the Rolls, and Mike always tries to have it for her if he can. When I think how she disapproved when he got it, it amuses me to see her turn around.

Sharon asked me to provide a reference for her, on her application for the police. She is fed up with the family, and has applied to a Yorkshire force, I think to be near you, and away from her father. A nice local inspector came to see me about her, and seemed happy. I think she has been accepted, but is doing odd jobs round here, to keep busy, and give her some money of her own. Her mother is supportive of her, and of course the boys are away. Arthur broke his arm playing rugger the other day, but it is a simple break.

Peter is always at work, and Jane is enjoying the kitchen she had fitted.

I think Francis is up to something, but he doesn't tell me much of what he is doing. The recent panic on the stock market has got him jumpy.

So, how are you keeping? Let me know how you are coping. Give my regards to anyone who still remembers me up there. Have you been in contact with Tom yet? If you meet anyone who remembers me in my younger (wild) days, and they tell you all the naughty things I did, believe them, they are all true!

Please give my regards to Nora Morpeth, she was always so kind when I stayed there.

Regards,

Jack Gough.

****

The Laurels,
Midsummer Upton

Dear Aunt Judith (may I call you that?)

Thank you so much for what you did for me. You have given me not only my freedom from a career I hated, but freedom to make my own choices, and to be independent of Daddy. The other thing that has happened is that Mummy listened to me, and we are so close now, and she is being wonderful, and even stood up

111

for me to Daddy. When Mummy gets adamant, Daddy usually backs down, and he has stopped saying nasty things to me now about kicking the modelling. It was never going to last for ever, and I want to be more than a walking clothes horse, anyway.

Daddy tied all the money I earned up in a fund, when I was under eighteen, and I shall have it, either when I am twenty five or when Daddy allows it. He says I will fritter it if I have it too soon, so he gives me an allowance out of the fund (which is my money anyway) and although it is quite generous, he disapproves of anything that is not essential. I saved a bit up and bought a car, and Mike helped me choose it. When I asked Daddy for some money to insure it, he said no, so I asked Mummy and she gave it to me. I tried to explain to Daddy that I didn't just want the car to go clubbing all the time, and I wanted to go places. He says I am too young to know my own mind. I am 21 now, and he is a dinosaur. I love him lots, but he can be horrid sometimes. I hope he will be proud of me one day.

I applied to several police forces, and one of them was Yorkshire. I went up to their HQ in Leeds last month, and did the exams and fitness tests, all of which I passed, and the interviews were held over the next couple of days. The last day they told me I had been accepted and I start on a local induction course in two weeks' time. I am thrilled! I know it is going to be tough, but I really want to make a success of it. Uncle Jack gave me a reference, and so did the headmaster of my old school.

I think Mummy is sad I won't be nearer home, but she understands.

I promised you I wouldn't cadge off you, but could I ask if I could come and stay with you before I go to the course, just for a day or two? It is a long drive from here, and the course is residential, so it would be for a night or two. After the course I go off to training school, and then, if I make it, I get posted somewhere. I know you will understand all this.

If the house is in such a state as Uncle Francis says, I don't mind roughing it. I shall quite understand if you cannot manage it, could you let me know?

Once I get my posting, I want to buy a place wherever I end up, with what you gave me. You have made life a lot happier for me, thank you.

Selfishly, I have been on about me, and I should have asked first how you are. Are you better, and are things OK? Can

I help at all? I am working at odd jobs here, to keep out of the family's way, and to pay Mummy back for the insurance. Mike lets me do some work for him, and I enjoy it. I also work in the Ring of Bells most evenings. The landlord gave me a pay rise, as he says I pull the punters in. Most nights there are a lot of men here, much to the disgust of their wives and girlfriends. I think I can live without being drooled over by a load of drunks every night, though.

Lots of grateful love, Sharon.

****

Porthwaite Hall

My dear Sharon,

Thank you for your lovely letter and your great news. Congratulations!

No, I would rather you called me Judy, not Aunt Judith. I prefer to rely on friendship, not relationship!

I said you were welcome here, and you are. I shall expect you here whenever you want to come, straight away if you like. Francis is talking through his bum, and there is plenty of space in a warm house and a choice of about twelve bedrooms for you. You will need a local base while you are on courses and at training school. Most of the others will be local, and going home for weekends, so would you look on this place as home? You may even take pity on other students who are far from home and bring them back for the weekend.

It will be great to see you. Come up sooner if you can. You can store any stuff here you need to, until you get your own place.

Your Dad will come round, eventually. I think he misses his little girl! Be kind to him, he loves you. When you have your passing out parade, which I am sure you will, I will invite your parents and the boys to stay, so they can attend.

Please give my love to your Mum. She knows she can stay whenever she wants.

I hate to tell you, but being in the police won't stop drunks drooling over you! You will deal with plenty of them! I expect a lot of policemen will drool too. With your looks, they will be round you like flies round a honey pot. I think that is a mixed metaphor, but don't trust any of them, especially the married ones!

Please, do me a favour, and discreetly let slip to Francis that everything is absolutely super up here. I'll explain when you get here. I am looking forward to your coming.

Lots of love,

Judy

****

Porthwaite Hall

Dear Jack,

Thank you for your letter. Things are hotting up here, and are going to get quite exciting very soon. I cannot say too much at the moment, but as soon as I can I will give you a blow by blow account. I am about to get very tough, and very angry!

I am quite ruthless if I have to be, and won't be taken for a fool! As certain folk are about to find out!

Thank you for the info, I had realised there are plots afoot, and I am in contact with Tom who has been most helpful.

Gregory McDuff sends his regards. It seems the two of you were hellions in your day. I think I can trust him, and he is being very helpful. He is an amusing man. When you come and stay, I'll invite him over. Nora remembers you fondly, and so does Toby and his wife from the pub. I think I have them on my side now.

I am taking on staff, and hopefully a secretary this week, so I'll have a bit more time to keep in touch. Sharon is coming to stay soon, and she is delighted to be in 'the job'!

Give my love to anyone who might think kindly of me. Can you tell them all that everything here is wonderful. It isn't but I want them to think it is. It might rattle one or two of them. Must go now, as I have a busy day ahead of me. I am girding up my loins, or something like that, to do battle, with Tom and his secretary, Celia, at my side, and Nora and Mary and others as the vanguard and Gregory in reserve. Don't worry, I have plenty of friends here already, and I think I know at least some of my enemies.

Love,

Judith Swallow.

****

Porthwaite Hall

Dear Mike,

Thanks for your letter, and thanks for the warnings, which are very interesting! Keep your eyes peeled for me, you are right, there is something afoot. I cannot tell you what is going on yet, but I will write soon. I am glad the business is going well. Sharon is coming to stay with me, thanks for helping her.

I won't divulge my sources. Love to the family. If you get any more info, give me a ring!

Judith Swallow.

****

Porthwaite Hall

Dear Dr Tippett,

Thank you for your visit, and your advice. I have a problem I need to discuss with you, of a confidential nature, could you spare me some time, and come for a meal or something. It is not really urgent, but I need your advice.

Judith Swallow.

Chapter Seven

Judith just had time to finish her letters and walk down to the post box to post them before everyone arrived. As she walked back to the house, Sam passed her in the car with the cleaning staff. Bill arrived on his scooter and Liam rode by on his mountain bike, grinning at her in a benign anticipation of lunch, she assumed. Sam drove back down the drive, picked her up and took her to the front door.

Lucy could be seen walking towards the house and they went to meet her. Judith saw a much happier person, she was no longer so timid. She was full of thanks, and Judith asked after the cat. Lucy assured her the cat was fine. Judith warned her not to let the cat out at night, as there were foxes which that had been known to take small animals. Lucy said she never let the cat out at night, anyway, and then asked if she could start work that day. Judith was happy with that, and asked her if she could do some laundry, and if she had any of her own to do?

Before anyone else arrived, Judith bolted into the kitchen, grabbed a bowl of cereal, and was gulping it down when Nora came in and made her sit down and eat it properly. She also insisted Judith had coffee and some toast and honey. She told Judith to slow down, and said she must take time to eat properly. Judith remembered and asked,

"Nora, is there a large black dog anywhere near here?" Nora shook her head. "No one keeps anything like a chimp, or monkey do they?"

Nora looked at her and said, "No. Nothing like that, the nearest black dog is a Labrador at High Beck Farm, about six miles away as the crow flies. It is very old. The next nearest is a Newfoundland at the nurseries just outside the village, on the other side. Why?"

"I just thought I saw one in the grounds last night, but I had drunk rather a lot of good wine. It's not important. You have collies at the farm, don't you?"

Nora nodded and added, "And they are never out at night, unless they are with us. They won't come near the house anyway, not on their own. Something here scares them off. There are foxes, quite big ones, in the grounds here. One of them is very dark, you probably saw that."

"Yes, that would be it. Nora, it is going to be a big day today, could you call a brief staff meeting in about ten minutes, in here? I want to speak to everyone, and that includes Liam. I have a lot of visitors expected, and could you get one of the ladies to get at least two of the guest bedrooms ready? Ones with bathrooms, if possible. I may have Clive's niece turn up any day, to stay for a while. We have quite a few for lunch, so can you keep the coffee coming? Mr Cummings is due here at eleven, and I doubt he'll be stopping, but we may have up to another four extra. Ah, Mary, is Jim around? I want a brief word with everyone, in here. Could he spare me a few moments?"

She got up without finishing either her coffee or toast, and was about to scurry off to the library, but Nora stood firmly in front of her and growled,

"No, you finish your breakfast. You look exhausted. I met Dr Tippett and his wife last night at a Parish Council Meeting, and he told me to keep an eye on you, so I will. I am sure you are losing weight before my eyes. If you want something fetched, Haley can get it. Eat your breakfast!"

Judith sat down, and Nora and Mary went off to round up all the staff, and they came in, in dribs and drabs, including Stuart, who had come to supervise for the morning. Everyone was invited to help themselves to tea, coffee and cake, and sat down at, or near, the kitchen table. This was a little cramped, and Bill and Sam put in two extra leaves, while Liam was sent to bring in some more chairs. Before everyone was settled, the door bell went and Celia arrived with a balding, red–headed man, with thick pebble glasses and a fussy manner, who was introduced as John Boyle, Tom's junior partner.

They sat at the table, and were given tea. Judith started rather nervously,

"Thank you so much for coming in, everyone. This is really the first time I've had you all together. I would like to say how grateful I am for your help and support, and the hard work you are putting in. I will normally call a weekly staff meeting for three o'clock on a Friday afternoon. That doesn't mean you have to wait until then to come and see me, but at those meetings, everyone has a say, if they want one. In the house, Nora is in charge. Stuart will be in charge outside. If you have a problem, take it to one of them. If you, or they, cannot solve the problem, I am here.

"I do not want anyone working for me who is not happy to be here I will ask that you come and see me if you are not happy. I hope, on Friday, to have your contracts of employment ready to give to you, so you can take a copy away to read, and discuss with your families, or advisors, anything you are unhappy with, or do not understand. Anyone who wants to ask questions can consult me, or Mr McDuff, who will be here. I would like to offer every member of staff, and their immediate family, a private health plan. This means spouses and dependent children and partners. This isn't because I am a particularly benevolent employer, it is because I need you all to be fit and healthy, so you can work harder for me! I propose that Dr Tippett and his partners will be the estate doctors, and will treat you all as private patients, but if anyone would prefer another doctor, please tell me. This will apply to the farm staff, as well, Jim, including families. Lucy, this includes all pre and ante natal care.

"Anyone not on a telephone? I want you all to have a mobile phone while here at work, and some of you will be asked to take them home with you. All houses and buildings on the estate will have a phone.

"This week I shall have to pay your wages in cash, and anyone wanting to be paid in cash weekly, please tell me. Otherwise, your pay will be monthly, direct into a bank account. If you want a savings scheme, we can sort that out, and I will be arranging a pension plan for everyone. Those on hourly rates will get overtime for evenings, early mornings, and weekends, unless they ask for time in lieu.

"While you are at work, you will be fed a lunch, yes, Liam, every day. During school holidays, and at other times, I propose to have a creche or youth club available here. After dark, no one goes out in the grounds alone, except with my specific permission. When you are working alone in the grounds, I want you to have your mobile phone with you. It is just too large a place to have an accident in. I too, will take a mobile or radio when I am in the grounds. If you need safety clothing or equipment, you will be provided with it, and I expect you to use it. I have asked the local Health and Safety to come out and talk to you all soon.

"If I, or any of you, think you need any training, approach either Nora or Stuart, and they will tell me. If you need training, you will get it. I would like everyone to do a First Aid course, and will be arranging that here soon. I also need a couple of you to be qualified life savers. The lake is deep and dangerous, and non swimmers shouldn't go in or on it.

"Any one who uses their own transport for work, or for getting to and from work, will either get a mileage allowance or petrol money paid. Liam, you will get a cycle allowance on top of your wages, to pay for repairs to your bike.

"Anyone wanting to better themselves, by doing evening classes, or day release, will be given every opportunity to do so, subject to the demands of the job here. If you have any problems, I cannot help if you don't tell me about them. If we need more help, we will get it. There will be other staff joining us soon, and any disputes between you all will be sorted out by me, Jim, Stuart or Nora. I want us to work together, not against each other.

"Right, that's what I am prepared to offer (it's all right, we will explain anything you don't understand.) Now I want to tell you what I want and expect from you. Anyone who steals, or takes anything from the estate, without clearing it with me or Jim or Nora or Stuart first, is out. Even small things, pens, dusters, linen, all count. There will be no betting or gaming here, unless I clear it first. Anyone caught stealing either from me, the estate, or each other, will be sacked on the spot. No exceptions. If there are thefts, the police will be involved. I would rather you did not bring large amounts of money or valuables with you. Everyone will have a locker, and if you must bring money or valuables, they will go in the safe until you go home. Do we have a safe here, Nora? No, then one will be provided. I would rather you didn't borrow from each other. If any of you have money problems, here, or at home, you come and see me, nobody else, and I will not tell anyone without your permission. If I cannot solve the problem, I may know someone who can. If you lie to me, or try to take me for a ride, then be assured, I will give you a very hard time. I don't want any lies at all. If you forget something, or make a muck of it, or accidentally break something, or think you are in trouble for doing something you shouldn't, and you come and tell me, I won't be angry. I might be a bit annoyed, but nothing is so bad it cannot be fixed. If you hide it, or lie about it, and I do find out, it could end up by your being sacked.

"If you overhear anything here, or see something that is private to me, or anyone else, you do not tell anyone except me or them. None of us wants our private affairs spread over the village, or the house or estate. Me, especially. If I, or Nora, or Stuart, or Jim tell you something, that is fine, but if I ask you not to say anything, I do not expect you to do so. This includes talking to the press, who I understand are already sniffing round, wanting to know about me and the estate. I will do an interview and will ask you, if you want to, to be in an estate photo for the press, if they ask. I want a photo of everyone on the estate, and if you find anyone in the grounds, or in any of the houses, who shouldn't be there, you tell someone. That includes poachers, people fishing or swimming in the lake or anyone hanging around.

"After the staff meeting every Friday, unless you have any problems, or want to talk to me, you will be free to go home, unless you are working overtime. Please, between now and Friday, I want you all to think of what you need, in the way of clothing, tools, equipment, safety gear, or anything else. Jim, can the farm staff make it this Friday?

"Good. From the managers, I need a list of tools, vehicles, equipment, stationery, cleaning needs, clothing, food, and all that. Nora, can you do an order from the shop tomorrow? I will need you to see me later, with Stuart, Jim, Sam and Lucy. We need to go through furniture, washing machines, cookers and all that for the houses, Mary. I will also need some idea of things like tractors, and I will be getting a minibus, and a couple of quads. Sam, I need to go into town tomorrow, can you take me in after picking the ladies up from the village?

"The reason these two people are here is, this morning Mr Cummings will be visiting me. I want certain people in the house, and the rest of you, to be seen to be working where he can see you, at least for a while. I want him to believe that you are all happy here. Can you all do that? Liam, please could you sweep all the patio around the house, especially near the library? When you have done that, go and weed the bit of the drive near the front door. Bill, will you work down the drive, towards the front gate. Sam, I want you to be in the house, start tidying the Lost It Room. Nora, Mary and Jim, can you be nearby, in case I need you? With Stuart, perhaps you could draw up some kind of work sheet, or something like that?

"Betty, would you answer the door, and if anyone else calls, refer them to Nora. I am expecting a Mr Wynn to be here shortly, and maybe Mr Barker, later. Betty, Mr Cummings will have a driver with him. After you have shown Mr Cummings into the library, take the driver into the kitchen. Please do not discuss anything with Mr Cummings, anybody, and whilst being polite, don't tell him anything! I know some of you know him, but I want to talk to him first."

Bill grunted, "Yes, and we don't like him either, I 'ope you be going to give him what for."

"Maybe, but leave it to me, I'll call you if I need you. Betty, there is the bell, it will probably be Mr Wynn, show him into the library if it is. Celia and Mr Boyle, could you go to the library, make yourselves comfortable? Haley, would you show them where the cloakroom is, and then the library, and then come back and help Mary with some coffee? Celia, the recorder is set up, can you check it, and I'll be in, in a minute or two. Bill and Liam, can you get started?"

Stuart jumped up, "Leave that to me, Judith, and I'll be back soon. I'm here all day, so I'll talk to you later."

Jim came over to Judith and said, quietly,

"Are you going to be all right, lass? If you are doing what I think you are doing, I'll come in with you. I must say, you really mean to get things sorted, and we want to help."

Judith looked up into Jim's freckled face, and saw genuine concern there. She could easily have agreed, but decided to stick to her plan. "No, thank you, but can you and Sam stay close, in the next room if you like? I have two, maybe, three minders, and I'll yell if I want you."

Judith used the loo, and then went in to the library, where Celia was talking earnestly to Mr Wynn, a sober grey–haired man in his early sixties. Beside him were three large document boxes, and another cardboard box full of files. He had a laptop computer open on one of the tables. Celia and John were seated at the same table, and Celia had the cassette recorder in front of her. Mr Wynn got up when Judith entered and shook hands with her.

"Mrs Swallow, thank you for letting me be here. Tom has told me everything, and I am appalled. I feel I have let you down so badly. I have been ill for eighteen months, and have come back to work this spring. I know it is no excuse, but I trusted him, as a partner, I had to. This time, it seems he has really gone too far. Are you intending to involve the police? I cannot blame you if you do."

The man was nearly in tears. Judith said, "Let's hope it doesn't get to that. He may have an explanation. I have asked you here as much for his protection as yours. Yes, what I have found has made me rather angry, but if there is a way to solve it, let us try to find it. I want to be fair. I understand you have really been a sort of sleeping partner of late but do you have any powers over him?"

"Sufficient to dissolve the partnership. I was going to retire this year anyway. Since Tom spoke to me, I have been doing some checking up and what I have found bears out your suspicions, not just on your account, but on seven others as well, none so big as yours, but I may call in the police myself yet, as I have some questions for him when you have finished. Mrs Johnson has shown me her notes. You have my full permission to smack him on the nose! If it is as I fear, I will get on to our insurers. In fact I already have. Tell me what you want me to do."

"Could you sort that out with Celia and John? I want some answers from him. If he doesn't want to answer me, then could you take over? Would you like tea, coffee, anything?"

As if on cue, Betty came in with a trolley and served all of them with a cup. Judith ran through what she intended to ask, and was advised what to say. The tape machine was tested and spare tapes put beside it. Liam could be seen sweeping up outside, and Bill was walking down the drive with a wheelbarrow, rakes and a hoe. The wheel on the barrow squeaked annoyingly. Judith felt a sudden sense of blind panic and was about to cry. The others were talking quietly together. She felt faint, and hung desperately to the table edge. She felt so alone and bit her tongue not to cry out in terror.

We are with you. You are here, we are here. We are strong, you are strong!

Judith froze, and looked over at the others, still talking to each other and totally unaware of her or the voices she had just heard. Liam was sweeping outside, as though nothing had happened. There was no one else near and no one had heard it. A voice in her head, not a voice she knew. She must be going nuts!

Whatever it was she thought she had heard had blotted out her panic. She felt stronger and more able than she had for months. After, she would speak to Dr Tippett. The door bell rang and she knew she could do this. She had never seen Mr Cummings, and he was shown in by a sour faced Betty who winked at Judith as she turned to go out.

Cummings was a giant of a man, about two metres tall, and weighing in at over twenty–two stone. He was overweight, and slightly balding, with a florid complexion, and a very expensive suit. His slip–on shoes were handmade, and his shirt was silk. He had a carnation in his buttonhole, and a Bart Simpson tie. She put him at about forty–five.

As they shook hands, she felt his sweaty palms. He smiled, and she saw at least two gold teeth. She introduced Celia and John as secretaries of hers and invited him to sit down. Celia poured coffee. Mr Wynn had gone out of sight, as planned, behind one of the high bookcases. John had a vapid, idiotic expression, and when he spoke it was in a weedy, weak tenor, not the fine, light baritone he had used earlier. Celia had turned into a prim spinster type, and sat on the edge of her chair, looking quite empty–headed. 'Damn them,' thought Judith,' "they might have warned me!'

"Mr Cummings, have you got all the documents you promised? I want to give them to an accountant friend of mine, to do my tax. They do not mean that much to me, but they will to him. He is coming here on the way down from Glasgow to London, so that's why I need them today."

"No, my dear, I'm afraid not. The caretaker of our document store has gone sick and has the keys with him, and my partner, Mr Wynn, has the other set, and he had an early appointment and forgot to leave the keys for me. I can send all the details you need to your friend by email. I can sort all that out for you. How do you like it here?"

"Very much. I will be very happy here. Why did you not send me the keys I asked for? There are a lot missing and we need them. The ones to the Folly, for example. I am longing to see it. It is the only part of the grounds not overgrown. Can you explain that? Have you got the keys?"

"Not with me, no. Let me know which ones you need, and I'll send them to you next week. They are with the documents. You won't want all that work all at once, will you? They are just empty buildings, everything of value is here in the house. Look, Mrs Swallow, you need an expert to deal with all this, and I will be happy to run the estate, until you decide what you want to do. You have only been here a few days. It is far too early to make such serious decisions."

"You sound just like my brother-in-law, Francis Heldman. Do you know him?"

"He sounds a sensible man, no I can't say that I do, should I?"

"All you business men stick together. You might. Are those your horses in the lower paddock? The foal is lovely. Why did you not tell me they were there?"

"I didn't want to worry you with little details. I thought I would save you the cost of getting the grass cut."

"You have saved on the cost of getting the rest of the grass cut. The place is totally run down, why?"

"You would hardly want me to waste your money if you wanted to sell it, would you?"

"But I told you I didn't want to sell it."

"You cannot make that kind of decision without someone to advise you, and you will soon see this place is more than you can handle, my dear. In a week or two, you will get fed up here, and want to go and travel abroad, to the sun, and by the time you come back, I'll have got the place neat and tidy. You could let it out for holiday flats, you know."

"Like you did with the lodges and the Folly?"

"Just trying to earn you a little money."

"How much did you charge?"

"I couldn't charge much, they are very run–down."

"Why are they run–down? I asked you to keep them up."

"It would not have been justifiable, to spend so much to get no real added value. I only have your best interests at heart. You must leave these things to the experts, you know, otherwise you could lose a lot of money."

"Is that why all the local people think I'm selling up? And they would have to leave their homes? That has really made me popular!"

"Oh, no, I never said that, I just told them it was a possibility."

"Why have the Morpeths had to wait for a new immersion heater for nearly six months?"

"The one they have is only five years old. It just needs a part, the contractor should have done it by now. I'll chase it up."

"Why did you not let them have extra staff when they needed it?"

"Farmers are all the same, they did not need any extra staff. They coped quite well without, which proves my point."

"They tell me they need a better tractor. Why not give them one?"

"The one they have is quite adequate."

"Why have you not been in touch with me for the last six months? I sent you my locations. I do not seem to have had any income at all since my husband's death. Can you explain that?"

"It will be paid into your account, as soon as you give me your account number."

"I gave you that months ago, by recorded delivery. The second time, by registered post."

"Oh, my secretary must have filed it. You must be quite a wealthy woman, but even so, it would take millions to get this place up to prime condition. You could never afford it. Let me sell it for you."

"Do you know someone who might be interested then? A rich someone?"

"I have a friend who would be willing to take it off your hands, at the right price, about three million."

"Isn't that rather unethical of you?"

"Only trying to help you, and save you worry. You have been through enough. Your husband told me he wanted to sell up, but you wanted the house, so he was going to let you see it, and then sell it and move on. He didn't want to tell you how much it would cost."

"I think the offer for the estate is insulting, criminal in fact. I gave you very specific instructions, and you have ignored them, because you think you know my mind better than I do. I think you don't want me to stay here because you have had a better offer. The place has been deliberately run down, so your friend can buy it at a knock–down price."

"My dear, you obviously do not understand these things. Mrs Holt did not understand either. It will cost two million at least to make it right. You can't afford that, now, can you?"

Judith finally lost her temper with him. Her inclination to hit him was almost overwhelming.

"Actually, Mr Cummings, yes I can. How dare you be so patronising? Now, let us cut the crap, and stop lying to me. Yes, I know you are lying, and can prove it. Either tell me what I want to know, or I call the police right now. Shall we start again?"

Cummings went even redder in the face and jumped up, banging his fists on the table. He towered over Judith, and she was terrified. He shouted at her, spittle flecks splashing her face.

"I didn't come here to be insulted, and I want an apology. You are a stupid woman, who has no idea what you are talking about, millions, indeed! You must be mentally ill. Where would you get millions from? I have done my best to save you money, and you just do not have any idea what is involved. You are not fit to be in charge of a place like this, the accident must have turned your mind. You need a doctor, not the police. These people must see that. I think someone should have power of attorney for you."

Judith, quaking in her seat, said in a deathly calm voice,

"Like one of my husband's family, for example?"

"Yes, either of your brothers-in-law would be suitable!"

" I thought you said you didn't know them?"

"I'm not staying here to be spoken to like this. I'll come and see you when you can be more reasonable. I'll see myself out."

"Fine, have a pleasant walk home, you should make it about supper time."

Cummings leaned over her and said in a menacing tone,

"You forget, I came by taxi."

Judith spoke calmly,

"And you forget, I employed the driver, and he will do as I say. If you insist on calling your own cab, use your own phone. The choice is yours. You will not use the phone here."

He became very agitated, and undid his coat. He looked at her as she would have looked at a poisonous snake. He raised his fist.

"If you touch me, Mr Cummings, I will call for help. If I do, I am sure you don't want to be ejected from here. Sit down, or get out. I am not frightened by you and your patronising, bullying manner. I know a lot about you. You have been cheating and stealing from me for some time now. You and your family, for whom I feel very sorry, have been using my buildings, letting out my premises, and allowing your friends to stay here, swimming in the lake, stabling your horses. You have the audacity to ignore my direct instructions, and deliberately devalued my property, to defraud me.

"Make your decision. If you leave, the police will catch you up about a mile down the road, I should think. You could always get one of your horses, but none of them could take your weight, and I doubt you could catch one. If you calm down, and are honest with us, maybe we can sort your mess out. Until we do, the horses stay here. They were on my land, eating my grass, and so far as I am concerned, they are my property."

He exploded. "You bitch, you fucking bitch, you scar–faced old hag of a fucking bitch, you wouldn't dare!"

"It isn't pleasant to have one's property appropriated, is it? Yes, I do dare. I may well seem to you to be a scar–faced old hag, but I do not need to resort to obscenity. I am not an overweight, fopishly–dressed crook, hiding under the veneer of respectability, milking his trusting clients, who he is too stupid to see are brighter than him. Sit down, Mr Cummings, you offend me greatly, but I have not finished with you yet!"

He hit her. She flew back out of her chair, and hit her head on the corner of a table. He kicked her in the shoulder, but was rugby tackled by Jim, Sam, Stuart and Liam who had rushed in. Mr Wynn and John pulled her out from under the considerable weight of bodies. Celia rushed to the hall and returned with an army of people.

It took some time to restrain Cummings, even with Bill joining in. He sensibly produced some bailer twine, and offered to tie the huge man to a chair. Judith called,

"No, just restrain him. If he moves, tie him, but keep him here. Liam, don't hit him, please. Mr Wynn, you take over, please, calm him down. Talk to him. I think he's on something. Gentlemen, please calm down. I don't want him, or anything else, damaged."

She tried to get up, and was assisted by many willing hands. It was Dot who took charge, and she helped Judith to a chair. Cummings was glaring at her and spat at her. She said,

"Mr Cummings, you're sacked. I never want you in my house or on my property again."

After a confused few minutes, Judith got up and limped out to the cloakroom, where she was sick. Mary made her lie down, and produced a basin full of hot water and a towel. Judith was shaking, but began to laugh,

"Mary, it's all right, I'm not having a baby!"

"No, Judy, but you are bleeding!"

Judith couldn't stop shaking and felt very cold, and someone fetched a blanket. She walked to the kitchen, and a wound dressing was place on her head. One eye was closing fast, and her nose wouldn't stop bleeding. Mr Wynn came to see her, and asked if she wanted to call the police.

"Not yet, and not at all, if possible. I think you should call a doctor, no, not for me, for him. No, don't call an ambulance. I'll explain in a minute."

Within minutes, or so it seemed, Dr Tippett had arrived. Judith insisted he see Cummings first, and then he came to see her. He stitched a cut on the back of her head, and insisted a cold compress remain on her face for some time. Judith soon felt better, and when her head stopped swimming and she could stand without rocking, she washed her face and asked Mary if lunch was nearly ready. The poor, bewildered driver had been watching the proceedings and came to speak to her.

"Excuse me, miss, but I don't approve of men hitting women, do I have to take him back?"

"Please, would you? I don't want him here any more. I think he is ill, you won't be on your own. Could you please take him to where the doctor directs, and then bring the others back? Jim will sort it, I think Liam and Sam should go with him."

Judith walked toward the library, but Dr Tipppet said she should sit down quietly. He left, and took Cummings, Sam and Liam with him. The car drove away. Judith suggested holding lunch until they got back.

The mess in the library was soon cleaned up. Judith went upstairs and showered and changed. Her bloodstained clothing was whipped away by Lucy, and when she came downstairs, she met Dr Tippett, Sam and Liam coming in the door.

Mary announced lunch was ready in the dining room. Bill was not sure, but didn't want to miss the fun, so he consented to enter the house, and everyone sat down to eat. The driver ate with them. Another place was laid for Tom who had arrived, and he was told in graphic detail, by several people, what had taken place. The excited hubbub was only interrupted by eating. After a wonderful bread and butter pudding, Judith knocked on the table, and there was an instant hush.

"Thank you all very much for your help today. I certainly did not expect things to turn out so dramatically! I am sure that Mr Cummings is unwell, and that was his problem. I am relatively uninjured, and I want to check that no one else is hurt. I am sorry if anyone was frightened or alarmed. I cannot promise a floor show like this every day, but I would like to thank my brave heroes, Sam, Jim, Stuart and Liam, for their brave rescue of me. Bill you were magnificent, and you, too, Mr Wynn. John, Celia, you should both be on the stage. Dot, I am impressed, thank you. You all did so well, I am very proud of you all. Doctor, am I right in thinking he has a drug problem? It would explain a lot. One of the things I forgot to mention this morning, is drink and drugs. I do not want anyone turning up for work on either.

"Now, I don't want this spread round the village. Talk about it between us, but not outside these walls. It could damage me if it got out, and it would hurt poor Mr Wynn here, and he has done nothing wrong. Will you all agree to keep it a secret? Liam, that means you cannot even tell your Mum. Yes, you can have another pudding, but only if you keep our secret! Is everyone all right after today's little adventure?"

The three cleaning ladies nodded in time with each other, and Bill muttered,

"Eh, lass, thee's all reet, I've wanted someone to bring him down to size for some time. If he ever sticks his nose near here again, I'll see him off."

Stuart added, "You won't be the only one, Bill. I'm just sorry we didn't get to him sooner. How did you keep your cool, Judith? I am very sorry, but we were all listening. I didn't know this pratt, but has he really been doing all that?"

Judith turned to Mr Wynn, and asked,

"Have you any idea of what the situation is? I only had my suspicions, but his attempts to prevaricate make me wonder just what's going on. Have you time to talk to me and Tom, Celia, and John, now? Dr Tippett, I know you probably need to rush off, but I think you could advise us, shall we go and sit outside on the patio? I feel the need of some fresh air, and a sit down."

Before she joined the others outside, she talked to the driver, and asked him to keep what he had seen and heard to himself. She tipped him generously, and he went off happily assuring her of his discretion.

On the patio they sat down, and Dr Tippett explained that he was arranging for Cummings to be admitted to a clinic, following his admission that he had an addiction, and had had for some years.

"The whole thing had accumulated, and he has admitted that you panicked him, and he is terribly sorry for losing control. He is desperately sorry, and doesn't know what to do to fix it. At the moment, he is pathetic, but he has left us all with a terrible mess. As he is one of my patients, I cannot discuss this any more, but I would ask you to try and realise how long this can take. Mr Wynn, he will need to talk to you, and he is waiting for the police to call. Have you any idea what action you are going to take? You should report the assault. I'm surprised you have not already done so. Mrs Swallow, I need to see you before I go, can we have a private chat?"

Judith went with him, and she explained she had written to him. He wanted her to visit the hospital, but she refused. He left, promising to call the next day, and they parted. Judith went back to the patio, and joined the group who were discussing the situation. Mary brought out some drinks, and after a while, Judith left them and went in search of Stuart, who she found in the barn. He went with her to the little office and asked her if she was all right. She assured him she would live, and asked him if he was able to be there on Friday afternoon. He made her sit down, and said,

"Actually, that is the main reason I came today, June asked me to ask you if we could move in on Friday, this Friday. I know it is sooner than we thought, but we have had her family around, and they have all helped, and we have a removal firm ready. It is half term next week, so the kids can help. I've arranged for them to start at the local school here, after the half term."

Judith was pleased, and rather surprised.

"Yes, of course you can, but I was hoping to get the place decorated before you moved in, but we can all help over the weekend, and you can use Sam, and the others. It will be very chaotic for a while. I am arranging for phones to be fitted, decorators, furniture to be delivered, all that, but yes. I can postpone the meeting, if it helps."

Stuart shook his head, "No, I'll be there. We will be here first thing, and the removal men can do all the heavy work. Can you manage without me in the morning, and can we all cadge a lunch that day?"

"I'm interviewing for a PA in the morning. Tell Nora how many extra there will be, and use Sam, Bill and Liam to help you. It would be quite handy to have them away from the house for the morning. Can you fix it all with Nora, and get her to order anything you need from the shop? If there is any furniture you need, borrow from the house. On Monday, I will need a big powwow between Nora, Jim and you, but I'll see you over the weekend."

She got up to go, but felt a little dizzy, grabbed at the table and dropped her stick. She had a raging headache, and stopped to draw her breath. Stuart pushed her back in the seat, and sat down beside her,

"Judith, sit down for a while. You have had one hell of a smack, and you are pushing yourself far too hard. I think you are more shaken up than you are letting on. What you did today took a lot of guts, and, if nothing else, you showed everyone what a strong person you are. The staff think you are wonderful, and already they want to do everything they can to help you. Liam is really upset that you got hurt, and he would do anything for you."

"You mean, he would do anything for a good meal! No, I'm only joking! I know he's a nice lad. How's he shaping up?"

"He's a hard worker, and doesn't mind what he does. Bill knows his job, and is longing to get onto the veg patch, but he has started on the front lawn, and next week we will start the back lawn. You've gone a bit pale, I'll get the car, and drive you back to the house."

"Stuart, please don't. I would rather just walk slowly back, it is just the after effect of a stressful time."

"Then I'm walking with you, you need to lie down for a bit. Come on, give me your arm. I'm not taking no for an answer."

Together they walked slowly back to the house, and as they walked, Stuart pointed out rare and interesting plants and shrubs, hidden in the undergrowth. He asked if he could, at a future date, look in the library to see if there were any records for the garden. Judith asked him if he had made any plans for the garden, and he told her what he thought it could look like in two years' time, adding that he had only considered the front garden so far. By the time they reached the front door, Judith felt much better and her headache had almost gone. Stuart walked her round to the patio and she sat down. He took his leave, and left.

Mr Wynn and Tom were discussing the finer points of fraud and Celia was taking notes. John was searching through a document box and in front of him was a cardboard shoe box containing numerous keys, some very old and large.

Judith listened to the conversation, and soon understood that they were reaching a solution, without her needing to join in. She sat for a while, and then announced that she was going inside, and would be upstairs if they needed her. Inside the house, Sam was with the decorator, and asked her for some colour schemes for several rooms, including her sitting room at the front of the house. She took some colour charts to the sitting room, and spent half an hour choosing what she liked, telling the decorator what she wanted, and he made a note of it.

She was thinking of going upstairs for a lie down, when the telephone man arrived, and went over her order and said they would be starting work on the installation on the Monday. When he had gone, she went up to her room and lay on the bed and watched the television and dozed lightly for a while. She felt utterly drained and her headache had returned. She took two pain killers with some water, and drifted off to sleep.

A light tap on the door woke her, and Nora came in with a mug of tea. She was amazed to find it was after six, and that everyone had gone home. Nora suggested she bring up a supper tray, and have an early night. Judith was too exhausted to argue, and gratefully accepted. She ate her supper, and went to sleep.

At about ten o'clock she woke again, and used the bathroom. She felt stiff, and wanted a cup of tea, so she went downstairs to the kitchen and boiled the kettle. She made a pot of tea and took it into the library on a tray. She read several notes left for her by the others and drank the tea. She needed to find some paper clips, and went to the desk, and started looking through it. In a drawer she found a photograph of Great Aunt Susan as a younger woman. She got it out and took it under a light to study it. She thought of the old lady and how little she knew about her. She wondered how she had come to the house, and whether she had ever had a partner. 'What had she been like, as a younger woman?' she asked herself. She tried to imagine the woman in her younger days, as she sat staring at the photo.

We remember!

Judith looked round, but there was no one there. The voices were tinged with fond regret. 'Who remembered?' she tried to reason.

We remember Zan. She was with us. Zan gone on. We remember.

'I'm going potty, too, this house has other residents, or I'm hearing things!' She wondered if she was concussed. The voices were inside her head. That did not come from outside her. She broke into a sweat.

You rest. You hurt. Sleep. Be better. We help.

She said, out loud, "Who are you, what do you want?"

We help. Sleep. Meet soon. Sleep.

Judith felt incredibly sleepy, and although she knew she should be alarmed, she felt at ease. She got up, and leaving the tea and biscuits on the table, she went up to her room, got into bed and went into a deep, relaxing sleep.

She slept late the next morning, and woke when she heard someone moving downstairs. Hurriedly getting dressed, she went down and met Nora coming up. Nora asked her if she was feeling all right, and when she explained that she seemed fine, Nora started to laugh. Judith wondered what the joke was, until Nora suggested she look in a mirror. The only mirrors Judith had seen were in the bathrooms, so she went back to her room with Nora and into the bathroom. Looking at herself, she saw she had two splendid black eyes and resembled a panda. She started to laugh, and once she started, neither of them could stop.

Quite what struck them as so very funny, neither of them knew, but Mary came in a few minutes later, somewhat mystified, and asked what was going on. Nora spluttered,

"It's not really that funny, I'm sorry, I shouldn't be laughing, it's not funny, it's not. Judy, stop it, you're making me worse."

Judith, by now lying on the bed, aching with laughter, managed,

"But it is funny. I look like an exhibit in a zoo. I wouldn't mind but I've got to see the bank manager today, and how is anyone going to take me seriously looking like this? How can I keep what happened here yesterday quiet, when the first impression they get in town is of a lame panda used to prize fighting, Oh, don't start me off again!"

Mary collected the tray, and tutt tutting to herself, left them to get over their giggles. They came downstairs a little later, and Judith went into the kitchen, but then remembered the teapot in the library and went in to fetch it. The teapot, tray and mug were there and an empty milk jug, tipped over on its side. When she picked it up it was sticky. There was no sign of the biscuits at all. She collected the things up and took them to the kitchen, had a bowl of cereal, and some toast and three cups of coffee. Sam came in with the cleaning staff, and Judith collected her brief case and went out to the car. She saw no signs of Lucy, and asked where she was. Sam said Lucy felt she would be in the way. Judith told him to fetch her as she might need her. She waited by the front door, while Sam took the car down to the stable block. Nora came out with a shopping list and asked if it could be fetched by Sam.

Nora found it very difficult to look directly at Judith, who knew this and peered out of black, puffy eyes with a michevious, sly grin. Nora bolted back into the house, where she could be heard trying not to laugh again. Lucy was full of concern for Judith, who insisted she looked worse than she felt.

It was a warm, sunny day, and the drive into town was pleasant.

Sam and Lucy talked happily about the flat and the future. Before long, Sam had dropped Judith outside the bank. She asked him to pick her up in an hour and told him to find a cafe or tea shop to take her to.

In the bank, she was ushered into an inner sanctum, where a charming manager went through her requirements and offered to come to see her the following week. She suggested Friday lunch time, so specimen signatures could be obtained from the staff who would be authorised to pay bills. The manager, a serious, rather pale man with blonde hair and light grey eyes, was so polite and never commented on her appearance. Their real business took about half an hour and she then withdrew sufficient cash for her needs. The bank gave her a lovely desk set, a bouquet of flowers and made her feel like a valued client.

Sam turned up at the allotted time. Judith made several calls at other premises, and they went to a cafe for some coffee. Then Sam went, at her request to a mains dealer to look at transport. Judith had already been in touch with the sales force, and together they looked at various minibuses and people carriers. They eventually decided on a large nine–seater, which Sam was happy to drive, and Judith finalised the deal. The next stop was for a four–wheel drive, a run around, for the estate. A long wheelbase Landrover was chosen, and its delivery was arranged. There was time to visit a sofa shop, a white goods shop and a computer shop before they drove back to the house.

Once back, she spent some time on the telephone and Dr Tippett came to see her. She explained her plans for the staff health scheme, and he readily agreed, and then insisted on talking about her. He had her notes, and examined her and gave her an exercise plan to strengthen her leg. Having sorted out her physical welfare, she broached another topic,

"I have a problem that is somewhat unusual. I have reason to believe that an attempt may be made to doubt my sanity, and to query my fit state of mind to run the estate."

She told him of the events leading to her arrival, and then told him what she had seen and heard since her arrival at the estate. She also told him of the letter to the psychiatrist and asked for his honest opinion. He agreed that she had been through a traumatic time, and also that it could have affected her, but he doubted it had made her mentally ill. He suggested he refer her to a specialist for an authoritative opinion. He added,

"Miss Holt saw things here, and so have others who have visited. Her sanity was questioned by the same people you have mentioned. She may have been eccentric, but she was sane, and I have often wondered if this place does not have some strange secrets. If you think you saw something odd, or heard things, then you probably did. There may be a simple answer. I doubt you are losing it, and from what I have observed, you are totally in control of your faculties."

They then chatted about other things. He left, assuring her she had little to worry about. She resumed her paper work and then walked for a while down to the summer house and returned in time for a cup of tea. She had a talk with Nora and Mary and asked them if they needed help in the kitchen with the cooking, as the daily meals seemed to be getting larger. Mary assured her that Sally could help and she was quite happy and would ask for help if she needed it. They discussed the interviews on the following day, and the ordering of various things for the house. Lucy came into the kitchen with a pile of clean laundry, which they all sorted while they chatted. Lucy suggested that during the half term, she would watch the children who were around the house, and organise them while their parents were working. They discussed which rooms they could use and what they could do. They allotted some of the upper bedrooms, one with a television, and Judith suggested Sam could organise a day out to a theme park.

Judith spent the evening writing letters and watching the television and had an early night.

Chapter Eight

Wynn, Cummings & Porter
Land Agents
The Chambers
Clipping Court,
Harrogate

Dear Mrs Swallow,

Following the events of Wednesday, for which I am most dreadfully sorry, I feel I should inform you of the developments since we last spoke. My partner, Gerald Cummings, has admitted to me that he has a drug addiction, on cocaine, and has had for some years. He has funded his habit from the funds of some of our clients, and to such an extent that it is far worse than I first suspected. I have had no option but to call in the police, and they have taken on the investigation. At this very moment they are here investigating. The other clients have been informed.

I know you wished to avoid involving them, but the problem is so great that this is the only way I see to move ahead. My other partner, Simon Porter, and I must share some of the responsibility, in that we were not aware of his criminal activity, and we should have been. The police have taken all relevant documents, and have searched Mr Cummings' house. I will be sending you all the keys, and have arranged for all items not seized by them to be sent to you.

May I come and see you, at your convenience? Explain how things are going? All Gerry's bank accounts have been frozen. His wife also has a problem with a drug habit, and is under investigation. I feel no sympathy for either of them, but I do feel very sorry for their children.

In his better days, he was very able and followed his father into our profession. Simon and I realise you will have legal redress against us, and we cannot seek to defend any action. We have, on Tom Barker's advice, agreed to work with him, with your permission, to repay whatever we can to you, as soon as we can.

Please, would you be kind enough to provide the police with a statement and any authorities they may need? I am, for many reasons, reluctant to see a prosecution against Gerry, but it may result in his being compelled to take the treatment he so obviously needs.

I do hope he didn't injure you too severely, and that you are not in too much pain. Let me know if I can help in any way.

Yours sincerely,

Albert Wynn

Porthwaite Hall

Dear Mr Wynn,

Thank you for your letter. I feel desperately sorry for you and your partner, and for the family of Mr Cummings. Of course, if you wish, I will give the police my full co-operation. It must be a terrible worry for you and Mr Porter, and your families too. I would very much like to meet you both, and I am sure that when the facts have become clear, we will be able to sort things out. I do not blame you for what has happened, and would rather not drag this matter through the civil courts, which will only line the pockets of solicitors and barristers.

I, too, feel sorry for the Cummings children. I doubt there is much I can do to help them at the moment.

I am not badly injured by Cummings' assault on me. The main injury is to my pride, as I currently sport two splendid black eyes, which will be gone in a few days.

Thank you for your offer of help. There are several things you can assist with. Could you please ring me, so you can help me sort them? The first is, I need to know what has happened to the income from the rest of the estate. There are many other properties in the total estate, and I need to know who has been handling these

What do I do with the horses on my paddock? I doubt that either Mr or Mrs Cummings will consider their welfare at the moment, and I would not want them to suffer. I know they are worth a lot of money. I can arrange to board them for a while, until their fate is decided. I could take them in lieu of money owed, if it helps.

I do not seek revenge or retribution against you, or your partner, Mr Porter. Nor do I seek revenge on Mr Cummings, although I do not see why I should go out of my way to help him much! I do not want him here again, or on any of my properties, and the staff have been instructed to call the police, if he appears here. You and Mr Porter, however, will always be welcome. I have seen, in the past, what drugs can do to families, and just how devious addicts can be. I know you have been ill, and I hope this will not knock you up! At the moment, I am sure he is most contrite, and seems a broken man, but this may change. I have seen such people turn on their friends and helpers, so be very careful! In a way, I regret challenging him, and I should have seen he was not right, sooner, but I had to know what he was up to.

We really need to talk, without prejudicing any police investigations, so please ring me. Maybe you could come out to see me next week, if that is convenient, to update me?

Yours sincerely,

Judith Swallow

****

Bank Chambers,
Howton
Yorkshire.

Dear Mrs Swallow,

I hope you are all right. That was a hell of a blow he must have struck you, did you go to hospital? Can I help at all?

After what happened yesterday, I have been in touch with Mr Wynn. He is quite devastated by Gerry Cummings' actions, and the situation is much worse than we expected. He has called in the police. I have to advise you to call in the police too, and that you have an excellent case against the company, and Cummings personally.

As you are well aware, Cummings has committed at least an Actual Bodily Harm, if not an Unlawful Wounding, against you. Unless you wish to be accused of concealing evidence or an offence, you should report it. The whole matter needs to be recorded, even if there is no prosecution.

John and Celia are devastated they were unable to prevent it. Celia wants to come and see you over the weekend, if you would like her to. I want to talk to you, as well. John would like to take lessons from you, in how to get someone to lose control, whilst remaining in

control yourself. He thinks you were wonderful!
Celia is hopping mad that she couldn't do more.

She is typing up the whole interview, and is
preparing our statements. I will come and be
with you when the police come, if you like. I
attach my home number. Could you ring Celia to
tell her if she can come and see you?

Yours,

Tom Barker.

****

Porthwaite Hall

Dear Tom,

Thanks for the letter. I will heal quickly, and have no lasting
damage. It did shake me up a bit though. I admit, I did want to
rattle his cage. I rather overdid it, it seems! I had no idea he was
potentially violent. He is in touch with Clive's bother-in-law, and I
am wondering what the connection is. I need to know what I do
with the horses on my land.

I've rung Celia, and you are all welcome to visit over the
weekend.

No, I did not go to hospital, it was not necessary. Dr Tippett
has been out, and seems happy. I am interviewing for a PA
tomorrow, and Gregory McDuff is coming out before lunch. My
head gardener is moving in as well, so I'm going to be busy, but I
would welcome visitors over the weekend, if you don't mind
simple fare. Bring the family, and some swimming things, if you
want to swim in the lake. I intend to!

It is a mess, and I'm reluctant to show my black eyes off in
the village, it will cause a lot of talk, so you will have to come to
me!

Ring me?

Judy Swallow

Chapter Nine

Judith was up at the crack of dawn, and had posted some letters, gone for a walk, eaten a good breakfast, and washed up the crocks long before anyone else arrived. She had arranged the library for the interviews, and checked the cloakroom and the drawing rooms, as waiting rooms. She walked down towards the farm and met Mary walking towards her. Nora joined them, and they planned the day. June and Stuart arrived and went down to the stables, returning fifteen minutes later for a coffee. Their children came too, and were soon exploring the front garden.

Mr Sandell arrived with a large grocery order, and all of them unloaded boxes and bags for the house, and the rest went down to the stables in the van, to be unloaded there. Sam went off to the village, and Dot and Haley to the stables to help. Betty helped Mary in the kitchen and Judith felt a little useless. She offered to peel potatoes, and complained that everyone was busy, except her. Eventually, she was allowed to do some vegetable preparation, and was digging in a potato sack when she looked at her watch. It was earlier than she thought, and she saw that everyone had come in at least an hour early to help.

She finished a huge pile of spuds and Mary called a coffee break and accused her of not having had breakfast. She explained that she had, but feeling hungry, she ate another four rounds of toast and jam. The front door bell went. Betty answered it and showed Gregory into the library, Judith joined him. Soon Jim arrived, having milked the cows, and Nora joined them. Betty brought in a trolley with tea, coffee, biscuits, and cake. They went through the interview candidates and prepared their questions. Judith asked Jim who could be employed to look after the horses, and Jim suggested Liam, who had worked as a stable lad for a while. It was decided to bring them up to the stables that day.

Gregory was most concerned about Judith's appearance, and had to be told the whole story. He was shocked and angry, and vowed to help if he could. He told Judith off for being too tough, and then they talked over the implications of the incident.

The candidates for the interviews arrived. There were five in all, and the first one was a pleasant young woman, who was undoubtedly efficient and capable. She appeared to have no sense of humour at all, and they asked their questions. She had good qualifications and excellent references.

She was shown round the house by Betty, while the second candidate came in. This was an older woman, married, with four children. Judith didn't think she really wanted the job, as she wanted all school holidays off, and was not interested in the farm side of the work.

The next was a cheerful lass of about twenty with a dreadful laugh, who wanted to be off duty by four each afternoon so she could work at a pub in the evening. After the first three questions, she couldn't stop talking, divulging personal information about her previous employers.

The fourth interviewee was so timid they could hardly get a word out of her. Her qualifications were good, but she had no personality at all.

Judith was beginning to despair, while they were waiting for Betty to bringing the final candidate. This took a long time, and then they saw why. A young man of about twenty-five struggled into the room on crutches. He was dark–skinned, of Afro–Caribbean origin. He had a wonderful smile and the most beautiful speaking voice. He introduced himself as Wesley Carpenter, and asked them to give him time to make the chair, as he was a little slow, and, he added, very unsteady! He had, he explained, had polio as a child and most of the time used a wheelchair, but could walk short distances. His qualifications were very impressive, but he said he had been unable to get a 'proper job' since leaving college.

As they spoke with him, he showed a good sense of humour and explained he had been bought up on a farm since his mother had married his stepfather. He had contracted polio abroad.

Jim asked him how he could get to work. He said he had an adapted car and could be independent, as he had a flat in town. He really wanted the job and asked a lot of intelligent questions. Gregory asked what special needs he would require, and for the first time he hesitated before replying. He stated that while some things would help to make his life easier, he could manage, and did not want to jeopardise the chance of a job, by making a fuss. From his manner it seemed that he had been turned down for jobs because of his disability.

He asked if he could bring a wheelchair in when he was offered a tour round the lower floor. Betty and Mary fetched it and Betty took him round the main part of the house.

The four interviewers discussed the applicants and Judith stated, "Quite frankly, the only one I think I can live with is Wesley. He wants the job, can do the job, and has a sense of humour."

Jim agreed, "He knows about the farm work, and I think I know his stepdad slightly, but I've never met his mother. I never realised she wasn't white, and I know one of their kids had polio. How will he get round the farm?"

Nora said, "I expect he will find a way."

Gregory explained, "There are grants and things available, and you will need to put ramps and disabled toilets in. The government are very keen on a certain percentage of disabled employees in any firm."

Judith added, "I don't think that is important. I'm not going to be employing the bit of him that doesn't work too well, I want the bit that does. If he thinks he can do it, and he's well–qualified and has what I need, then I'd like to give him a shot. He's the most human of the five."

They discussed all the candidates again, and then Gregory went and told the remaining four that they would be notified within five days. Wesley, returning at some speed in his chair down the corridor, apologised for being so long, but he had found the patio, and thought the house was wonderful, and the view even better. The others left and Wesley was invited into the drawing room, where he was asked a lot more questions.

Judith asked him to stay for lunch and he seemed surprised and accepted. She asked him what salary he would expect, and discussed with him what he would be expected to do.

Before lunch they went out onto the patio, and she talked alone with him. He was frank, and seemed to be without any bitterness about his limited mobility. She asked how many jobs he had applied for, and he told her of quite a few, and explained he had got to interview on several, but had never been taken on. She asked him if he had been told why not. He explained that he had been given a number of reasons, but he suspected it was because of his disability.

He was well–educated, had an interest in music, and played the piano and guitar. She asked if he truly wanted to work so far from a town, and if he could work alone. He explained that he hated crowds, and liked to get on with his work.

"Wesley, if you worked here, I would have to rely on you, and I would expect you to keep the private stuff private. Could you do that?"

"Sure, who would I tell? If you employed me it would mean you trusted me. I wouldn't want to lose that. You would be the first person to believe I could do it."

"Can you foresee any problems working out here?"

"Only if my car breaks down."

"I would like you to meet the rest of the staff over lunch. Is that OK?"

"Sure, Mrs Swallow, even if I don't get the job, it would be interesting."

Stuart and his family came in for lunch, and soon they were joined by all the others. Wesley was introduced, but Liam needed no introduction. It was obvious that he knew and liked Wesley and that Wesley felt the same way. Over lunch Stuart discussed botany with

Wesley, to some depth, and they argued intelligently over some obscure rose. Nora talked to him about keeping household accounts, and Jim about farming. Wesley took the time to talk to everyone, even the children, who he amused with an adventure story.

While everyone had tea or coffee, Judith asked Mary, Jim, Gregory, Nora and Stuart into the Butler's Pantry, and said she was of a mind to employ him. They all agreed. She asked Gregory what a fair wage would be for the work expected, and he named a sum considerably more than Wesley had asked for. They returned to the kitchen, and Stuart, Jim, Liam, Sam and Mary went off to bring the horses up to the stables. Wesley offered to help, as he loved horses, and riding was about the only exercise he was good at, except swimming. For Judith, that clinched it.

She invited him onto the patio again, and said,

"Wesley, I would like to offer you employment, initially on a two month trial, so you can back out, if it doesn't suit you."

She told him of her proposed salary, and of the conditions imposed on all staff, and the benefits she was offering.

"Can you think it over? How long do you want?"

He looked up at her, and struggled up out of the chair. He said "You mean it? When can I start?" He grasped her hand and shook it.

"Right away, if you like, but whenever you are ready. Would you like to take a day or so? It will be pretty hectic, at least for a while. You'll be my right-hand man, and at my beck and call. I can be a slave driver!"

"That's all right, my ancestors put up with it, I'm sure I can. I won't let you down, Mrs Swallow. You don't mind I'm disabled, or that I'm black?"

"I'm not employing you for your physical strength, or because of your colour, I want your loyalty, your honesty, your skills and your brains. I want you to be straight with me and to help me run this place. When do you want to start?"

"Now, if you will let me. What do you want me to do this afternoon?"

"Can you take notes at the staff meeting?"

"Sure."

"Any questions you want to ask?"

"Just one, for now."

"What?"

"How did you get those splendid black eyes?"

They returned to the kitchen, laughing.

The staff meeting was held in the drawing room. Judith told the staff what the plans were for the next week, and asked for comments on

141

how the last few days had gone. Gregory handed out contracts for the staff to take home and study, and Judith was given long, and comprehensive, lists of what was needed, or desired, by all the managers. The farm workers came in a little later. There were four of them, and they, too, were given contracts.

Haley asked if they could have work clothes, in the form of tee shirts, sweatshirts and slacks as well as overalls. This produced an animated discussion about the design and motif of such clothes.

Judith handed out wages to everyone for the week, and offered overtime for anyone wanting to work over the weekend. Liam immediately offered to work, and Bill asked not to, as he had commitments at home. Lucy and Sam both volunteered, as did Dot and Betty. The farm workers came and introduced themselves. Jim asked if he could be excused on Saturday afternoon, and Judith said she knew he had cricket. Wesley asked to work on, and Liam asked if they got lunch. Sam ran the cleaning staff home. Lucy went off with June, and Nora and Mary offered to cook over the weekend, provided the twins could come to the house. Gregory asked to return on the Monday and then left.

Stuart, Nora, Mary, Jim, Judith and Wesley then had another meeting. They planned the week and Wesley noted down various tasks. The meeting moved on to equipment, and where to order it. It was after six when they all went home and Judith was exhausted.

She raided the fridge and ate a light supper. She saw the box of keys that had been left by Mr Wynn on the Wednesday. Looking through them, she found a bunch that were marked 'cellar'. She got up, and went into the Lost It Room and tried the keys in the doors which were locked. One door opened, and steps led down. She found a light switch and switched it on. She went down the steps, with difficulty as they were uneven and steep. The cellar was well lit, and as Jim had said, dry. At the bottom of the steps, Judith found a large room, full of old furniture and machinery. An old sewing machine stood in front of a pile of pictures, and a collection of trunks and boxes. They were dusty but there were no cobwebs. She wandered past the piles of unwanted furniture, under an arch into another room, similarly filled, and went left through another arch. This room had a door through which there were chinks of light showing. One of her keys fitted this, and the door creaked wearily, as it opened into another area, which had glass doors overlooking the lawn at the back of the house.

As she progressed, she found another three of these rooms, and she explored many chambers under the house. There was so much old furniture, gardening equipment, a very old motor bike in pieces, some croquet mallets, and an artificial Christmas tree. The rooms led round the edge of the house, and returned to the foot of the stairs. Under the centre of the house was a huge chamber, from which most of the outer basements could be reached, through low archways. In this central room was a lot of furniture, a huge old table was laden with candles, candle sticks, and some torches, none of which worked, but a large box of batteries enabled Judith to get two of them to work. She switched on one, and as she passed the beam around the room, the light was reflected from something in the corner. She went over and pulled an old blanket off a large, rather fine, free–standing mirror. It was very dusty, and, remembering the acute shortage of mirrors in the house, she went and found a bucket in a nearby part of the basement. In one of the rooms was a sink, and in a small side room she found a toilet. An old box of rags was nearby, so she filled the bucket with water from the sink, found some washing up liquid under the sink, and returned to the mirror and began wiping it down.

It was a beautiful mirror, and rather old. It was too awkward for her to move on her own, although she tried. Turning back to clear a large cardboard box out of the way, she stumbled on something, stepped back and kicked the bucket over. She swore, and watched in amazement as the water flowed, not all over the stone floor, as she expected, but straight down a thin crack in the floor and disappeared. Curious, she cleared the area, bit by bit, and under the dust she found a wooden trapdoor, and an old, inset brass handle. She fetched the two working torches and pulled hopefully on the handle. She expected it to be very heavy but it was unexpectedly light and she dropped one torch, which promptly went out. The second torch was not too reliable, so she fetched a candle lantern from the table and a couple of extra candles. She lit the lantern with her cigarette lighter and went to stare down into a black hole revealed by the trapdoor.

She felt intense curiosity. She sat wondering if it was altogether sensible to continue. Looking around, she saw an old Mercedes car handbook, and it reminded her of the accident. She remembered the children who had been killed, and that made her remember the loss of her own baby. She made her way down some solid, but old, steps into a cold, dank room. As she got to the bottom of the steps, she held up the lantern to see where she was. There was some sort of circular structure in the centre of the room and she moved towards it. She was amazed to discover this was a well, from which she could hear water running. She peered down it. It was not that deep, and she saw sluggishly moving water swirling round at the bottom. There was a steel rod at the side of the well with protruding spikes, obviously used as hand and footholds. She moved away and, with the lantern, went to the far side of the room.

Behind her something moved. She heard a faint rustling, and knew there was something alive in the room with her. She froze. For some time she waited, but when she stepped towards the noise, she heard it again, and something black moved in the corner. She experienced a feeling of panic and fear, but it was not from her. She said, softly,

"Please do not be afraid, I will not hurt you. Whoever you are, I wish you no harm."

You are unhappy.

This time it was a single voice.

"Yes. I am. I remember a bad thing. A child died."

We understand. You have come. We wait. Zan say you come.

"May I see you?"

Other light hurt. Flame not hurt.

From the shadows came the strangest creature Judith had ever seen. She watched as a black animal, the size of a greyhound, walked slowly towards her. It had huge eyes, black, and it crouched, walking mainly on short and strong hind legs. There was something monkey–like about it. It seemed mottled, and then she saw that it had shiny black scales, between which she thought was some kind of fur. There were no ears and the head was small and round. The mouth was wide and full of the most alarming, sharp teeth. The paws, or hands, had prolonged digits, three that she could see, each with a massive claw. There was a long, prehensile tail, and the front limbs had sinews showing under the smaller scales. The whole creature was moist. As it approached she saw it was not black, but a deep purple shade, with tones of mauve.

It seemed to undulate, as it moved towards her, stopping more than two metres way. She knew she should be terrified, but she wasn't. In a bizarre way, it was beautiful.

From the well something moved, and she could hear movement in the water. She nervously turned, to see another creature come over the top of the well and slither, with a rustling sound, onto the floor. It was followed by several more, all different in shape, and coloured differently. One had massive teeth and jaws, and another was small and round in build.

She felt faint, and sat down on the floor, putting the lamp down and feeling in her pocket for the other torch.

They advanced towards her and stopped in a loose circle around her.

"What are you? What do you want with me? I can feel you mean me no harm, but why are you here?"

We are here. We were here long ago. Do not fear. You have come. Zan say you come. Zan gone. Sad. She say you to be friend.

Judith saw a picture of Great Aunt Susan in her mind. Into the picture came some of the creatures, and she saw they were sitting in the library. Susan was much younger. Some small creatures were playing with a ball of wool on the floor, and the larger creatures were lying relaxed beside her.

"You can get into my mind!"

You can hide nothing. You are the one who will come. Here is our place too. We wish to be allies. You must tell no one. We die if you speak of us. Man come and hunt and kill and hurt with light. We must not be found.

Judith asked, "Then why let me find you? Why trust me?"

Zan say you be friend. We need friend. You keep secret, if you tell, you die, we die: too few in our colony. We must survive.

Judith felt quite bewildered. She had nothing to judge any of this by. She wondered if she had flipped, and if it was a dream.

Not dream. We wait for you. You tell name.

"My name is Judith Swallow. How are you called? My friends call me Judy."

She felt their thoughts meld, and then,

We, the Garr. You, we call Zood. We have a message for Zood, from Zan. We get. You stay.

Two of the smaller creatures jumped down the well, and splashed into the water. More creatures came from the well. One of them was very large, and the others moved deferentially, to make way for it. Instead of being dark, it was a lilac colour. It was like the first in shape and form, but bigger. Its eyes were black, but as it looked closely at her, a covering over the eye peeled back, and revealed a reptilian eye. The thoughts were clear and strong from this animal.

I am named Goy. Zan was friend to Goy and Garr. We live here long time. Before man come. Then we try to live with man. Man hunt us, with crossed stick. We hide from man. Long time. Hide from man. Always we have friend. Help us protect Garr. Garr very few. Before Zan, Zelss. Before Zelss, Zagath. You help us.

It was not really a question, it was a fact. Knowing every thought would be read, she tried to make sense of these creatures. They were not animals, they were intelligent beings. She could sense their desperate fear of discovery and their despair of extinction. The smaller Garr returned with a package, well–sealed, and without any label. The small one handed it to Goy, who approached Judith.

"May I touch you?"

Judith felt silly, but wanted to check these beings were real. Goy came really close, and put a paw on Judith's arm, and then touched her hair. Judith tentatively touched the scales, which were damp and rather slimy. The fur between the scales was a beautiful amethyst shade, and was very dense and soft. On the underside of the paw were pads of sticky leather, concave and pliable. She realised they were suckers, used, she supposed for climbing.

We climb. We live below the ground. We need water, and light hurts our eyes. You tired. Message in gift. We will not harm you. Go up to light. We call you soon. After strong light we come, when you alone. If other man there, we know, will not come. We have other gift, drink and not hurt.

Judith said, "But I have no gift for you. What can I give you in return? How will I know if you call me?"

You give sweet food. where food lives. We speak in your head. Be serene. Rest. Drink.

Judith had a picture of the kitchen, and of a box of cereal, and a sugar basin. A small Garr approached with a glass bottle, containing a deep blue fluid. She was urged to drink, and to finish the bottle. It tasted foul, but she didn't want to offend. She got up and went to the steps and climbed up them.

Close door. Cover, so no one finds. Be calm.

Judith closed the trap door and left the cellar. She went up to the Lost It Room, and switched the cellar lights off. She locked the door, went into the kitchen, and put the cereal and sugar on the floor. She added some chocolate biscuits and some Kendal Mint Cake. She went to the dining room, poured herself a large brandy and returned to the kitchen and ate some cold tongue and salad. She loaded the dishwasher and was startled to find it was nearly midnight. She went to bed but could not sleep. Her mind was racing, and her heartbeat too. Gradually, either the brandy or the blue fluid worked and she fell asleep.

She woke early and got up feeling better than she had for months. She didn't ache, and her leg hardly troubled her. She showered and brushed her hair, and looked in the mirror. Her bruising was fading fast and she had lost the tired rings under her eyes. She felt full of life, and went down to the kitchen. The cereal and all the other food she had left had gone. In its place was a bottle of blue fluid. She picked it up, and looked at it.

Drink, it will heal.

She drank the fluid, wondering what was in it. The taste was so foul that she went to the fridge and drank some orange juice. The sun was up, and she took some toast and jam out onto the patio, and sat down in the warm sun.

She opened the packet she had been given the night before and took out a long letter and a pendant on a chain. It was very old. The chain was strong and beautifully fashioned. The pendant itself was an intricate miniature of one of the Garr. Its eyes seemed to be of black crystal, and the claws seemed to be small opals. It was a fantastic creature, beautifully sculpted, and very light. Putting this aside, she removed a key from the package and an old map. Turning to the letter, she recognised Susan's hand writing. She read the letter.

Porthwaite Hall

My very dear Judith,

The fact that you are reading this will mean that you have discovered the secret of the Hall. It is a secret I have kept for many, many years, and the time is coming when I have to pass my guardianship on to you. I know that my heart has been failing for some years, and my time is near. Even the blue healing potion cannot help me much longer. I will explain about that later.

When I first came to the hall as a young woman, I had cancer and did not expect to live long. My fiance had been killed in the war. He was in the navy, and was lost at sea. I was left this place by an aunt of mine, who I hardly knew. Aunt Elsie was known as an eccentric, and had lived here many years. She left me a letter, similar to this one, which I enclose.

My cancer went and never returned. I began to feel well and life was good. When I first came to the house, I was very frightened and very unhappy. I expect you have been frightened of things you may have heard or seen. Do not be. All will be explained.

The Garr are an ancient race I think they predate the evolution of man. I suspect they evolved from the dinosaurs, and they have always been in man's folk law. Once they were plentiful and people explained them as fairies and goblins. People even worshipped them and often left offerings to them, mainly of food. Local farmers used to leave them dead lambs and calves. The church put a stop to that and persecuted them. They turned them into demons and hunted them almost to extinction. Nowadays the threat to them is of discovery, and modern technology.

The Garr live underground and cannot stand exposure to the light. They must stay moist. A large colony lives in the cave system under the house, which has remained undiscovered because it has been private for years. All, or almost all, of the entrances are locked in some way. I am sure the Garr know of other ways in and out which they keep to themselves. The Garr have protected and sustained me for years, and in return I have guarded their secret. It has been a happy duty and I have never felt alone.

The Garr have their own ways and will do anything, and I mean anything, to protect themselves. They wouldn't hesitate to kill, to ensure their survival. The fact that they have revealed themselves to you means they have chosen you, and you cannot escape this burden, until a successor has been chosen. You may ask why you? I have passed this burden on to you. Their guardian has to be female and has to be able to speak within the mind. I understand this is known as being telepathic. I knew you had this power when I met you, and I knew someone would come. It always happens that way. In your turn, a successor will arrive. You will know who it is, instinctively.

I do not know when you will get this letter. It may be years in the future. I believe that for some reason, Clive will not be with you, and I am sorry. I hope you were happy together.

This house is very old, older than records, certainly. Try not to disturb it too much.

The guardianship has its benefits. The massive wealth I have left you is compensation for a lifetime's work. If you need wealth, it will come. I am very old now, and have little energy to keep the estate as it used to be. I have only held on until you could come. I am very weary and want to go. Please, could you care for the estate, and for the faithful staff who have served it so well? Beware the rest of Clive's family. They have tried to prise my wealth from me.

The Garr are not demanding. All they want is a safe haven, and their secret kept. Occasionally they ask for something, last time it was for an antibiotic. Somehow they manufactured a copy. Give them what they ask for. They will repay you. They will respect your wishes, as long as they do not endanger them. Animals you care for will be left alone, but if you do have a dog, have it from a puppy, and let it make friends with the Garr. They tend to dispose of animals who yap at, or chase them. Cats usually run away from them.

The blue elixir they may already have given you is not addictive and has amazing healing powers. I have no idea what is in it, and you should never give it to anyone else, in case they try and analyse it. The Garr may give you some for others, if they know it will be disguised and used only for people you love or care for. Whatever you do, do not tell anyone about them. There is one person who knows something and he will never say anything. The Garr know who he is, and will not reveal themselves, or speak to him, but accepted some time ago that I needed him to know.

There are many secret ways in and around this house, that the Garr use. Please help them keep them secret. You may have found the cellar, and I enclose a key for the trap door. They have access to most of the rest of the house, but will avoid areas you ask them to, should you have guests.

Your guardianship is likely to last a long time, and it does not mean you are tied to the house. Foreign holidays were a great pleasure to me, and I always told them where I was going. There are other colonies all over the world, but only in temperate zones. They cannot stand heat and need water. Caves are their natural homes, so limestone areas are where they concentrate. They described to me Martel's descent into Gaping Gill.

You can hide nothing from them, they are always in your mind. They consider humans as frail creatures, weak, and like the young. They are very wise and live a long time. If you need help or advice, ask them for it. Their understanding of our society and motives is somewhat limited and a little simplistic. They cannot comprehend the idea of property or wealth and do not understand theft. Much of the wealth they have provided their guardians, is, I believe, the results of foraging in cellars and old graves. They can extract minerals and precious metals from deep under the ground, and have much treasure stored away. The pendant I enclose is probably over a thousand years old, and has always been worn by the guardian. Should you ever see anyone with another, they will be guardians of their own colony. The eyes are black diamonds, and the claws are opals. The metal will never tarnish, and is very light. Put the pendant on, and, should you ever lose it, it will be returned to you. I lost it swimming in the lake once, and two days later, it was back in my room.

The young are playful and play tricks. They do have a sense of humour and can be affectionate. They never stop growing and the eldest ones are trapped underground by their size. They regard death as a natural progression and can suicide at will. Their blood, which is corrosive if not oxygenated, dissolves their bodies, so science has never caught up with them. Should one be injured, they may ask for your help. Wear gloves, as their blood will burn. They are limited physically by their lack of a proper opposing digit and may ask you to help in that way.

When you put on the pendant, the other keeper of our secret will make himself known to you.

I am sorry to pass this burden on to you. I have given you a life sentence, for which you never asked. Barring accidents, you will live a long and, I hope, a happy life. I doubt you will have a lifelong partner, but you will never be lonely. Forgive me, and thank you for coming along when you did. I found it helpful to be known as a benevolent, if slightly eccentric, old woman. I know the estate will take a lot to bring back. If you are the person I believe you to be, it will thrive.

I know my end is very near now. So do the Garr, who are with me, mentally and spiritually, and will be, when I go. If there is a heaven, they will be there. I have asked for my ashes to be scattered down on the lake. I go happy, knowing my greatest friends will be safe with you, and in many years, your successor. I believe the modern phrase is 'Live Long and Prosper.'

All the luck and strength in this world, and the next.

Susan Holt (Zan)

****

Judith was weeping by the time she finished the letter. All around her she felt the combined grief of many minds. She sat and howled for some minutes.

Zan gone, Zan at peace. We were with her. Zan not alone. Zood not alone. Be tranquil. New life, new hope. Weep no more. We sing at large water. We honour Zan. You honour Zan. We are with you.

Judith picked up an old document from a pile of old letters. She read it, slowly.

Porthwaite Hall.
July 1942

My dear Susan,

You will have discovered my secret, and why I left all my property to you. The Garr will show you my notes, explaining about them. They have them in safe keeping, as it is not safe in this house, while we have all these servicemen here, convalescing. In this, Britain's darkest time, I have placed on you a heavy duty, to add to your grief. You are the one I, and they, have chosen. Do not fight them, and care for them as I have. They have kept me alive long beyond my three score years and ten, and I am tired, and wish to go, and have served them, and I believe my country, and God, well. Keep my staff safe, and you will want for nothing. In your time, pick a brave and honest successor, and promise never to betray our secret. The guardianship was passed to me by my grandmother, Agatha Eccles.

God bless you, Susan, may your life be as happy and fulfilled as mine. I will not be alone when I die. The Garr are with me, as they will be with you, in your time.
God save the King, and M. Churchill.

Elsie Ivy Garreton (Zelss)

****

Judith wondered what these women had been like. Pictures came into her head of two women, one small, and with fair hair, in thirties dress, and another in Edwardian dress, taller, and rather austere, in a hat. Again she felt a communal grieving.

We remember. We sing at hole in dirt, at place of crossed sticks. We honour them.

She looked reverently at the pendant and wondered what metal it was and who had made it, and looked at the clasp. It was intricate, and it took her some time to undo it, and even longer, in front of a mirror, to fasten it. It would not come undone easily. It was so light she barely felt it, and she noticed that it was instantly warm. She folded the letters and the map of the area marking entrances to the cave system, and replaced them into the wrapping. She needed to hide the letters safely, so they would only be found by her. She tried to think of a place and instantly she had a picture of part of the library, so she went there and pulled out a book on a lower shelf. Behind was a small opening and she placed the packet inside and replaced the book. A few moments later she heard a click from the area, and removing the book again, found the hole was blocked.

She felt relief and went upstairs to make her bed, and tidy her room. She went down again and met Jim and Liam, who told her they were taking the horses to the farm to eat off a paddock there, where they could be housed at night in a set of cowstalls. They all went down to the stables and Judith led two of the mares, a bay and a dapple grey, back down to the farm. The grey was affectionate and a little plump. Judith suggested she might be pregnant. Liam took a look at the mare when they reached the paddock and agreed. He was very good handling horses and they were placid around him. The foal had trotted happily after its mother, a flighty chestnut, and once in the better grazing, cavorted around. They walked back to the house and Judith put the kettle on. Jim looked at her and said,

"Judy, you seem much better, you are not limping so badly, and you have not got your stick."

Judith looked for her stick and remembered leaving it in the library. She was pleased and replied, "Yes. The leg does seem much better. I feel good. Now, what needs to be done today? Did you want to run through your list for the farm?"

Jim, thoughtfully stirring three spoonfuls of sugar into his tea, nodded.

"I realise I cannot have everything on the list. The tractor is the most pressing need. It is fine for light work, but not for the heavy stuff. I could look round for a secondhand one, but you never know what you are getting. Could you run to a new one?"

He was soon expounding the virtues of a John Deere, and a Ford, and a Mercedes, and a Case. Judith stopped him, and confessed she didn't have a clue what he was talking about.

"What is the one you need, that can do everything you might want?"

"The John Deere, but they are very expensive, even secondhand."

"Then get one. Don't muck about with an old one, get it new, with a guarantee. Get what you need to go with it. Is there a local dealer? Then go and ring them now, and buy one. Do they also deal in quad bikes?"

"Yes, they do. We could use a second quad. I was really wanting to talk to you about a full–time shepherd. If we had one, we could get the sheep up to a decent standard and we would keep more lambs at lambing time. If we get a shepherd, we will need to find him, or her, accommodation. There is the other farm house empty, it has been for a while. It is smaller than ours, and needs doing up, but it would help the farm to have a good shepherd."

"Did you have anyone in mind?"

"No, we would need to advertise."

"Then do it, get Wesley to sort it. Do we need a student at lambing time? If we do, get us on the list at the local agricultural college."

"They all cost, you know. We would need a good quad for the shepherd, too. Shall I get Wesley to sell the old tractor?"

"Only if Stuart doesn't want it for the grounds. It might be handy to have a spare. See what he says. The phone is there, ring the dealer now, and get what we need as soon as you can. Get a good deal if you can, but don't sacrifice quality for the sake of a couple of quid. I do not expect anyone to do a job without adequate tools. Go on Jim, order your tractor!"

Jim went to the phone, rang the dealer, and came back, almost bubbly. He thanked her, and said something about being the envy of the neighbourhood. He strode off down the drive, whistling happily to himself. Wesley arrived five minutes later, followed by Sam. Judith asked Wesley to make a list of what alterations he would need, and what he needed for his office, which she suggested might be situated in the room between the sitting room and the music room. She asked if he needed the cloakroom altered, and took him to the room to see it. Sam followed and began moving the boxes. Wesley looked at the room, and said,

"Who will I be sharing this with?"

"No one, except occasionally, me. It will be your office. You choose the decor and furniture, get yourself a decent stereo, and a good computer. You choose, but make it good enough for the job. There is a catalogue or two there, pick what you like. I will be ordering from both, my private sitting room will be the next room, and I will need some stuff for there. The decorators will show you some sample books, and you had better choose your own flooring, carpet, or whatever you want. Sam, can you do ramps for outside the door here, to the terrace, and on the front steps, and anywhere Wesley might want to go? Wesley, you had better have a new chair for here, so you don't have to lug yours in and out of the car."

Wesley looked a bit taken aback, and said, "Are you saying that I can play my music at work, and I can choose the colours, and I can have my own pictures?"

"Yes, I am. You have to work in this room, and so it had better be how you like it. Can you get in and out of the cloakroom easily? If not, we will alter it. Just get what you need, filing cabinets, desks, and I don't want cheap tacky ones. Get something comfy, and a bit stylish if you can, as you will be representing the estate. I am having a safe fitted in here and the phones should be in this week. Do you want your own fridge and kettle? If so, get it. You get free coffee, lunch and tea, and can make yourself a drink whenever you want. The room will be cleaned daily. Sam, could you start on the ramps? Can you make sure Wesley can get down from the patio in his chair, and round to the drive, as well as out the front door. Please find a spare key to all the doors into here, and give a set to him."

"I'll get my tools, and find the keys."

Sam left and Wesley said,

"I don't need to go out on the patio, but it would be nice. Can I choose a carpet too? Could I have a blue one?"

"Wesley, you have what you need. You can have a green one with pink spots, if you must, but you will have to live with it. We will get these boxes shifted, for starters, and then you can plan it. Until we have done so, could you charm someone out of some coffee for us?"

Wesley grinned, and said, "There is something I want to talk to you about. I should have said yesterday. You said staff got free medical treatment, as private patients. You obviously won't want to include me in that, it wouldn't be fair, as I already have problems."

Judith looked at him.

"Wesley, why should you be any different to any other member of staff? That includes you. If you need treatment, then you will get it. I cannot afford to be without you for longer than necessary. If you want your own doctor, then we will use him. Who is your doctor?"

"I go to Dr Tippett. I think he is the local one for here."

"That is simple then. I need you, and I need you to be happy at work. I don't want you to be worrying about waiting lists, or cost of prescriptions, or waiting round surgeries for hours. If you do the job right for me, then I will do right by you. Start taking me for a ride, and you won't find me so kind. Mr Cummings found that!"

Mary and Nora appeared with Sally and the twins. Sally went to the kitchen and the boys helped move the boxes. Sam and Liam got the boxes unpacked, and soon the room was cleared and Dot and Betty were cleaning it. Wesley went into the library to work, and was soon making lists and costing them. He was put in charge of the telephone. Judith was compiling her own lists, and soon they were working together to cross reference with suppliers. Stuart and his family arrived, and they helped with the boxes. Lucy sorted the linen and clothes, and a huge pile of clothes appeared at the foot of the stairs in a wicker laundry trolley. Nora asked her why she didn't take it up in the lift and everyone turned and looked at her in surprise. She found a key to the other door in the Lost It Room, and revealed a large lift. This went to the top of the house, with an exit to each floor. On the floor of the lift, Judith noticed some cereal flakes and removed them when no one was looking.

Lunch was a hurried affair and Sam had finished the ramps by early afternoon. Wes, as he asked to be called, had worked hard at the lists, and everything was set up for Monday. Celia turned up and Judith went down to the lake with her. They chatted, and walked back to the house.

The rest of the day was spent checking prices and lists and generally tidying up. Judith helped sort linen, and sorted through some of the boxes of her belongings. She started going through Clive's belongings. She sorted out his clothes, which distressed her, and made a huge pile of them. She kept very little and went and found Nora and asked her if anyone would want any of the clothes, or would be offended at the offer. They looked them through.

June had taken her son, Julian, and Chris and Tim, down to the lake for a swim. Sally had teamed up with Stuart's daughter, and they were playing music in the music room. Sam was fixing a rail in the downstairs cloakroom. Stuart came to see Judith, and asked what she wanted done in the conservatory and the vegetable garden. They discussed what to plant for the next year, and he mentioned that there was a lot of fruit needing picking in the gardens, and he wanted to know what to do with it. Judith suggested that all the staff take what they need, and then she would ask Mr Sandell if he would take any. Stuart said he would enquire, and suggested the children help pick the fruit.

Jim returned from the cricket match, again jubilant at having won. He invited Judith to the farm for supper, and after everyone had gone home, Judith walked to the farm and had a splendid meal. The twins had enjoyed their swim in the lake and had already planned the next day with Julian. The meal was relaxed and Judith was shown round the farm on the ancient tractor. The dairy herd was examined and the horses had settled in. Jim took her up onto the moor and they checked the sheep, who were hefted to that area. As it got dark, Jim dropped her off at the house, and she had a quiet evening watching television. She did not forget to leave food out and had a quiet and peaceful night.

Chapter Ten

Sunday started quietly. Judith still had the residue of black eyes, so did not go to church. Tom rang, and asked if he could bring his family over. June and Sam went with all the young people to the lake for a swim. Celia arrived with Tom and his family. Tom asked,

"How are you? You must still be shaken up. I hope you can relax today. It's a lovely day, very warm. You seem to have brought the good weather with you!"

Judith smiled and said, "Yes, an Indian summer, but remember, one Swallow doesn't make a summer!"

Soon the place was full of staff and their families, and everyone went down to the lake. Judith took her swimming costume and a mound of towels, and was just leaving when Wesley turned up and joined the group down by the lake. It was a beautiful, hot day, and some food was fetched. The children were soon exploring the woods, but the adults mainly sat and relaxed. When the sun finally lost its strength, they wandered back to the house. Judith suggested a drink and opened some wine and anyone not driving was offered some. Jim only had one glass and Wesley opted for fruit juice.

The children were playing the banister game and some cushions were placed at the bottom of the stairs to prevent too many bruises. Eventually they got bored and the party broke up. Wesley said he had a date and went home. Mary tidied the kitchen and Judith saw them all off and then wrote some letters, watched the television and went to bed.

Monday began with a lot of telephone calls. All day the house was invaded by tradesmen, the decorators arrived in force, and furniture and equipment were delivered. The drive was packed with vehicles, and the telephone company started work. Wesley took it all in his stride, and took most of the burden off Judith. Liam came in to help Sam move furniture and Betty was in her element directing their every move.

Sharon rang to say she was arriving the next day. Dot got a bedroom ready, and Stuart suggested someone pick some flowers. Judith volunteered and was glad to escape the chaos for an hour or two. She returned, having discovered yet another walled garden and quite a bit more of the grounds. Haley asked if she could arrange the flowers, unless Judith wanted to. Judith hastily accepted the offer as her flower arranging skills were minimal.

Bill was mowing the front lawn and Liam went out to strim some of the rough areas. Gradually, a pleasant area was being revealed. Sam came to search for the keys to the second gate, and eventually found them. Judith drove down to the village, and sorted out an account with the garage, and popped into the shop. Mr Sandell was delighted to see her and introduced her to most of his family. She made some private purchases.

She returned to the house and surrendered the Astra to Sam. The house reeked of paint, and there were strangers all over the place. It was another hot day, and the front lawns were looking quite respectable. When Judith felt harassed in the house, and was in the way in the kitchen, she took a book and a rug and went and sat on the lawn to read.

Someone shouted that lunch was ready, and the staff went into the kitchen to eat. The decorators and telephone men asked to eat their sandwiches on the terrace. For a while, there was peace, but after lunch the noise and bustle began again. Wesley called her to the phone, and Tom asked if he could come over to her that afternoon with the police, who wanted her statement. She agreed and went in search of an unoccupied room and found one in the drawing room. She asked for a tea and coffee trolley to be brought in, and was reading in there when Tom arrived. They were soon joined by a woman detective sergeant. They sat down and Judith made her statement, which took most of the afternoon. The officer left and Tom promised to call in during the week.

Wesley came in with a sheaf of messages, and updated her on the day's developments.

Lucy came out of the house, and asked if it was in order to take the children up to the moor for a picnic the next day. She went off to clear it with Jim, and then returned. Stuart had asked her if the children wanted to earn money picking fruit the day after, and they had all jumped at it. Lucy had lost her timid demeanour and was actually seen laughing on occasions.

She scurried to the flat, to see if her furniture was in the right place, and to try out the new kitchen equipment that had been delivered and fitted that day. Sam came, and asked for permission to use the car that evening, to fetch some things for Stuart from the nurseries. Judith asked if she could come too, and jumped in beside him.

Judith helped collect plants, pots and seeds, and they came back to the stables. Sam asked Judith into the flat, and Lucy was delighted to show her how it had improved. Sam wanted to build some bookcases and a built–in wardrobe, and to make several improvements, to which Judith readily agreed. She stopped for a cup of tea with them, and cuddled the cat, a little tabby and white, for a while, and then looked at some embroidery Lucy was doing. She finally got back to the house, in time to have a nice relaxing bath, watch the news and head off to bed.

The next day was similarly busy, and Judith was finally able to start furnishing her sitting room. She picked the carpet she wanted from a sample book brought out to the house by an optimistic salesman. She took him to see Wesley, who picked what he wanted, and then, gathering Nora, they went round the house, and the salesman was overjoyed before they even got to the second floor. The poor little man spent the rest of the morning measuring up, and returned to Judith to confirm all the order. He was thrilled to telephone his boss, and then announced they could deliver and fit within the week, as such a large order would take precedence over all others. Judith gently explained that the houses and flats were yet to sort, and Sam took him away to measure those, and then he was invited to lunch, so he could confirm colours with the occupants. The salesman must have thought it was Christmas, and was quite overwhelmed with the order, or more accurately, as Stuart pointed out, his commission.

The telephone engineer asked if he could explain the switchboard and the phone system to her, so a group went to Wesley's office with Wesley, while the system was explained. Lunch was a choice of meat salad or pasta, and Liam needed no encouragement to try both. No one hung about, and they soon got back to work. The carpet man, now grinning from ear to ear, rang an interim order through, and offered a discount for bulk. A builder arrived and went up to fix the attic floors with Sam.

Sharon arrived a little later, and Liam offered to carry her cases for her. He seemed a little struck with her, and she was very sweet to him. Bill could be seen hovering in the background, and when Lucy came back with the children, Tim and Chris insisted on taking her on a tour of the house.

Finally, the house was quiet and Sharon and Judith got to talking. Sharon needed to go shopping the next day, and was full of news about the family. They spent a pleasant relaxed evening, and the next day went into town in Sharon's car.

On their return to the house, in the late afternoon, they were assisted by Betty and Liam, who carried the shopping, and then after a brief shower, and a check to see what had been done, Judith took them to the Ugly Imp for an evening meal. Toby and Dee welcomed them, and Sharon made quite an impression on most of the cricket team, who were holding a meeting there. Amongst the team was John Arrowsmith, who talked about the police with Sharon. Toby came to talk to Judith while Sharon socialised.

Toby was good company and a good host. He provided her with the village gossip, most of which seemed to be about her. It was common knowledge that the Cumming's had been arrested, and that drugs had been found at their house. To her surprise, Judith heard nothing of the incident at Porthwaite Hall. She had expected something to leak out. Toby gave her a list of things that needed doing to the pub, which she had asked for. He said that they could be financed from the profits, but needed her authorisation for them.

When they left, they drove back through the back gates, into the grounds and up past the barn. As they approached the house, a figure ran away into the grounds and went into the undergrowth. It was human and any chase would have been pointless. Together they checked the building, but could find nothing amiss. They had a drink and Sharon went to bed.

Judith went to the library and checked any messages from Wesley, and wondered who had been in the grounds.

He come, he try to enter. Bad boy. He come to take. Do not trust. He means you ill.

A picture of the cowman's son, Brian Hall, was put into her head. She wondered what he wanted.

He want paper and metal round things.

Judith was a bit puzzled by this and a picture was put into her head of money.

"Oh, I see. Is he not afraid of this place?"

He is, but he needs for powder to make him good. Man who gives powder is not here.

Judith saw a picture of Cummings, in a car by the barn, with Brian and two other youths, exchanging packages and money.

"You mean he was dealing drugs here. Is he here now?"

Not now. Gone. Big man not here now. Zood not want this, Garr stop them. We tell if they come. Zood has friend. Many man come in light. House change. Zood not let us be found.

"No, I will keep your secret safe. There will be a lot of activity for a while. I read Zan's letter. I understand now, more than I did. Tomorrow we pick fruit off trees. Do you like fruit?"

We take all time. Rotten is best.

"You mean you like rotten fruit?"

We like. Also old meat. We eat old to make easy .

Judith saw a pile of rotten meat in a cave, and rotten fruit. She saw the Garr eating it. She was shown a picture of a primitive stomach, and suddenly realised they could only digest semi–rotten food. The picture faded, and was replaced by pictures of a dead calf.

"I see. Thank you for the drink, I feel much better. There are a lot of things going on, tell me if anyone is bothering you, or if you need anything."

We will tell. Big man keep powder in tower by big water. Secret.

The voices had gone. She thought about it and realised they meant the Folly. She wondered what to do. No one could find the keys to the Folly. She would have to be very careful. She finished her paperwork and retired to bed.

In the morning, they went down to the lake and had a swim, and then went to join the others in picking fruit. Judith noticed an absence of windfalls and rotten fruit. Everyone worked hard, and baskets of fruit piled up. Stuart ferried them away, either to the houses or to outside the barn. Mr Sandell came and collected some. By the end of the day, everyone was sticky, hot and dirty. Sharon said she had enjoyed herself. During the evening Judith helped her sort out her clothes and belongings for her course, and they stored some things in Sharon's room, which was like the Chinese Drawing Room. They went to a bedroom at the back of the house, to watch a good film on the television there.

He comes. With metal bar. We watch. Do not show light.

Judith saw the picture of Brian with a crowbar, skulking towards the house. She could hardly explain how she knew about it, so she left the room, and went to her unlit bedroom, and peered out of the window. She saw him, heading around to the side of the house, towards the music room and office area.

We will frighten him. Stay away, with friend. Zood not be there.

The instructions were very emphatic, and she returned to the television. She found it hard to concentrate on the film, and Sharon asked her if she was feeling unwell, as she had gone rather white. Judith said she had a stomach ache and left under the pretence of looking for some remedy. She moved quietly to an unused bedroom above the library and peered out of the window. Brian was trying to prise open the library French windows. He was unaware of several dark figures on the edge of the terrace.

Zood. To room. He run to us, in dark we frighten him. Not be seen or he talk of us. Then call help. Men with talking clothes and sticks.

Judith rushed and fetched Sharon, and got her to call the police. Then she crept downstairs, into the library, and as Brian finally got the door open, she faced him and said,

"Good evening, Brian. Wouldn't ringing the door bell be a little more polite? Do come in and wait for the police."

Brian had expected the house to be empty, and jumped as she spoke. He dropped the crowbar with a loud clang, and as Judith approached him, he hesitated momentarily, before turning and running off across the terrace. Sharon, who had silently come up behind Judith, went to chase him, but Judith grabbed her arm and said,

"No. If he can see where he is going, he's cleverer than I thought. I know who he is. Don't you risk tripping or falling."

As she spoke, an anguished howl came from the bushes, followed by a series of terrified yelps and whimpers and cries for help. There was some rustling and commotion from the area, and then Brian crawled from the bushes. He got awkwardly to his feet. Judith went to him, but he managed to limp off towards the drive. His language was obscene and rather limited, and he declined her invitation to wait inside. He had been severely scratched, and, she suspected, bitten, as well as bruised.

She stopped Sharon, and asked her not to pursue the lad. Sharon went and put the kettle on in the kitchen, and they waited for the police to arrive.

"I don't really want him caught, Sharon, I don't think he will come back in a hurry. He got the fright of his life, and getting tangled up in the undergrowth was rather silly. Nothing has been stolen. He is the son of an employee of mine, so can you keep quiet about my knowing him."

Sharon looked out of her amazingly beautiful face, and said,

"If that is what you want. There are things I don't understand and I think you know more than you are saying. Tell me later. I will go and make the tea. Shout if he comes back."

There was slight anger, tinged with amusement when the voices came to her.

Very stupid boy. Wants powder badly. Now hurts bad. Very scared. He go to farm where father live. We go. Talking clothes come. One wants friend. You call love.

When the police arrived, Judith realised why the Garr referred to them as having talking clothes. Their radios were chattering. John Arrowsmith arrived, and with two other officers they looked at the forced door, and made a brief search of the shrubbery. None of them seemed too keen to hang around in the garden and when Judith said Sharon was making tea in the kitchen John was in there so fast, that the other two wondered why. Judith explained that he and Sharon seemed rather struck with each other. They joined them in the kitchen, and a crime report was taken by the older policeman, while the two younger ones almost ogled Sharon. The older officer, Jake, mentioned in an undertone,

"Something tells me you might have several follow up visits. She is beautiful, isn't she? Did you say she is joining up?"

"Yes, tell me, is John married? They seem very taken with each other. She is lovely, inside and out, and I don't want her hurt."

"Yes, he is single. Nice lad. Do you want me to get someone out to fix the door? I think this is the first time I have been to an intruder call here. I came out to the lady's death, before the doctor certified death from natural causes, but the locals seem scared of this place. Now we have two incidents in several days. Are you the one that slime ball punched? Your bruises have healed quick, I can only just see them."

Judith replied,

"Yes, I heal fast. It must be the fresh air. No, don't bother, I'll get Sam to look at it in the morning. Tell me what you know about Cummings."

They left Sharon with the other two and went to the library. Jake told Judith a bit about Cummings, and then Judith asked about the drug scene and Jake replied,

"We have quite a few problems, not like the city, but some of the ne'er do wells seem to have a drug problem. We know there is a dealer in the area, but we have no idea who. There have been two burglaries at chemists in the town in the last week, drugs taken on both occasions. It is a new problem here. I wondered if their supply has dried up."

He looked thoughtful and said, "I wonder, there is only one person not around recently, and we know he is a user. Could you keep your eyes and ears open? I had never considered Cummings, but it would make sense."

Judith decided Jake was a lot smarter than he looked. He was a large, solid man, of about fifty–five, and soon they were chatting. He mentioned belonging to the local Operatic Society, and she asked about it. He invited her to come and join, they were just beginning rehearsals for Patience. He mentioned that they were desperate for a rehearsal hall. She wondered if the ball room would be suitable, and offered its use. They went to look at it, and she explained there was a grand piano available. She asked if the Hall wasn't too far out, but he said it would be ideal.

He asked if he could call and see her the following day, saying he thought he might have company, if Sharon was likely to be there? They laughed, and went to find her.

After some more talk, they got a call on the radio, and had to leave. Sharon seemed quite flushed, and while they cleared up in the kitchen, avoided saying anything about John. Returning to the television, she asked,

"So tell me, how the heck did you know there was someone out there? I didn't hear anything, and neither did you. If he got his injuries by falling in the undergrowth, I'm a Dutchman. Something got him, and you knew it would. That's why you didn't want him caught. It's all right, I won't say anything, but are you really safe here? Why don't you get a dog? Or do you already have a pack of them out there?"

Judith felt that Sharon would be an excellent officer. She thought carefully before replying,

"I cannot really explain, I just had a feeling. I've sort of been expecting something like this, it was inevitable, I suppose, someone would think there was something worth taking. This is a strange house, and it is looking after me very well. All I can say is I think it is benignly haunted, I and my friends are safe, but it doesn't like intruders. I think the lad was drugged up, and he is not likely to trouble me again. I was thinking of getting a puppy, probably a Water Spaniel, it is a breed I like, and they are very bright. I had one for years!"

"Judy, can I stay here some weekends? I can't go home, it's too far, and I would rather not stay at the training school on my own. Did you mean it when you said I could invite a couple of friends? I'll contribute towards my keep."

Judith smiled, and commented,

"You know, one of the good things about being wealthy, is that you can have your friends round when you want to. I think I might just find room for you here! And your friends. There were, at the last count, twenty–seven bedrooms. Come here whenever you like. You can use the facilities. It won't be long before you have your own house. Then I'll come and visit you! Look, it's way past one, I'm off to bed. Goodnight!"

The carpets arrived first thing, in two large lorries, with an army of fitters. While Judith made coffee, she decided they needed a hot water boiler instead of kettles, which were inadequate. She thought of a large samovar, and how useful it could be. She was alone in the kitchen, and was putting another kettle on the Aga.

You have. We show.

She went down to the cellar, and under a pile of old kitchen implements, she found the samovar. It was made of silver and was ornate and she thought it was Russian. She took the opportunity of locking the trap door, and struggled up the steps with the bulky item. She pulled it into the kitchen, and Jim came in. He helped her and looked at it with astonishment.

"Look what I found, it might be useful. Help me up with it."

They put it on the table. Jim looked at her, and said,

"Whatever is it, and where did you find it? I've never seen it before."

Judith explained what it was, and that she found it in the cellar. They got chatting, and then she asked, "Jim, have you had a calf die in the last three days or so?"

"Yes, I have, a bull calf. It was very weak, and it was probably the best thing. It was one of twins, the other is fine. How on earth would you know that?"

"I just do. What do you do, do you have a dead pit?"

Jim shrugged his shoulders. "Yes, it is just on the border of the farm land and the moor, but something gets to carcasses, we seldom have to move them up to the pit, they disappear overnight. It's always been that way here. Strange, but handy. Miss Susan said not to worry about them, they would go, and not to ask questions."

"I think I'll say the same. We had an intruder last night, young Brian Hall, he got in though the library windows, but ran away when I challenged him. He fell over in the undergrowth and I think he hurt himself, but he didn't stop long enough to let me see. We had to call the police, but I didn't tell them I knew who it was. Would it be any use talking to him?"

"That explains something. We got broken into last night, things from the kitchen went, but it was our fault, the door was unlocked. Whoever it was, knew what they were looking for. A bit of cash in an old salt box, kept in the larder, and some catalogue money from the drawer. He's been to our place often enough. There were blood stains over the sink and in the porch. I think I'll pay him a visit, and get it back before he spends it. Did he take anything from here?"

"No, but he left this." Judith produced the crowbar.

"Cheeky sod, that's mine! It is from my barn. No wonder the dogs were creating. I hadn't missed it. Can I take it? If it wasn't for his dad being a good cowman, I'd wrap it round his nasty thieving head. Are you all right?"

Judith grinned, and said, "Oh yes. I'm fine, quite enjoyed the encounter, actually. I have a vicious streak, but I think he might be feeling a bit sorry for himself, he took a hell of a tumble, can't think how he did it. No, I didn't lay a finger on him, nor did Sharon, he managed it all by himself. Unless I am wrong, he is sailing very close to the wind, in several directions. I think he might be on drugs, and he knows Cummings. I cannot kick him out because of his dad, but I don't want him here again."

Judith made a tray of tea and coffee, and took it out to the hall for the carpet fitters. Back in the kitchen, Nora had arrived, and Judith asked, "Look, I really want to find the Folly keys. I need to get in there. Have you any idea who has them, or where we can start looking?"

Nora piped up, "The last person I saw with them was that nasty friend of the Cummings, who was staying there. He said he would give them to Cummings. He was there a while, and had a lot of luggage. He didn't leave with much, so he may have left some stuff there. He might have them. I think he was Dutch."

"In which case I'll get a locksmith to change the locks. I'll get Wesley to do it for me."

Sharon came down and helped get breakfast. Sally helped with preparing the meal, and then took Sharon and Charlotte down to see the horses. They had some tack, and were going to ride the quieter mares.

When everyone came in for coffee break, Liam, Sam and Bill moved the piano into the ballroom, and then fetched chairs up from the basement, and Betty and Dot cleaned them. Judith was called away for a visitor, Dr Tippett. They went to the terrace, where he commented on how much better she looked. They had a general chat and then he looked closely at her neck. He touched the pendant and looked thoughtfully at her.

"Shall we go for a walk?" he suggested, and went round the house to the front lawn, stopping out of any possible earshot. They sat down on a stone seat.

"I see you know about what Miss Susan described as The Cellar Pets. The Garr. She told me all I needed to know, but, sadly, they won't talk to me. I couldn't say anything the other day, until you knew. Are you very upset?"

"Not at all, far from it, they are already protecting me. It was a shock, and I still think I am dreaming, but I accept the job. I don't actually have a choice."

"Am I right in thinking you have drunk some of the blue stuff? You are so much better."

"Yes, I am. Will I always have this limp? It doesn't hurt so much now."

"As one of your legs is shorter than the other, yes, but you can do most things in time. I do not believe even the Garr can fix that. Sorry! I hear you have taken young Wesley on, he is a remarkably talented and well–adjusted young man. It is nice to see him get a chance at last. He was someone I wanted to talk to you about. He says you have offered him private treatment. Is that true?"

"Yes, I don't see why he should be any different from the rest. Is there something you can do for him?"

"There might be, but he could never get it on the NHS. There is a treatment in the States, which, with an operation, might make him more mobile. It will be very expensive, and he has always said he, and his parents, could never afford it. Shall I make an enquiry?"

"Yes, please do. Let me know. How is Mr Cummings?"

"That was the other thing. He was arrested and bailed. He's done a bunk. He was going to a de-tox clinic, but he never turned up. His wife has gone, too. I think, from what the specialist tells me, that he is quite unhinged, and may be quite desperate. To be frank, I fear for his, and your, safety. He may just turn up here. He will be desperate for a fix, and I am worried he may have hidden something here. I don't want you here on your own. I think the Garr will protect you, but he is a dangerous man. He's not in his right senses, certainly. Can you get someone to stay here with you? I think the police may be out to see you

165

soon."

"Thank you for the warning. Sharon is here at the moment, until Sunday. What happens if he finds his stash? I might be able to look for it. I think I know where he will go. You think he is in danger?"

"No, I think you are. You burst his nice little bubble, and precipitated his problems. I think he blames you. We all know he is the author of his own problems, but he doesn't see it that way. You were the one who rumbled him. He underestimated you, and that hurt his pride. Now his life is collapsing round his ears, and all he can do is to blame you. From what the police tell me, after what they found in his house, he wasn't just fiddling you, there is some suspicion of money laundering. And the drugs, which may have caused the whole problem. Could he have money here in the house, or on the estate, hidden somewhere? His disappearing like this, makes me think he is making a run for it."

"Yes, I know he has been dealing drugs here. The Garr told me. I can find out, but I cannot say how I know, as you well understand. I know the Garr will protect me, at night at least."

Judith told him about Brian Hall, and he laughed. He promised to treat Brian's injuries (if requested) with a stringent antiseptic like iodine. He suggested Jim deal with it. They walked back to the house, and he declined lunch and left.

Judith went and talked to Wesley about progress with the carpets. Several deliveries had arrived during the morning, including a stacking system. Wesley had his office nearly finished. The carpet was sea green and the walls a refreshing duck egg green.

She asked if he had managed to sort out matters for the staff meeting that afternoon, and he produced them, as if by magic. His computer was large, and quite incomprehensible to her. Betty asked her to direct where some of the settees that had been delivered were to go. Judith told her and Betty instructed the removal men to place them accordingly. The mobile phones, the pagers and radios had arrived, and Wesley took charge of them, logging serial numbers, while plugging in chargers, Sam erected some racks for him in the Lost It Room, which was clean and tidy and was taking on the shape of a staff room and general office. Bill even condescended to go into it. The lockers had arrived and were placed on one wall. Three safes had also been delivered, one for Nora, one for Wesley, and one for Judith. These were concreted in to appropriate places, and a small personal safe was hidden in a wall upstairs for Judith.

Piles of safety clothes and work wear arrived, but no casual wear.

Just as she was about to sort it, Haley told her there were several people to see her, in the big drawing room. The piano tuner turned up, and went to the ball room to tune the piano with Sally and Charlotte. The twins were fighting with cushions in the hall and Julian was with them. Mary came like a tornado from the kitchen, and marched them all into the scullery to polish some shoes as a punishment. More deliveries arrived, and amidst total chaos, Judith fled to meet her visitors.

Seated in the drawing room was a very tall, slim, athletic man, with a pugnacious jaw, and black hair, and pale grey eyes, dressed in a very smart suit. Tom Barker was with him. The woman detective came in to join them. Another car pulled up. Judith could see two marked police cars in the drive, with Jake and John standing by the front door, and two police officers in what she took to be riot gear, with them. The piano tuner was working in the next room, and there were delivery men everywhere.

The tall man was introduced as Detective Superintendent Carlton, from the Serious Crime Squad. Another man, who came in, was an inspector from the Drug Squad. She began to feel alarmed. She found Superintendant Carlton very intimidating, and rather disliked him. Another man was shown in by Haley, and he was from Customs and Excise. They asked to go somewhere private and talk to her. Knowing the dining room was being prepared for lunch, and almost everywhere was occupied, she went to the conservatory, which she discovered had been transformed. It was warm, and the plants were watered, and when everyone had found a seat, and coffee or tea had arrived, the doors were shut and she was told why they had arrived in force.

Dr Tippett had rather underestimated the problem. Mr Carlton explained that Cummings, and some others, had been involved in a number of big time crimes, including money laundering, drug and currency smuggling, and robbery. As a result, a security guard had died in one robbery, and a search of Cummings house had revealed most of these links. They were convinced that Cummings had secreted vital evidence, drugs and money in or on the house or estate and would be back for it, and probably not alone. They wanted Judith to go into protective custody, but she refused, and asked,

"But why would he leave all this stuff at his house?"

"Because he thought he was above suspicion, I suspect. We know he was not the ringleader, and we believe he was involved through his habit, and was blackmailed into it. He had the perfect set-up. No one suspected him, and he had this place empty and available. It was only his greed, and contempt for his clients that let him down. If you hadn't confronted him, he would have made a getaway. Will you help us? Have you any idea where he is, or where he might have hidden anything? We think something big is going on, and that was what he was waiting for. Hence his desperate attempts to delay you. We think he

167

wanted this place to work from. We don't know why, but we are worried."

Judith sat, dumbstruck, and thought it through. She asked, "Can you give me five minutes? There are some people you need to talk to. No, I'll go Tom, I need to get my head together."

She went and found Nora and Mary and asked them to help, by saying what they knew. Jim walked in, and after a brief discussion over Brian, they agreed to tell the police about him. The whole thing had got out of hand. Jim went to the conservatory, and Judith, dodging sofas going into the lift, went down to the cellar. She went to the centre chamber and sat down and said,

"I need your help. Please talk to me."

We are always with you. You troubled. How Garr help? Be calm. You have mixed mind. Not easy Garr help.

Judith composed herself, and asked, "Do you know what is inside the Folly? Can you get in there?"

We know. We go there, from under. You seek something?

"I need to know about the powder, and paper like this." She tried to imagine a large amount of money, and cases in which it might be found.

You want this.

A picture of a number of leather holdalls, under an old marbled–topped table in an upper room came into her head. A Garr paw pulled back the top of one bag and it was full of packages of white powder. In another bag were wads of money. In another were velvet bags and crystals, possibly diamonds.

You want them with you? We fetch to Zood.

"No. If you do that I shall have to say how I know they are there. Do you know where the key to the Folly is?" She pictured a key.

We know. Big man put in wall round big water. We know. Zood not happy. Zood in danger. How Garr help Zood?

"Where in the wall?"

Judith was shown a place in the dam, almost under the seat where she had rested.

"I do not know how you can help yet. I will speak in the mind with you, when I know. Can you hear me if I do not speak out loud?"

Think clear. We hear. Think slow. You have strong voice. No need make noise. We hear if you speak. Zood not be hurt.

Thank you, you are good allies. Zan said you were good friends. I am in trouble, and we are in danger from big man and others. You too. Be careful, many people will be around and watching, with light that shows in night, infra red. Don't reveal yourselves.

We hear. We understand infra red. Garr use to see in dark. Zood

168

do well to warn of danger.

Judith went back upstairs, to find Tom searching for her. He was worried, and said,

"Are you all right? They were beginning to think you had done a bunk. In fact you made them suspicious of you. I said I thought you might be being sick, and said I'd fetch you. Come on."

Judith dashed into the cloakroom, threw water over her face, and emerged as the drugs inspector came out to find them.

"Sorry about that, I am sometimes sick when I am scared. Some coppers do it at accidents. It can be embarrassing, I do it when I'm frightened!"

Tom gave her a strange look and they went back to the conservatory. Jim, Mary and Nora were sitting quietly on a wicker settee, looking shocked.

Judith sat close to them on a box, and said,

"I have been thinking. We have searched the whole house since I got here. We have found nothing, but the only place we cannot get into is the old Folly, the keys are missing. I think you will find what you want in there, but we can't get in. I have called a locksmith. There is no way you have time to search the house, but you are welcome to try. The only other place is the basement, and from the covering of dust, nothing has been down there in months, except me. I had a good look when I got here, I did find a samovar there this morning, which I brought up. Jim, you helped me. I am sure the Morpeths will confirm that nothing is in the house."

She fielded a penetrating look from Nora.

"Look, there are tradesmen, children, not to mention my alarmed staff. I don't want everyone terrified and I am not leaving here. What do you want to do? You must have a dozen of you here, at least. I am almost sure that the Folly is where you should wait, but you can be seen going down there. Bring your troops in, they can use the attic floor, and you can watch the Folly from there. I am sure that we have looked everywhere else."

Nora added, "Yes, so am I. He never brought anything into the house, and never went to the basement. We would have found anything he left. Judith has been over every inch of the house. We haven't had the key to the Folly for months. I am sure she is right. Are we in danger at the farm?"

Maps were produced, and Mr Carlton considered the location, and then went up to the attic with Jim. Nora spoke quickly to Judith, who then asked their visitors,

"As you are here, you will need feeding. Bring everyone in, put the cars out of sight, and we will have lunch in half an hour for everyone. Meanwhile, I will ask the boys to show you the cloakroom, and where you can change, or put your things."

Judith went to the front door where Sharon was talking to John, and Jake who came over and talked to Judith. Sharon was briefly told the situation, and then Judith went back inside. Mr Carlton came and spoke to her, and called in all the officers, who went to the attic rooms, and waited there, some of them watching the Folly. The vehicles were hidden from view and Mr Carlton walked out onto the lawn with Judith, with an escort of a policeman who was armed. Judith was asked who was living where, and who would be resident on the estate after dark. Mr Carlton suggested that all estate residents should be brought to the house for safety, where they would be guarded. He let slip that one of the suspects in custody had told them that a premises on the grounds was involved, and that the people doing it were going to be 'tooled up'.

Judith told him everyone involved and offered to put them all up in the house, and Stuart, June, Sam, Lucy, (and the cat) were fetched in from the stable block after getting some night gear.

Lunch was done in stages, staff first, then the others. Gregory came to explain the contracts to the staff. Beds were made up in many of the bedrooms, and the cat was given an earth box, water and a meal, and promptly curled up on the four–poster.

Please be kind to the cat. She doesn't understand. We are all scared. I'm sorry about all these people.

Garr know. Cat safe, will not see Garr.

Mr Carlton did not want anyone outside in the grounds, at least for a while, so Judith asked the children if they would like to start clearing the cellar. Mary said she would supervise them. She went to organise them. Jim came and explained he had to do things on the farm. The cows had to be milked and the dogs fed and exercised.

Mr Carlton asked if he could take an officer with him, as that was agreed, but Jim asked if he could be in country clothes, not uniform. They explained that Cummings and Brian knew each other, and Brian's father would be doing the milking. Just as an officer was about to go to town, Judith remembered Clive's clothes, and a selection was made from them.

At half past two, every officer was upstairs, and the staff and farm workers met for their meeting, where Judith kept things very short. Gregory set up in the library and the staff signed their contracts, and he explained any points they did not understand. Sharon went to the basement to help the children, who were having a wonderful time, making more mess than they were clearing.

Reg Hall asked for a private word with Judith and apologised for Brian. Jim had spoken to him and Reg had got back from Brian what had been taken. Reg offered to pay for any damage Brian had done, and asked Judith if she wanted him to seek another post. He was profoundly embarrassed, and Judith reassured him that she needed his skills and his job was safe, but his son was not welcome while he behaved the way he did. Reg said he wished he could control the boy and was at his wits end.

The whole staff met again and Judith was pleased that everyone wanted to stay. The major discussion was then started on a design and logo for some sort of casual uniform. Judith had prepared several designs, and her favourite was selected, and agreed. It was on a black background with a small version of the carved coat of arms on the front of the house. Liam asked what it was and Betty said,

"It's a goblin, they are meant to be lucky. I think it is rather sweet."

It took some time to explain to Liam what a goblin was, but he accepted it was like a male fairy, and when he realised only special people could wear it, he was happy. Judith asked them all to say nothing about what was going on, to anyone, and stressed that her safety could depend on it. That produced a stunned silence and they assured her of their discretion and Liam was bribed with a whole gateau. Sam ran some of the staff home, and returned to help the workmen finish clearing up. Soon, the carpets down and with some of the rooms decorated, the remaining staff got things in place and they planned the evening. Jim and Mary went with the policeman and Nora to the farm and fetched clothes and night wear.

Judith was quite distraught at seeing someone else looking so like Clive and went into the library to compose herself. Wesley came in and said he would like to stay too, as he knew he could be useful in some way. He wanted to do what he could to help, and could at least man the phones, but it was Tom who explained that everyone might have to move fast in an emergency and he reluctantly agreed to go home but asked if he could ring to see what had happened. Tom and Gregory left, and the children were evicted from the basement, very dirty. They all went and had baths, much needed in the three boys' case, and June, Lucy, Mary and Nora prepared supper. The police contingent, which had grown to nearly twenty, came down for supper in shifts, and Mr Carlton spoke to them all about not making it obvious that there were more people than Judith and Sharon in the house.

He took Judith aside and asked her what her normal routine was. She told him what she would normally do and asked,

"You think I am going to be the target, don't you?"

He nodded, and promised her she would be protected. "We don't even know exactly what they have planned have you much money here?

171

No, then there may be something of great value in the house, a picture, or china. It may not be here. I just don't want anyone getting hurt. We cannot protect the other buildings as well. If everyone is in one place, we can keep them safe."

"Rather than endanger anyone else, including your officers, would you not be better using me as bait?"

"I had thought of it, but no, I need you to act as normal. If you are in danger, keep as still as you can and don't make any sudden moves. Wear this bullet proof vest, please."

Judith put it on under her jumper, and went and gave one to Sharon. They joined the families in the sitting area she had made in the sunken landing. She went downstairs to the library, and read a book. Sharon joined her and they played canasta for an hour or two. When she went up, the children were in bed, and the adults were talking quietly. She made cocoa and served it and by eleven, she was the only one still up. Mr Carlton came and sat with her with an armed officer. He tried to put her at her ease, but she found him very powerful and rather cold.

Zood. They come. By wall round Big Water. Five, and another on stones. Big man is with them. They carry metal sticks that make noise. All wear black.

She saw a picture of men by the seat on the dam. Another was waiting by a van near the lodges.

"Don't ask me how I know, but there are five men by the dam, and one waiting by a van near the lodges, just off the drive. They have guns and they are all in black. No, I think the one by the van is a woman."

Carlton gave her a startled look and listened to his radio earpiece.

"There is one by a van near the lodges. Take him or her out, quietly. You have the five. By the dam. Keep me informed."

"You're right, and thank you. Are you psychic?"

"Something like that, yes. I cannot say how I know."

They waited in silence for about ten minutes and then Carlton said,

"All received, take her and the van straight to the nick."

Zood. Four in Tower. One hide behind door with metal stick. Wait for men you like. Garr watch.

"Superintendent, tell your men to be careful. Four have gone up into the Folly, one is hiding behind the door, with a gun, waiting to shoot."

"Thank you, yes, they have seen him. To all units, let them get back to where the van was, and get them there. Move now."

A few minutes of agonising tension passed.

Zood. Big one come to house. Four to where other taken. Zood, danger. Big man sick in mind. Want kill Zood. Make fire with

package.

"He is coming to the house. I think he has a fire bomb. Are you on him?"

Carlton nodded, and then there was a commotion down stairs and a big bang. Policemen came from everywhere and Judith followed them downstairs. There were flames all over the terrace and a pile of men fighting by the library window.

Cummings was taken in handcuffs to a car. There were two of the several bags Judith had been shown, with him. The fire was soon put out, but there was some damage and a lot of broken glass lying around. Jake took her inside and soon Jim, Stuart, Sharon, and Sam rushed in.

June came down to say the children were still asleep, but Sally and Charlotte wanted to come down and Lucy was preventing them. June went back to say they had to stay up there, at least for the time being.

Judith left the police to sort themselves, and fetched a bottle of whiskey and the brandy. They sat round the kitchen table, and all had a drink.

One by one they went up to bed, but Sharon stayed with Judith, who waited until Jake came in followed by John Arrowsmith, who was instantly mesmerised by Sharon in her negligee.

It took a couple of hours until the police left, promising to be back in the morning. Jake said he'd pop in anyway, and dragged John away. Judith locked up and left some food out and was asleep as she hit the pillow.

She was woken by children running along the landing. She got up and limped downstairs. The terrace by the library was taped off and she went to her sitting room. She felt exhausted and reached for the phone and rang Wesley, who asked if he could come in.

Superintendent Carlton arrived, with a contingent of officers and she found coffee for them and went into the conservatory with him. He thanked her and her staff, for their help, and told her that they had a total of twelve in custody on charges of murder and lesser offences. They had recovered a vast fortune in drugs, and more in currency and diamonds. He took a statement, and explained they would be out of her hair soon.

He informed her that the local officers would be paying periodic visits to check all was secure. She mentioned that they seemed to be doing that anyway, at least while Sharon was there, and he laughed and said he had noticed. He promised to keep in touch and they went to the library. There were scenes of crime officers on the terrace, watched by an excited trio of little boys. When they had gathered what evidence they could and taken photographs, the boys were allowed to help and had their photos taken.

Jim came back from the farm, reporting all was well. Wesley arrived and introduced his girl friend, and they went down to the lake. Sharon went with them and Judith helped Nora with a picnic lunch. The boys, having been left by their police friends, went to play detective in the woods by the lake. Sally and Charlotte went with Lucy, Sam and June back to their houses and Mary went to the farm. The police went to the Folly and continued the search there.

Judith was glad to be alone in the house and sat thinking for a while. She woke up when Nora called for her to say lunch was by the lake. Judith said she'd be down soon.

Thank you for your help. Are you safe, no Garr hurt? We should have peace soon.

Go to food place. Drink. Garr safe. Battle over. Zood weary. Eat at big water. Sleep in light. Speak later. Garr happy. Garr safe. Garr have gift when light go.

She went to the pantry, found a small bottle of the blue fluid, drank it, collected her costume and towel, and walked to the lake, ate, and watched the children swimming with Wesley, and his girl friend, Sonia, and slept in the sun. When she woke, she went to the Folly and met the police, who were leaving, and handed her an ancient key, and she went in.

She knew the Garr were close. The Folly was at least as old as the house, a strange stone tower, with two semicircular rooms on each floor, of which there were five. It was quite small on the top floor and the view was magnificent. The circular stairs ran inside the outer wall, and a fireplace in the centre of each floor served both rooms. There was a shower and small toilet, and it made a pleasant, if strange dwelling.

She locked the door on leaving and went back to the house with the others.

Sharon packed her case that evening and loaded the car. They went to the Ugly Imp for supper in the Astra and Judith was not too amazed to meet John Arrowsmith there. He joined them, and then while he talked to Sharon, Judith told Toby, and most of the rest of the pub, what had happened up at Porthwaite Hall.

Sharon had a bath, while Judith left a small offering in the pantry. She had washed the bottle and put it beside the biscuits. A small packet was by the grating, and she put it in her pocket. Sharon made cocoa, and they went up the stairs to their separate rooms. Judith opened the packet and out fell a wonderful ring, made of the same metal as her pendant, and with a huge, almost black, diamond. It was exquisite, and very unusual. She put it in the safe.

Thank you Garr. It is a wonderful gift. I shall wear it often.

There were many. Not miss one or two. You have it. Garr change

it. Big man not take it. You keep Garr safe. Sleep.

Judith vowed not to wear the ring when she gave evidence at court and felt rather guilty. She dreamed of caving through a diamond mine, with the Garr beside her.

Chapter Eleven

Judith and Sharon spent the morning walking round the lake, and in the woods where they found a secluded clearing surrounded with dark pine trees, where they sat. As they returned past the lake, they met Stuart and his family going for a swim. Judith cooked a lunch for the two of them and they sat in the front garden until Sharon had to go. They loaded her car, and Judith gave her a few small presents and some food. As Sharon drove off, Jake turned up to check on the welfare of the house. And Judith made tea and they arranged for the committee of the Operatic Society to visit during the week.

Judith made it to church for the evensong service and sat in solitary splendour in her pew. After the service, she looked round the church yard and found the graves of Agatha Eccles and Elsie Ivy Garreton. She saw that Agatha had died at ninety–seven, and Elsie aged ninety–two. If she was to live as long, she had another fifty years to go. She wondered what she would do in the forthcoming years, and how she would fill her time. She drove back to the house, and listened to music until she went to bed.

On the Monday, the house once again became chaotic, and builders, decorators, carpet fitters and telephone engineers moved around. Judith took herself to the basement and made an inventory of what was there. She found cases of old paintings, most of which she thought were hideous, but which seemed to be good. They were dirty and in need of restoration. There were trunks full of ancient clothes, and in a leather case, she found jewellery, and looking closely at it, saw it was genuine, and possibly valuable.

Nora came and found her and said coffee was brewed. Judith went up to the kitchen, and over a cup of coffee, and some biscuits, they talked amiably of mundane matters to do with the house. Nora asked if the police had been back and said the boys, who had gone back to school, would be celebrities. Judith asked if everyone was over the weekend's excitement. Nora said no harm had been taken, and then said,

"You are an amazing woman, Judy. Since you have been here, life has been really exciting. We normally have a pretty mundane life, but not recently. You get things done, I give you that, and you lie convincingly when you need to. We both know you hadn't searched the house, or many of the outbuildings. You had me believing you, and I knew different! I know you had your reasons, you didn't want the staff or children upset. You are so like Miss Susan, it's uncanny. She used to explain how she knew things, by saying she had second sight. I reckon you have it too. You knew the hiding place was the Folly, but I know you had never been there." "What are you going to do with the house, once we have it sorted? I am sure you have plans, and I cannot see you doing nothing for the rest of your life. I've often thought it should be used for more than just a dwelling."

"Yes, I have plans, but they are not formulated yet. Thank you for covering for me, I shouldn't have expected it. In a way, I do have second sight. I cannot explain it, but sometimes I have more than just feelings, I know. This house has accepted me, and I want to stay here. I do hope to start some of my hobbies again. I used to enjoy spinning, and designing knitwear, and hoped to keep some rare breed sheep, for their fleeces. I expect Jim will be horrified at the idea, but I will sound him out. I would love to make the whole estate into a working place where we can sell organic fruit and veg, and plants, like a nursery, and possibly run courses here. We have the accommodation. Students who want to learn about estate management, or gardening, something along those lines. We could run First Aid courses, residential, and business courses. I want to use the place for good, but make it pay for itself. You said it used to be open to the public, the gardens anyway. I know Stuart would like that."

Nora nodded, "Yes, I think you are right. Jim won't be so hard to convince, he has always wanted to go organic, but never could afford it. He wanted some rare breeds, but Miss Susan took the advice of Cummings, and that was that. Now we are taking in the other farm, he will need to buy in more stock. With a shepherd, life will be easier for him. I'll tell him to talk to you. Oh, can I move into the South Lodge this week, now the decorators have done? Thank you for getting it kitted out with all the kitchen things and carpets."

They made plans for the move, and after their coffee, they did a tour of the house. Wesley said Sharon had phoned to say she had settled in and would be in touch. Judith caught up with her letters, and asked if Mr Sandell had done a delivery that day, and when told he would be arriving later, she rang him and ordered some papers and magazines.

Jake and two women turned up, and he introduced them as members of the Operatic Society. They were delighted with the ball room and asked to use it on Wednesday evenings, from seven to ten. Judith showed them the facilities, and they asked to use the kitchen for tea making. Judith referred them to Mary.

The Reverend Pike turned up, and asked Judith to a social event in the evening, in aid of the church hall roof fund, and apologised for not asking her before. Judith asked if she would know anyone and the vicar said she was sure to. She agreed and he left. Lunch was announced, and when everyone was seated, Judith told them what had happened, and told them they were no longer restricted to not talking about it. Dot asked,

"Are you all right, Mrs Swallow? It must have been very worrying for you. Were you not very frightened?"

"Yes, I was, and without you all I would have been terrified. I want to thank you all for your help, understanding. and support. The police have also asked me to express their thanks. I thank all of you for your hard work around the house. Every time I go into a room, it seems transformed. The gardens are starting to look good, and the conservatory is wonderful. Thank you, whoever put fresh flowers in my room this morning. Was that you, Haley? Tomorrow the new van should arrive, so if Bill or Liam want a lift, it is available to you. Wesley, has your chair arrived yet? It is due today. This afternoon, I want you to see Wes, and get a radio or mobile phone from him, so we can keep in touch. Stuart and Sam will have mobiles and everyone will have a radio. All the lockers have arrived and you can either take your keys, or lodge them with Wes, in his safe. Jim will have a mobile, and should be getting the new tractor this week, and the old one will be available for the estate. I have ordered the uniform sweat shirts and they will be here soon. Overalls too, and I have had your names put on them. I will wear the same when I am around and working. Any questions?"

There were a lot of questions, and soon the talk became general. Judith asked Nora what she should wear to the church social that evening, and Nora said she was going and would pick Judith up. Mary said she would like to, but Sally was at orchestra practice, so she had to stay with the twins. Lucy offered to babysit, and they all agreed to go in Jim's car. Nora confided that a few people brought a raffle prize of some sort, which put Judith in a panic. She wondered what she could take, and finally they came up with a couple of bottles of not too expensive wine, which were in the pantry. Jim came in halfway through lunch to say a cow had got stuck in a gate, and asked for help. Liam and Bill went with him and Judith offered to go too.

When they got to the cow they did a lot of pushing and shoving, and the cow did a lot of kicking and bellowing. Finally, by removing the gate from its hinges and moving it around, the cow was freed, but not before several of them got covered in muck, and well and truly bruised. The gate was replaced, and they rode back on the trailer, smelling very bad, and comparing bruises. Jim offered to hose them down in the yard and they stood while he did so. They then hosed him and this caused much amusement. Bill said,

"Eh, lass, thee's got guts. Anyone who will give a hand, and don't mind getting shitty, is all reet by me!"

They walked back in soggy silence to the house, and had to face the laughter of Mary, who fetched dry clothes from somewhere for Bill and Liam, and made them strip in the laundry room before letting them in. Judith, wrapped in a towel, made it to her room, and showered and changed. Lucy gathered up the dirty clothes and washed them. Liam fitted very well into some clothes of Clive's. He went back to the gardens with Bill, and Judith asked Wesley to get an estimate for a shower room for the staff.

By the time Judith was picked up in the evening, she had regained her composure. She had rather enjoyed the afternoon, and wished she had something more practical to do than just organising, and it got her thinking.

The social was fun, and she met several of her neighbours. Bill was there, giving a blow by blow account of the cow episode, and Liam was helping with the seating. They asked Judith to draw the raffle, which she fortunately did not win, and Jake asked her for a dance. She declined, because of her gammy leg, but asked where Jake's wife was. Jake explained that he was a widower, and his son was away at university and his daughter was a nurse, at Jimmy's in Leeds.

When they left, the vicar thanked them for coming, and Jim drove them back and then drove Lucy home. Judith had a slight headache, which she put down to the weather being very close.

The fine weather broke with an impressive thunder storm, about three o'clock in the morning. The rain came down in stair rods. Judith watched the storm from her window and wondered if the Garr would be in danger from flash flooding.

Garr safe. Come to house. Water soon fall.

She 'saw' the Garr in the basement, so she got up and went down to the basement, unlocked and opened the trap door. She lit several candle lanterns. Soon after that the electricity went off and she was glad of the lanterns. Slowly the Garr emerged into the basement. She sat on an old chair, as dozens of them came into the chamber. She recognised Goy and others, but was startled to see several new types. The larger they were, the paler they seemed. One large warrior type was a delicate rose pink, with darker, wine red fur. It had huge teeth and massive claws, and spine–like spikes down its back. It looked very frightening.

I am named Grreth. I protect. I not hurt Zood.

Judith was relieved. Another type seemed to have elongated and rather spade–like feet, and massive upper limbs, with huge muscular shoulders, and a short tail. It was a delicate leaf green, with darker green fur.

I am named Glot. I dig. I build. I move rock. I not hurt Zood.

There were many smaller, but darker versions of these Garr. The small, rounder ones came closer, and a larger version of them came to

179

her.

We get food. We gather. We feed Garr. I am called Glate. Young called Glave, Galak, Glire, Gan, Gode. We take sweet food. Zood give, we take for Garr.

Do you want food now? Come up to the kitchen and get some. There is no one else in the house. The lights are off.

The minds joined, and then several voices said,

Garr come. Garr bring others. Garr that make object, gift.

Judith watched, fascinated, as yet another type emerged from the cellar. These were long, sinuous creatures, with long, thin digits, and tiny claws. They had four digits on each foot, and a basic thumb. The largest was about two metres long, and almost silver in colour, with dark grey fur.

I am called Glyff. I make. I make for Zood.

One of the tiny, round foragers came to Judith and touched her on the leg with a gentle, damp paw. It looked into her face and put the paw up to her face, very tentatively.

Zood. I Glant. Friend. Touch?

Yes, you can touch me. Do not be afraid.

Glant touched her very gently, and then examined her hair, and her fingers and hands.

Hot. Dry.

Gradually several of the young touched her, and examined her ears and hands, and peered into her mouth. One sat firmly on her lap, and rolled onto its back.

Glosa. Zood touch Glosa.

Judith gently rubbed the fur on the baby's belly, and tickled it. It wriggled pleasurably, and produced a musical, high–pitched croon. The other small Garr, of all types, approached, and soon Judith was playing with them, and tickling all of them, to a harmony of croons. They were very musical, and she felt real affection for, and from, them. The larger Garr watched, slightly amused, and with pleasure. Judith laughed.

Zood like young. Young like Zood. Garr like Zood.

These are your young. Are you all here?

Elders in upper caves. Too big to meet Zood. Many Garr with Elders. Elders wish Zood well. Garr come for food?

Judith gently detached several small Garr from her, and carefully got up and moved to the stairs with the young scampering around her. The rest of the Garr followed them. She opened the doors through to the kitchen, and got several packets of food from the meat safes, and put them on the kitchen floor. She fetched a candle lantern, and switched off all the lights in case the electricity came back on.

Zood cold. Get clothes. I am going up to my room.

The elder Garr remained in the kitchen, while Judith took the candle lantern to her room and put on some warm clothes and a pair of slippers. Several young Garr came with her. When they moved, she heard a soft rustling sound. She returned to the kitchen with her playful escort. The older Garr were waiting.

We go down. Zood come.

They went down to the basement, the Garr bringing the food with them, some carrying it in their jaws, others using one paw. The young ran round the basement and one found an old tennis ball somewhere, and they all played with it for some time, offering it to Judith to throw for them. Finally, the older Garr called to the young.

Water down. More room in caves. Garr leave. Zood enjoy Garr young. Young enjoy Zood. Zood sleep. Zood tired. Light soon come.

One by one they went to the cellar, and she heard them splashing into the water.

Lock door. Zood sleep.

Judith replaced the trap door and locked it. She tidied up the lanterns and then the kitchen, and went upstairs, fumbling in the dark. As she reached her bedroom, she saw the first signs of light outside. It was after six. She tried the light, and it came on several minutes later. She fell into a deep and satisfied sleep.

Superintendent Carlton rang her in the morning to ask if he could come and see her, and turned up with another officer, just after ten. They went to the library, and he told her that they had interviewed the prisoners and had charged most of them. All had been refused bail, but he needed to make further enquiries on several matters. Judith asked him how she could help.

He looked at her and said. "Cummings has made several allegations against you, which we need to clear up. He says that you knew all about the operation, and had done for months, and you suggested the Folly as a hiding place. The others involved did not trust you, which is why he was made to try setting fire to the place, to scare you into silence. He denies trying to kill you. Have you any comment?"

"Yes. I have no idea what he hopes to gain from this. My only meeting with him was witnessed, and the only phone call overheard. You are welcome to examine all my phone bills, on my mobile, and on the house phones. I would hardly expose him if I was in with him. I have nothing to hide and totally refute any involvement. I know he hates me, but I thought he was a bit brighter than that. Can he offer anything to back his story up?"

"Nothing at all. We do not believe him, but we need to have answers to these allegations. There are several dates he said, when he met you in London, and once in Bristol, and before your husband's death, he says he met with him, Clive Swallow, in London. Can you tell me where you were on the following dates?"

Judith fetched her diary, and Clive's old diary, and was able to provide alibis for most of the dates. The day she was alleged to be in Bristol coincided with the day she had been to the hospital there, whilst staying with Clive's mother. She explained that Mike had taken her there, and that she had been with someone all day, and gave details. She was very grateful that she had always kept a comprehensive diary. He asked to borrow it, and she agreed but asked for a copy.

"Do you know a Francis Heldman?"

"Yes, he is my brother-in-law. Why?"

"Tell me about him."

Judith told them, and what she thought of him. It wasn't hard to work out where Cummings had got some of his information from, and she knew why they would want to discredit her. She told Carlton all about the family and asked how Francis was involved.

Carlton told her of correspondence found, indicating Cummings having invested a great deal of money through Francis. The investment had been unwise, and a lot of money had been lost. They suspected Francis of deep involvement with money laundering, and the police were visiting him at that very moment.

Judith remembered Ingrid saying Francis needed help with some investments, and was glad she had not trusted him. She fetched copies of the gifts and their attached conditions, and asked what she could do to clear her name of these spiteful allegations. She offered access to all her bank accounts and assured him that every penny she had could be accounted for.

Cummings' secretary had been interviewed, and had confirmed their suspicions of Cummings' fraud and false accounting and Carlton explained that they merely needed to eliminate Judith. She thought he was suspicious of her and his gaze gave her the shivers. She decided he was a very intelligent and rather dangerous man.

"The next thing he'll be saying is that I am mentally ill, and should be committed. I wouldn't be surprised if it hasn't already been suggested," she said angrily. From the look on his face, she knew that it had. "Who has said what?"

Carlton looked at her, and said, "Yes, we found a letter from Heldman to Cummings detailing how you could be committed. He mentioned a Mr Chatterton, a specialist in mental illness, who could be relied upon to prove your insanity. Have you ever met this Chatterton?"

Judith thought back, and then said, "Yes, actually, I have. He came to see me at the convalescent home in Malvern. He said I had been referred to him by the Birmingham Hospital, after losing the baby in the crash. He offered me counselling. He told me it was routine. I thought it was a bit odd, but wasn't really in a state to argue. He did ask some very strange questions, and I stopped answering them and asked him to leave me alone, and wouldn't see him again. He said he was worried about me and tried to make another appointment. I left soon after, but he contacted me in Hampshire. I wrote to him, and thanked him for his concern, but refused to see him again. I did wonder how he then contacted me in Wales, as I hadn't told him where I was going and my friends in Hampshire said they hadn't told him. I had told Cummings where I was, though. What the hell is going on?"

Carlton replied, "You are a very rich woman, and I think you may be the subject of a sophisticated attempt to get your money from you. Cummings says you deliberately provoked him, and made irrational comments, and he alleges you are mentally unstable. He suggests that you would be an unreliable witness. Have you ever had a mental illness?"

"No. I think before we go any further with this, I want my solicitor here. As you have not cautioned me, you will not be considering detaining me, but before I answer any more questions, I want Tom Barker here. I am going to ring him now. You can listen in if you want."

She picked up the phone, and said,

"Wes, could you ring Tom Barker for me? Tell him or Celia it is very urgent."

She replaced the receiver, and went to the tape recorder, and inserted two tapes, and said,

"If you don't mind, I'll tape the rest of this. You can have a copy if you want one. I understand you have your job to do, and have to make enquiries, but this is getting very alarming."

The phone rang and Judith said, "Thanks Wes, could you get some coffee in here? Tom, thank goodness you are in. Can you come? The police are here and are asking some very unpleasant questions and I need you. Can you come now? I won't say any more until you get here. Thanks, sure you can bring her. This is really scary."

Carlton said, "Mrs Swallow, I do understand. I believe you are the victim in a huge fraud. I understand your anger and concern. Of course you should have Mr Barker here, if you want him. I am sorry I have upset you. I never meant to. I do think you should know what is being said. You know, as a retired officer, that I must clear all this up. I do not doubt your sanity, I just need to disprove their wild allegations, to the satisfaction of a court. I will go until Mr Barker arrives, if you want."

Judith calmed down a bit, and said, "No, that will not be necessary. Let's talk of something else. Here is some coffee, thank you,

Betty."

Carlton got up and took his cup from Judith, and smiled down at her. His smile changed his whole face, and for the first time, she almost liked him. Carlton looked at some of the books on the bookcases and said,

"I see you've some rare books here. Have you had time to catalogue them yet? Some of them are very rare. There is a very early Bible here, and a very old copy of Grimm's." He was trying very hard to put her at ease, and she looked at the books with him. His presence was almost overpowering.

"No, I have not had time to look at what is here. Do you think I should get an expert in to look at them? I shall take good care of them. When I have some time, I mean to read some of these books. Oh, here is a journal of the plants in the grounds, my gardener will be thrilled! He tells me there are some rare plants here, and was raving about Clematis Orientalis Tibetensis, whatever that is."

"It is a yellow flowering, rather pretty, climber. I didn't know it grew up here. If you are still speaking to me when this is over, I wonder if I could buy one from you? I love plants and have a big garden. Nothing like this one, of course. I would like to talk to him at some time. Is he interested in roses at all?"

Judith laughed and replied,

"Mr Carlton, you can have one. He is mad about roses, I'll introduce you. I know you are only doing your job. It isn't you I am angry at, it is the situation I find myself in. I feel very vulnerable, and I am furious that is so easy for others to make such allegations. I need the loo, and I will be back in a minute. Is that OK, or do you want to come with me?"

Superintendent Carlton assured her that he had no problems with her using her own facilities, and said he would wait in the library. Judith went to the cloakroom, and sat down.

Zood fear. Garr with you. Garr help?

Zood angry, help coming. Big man makes trouble. Big man lie. Family betray Zood. I will explain later. It's complex.

Judith returned to the library, having washed her face and hands, and having had a drink of water. She talked about the gardens, and the way the estate had been run down, and how she hoped to open the gardens to the public.

Tom and Celia arrived quite quickly and Carlton explained what had been said. He apologised again for upsetting Judith, and went through all the allegations made. Tom looked concerned when he heard of Chatterton's involvement. He asked for transcripts of interviews, and any allegations made. Celia came over to Judith and sat beside her, and squeezed her hand.

"I would be alarmed over this. Are you very upset?"

"Yes, and very, very angry. How could he say this? Can I get them for slander? I'm not mentally ill, am I? What was Chatterton doing? It seems highly irregular. I have nothing to hide, they can't put me away, can they?"

Tom got up and came over, and said,

"Judith, listen. Stop panicking. I think I see what they are trying. They hope to make you break down, and be unable to give evidence. Superintendent Carlton and I are agreed that you are the victim here. Tell us again all about Chatterton and Heldman. I'll stop you, if I think anything you say is incriminating or putting you at risk."

They went through everything again, and Judith told them everyone who she had seen since the accident. The whole interview took some time and was recorded, with the consent of Carlton, and he took copies of the tapes. He gave her a receipt for all her diaries and paperwork, and promised she should have copies that day. He talked with Tom, while she went and organised a lunch for everyone. When she returned, Tom looked worried and said,

"Judy, Superintendent Carlton is worried about your safety. Until this is resolved, he wants to put a personal protection officer here. Your evidence is going to be vital and he wants you safe. Is there any chance you would be prepared to go away for a while, to somewhere safe? No, I didn't think so. Would you mind a house guest for a while?"

Judith thought about it, and asked,

"How long for? Am I in that much danger? I think I am safe enough here, there are plenty of people around during the day, and I am safe enough at night."

Carlton said, "Maybe you are, but if you leave the grounds, I want someone with you, and I want someone close, especially at night. They don't have to be here in the house, but they need to be very close. You could have a radio, and call them in if anything unusual happens, or you are worried. You obviously have a way of knowing who is around, and trust your staff. Is there somewhere a couple of officers could stay, close by?"

"They could use the Folly, is that close enough? All this is going to be expensive, and so you must think there is a real threat to my life. I won't refuse, if that is so. I do not want any of the staff worried, and Jim and Stuart, and Mary and Nora would all have to know, and Sam as well. Could we pass them off as friends staying in the Folly? Is that all right? Tell me what I need to do. The most important thing is that the staff, and their families, are not put in any danger."

Betty said lunch was ready in the dining room, and they went through. Betty served them, and then left. The staff were eating in the kitchen. Tom and Carlton thrashed out details, and after lunch, Carlton left and Judith went up to her room, to think about the whole, miserable problem. She tried to think what to do for the best and then went down to find Tom. Celia was in the library and said Tom was talking to the staff. Judith felt she was no longer in control of her life. She was tired, angry, and had a headache. Her leg ached, and it was raining outside. She felt desperate. She could feel the Garr and their concern for her.

Wesley came in, in his chair, and told her he knew what was going on, and had arranged for every visitor to sign in and out on a log, and gave her a radio to ensure she could talk to him, wherever she was. He asked what he could do to help and did she want him to stay at the house. Judith burst into tears and cried miserably for a good five minutes, while Celia found tissues and Wesley put his arm round her. She apologised for breaking down and told them she would be all right. Wesley said he would take care of the normal household affairs with Nora, and that everyone was concerned about her.

He informed her that Jim had offered to get his shotgun, and Stuart was designing mantraps for the garden. Liam wanted to stay on guard by the back door, and Bill was going to take the front. Sam had volunteered to use his army experience, and tear any intruder limb from limb. He added that Liam was worried about missing meals, but had accepted that he could go without sustenance for a while, and that it was worth it. Wesley made it sound so amusing that Judith began to laugh and then Celia and Wes joined in.

She cheered up and thanked them both

"Wes, you daft sod, thank you, you are kidding! I'll be all right now, and you have helped me to put it in perspective. We have to take precautions, but if the staff are turning this into Colditz, no one is going to get any work done. Let's sort all this out. Has everyone got a radio or mobile? Call them in for a meeting."

Wes grinned and told her everyone was in the Lost It Room already and Tom was with them, so they went with him, and found a heated discussion going on between Stuart and Sam, about who could get the first blow on any intruder. Her entrance silenced this, and she told them that the police had it all under control and she was well protected. She left Tom and Wes to explain about what to do with any unidentified intruder, and said that when the police returned, they would talk to them all and tell them how they could help. Jim announced that they would take it in turns for someone to be around until late evening every day, and everyone volunteered to take their turn.

Judith thanked them, and told Wes she wouldn't need him to stop over, but would be grateful for his company some evenings. Wes asked if he could play the piano in the ball room sometimes, as his flat was too small for a piano, and he only had a keyboard. Judith was delighted to agree and told him that the Operatic Society would be there the next evening. Dot announced she would be there too, and asked if she could stay on at the house, rather than go home for her tea and then come back. Bill said he was in the same position, and Sam said he wanted to join. Lucy offered to do teas and coffees and they all arranged for Sam to pick them up and drop them off the next day. Nora said she would be there, and they were discussing Patience, when the door bell went and there was instant silence.

Sam went to the door and came back, grinning, to say the minibus had arrived. They all went out, Judith signed for it, and they admired it. Jim dashed back to the farm, and soon he arrived with the old tractor, which he handed over to Stuart, announcing he had a new tractor now and Stuart was welcome to the old one.

Jim and Stuart went to the farm and brought two quad bikes back and Judith had a go on one, up and down the drive. She was a good motorcyclist, and it didn't take her long to master the differences of a quad, and she even won a race against Stuart, but lost to Jim and Liam. Bill said he was too old for all that, and they should be ashamed of themselves. Having behaved in a suitably juvenile fashion, Judith felt less tense, and they all went in for a cup of tea, and the staff went happily about the end of day chores. Two police officers in plain clothes turned up and introduced themselves, and gave Judith a file of papers. They came well provided, and Jim took them to the Folly, and then showed them the grounds and the house and found keys for them.

The afternoons antics had lifted a lot of the tension, and Mary cooked a tea, and the boys and Sally ate with them in the kitchen with Wesley and Lucy. Sam joined them after taking the other staff home.

Wesley went to the Ball Room, and played the piano, very well, for a while, and then Sally joined him and they played a duet together. Judith went to her sitting room with Lucy, who fitted some new curtains she had made, on the windows. Judith sat down and composed herself.

How much of that did you understand?

Some. Zood afraid. In danger. Men help. Men go to tower by big water. Friends angry. Garr warn if bad man come. Zood safe.

Thank you, Garr. There will be many people here tomorrow evening. They will go late.

We know. Men in tower have metal stick that make bang.

I know. They are here to protect me.

Friend in house. When go, young Garr wish to play with Zood. With round thing. Zood want?

I'd love to. I will unlock the trap door later.

Young Garr have other way. Old Garr big. Need door. Music good. Garr like.

The voices went and Judith went to the ball room, and listened to Wesley and Sally. They found a score of Patience in the music room, and Wes played some of the songs for them. Judith sang with Sally, and Wes joined in with a fine bass voice. Jim turned up and walked Sally home and Wes got into his car and went home.

Men from tower come. Speak with Zood.

Judith waited by the front door and soon the two officers came in. She asked if they had all they needed, and made a cup of coffee. She found them a flask and some cake. They went through messages and codes with her and she showed them where she slept. They left, after checking the outer doors.

Men gone to tower. Zood come? Garr warn if man come.

Judith, armed with leftovers of meals and some sugar, went to the basement, lit a candle lamp, and turned off the lights. She found several balls, including a football, unlocked the trap door, and waited. The Garr came quickly, mainly young ones, but a few larger ones as well. They took the food, and the young played happily with the balls. Several, including a young 'maker,' climbed onto her lap and offered their bellies for a scratch. They crooned happily and soon she was covered in damp, happy young. She listened to their crooning, and recognised strains from Patience. One young 'forager' fell asleep in her lap. It woke suddenly, and jumped off, baring its teeth, until it was reassured by the others, and then crawled apologetically back on her lap for another scratch. She stroked it and it snuggled into her arm, but soon got down.

Galak hot. Dry. Drink.

It scampered off into the cellar, and she heard a splash. After about an hour, the Garr went.

Goy, who she recognised more by the tone of its mind, than physically, approached her.

Zood sleep. Drink. Garr heal Zood. Agitated in voice. Garr heal.

Judith shut and locked the trap door and hid the balls in a box. On the table was a bowl with blue green fluid, which she drank. It tasted just as bad, but slightly different to the blue fluid she had taken before. She put out the candle and went upstairs. She radioed to the officers that she was going to bed, and they wished her good night.

Chapter Twelve

Although she was still worried, Judith was calmer the next day, and in the morning she met the police officers at breakfast, and told them she would be visiting the bank during the morning, and she arranged for Sam and Wesley to go with her. One of the officers, a cheerful Scouse lad, called Geoff, came with them, and they went in the people carrier. At the bank, she introduced Wesley and they obtained specimen signatures from him and Sam.

On the way back they went to a sign writer and he arranged to paint the Porthwaite Hall motif on the vehicle later in the week. They also stopped at a tee shirt printers, and picked up piles of clothes in large boxes. Geoff nearly had kittens when Judith exposed herself to the general public, and helped load the boxes. He stood hovering, while she and Sam loaded the van and then got Wes to keep watch, when he helped them.

At the house everyone helped unload and the boxes were taken to the Lost It Room, and sorted. Geoff and his colleague went off. Tom rang and said Superintendent Carlton would be visiting the following day and he and Celia would be there.

Wes asked if he could stay on for the evening, and help with the Operatic Society, and suggested issuing all visitors with badges, at least until they knew everyone. He made some calls, and Sam returned to town, and fetched a load of stationery for him.

The staff cleaned and set up the ballroom during the afternoon, and Bill and Liam arrived with logs, and kindling for the fire. They had also found some coal and Judith laid the fire, ready for lighting later. Nora assured her the chimney had been swept and there was no fire danger. Judith looked up the chimney and saw it was very old and huge. She paused.

We intend to light a fire in the chimney. I do not want anyone hurt. Do the Garr use the chimneys?

Sometimes. Garr thank you for saying. Garr not there when fire light. Many passage through from fire. Garr close. No smoke in home.

'Interesting,' thought Judith, 'that is how they get around.'

Judith also laid a fire in the drawing room, and prepared the Chinese Drawing Room as a cloak room. She checked the cloakroom for loo roll and towels, and Nora cleared the bathroom at the top of the stairs.

Nora had prepared sandwiches and had finally learned to work the, now gleaming, samovar, polished by Lucy. Jim had found the hot water heater in the summerhouse, and there was a frenzied hunt for cups and saucers. A search through the dining room cupboards provided plenty, which were then washed and dried by Judith and Lucy. The twins, now firm friends with Julian, were conscripted into helping and Sally and Charlotte helped with a high tea. Geoff appeared with a new policeman, and he suggested they pass themselves off as staff, and help Wesley.

Judith took all the staff into the Lost It Room, and issued them with their black sweat shirts, Wesley got them to check the sizes and sign for them. Liam was thrilled with his and especially with his name embroidered over the motif. Judy put hers on. Bill was shocked that hers just said 'Judy'. He didn't mind that his said 'Bill'. Judith also gave them another set, which gave their initial and surnames, as she explained, for more formal occasions! She gave them the choice of what they wished to wear.

The children were thrilled that they had not been forgotten, and they each had a personalised tee shirt, sweat shirt, and jacket, as did everyone. Judith also issued plain black slacks to everyone. In another box she found white tops, with a black motif.

The two police officers were loaned an unnamed sweat shirt each and given badges by Wesley.

They all had tea, and Sam went round and put the lights on, and switched the lights on up the drive, and to the main gate. Judith insisted he show her the light switch, as she had never found it. It was still light, but a miserable day. Sam and one officer went and checked the back gate, and put the house vehicles in the barn. The boys were detailed to direct the parking with Geoff, and the girls were asked to do coats.

At just before seven, Jake arrived with the two women Judith had already meet. They were delighted with the preparations and met Wesley. They went into the ballroom, and soon a string of people, some of whom Judith had already met, came and were each issued with a name badge. The telephone rang, and Wesley came in with a message for the musical director, Margaret, a short, very dumpy woman, with a bossy manner. She rushed to the phone and then came and told the company that their pianist was ill. Wesley offered to play for them and sat at the piano and played through some phrases. Margaret was pleased and impressed. Judith lit the fire.

At seven thirty, they began singing. Judith, with the altos, was next to Nora, and Bill was behind with the basses. Sam was in the tenors, and Dot, and Dee Jugg, were in the sopranos. Chris and Tim sang with the trebles, and Julian with the altos. Stuart slid into the room and joined the tenors. Judith decided she had a very musical staff when Jim came over and joined the bass line.

190

Even Geoff joined in, standing at the back, with Jake. The other policeman was outside by the front door. He had already admitted to being tone deaf.

They had a sing through of the main songs, and were well into 'A magnet hung in a hardware shop', when Judith was aware of an additional, very soft harmony. The Garr were adding their own contribution. Margaret stopped them. They began again and this time the Garr hummed louder. Judith thought she was the only one to hear it, but Margaret stopped them again.

"That is an excellent harmony, but it is not what is written. Whoever is doing it, please stop." She glowered at the children.

I love your singing, but she can hear it. I will play music for you later. Garr sing well.

Garr know. Fat one can hear. Garr stop.

There was regret in the voice.

By half time, and tea, everyone was relaxing, and Judith mixed. Tim and the other boys and some girls started the next half with a bout of giggles. Margaret scowled at them, and when they started laughing again, they were banished to help in the kitchen. At nine thirty the rehearsal stopped, and Judith offered those not driving, a beer or lager or wine, and coffee or tea to the drivers.

The few stragglers left by ten thirty. Wesley played over 'The Soldiers of our Queen," and Judith heard the Garr join in. He left, and she went to bed after the police officers had checked the doors.

Superintendent Carlton arrived first thing next day, Tom with him. He explained that they had arrested Francis, and had interviewed Chatterton, who had admitted seeing Judith under false pretences. Francis had broken down and admitted everything, putting the blame on Cummings, who was still alleging Judith was involved. Carlton asked Judith if she had any more information. He then asked her if she would see an independent psychiatrist, so they could counter any allegations. He obviously expected her to be angry, but she was happy to agree.

"If it will help me, and you, of course. Maybe the fact that I have done it will take the wind out of their sails. Do you honestly think I am in danger? These policemen are lovely, and doing their job well, but there must be more important people to protect."

"We have more information, I'm afraid. Without you, our evidence is limited, and they want you unable to go to court. We can either play the waiting game, or tempt them into the open. We know there are another two main players, and a few small–time crooks connected. You spoke the other day about acting as bait, would you actually do that? I wouldn't blame you if you didn't want to. I would use you only if I had to, and we could try to ensure your safety. There are risks, as you know. I cannot afford for them to succeed. I have no right to expect, or even ask you, but something did occur to me. Would you listen and tell me what you think? I have a further statement prepared, based on what you said the other day, which I need you to sign."

The three of them talked for some time, and evolved a plan. Judith was adamant that no one else should be put at risk, especially any of her staff and their families. Finally they reached a workable plan, and she then read through and signed her statement. Carlton walked out to his car, and when he and Judith were alone, he said,

"Are you quite sure that you can 'read' what is going on, in and around the house, after dark? I know you did it the other night, and I still cannot fathom how you did, or even what you did. Would you like to tell me?"

"No. I cannot tell you, and will never do so. Around the estate, after dark, I just know. It won't work any distance away, though. I will deny it if you ever bring it up again. Just say I have a slightly different mind, and I am in tune with the ghosts in this place. Oh, look, there is Stuart, the head gardener. I'll introduce you, and you can bore each other to death about roses."

Tom talked for a while, and then Judith went for a walk down to the lake. It was a drizzly wet day, and she felt very alone. For nearly an hour she watched the rain as it made circles on the water. A large fish jumped in the middle of the lake, and she could hear a bird call in the woods near by. The lake was beautiful and peaceful. She felt at home there, and in the house. She belonged to this place and had such a responsibility towards it. The bird called again, an alarm call. She heard a stick break and someone moving in the woods by the head of the lake. Quietly she crawled back to a large bush, and lay behind it in the long grass, and watched as a stranger, a man, came to the edge of the woods and got out a pair of binoculars and watched the house. Judith lay still and watched him, as he moved on through the hay meadow, towards the trees by the Folly. He stood under the trees, a little way back from the lake edge, and waited. She saw him light a cigarette. She wondered if he was a police officer, and waited for some minutes. Some birds flew up from around the Folly, and Brian Hall came to the lakeside and waited and the man came to meet him. Brian was gesticulating towards the house and the man pulled him back into the trees. From her location Judith could see him hand something to Brian, and they walked off behind the Folly. She waited, and as she lay in the grass, she could not think of a way to get close enough to listen or watch.

Garr know. Garr hear. Bad man go to cave in drop above trees. Boy smell. Man have metal stick that bang. Boy do as man say, take

powder. Man sleep in cave. Watch for Zood. Want boy to bring you to big water, when light go. Use metal stick that bang. Watch with in vra red. Boy frightened. Want powder.

Will they see me if I move?

Zood wait. Garr make rock fall outside cave. Little rock. Bad man, boy that smell in back of cave for shelter. Zood move. On ground. Zood wait. Not move yet.

Judith waited, aware of being very wet. She was lying in a hollow, which was fast becoming a puddle. She remembered she should have a radio with her, and wondered how long it would be before someone would miss her and panic. She felt a complete fool.

Some time later, she heard the rocks begin to fall. The noise echoed over the lake and she tensed up. She had worked out a route to get out of sight. She was very aware of her need to be safe.

Zood, go now. Zood run. Garr watch.

She didn't stop to think. She ran until she was safe in some yew trees, where she lay gasping for breath. She was shaking.

Zood safe. Friends worry.

Judith got up and walked to the kitchen door and went inside. Sam saw her and shouted to Wes that she was all right. Judith sat down at the table and gasped, "I'm all right, I'm sorry if I gave you a fright. Have I missed lunch?"

Jim came in with Wes, and came over to her. He put his hand on her shoulder, and said,

"Something has happened. You are soaked, and very cold. Why did you not take a radio? We were just about to call the police. Something has scared you, lass, and I want to know what. You are shaking. Mum, get some dry clothes, she's drenched. Mary, get a towel. Get someone to run a hot bath. She is almost hypothermic."

"First I must make a call, Jim. Then I'll tell you. Before I do, I want everyone indoors and out of the grounds. I'll explain. What time is it? Everyone will be coming in in ten minutes, so I have time. I'll use the phone in my room. I'll shower and change there. She got up, and limped upstairs, her leg hurting and feeling weak. Jim walked with her, and stubbornly stayed outside her room, while she showered and changed. Once in warmer, dry clothes, she went out to find him sitting on the landing, and Mary bringing a hot cup of tea up. She took it gratefully, and went into her room, and rang Superintendent Carlton on his mobile, and then went out to face Jim.

Jim was more than concerned, he was angry, and his concern for her had fuelled his anger. She listened while he told her how worried they had all been. Mary tried to stop him, but it just made him worse. Judith saw his anger for what it was, and privately, totally agreed with him, and listened patiently until he ran out of things to say. She said,

"Jim, I'm sorry, I really am. Thank you for your concern, and you are quite right. Something did happen, and I should have realised how stupid I was. I'll tell you when Mr Carlton comes. Please don't have another go, I will explain. I'd rather just tell it once, I haven't exactly been enjoying myself out there!"

Mary interrupted, and said. "Jim, leave off, let her calm down, and drink that tea. She'll explain when she is ready, I'm sure."

"She'll explain now! We can't afford to have anything happen to her. Judy, we really like and respect you. You mean so much to us, and all the staff, who would do anything to help you. You must share some of this, we want to help. Don't shut us out. We worry about you!"

"I know you do, and thank you. I have turned your lives upside down in the short time I have been here. I never meant to put any of you in danger, and I am really praying no one gets hurt. I feel it is my fault, and if I had acted differently, it wouldn't be like this. I feel so helpless."

Judith burst into tears, and cried for some minutes, while Mary comforted her and Jim sat in horrified silence, until Mary said,

"Jim, go and ask Mum to serve the meal. We'll be down as soon as we can. A meal will not hurt her or us. If the police are coming, I want her warm and fed, before they get here. Go on, please."

"I didn't mean to upset you, Judy. I was just anxious."

He went downstairs, and Judith washed her face, and soon managed to walk down to the kitchen. The staff were waiting there, and they looked at her in an alarmed, concerned silence as she sat down. Liam could not contain himself, and burst out.

"You tell me who upset you, Mrs Swallow, and I'll punch them on the nose. I'll go now, where are they?"

"Thank you Liam, but I'd rather have lunch. Could you all clear some of the basement this afternoon, I need to see what is down there? I'll be down as soon as I can. Let's eat, it is my favourite, shepherd's pie."

"You can have mine, if you want second helpings." Liam offered. Judith knew what the offer must have cost him, and smiled at him. He beamed back at her.

Lunch was rather subdued, and when the door bell went, Judith went with Sam, Stuart, Wesley and Jim, to the library, where Superintendent Carlton and another officer were waiting. Judith sat down and explained how she had seen the man, and the prearranged meeting with young Brian. She then said she had followed them to the cave and had seen them in there.

"I couldn't get away without being spotted, and had to wait for a while. Fortunately, some small rocks fell by the entrance, and they went back in and I got away then. Some animal or something must have set it off. I got so far, but they came out again, and I lay in the grass, which turned out to be a puddle, and waited until they went in again. Then I got scared and ran, forgetting my bad leg, and that shook me up."

Jim asked, "There are three caves up on the cliff, by the path, which one was it?"

Judith did some quick thinking.

Man in lower cave, with dead tree by edge of cave. Water come from cave. Path into two by cave. Rock across path.

"I only saw one, there was a small stream coming from it, and a dead tree in the entrance. The path divides, and there is a large rock across it."

"Yes. I know it, it goes back, and an easy climb comes out into the top cave entrance there, at the top of the cliff. They would have a good view from there. You can get out onto the moor from the easy passage that leads from the top cave. It takes the stream from the moor in wet weather. The other cave goes back a bit, and then closes down, it's all part of the same system, it has to be. The middle one has always been called Echo Hole, because you can hear every movement from in there." Jim got a map and pointed out the location.

Carlton asked, "What else did you see in the cave, Mrs Swallow?"

Judith was given a picture, from somewhere in the back of the cave, looking out. It seemed rather distorted, but she observed quite a lot before it faded.

"There was a sleeping bag, some rations, a rifle with sights, and a small handgun. The man was wearing dark clothing, and had binoculars, and was carrying a bag. He smokes, cigarettes, and is fair, with a moustache."

"You must have got pretty close to see all that?" Carlton was staring at her, and it made her uneasy. He had a very penetrating gaze, and she knew he was doubtful about how she had got so close. She felt a shudder of fear, of lying to him. Somehow, he knew that she was not being totally straight. He lifted one eyebrow and waited for her to continue. She looked away and continued,

"Yes, I didn't know about the cave until I was almost on top of it. I could hear quite a lot of what they said." She hoped the Garr would help her out here.

Man say, "You know what you have to do. Get her down here at dusk, and bring her to the lake by the boat house, then make an excuse, and go behind the boat house, and wait until I do it. Then get the fuck home. If you fail me, you get it instead, and I will shoot you before you get ten yards. My mate will be by the dam, and if I fail, he'll do it. We will be going back on the moor road. Wait by the standing stone, and you'll get what you want." ***Man lie. Not wait.***

Man see long way. Know Zood. Then say, "You want the stuff, we'll get it for you. You know what to do. She'll fall for it. Make sure she's alone. We'll see anyone else. Shit, what's that, I thought you said this place was safe. Get back." ***Garr help***?

Judith repeated what she had 'heard', and added, "They seem to have got some plan, and know me. You want them to try, don't you? If they do, then you can hold them. I don't want them to get bail. Can you let me have body armour? Then I can pretend to go down. You can get them on the moor road, wherever that is."

This provoked a heated argument, with Jim and Stuart protesting at the idea, Sam telling her not to be silly, and Wes trying to ask something. Jim got angry, got up, and paced up and down the room. Stuart asked how they could help, and Carlton eventually calmed them down. Judith, whose leg was hurting quite badly, just sat and observed them, wondering how she could escape. Carlton frightened her more than her situation. She wanted to be away from him.

The argument went on for some time. Carlton turned to her, and said, "Would you really be prepared to do that?"

"Of course she can't, it is much too dangerous, you can't let her!" Jim was really agitated.

"Hang on, everybody, I have an input into this, hear me out. This is my home now and I have grown to love it already. I don't want to live for months in fear of someone getting hurt, or with guards everywhere, and feeling like a prisoner. I can't stand waiting for weeks, until they get another chance. I would rather bring it to a quick, if exciting, conclusion, than let the fear eat into my soul. This way, no one else is going to be hurt, and you and your families are safe. Imagine what months of this will do to all your families. If I have the best body armour, I stand a good chance of getting away with it. They might even miss, but I would go down, anyway. We can hardly creep up on them now, and they have the high ground. We don't even know where the second one is hiding out. The risk is mine, and so should the decision be. I wouldn't mind a paramedic standing by, just in case, though!"

Carlton looked at her with a dawning respect. Once again, he smiled at her. "I wish there was another way, but she does have some valid points. We need to put a wire on you, and provide you with head protection. I want everyone else on the estate well guarded, and that means bringing you back here, as we did before. It looks like tonight is the night, I don't see them hanging round to be discovered. It seems that this Hall boy has provided them with the local knowledge. He was police bailed yesterday. If we could prove a conspiracy to murder, Cummings' allegations would be thrown out."

Carlton went out with the other officer and then returned and talked through the protection of the families. Judith announced she was going to have a lie down while they fought it out, and would come down for their instructions later. She went up to her room, took a couple of pain killers, and lay on the bed.

Do you understand what is planned? I do not want you hurt, but I will need the Garr to watch for me.

We know. We hear. Garr read thought in head. Garr with Zood. Zood warrior.

Can I ask you something?

Zood ask.

You hear the words men speak, and can say them, but you speak in my mind very simplistically. Why?

Garr understand, not words, but seeing and words. Not need to speak like man. Zood sleep. Zood hurt. Garr watch.

Judith did exactly that.

Chapter Thirteen

"Judy, wake up, it's gone four, and Superintendent Carlton needs to talk to you. I've made tea, and we are all meeting in the library. His sergeant is organising us in there, can you come down? Are you fit enough?"

Judith got up and went down with Nora into the library.

Please listen to this, it could be important. I am going to need your help today. If things go well, we can get rid of this threat to you and me. I am very frightened, and need you to tell me what is going on. Will you help me?

Garr be with you. Garr help Zood. Zood help Garr. Garr listen.

Carlton came towards her and asked to go somewhere private, so they went into the Chinese Drawing Room. They sat down,

"May I call you Judy? Call me Dennis, I need to talk to you seriously about this. I admire you immensely, and I appreciate your reasoning and courage, but I would rather you didn't do this. I wish we could eliminate the danger you are in, and I will offer you protection for as long as you need it. My chief constable, Mr Elgar, has asked me to try and talk you out of it. We can get a woman officer to take your place. We would not normally allow anything like this, and we can pick these three up and frighten them off, but as you so accurately pointed out, they wouldn't stay in custody very long. Are you still determined to do this?"

"Dennis, let me ask some questions first. Then tell me you still don't want me to do it, and convince me there is another way. If I could see another way, I would take it. Does any replacement officer have the 'sight' I have? Are they so like me as to fool Brian Hall? Could they limp the way I do, and look enough like me to fool anyone? Why should a complete stranger be asked to solve a problem that is essentially mine? If they don't succeed, or think they have succeeded, will they not be waiting for another opportunity, when I am less prepared? Would you want to wait for months, wondering where, when or how the attack is coming? Wouldn't you rather get it over with? Can you afford to protect me for an indefinite period? Remember, I know how much this sort of thing costs. Can you really afford to turn down my offer? How else are we going to get these animals behind bars. Shall I go on?"

"Point taken, Judy. You have thought this through. Now I have some questions for you. You are aware that we cannot totally protect you, and there is still a danger of injury and death? You would have to wear a wire and body armour. You must do it exactly the way we have planned. We must know what you can see. Once you go down, you must not move, possibly for some time. You will feel totally isolated. These men mean business. Can you keep your nerve? Will you panic? Will you trust us? Can you trust us?"

"Yes, I will trust you. No, I doubt if I will panic. Yes, I'm very frightened. Yes, I know you cannot guarantee anything. Yes, I can play dead. Yes, I will talk to you. Will you be able to protect everyone else? I couldn't accept anyone else being hurt, in my place. My staff and their families are also my friends. A few months ago, I thought I didn't want to live, and I had nothing to look forward to. Now I have everything to live for, but I won't live much of a life, if I am expecting a bullet in the back all the time! Please, please let's get this over with. The sooner the better. This has got to be the best chance we will get. I am no heroine, I can assure you. I'm not trying to impress anyone. What are you going to do if they do get away?"

"You are determined to do it? I cannot talk you out of it?"

"Yes, I will do it. No you cannot."

"Right, in that case, I will brief you after we talk to the others. Let's go and see them now."

The Morpeths were in the library, with Wesley, Sam, and Stuart. June was with everyone else in the drawing room, including all the children. Dennis started by asking his sergeant to explain how the staff could help. They would be taken, with their families, to a hotel for the night, except Jim and Sam, who wanted to stay and help. Stuart had also asked to stay, but had been asked to help in another way, by going with officers to a control room, as he knew the layout of both the grounds and the village, and the moor. Jim would be in the farm house, ready to move with officers to block any roads or paths with the tractor if necessary, and help them with local knowledge. He would also appear around the farm, to make it look as though all was normal. Sam was staying with officers in the house, on the roof. He was to drive them away to be met by other vehicles, who would take the staff to several hotels at least for the evening, and, if necessary, overnight. They were being told it was a staff outing, and would be taken to whatever entertainment was acceptable. Sam would return, and park the bus as usual, when he would go to his flat, and then make his way to the house. Officers would come, concealed in the van with him, and unload in the barn.

Dennis asked Judith if that was acceptable, and for permission to use the van and the house. Jim said,

"Thank you for looking after our families. The officers are already in the boys' bedroom. Judy, can I talk you out of this?"

"No, and I see I'm not going to talk you out of your part either. None of you. What is Wesley going to do?"

Wesley grinned, and said he was going to the police station, to help co-ordinate there, as his car had to go as normal, and he didn't want to slow anyone down. He was going to hang on until the police were ready, and would play the piano as an excuse for staying on. It should be easy for Brian to know he was there, and then watch him leave.

Dennis said he was going to put his car in the barn and sneak into the house. Judith, with a sinking feeling in her gut, was too overwhelmed to say anything, except to thank them all. They all took mobile phones, and one by one, left, until she and the officers and Wesley were left. Nora brought in a light tea, but Judith was not hungry.

The sergeant asked her to wear casual, loose fitting, clothes, that would disguise the armour, and they went upstairs to raid her wardrobe. He produced some body armour, a bullet proof vest, and leg protectors, and a variety of headgear. Once she had put it all on correctly, it weighed a ton, and she selected a baseball cap, as the only item that did not look totally silly. He fitted a tiny microphone to her and tested it. She learned just the right volume to speak at and then tried to talk to the Garr. She had feared that the armour would inhibit her ability to talk to them.

Can you hear me clearly, does this make it difficult ?

Garr hear well. You wear scales like Garr. Garr approve. We watch. Garr hear what Zood and Niss say. Elders tell to let us speak to Niss. He will hear Zood. Niss see what Zood see. Garr will speak to Niss if Zood need. Zood not fear Niss, Niss like Zood.

How will I explain that? We cannot trust him.

Zood say nothing. Niss never know. Niss wonder. No tell. Niss has mind Garr can reach. Trust Garr.

I offer no explanation, and as he will never see you, he cannot prove anything. I see. He will always wonder. Will you not endanger yourselves by this?

Niss special. Time special. Garr do this long ago. Niss clever. Niss never say. Zood in danger. If Zood die, Zaron will hear Garr.

Yes. Zaron will be your new guardian if it goes wrong tonight. Is the man still in the cave?

Man not in cave. Garr say when come. He will come to cave. Leave food there. Leave cloth there. Garr tell when man come.

Has he left his stick that bangs there?

Stick there.

Judith pictured bullets, and immediately received a picture of bullets, by the rifle.

Can you get to the cave, and change those bullets for other ones that will not kill?

Garr will. Soon.

Can you show the gun and bullets in a picture to Niss, and make it seem the picture comes from me?

Garrr try.

Judith went downstairs and took Dennis aside. She said,

"Dennis, listen. I want to know if you could get me some blank bullets quickly. Don't ask why, but I want to show you a picture of a gun and bullets. The ones in the cave. I'm not going to explain, and you must keep it to yourself. No, not a photo. Sit down, shut your eyes and clear your mind completely. Just do it. It could save my life. I want to know what they are."

She sat next to him and cleared her mind. A close up of the guns and bullets in the cave came very sharply into focus. She mentally pushed it towards him. He gasped and she felt him looking through her mind into the picture.

"Got it. I see what it is."

The picture faded. Judith opened her eyes, to see him pale, and looking at her in total amazement.

"Can you get me that number of blanks, very quickly?"

"Yes, I can. But how do we get them there without being seen? How did you do that?"

"Never mind, just do it. We don't have much time."

Dennis lept up, rather shakily, and went to the telephone in the library. He returned a few minutes later, and said,

"They are on their way. About twenty minutes, by motor bike, unmarked. We cannot get them to the cave without being seen. It could blow the whole operation. You certainly can't go. They may come back at any time. How did you do that? You got into my mind, it was like I was really there. I've never been so scared in my life."

"It is nothing new, it is called being telepathic. I am too. That is how I see things. Around me, you probably can, too. I am going to get those blanks there by a similar means, it is called telekinesis. It is a lot harder, but I cannot put one in the gun. It is too difficult. There are limits. If the gun is already loaded, I'll have to trust the body armour. Would you like a brandy? It can be quite a shock, the first few times you use it."

"Yes, a small one, please."

He sat down, and she fetched him one from the dining room. She gave it to him, but he was still looking shaken, when the sergeant came in, and asked her,

"Have you turned off the mike, it isn't working?"

"Oh, yes, sorry, I get all coy about being in the loo. I'll switch it back on, is that working now?"

After a bit of fussing, he went back upstairs. Dennis looked at her suspiciously and finished the brandy. He ran through the plan, and she showed him on the map, the positions she thought he should watch most carefully. She suggested they watch the dam, the Folly, the boat house and the cave. While she had been asleep, equipment had been delivered, including telephoto lenses, video cameras, night sights infra red cameras. It was set up in the attics, at Jim's farm, in the unoccupied stable flat, and the lodges. A motor bike pulled up, and a package was delivered. Wesley brought it in and handed it to Dennis, who checked its contents and handed it to Judith. She nodded and said,

"I need to take these, I'll be gone ten minutes or so. No, I need to be on my own, don't follow me. I have to have total concentration. I won't leave the house."

She got up and went into the kitchen. No one was around.

Do you need me to go to the cellar?

Zood go to place for food. Take metal from paper. Put by ground. Zood wait. Garr know what Zood want. Garr show when in cave.

Judith went to the pantry, unwrapped the blanks, which looked just like the real thing, put them by the grill, and waited. Within seconds a small Garr swung open the grill, and put the bullets in a pouch, seemingly made of leather, and passed it to another paw behind the grill. The Garr looked up at Judith. Its eyes were almost covered with a heavy opaque lid.

Garr help Zood.

It went back through the grill, which closed silently.

Try not to get them wet. They need to be put in place of the others, exactly, so man doesn't see they have changed. Hide the others, and, if you can, swap them back after the man has left, or has made the stick go bang.

Garr know. Soon we put them in cave.

Judith had an impression of blackness, and then of water, then more blackness. A filtered, weak light for a few minutes, and then blackness again.

Zood with Niss.

Judith went back to the library. Dennis was talking to Wesley and Judith asked,

"Is everything set up ready? Dennis, how long will it take to get everything in place?"

"Not long. How long will you need? The other officers are waiting, some are already in place. I think it is time for Wesley to play the piano. I need to run some last minute details past you, and then

202

'leave'. I will come back very soon, via the conservatory and into the ball room. Then I will go upstairs and the other officers will follow me. Could you make sure the door is unlocked?"

Wesley collected some of his papers, and left, saying,

"Judy, be careful. I wish I could stay and help you, but I know there is nothing I can do. I'll see you later, when I go. Any requests, music wise?"

She knew he was worried, and that he desperately wanted to help, and how helpless he felt. Since his arrival at the house, she had been impressed with his many abilities, and now it seemed he was coping under pressure better than any of them.

"Something stirring, to bolster up our spirits, anything you like. Not 'One Fine Day'. That always makes me cry, I leave it to you. I'll be in soon. Thanks."

He wheeled himself off and she realised he had a new wheel chair. It had arrived at last. As soon as he had gone and the door had been shut, Dennis said,

"Did you manage to do it? You turned the mike off. You must not do that. We need to be able to hear you at all times." *You are the most accomplished liar I have ever met!*

"I will tell you when it is done. I have to do it in stages, it takes a lot of effort. What are the plans then?" *Am I? What a thing to suggest!*

For half an hour they went through every scenario they could think of, and the sergeant came in and checked everything with them. Dennis left and the sergeant went upstairs. Judith went to the conservatory, checked the doors were unlocked, and drew the curtains in the drawing room and the Chinese Drawing Room, and put lights on in both rooms. She went into the ballroom, and took a cup of tea in to Wesley, who played a selection of Sousa, Chopin, Copeland, and Grieg for her. He then ran through some of the songs from Patience. Judith heard the Garr join in, and as Wes played on, they became bolder and more inventive with their harmony.

Dennis knocked on the door as arranged, as he and several officers came in through the drawing room, and went upstairs. Wesley played on, but they were disturbed by the telephone ringing. Judith was expecting Dennis to call her on her mobile when he was ready, and Wesley should leave, so this call was unexpected, and she took it in the Chinese Drawing Room. It was Ingrid, hysterically wanting to know what Judith had against Francis. She said he had been arrested, and she wailed that she knew he was innocent and Judith could help. She just had to get him off, for Clive's sake. Aware that every phone call from and to the house phones was being recorded, Judith asked what was going on and feigned innocence about Francis' involvement. Judith

203

assured her that she could only tell the truth and eventually Ingrid calmed down a bit, and after mentioning that Judith owed the family some loyalty, she rang off.

Jim rang through from the farm, to say everything was ready and to check she was safe. She reassured him. Wes asked about the calls, when she went back to the ballroom, and she told him some of Ingrid's comments. He laughed, and hoped he would meet Ingrid, when he would put her right on a few things.

"One advantage to being in a wheelchair, is that you can be as rude as you like and seldom get smacked! I shall enjoy bringing her down to size. Just say when."

The house phone went again and Judith answered it. Nobody spoke and she heard a click as the phone was put down at the other end. She spoke to Wesley and said, "No one spoke, it looks like things might be progressing."

Her mobile phone rang and Dennis told her Wesley should leave. She said,

"Could you play 'The Soldiers of The Queen' for me?" Wes nodded, it was their prearranged signal, so he played it, and then closed the piano and she walked beside him and saw him to his car. Once in the driving seat, he looked up at her, and whispered,

"Take care, see you tomorrow."

As he drove off, Judith felt very alone. She turned and walked back into the house and went to the ballroom and switched off the lights, and then turned off the lights in the two drawing rooms.

Zood not alone. Garr with Zood. Man from cave come over top ground. Man follow, man who stay in Tower. Friend of big man. Tower man have short stick that bang.

Judith spoke softly into her microphone,

"Two men are approaching over the moor. One is our friend from earlier, the other is the Dutchman who stayed at the Folly earlier this year. He has a hand gun, I think. I will tell you when they are in place, and where they are."

Man not friend, foe. Garr put in cave. Man not know metal change. No metal in stick. Garr look.

Judith said,

"The things I took earlier are there, in place. I am going to the kitchen."

She wondered how she would explain irony to the Garr. When she got there, she took some food into the pantry and placed it by the grill.

Food in pantry for Garr.

Garr thank Zood. Zood worry. Man in cave, take stick. Lie on cloth in cave. Put metal into stick. Tower man go though trees.

Judith waited, wishing her stomach wouldn't rumble, and would stop doing somersaults. She wondered what Brian would say to get her down to the lake.

She helped herself to a chocolate biscuit and dunked it in her coffee. She tried to think of something that would calm her down, but her mind kept jumping all over the place.

Zood watch.

She was shown a beautiful view of the lake by moonlight, with the Garr swimming and playing in the lake. She saw one catch a fish, and knew she was being shown a time gone by, that they had enjoyed. Their efforts worked and she felt more tranquil.

Do you like fish? Does it have to be fresh? I'll get the lake restocked. Would you like that?

Garr like. Zan gave Garr. Zood give Garr. Tower man wait by little tree by wall by big water. Tower near.

"The second man is on the Folly side of the dam, waiting. The man in the cave has loaded up, and is lying on the sleeping bag, in the cave entrance."

It was not even dark outside, and Judith decided she needed the bathroom, before anything happened. She went to the cloakroom and spent some time getting her body armour right, after she had finished. She went to the sitting room and tried to read a book, but gave up.

Boy that smells comes. Door at place to eat. He wait, afraid. He come.

Judith went to the kitchen, and cleared her coffee mug away, and then put the plate of biscuits on the kitchen table.

There was a knock at the back door, and she felt a rush of adrenaline, as she took her time to answer it. She collected her stick, and opened the door. Brian was standing there, sweating profusely, and obviously very agitated. His pupils were dilated and he was flushed.

"Hello, Brian, I didn't expect to see you. At least you knocked this time. Whatever is the matter? You're shaking like a leaf. Is something wrong?"

"Yes, Mrs Swallow. I have been having a chat with my dad, and he has told me I need to come and see you, and apologise about the way I have been. I think I must explain. Mr Cummings got me hooked on drugs, and I have been a fool. I want to start again, and Dad said you might know somewhere I could go, to get off it. Will you help me? I know I shouldn't expect it, and I'm really sorry. If I don't sort myself out, he says I'll end up in prison. He's going to chuck me out."

"I don't know, Brian, I might, but you will have to show you mean it. Why come now, today?"

"I don't want anyone else to see, or know. No one likes me round here, and Mr Morpeth said I wasn't to come near you. I'm scared of him seeing me. I thought if I could talk to you alone, you might listen."

"I'll think about it. I don't like those who try to break into my house. Or anyone who steals from me. I won't have it. Has he chucked you out yet?"

"No, but he will if I don't get sorted. Look, I know where Mr Cummings hid some of his dope, and if it stays there, I'll want to use it. I can't hand it in, but if you found it, you could take it to the police, couldn't you? If it's not there, I won't use it. I'll show you where it is, if you like, now, or I'll lose me nerve. Mr Cummings will kill me if he knows. Will you come?"

Judith pretended to think about it. She asked,

"Is it far? I'm not up to a long walk. If you are being straight with me, I might help, and I certainly don't want drugs around the estate. Does anyone else know about this?"

"No, it's by the lake. I'll show you. You could tell the cops you found it there. Please come."

"All right, I'll get a jacket." She picked up her jacket from the back of a kitchen chair, put it on and left with him. She walked slowly down to the lake with him. He said little, and wanted to hurry.

"Brian, I cannot hurry. I have a bad leg. Slow down."

"Sorry, I forgot."

As they approached the lake, and made their way towards the boat house, Judith's stomach was tying itself in knots, and she was fighting the desire to turn and run for cover. She began to sweat. Brian took her to the jetty, and pointed out a small box hidden under it. It was just out of reach, and he said,

"I'll get a stick, wait here." He went off round the boat house.

Zood ready. Man use stick. Now.

Judith heard a shot ring out, and dropped onto the jetty, and rolled onto her front. She pulled a small string in her coat cuff, which opened a sachet of artificial blood in her jacket, both at the front and back, and felt the liquid seep through the cloth over her back and under her. She lay still and Brian came up to her. She saw through the Garr's eyes as he looked nervously around and came towards her. He gave her several hefty kicks in the back and sides, and then tried to turn her over, but when he put his hand on her 'bloody' coat, he lost his nerve, and stepped back. He said,

"You stupid bitch, you fell for it. I'm glad you're dead. You are dead, aren't you? He kicked her viciously again in the side, and then ran away, back up towards the house.

Judith lay quite still and whispered softly,

"I'm fine. A few bruises, nothing worse."

For a long time she waited, feeling very uncomfortable. She opened her eyes slightly and could see the water through a crack in the jetty. She waited.

Zood not hurt? Man in cave take things, and leave. Man wait for Tower man. Tower man come to cave. Boy that smell gone to house. Man wait, watch. Zood not move. He come. Leave stick and metal by cave. Garr change metal when he go.

Be careful, he must not see you.

Garr know. Men come. Look at Zood.

Judith closed her eyes, and hoped they didn't intend to deliver a coup de grace. She heard them approach some minutes later.

"Don't touch her, forensics. When that stupid boy comes out of the house, he should get picked up for burglary. They'll find traces on him. I've left the gun up by the cave, and it's clean. He'll get convicted, he is so doped up they won't believe a word he says. She hasn't moved in half an hour. She's dead. Let's get out of here. We'll be in the Smoke by morning when they find her. Come on, we don't want to stick around. Job well done."

Judith hoped the mike had picked that up.

The men left and she heard them move up through the wood and past the cave. She was shown them moving across the moor in the twilight, and then they faded from her view.

Men you like come. Zood stay still. They come with Niss. Boy in house, take paper from leather pouch. Zood wait. Men in house watch boy that smells.

Judith racked her brains to think what the paper in pouch was, and they showed her purse in Brian's hand. She heard running footsteps coming towards her and Dennis said,

"It's all right, Judy, you're safe. They have driven off, and we have a block set up for them, where it is safe to arrest them. Well done. Are you hurt? Hall will get a very nasty shock in a minute or two, when he leaves the house."

Judith spoke,

"Good. I really don't like that young man. Can you help me up? I have been lying here so long, I'm really stiff. That little bastard got me well and truly in the ribs when he kicked me. I am surprised he never felt the body armour, which is **really** uncomfortable."

Willing hands helped her to sit up, and then got her to her feet. Dennis looked very relieved, and they sat her down, while a paramedic checked her over. He was a cheerful, blonde man, and as she took off the vest, he winced as he saw the bruises on her back and side.

"Can you walk?"

"Yes, but I have cramp in my foot, let me move around for a

while. That's better. Yes, it is a bit sore, and it will ache for a while, but I'll live. Did you hear what they said, when they came to check I was dead? Good! What do we do now?"

"We need you to be dead for a while longer, I am afraid. Would you mind? I need them to think they have succeeded, and I know you have been through a lot, but I want to make sure we have all of them. Your delivery, critically injured, by ambulance to the hospital, would do the trick. Then we can see if anyone comes to finish the job. You won't be there, some one else will."

"How long for? I don't want the staff distressed, and I think they will be, if you tell them I'm near dead. Then I suppose you want me to hide up somewhere for days. I don't want to leave here. It would be interesting to watch the family gather like vultures, but no, I will not do that. I'll be dead for two days, no more, and that is my best offer. I'm tired, cold, stiff and sore, and I want my bed. Come on Dennis, I've had enough."

"That is more than I hoped for. An ambulance will take you in, and I will follow, and as soon as you have been checked in, we can bring you back. Will you keep your head down here for two days? I know we can trust the Morpeths, and your gardener and young Wesley. It's Friday tomorrow, and by Sunday we should be well clear."

He listened on his radio earpiece, and then said. "Hall is just preparing to leave the house, with a few bits of your property. It would be perfect if you came up in the ambulance while he was waiting to be taken into the nick. We have an ambulance ready. It's on its way. This paramedic here is to be trusted. We are just about to 'find' you, so lie back down, and we will cart you off. Can you remember how you were? Thanks Judy, we owe you big time."

Judith grumbled, "Yes, you do. This is like a bad comedy. You will bring me back soon? I don't want to leave the house."

Dennis helped her lie down, and then retreated, and disappeared. She felt dirty, wet and exhausted. The adrenaline rush from earlier had gone, leaving her feeling quite drained. As she lay she watched the water glinting beneath her, and then saw something surface beneath her. A small 'finder' Garr was under the jetty, and even though it was very dark, she was sure she saw it wink at her.

Zood not fear. Garr with you. Men come. Boy that smell is with more men. Boy frightened. Men find paper, boy fight men. Boy lose. Niss come now.

Judith heard a vehicle approaching, and then heard Dennis shout, "Over here." People ran towards her, and she shut her eyes and went limp, as the paramedic from earlier said,

"I have a pulse, a very weak one." He tore her coat open, and put a wet dressing on her chest and back, and they put her gently on a stretcher, and carried her to the ambulance. She remained totally relaxed, and then they were moving in the vehicle. It was a bumpy ride, and she heard the sound of gravel under the wheels. The ambulance stopped, and the back doors opened, and someone got in or out. Then they were off, and when they left the gravel, the ride was smooth. It seemed to go on for ages, and then the two–tone horns came on. Once they reached the hospital, the doors opened and she was taken out. She could see the lights through her eyelids. They went down a corridor and then into a room. Someone taped a tube to her arm, and she was then taken on a trolley to another place. After twenty minutes she heard Dennis say,

"You can wake up now, we're safe. Well done!"

She opened her eyes, and sat up. Several police officers were there and a person in a white coat, who introduced himself as a doctor. A policewoman smiled, and said,

"Hi! I am going to be you for a while, but I need your clothes and your bandages. Someone has come in with some fresh clothes for you. You look really badly injured. I am so glad you decided to be unconscious, I won't have to wriggle and moan!"

The doctor insisted on examining Judith, and felt the bruises. Judith winced. He advised rest and warmth, and suggested she have a stiff drink when she got home. Judith swapped clothes and the policewoman put them on. The wet pads turned out to be wound dressings saturated in artificial blood. Judith was offered a shower and took up the offer. Somehow her hair was saturated in the 'blood' and she did moan a bit about that.

Cleaner, fresher, warmer and less sticky, she went back into the room and Dennis apologised about her hair. He explained that it would be easier to disguise the decoy, with an apparent head wound. Judith was given a cup of tea, and some pain killers. Her stick was produced, but kept at the hospital, and replaced by another. Wishing the decoy luck, Judith was smuggled out of the back of the hospital, and into a van, and Dennis soon joined them. He asked her to go to a police station with him and she said,

"Yes, provided it has a bar, and you are buying!" They drew up in the back yard of a large city police station, and while they were waiting to be let in, a van load of drunks arrived. They waited until the drunks, some of whom were quite amusing, if a little crude and rude, were taken inside.

"This takes me back to when I used to do this. I don't miss it. I enjoyed my time in the job, but I have a new life now, and a new challenge."

Upstairs, in a nice warm office, Judith had her bruises photographed, and then Dennis took her up to the bar and introduced her to a group of officers who looked after her, while he went off to make some calls. She was talked into a darts game and won. She was listening to the after shift chat, when Dennis came back. He smiled and said,

"There was a reporter from the local radio station in casualty when you came in. He even got a photo. I am sorry if this worries you, but it is exactly what we need, especially as they found out of their own accord. I will need to issue a statement, I would like to say that after a shooting incident, you are critically ill, in intensive care, and are on a life support machine. Is that all right with you?"

"Please don't give my address, I don't want the press hanging round the house, or bothering the staff. Have you got the two men yet?"

"Yes, we ambushed them and had an interesting stand off. They both had hand guns, as you said. They are all three in custody, in different stations, and will be interviewed in the morning. Now, do you want to go home? If you do, I insist on you having at least two officers with you, and not to show yourself. If you like, we can put you up here, in town, at a good hotel. You still get a body guard, whichever you choose."

"I'll go home then, they can stay in the guest bedrooms. I must ring Jim, Wesley and Stuart, to tell them I am all right. Can I do so? They will be worried sick. Sam too."

"They already know. I told them myself. They were all brilliant. They send their love. They will keep the secret. Your staff adore you, and gave me a very hard time over putting you at risk. Have you really only been there three weeks? I will have to come and see you tomorrow, you need to make yet another statement. I'll bring a stenographer. We will talk over the whole thing then. Could we use your house for a debrief? There will be a whole team there anyway, forensic teams, and a statement–taking team, and I have to offer you counselling and support. The force psychiatrist is coming out, for the whole team. We will pay for the hire of the facilities. You have a wonderful house. On Saturday I want to ask the three boys, and the girls, if they want to come over the police headquarters and show them the horses, where we train the dogs, a ride in a traffic car, you know the score. I thought they would enjoy it, and it will get them out of the way."

"You will be their hero! They have been playing detectives and policemen all week! By all means use the house. My niece, Sharon, is at training school here at the moment, she might want to help show them round. They know and like her. She too, will be worried. Can you tell her?"

He took Sharon's details, and went off and came back minutes later with Sharon. She turned a few heads as she entered the bar, and rushed over to Judy and hugged her. Dennis asked her if she wanted to show the children round, and she was most enthusiastic. Judy pictured Sharon staying at the house, and helping on the Sunday. Sharon, without thinking said,

"I wish I could, I have to be back here Sunday evening, so I won't be able to stay late. You need permission to come in on Monday morning."

"I think it is a good idea and you shall have your permission."

Sharon left soon after, as she said something about lights out. Dennis was looking rather puzzled and shook his head. When Judith asked what was wrong, he said,

"You are the most alarming person to be with! I heard you ask Sharon and answered before I realised you hadn't spoken a word. She is obviously telepathic too. Does it run in families? My mother had what she called the 'sight'. Her mother had the reputation as a witch. I never knew I had it, but you sent a very clear picture. I can't say I am that comfy with it, but I would like to talk to you about it sometime. Come on, let's get you home, you look shattered. Your guards are waiting downstairs, let's go."

He picked up her stick and she moved painfully towards the lift. She was worried too, as she thought it was the Garr who did the thinking magic.

There were still a number of officers and activity in the house when they got back. Dennis saw her in and left. She showed the two officers, a man called Bert, and a woman called Dawn, to their rooms, and then the kitchen. She said she would call them if she needed them and went to bed. She lay in bed and waited.

Garr welcome Zood. Zood sleep now. Speak in light. Garr have fun.

Judith drifted off to sleep, and dreamt of caving in a diamond mine, and finding the biggest diamond in the world, which was shaped like a huge bullet.

Chapter Fourteen

It was very hard to wake, and once awake, she felt so sore and stiff, she stayed in bed until she needed the loo. Her ribs ached, and she felt uncomfortable all over. She watched some television, and when the local news came on was interested to see that she was still on the critical list. The picture of her looked gruesome.

She heard movement outside her room, followed by a knock on the door. Dawn came in and they chatted, and Judith said she would be down in a minute and got dressed. She used the stairlift to get downstairs, and took them to the kitchen where they got themselves breakfast. Judith prepared a full fry–up, and Dawn did toast, while Bert made coffee. Judith went and fetched some cereal from the pantry and saw the familiar bottle of blue liquid.

Zood drink. Zood hurt.

She drank the foul fluid and went out with the cereal. They were sitting talking over the dirty dishes when there was a ring at the front door. Judith dived into the pantry and waited.

Thank you, Garr. Goy are you there? I need to ask you something.

Zood, Goy here.

When Zood asked you to show Niss a picture, what did you do?

Garr not show. Zood do. Zood have power. Niss have power, Zaron have power. Not need Garr to talk in mind with Niss, Zood, Zaron. Garr hear all.

You mean I can communicate without you, between some other people? Why did I not know before?

Zood never try.

Judith waited until she heard Dawn call,

"It's OK, it's our lot. Come out, is it all right to give them coffee? The super will be here soon. We knock off then, and come back this evening. Have a fun day, being dead, and take care of yourself. I love the house, and thanks for breakfast. Do you want us to bring a take away this evening?"

"What a brilliant idea, anything you like."

Zood, Niss come.

Dennis came in, with yet more officers, and Nora and Mary who went to the kitchen to make lots of coffee for them. Nora hugged Judith but said nothing. She mouthed 'later' as she fetched a large tin of coffee from the pantry.

Judith took Dennis to her sitting room, and they sorted out which rooms they would need. She then went back to the kitchen, to ask if

Nora and Mary could feed the police as well, and if not, she would get Dennis to get caterers in. Nora went off to talk to an inspector and returned to say they could manage, if they put all the leaves in the dining room table and used the large dinner service. The staff would eat in the kitchen and then help serve the officers.

Dennis was most grateful and asked for a bill, which he would get paid. Judith tried to say it wasn't necessary, but he insisted, something he was very good at. He then asked if he could take a statement from Judith, and if they could use a room where they couldn't be seen from outside. Sam arrived with the cleaning staff, who were delighted to see Judith in one piece, and with Bill and Liam. Wesley came in and told Dennis that he had seen a press van, with a camera crew, setting up by the lodges. One of the inspectors was sent out to put a guard on the gates. Stuart and June came in to say they had already turned two lots of the press out of the back drive, and Stuart had locked the back gate. Sam went and fetched Lucy, and Wesley rang Jim to see if the press were bothering him. Jim told him they had been, until he began muck spreading, when they had hurriedly left!

Wesley got together with the administration officer, and soon they had everything organised. Judith went to the landing sitting area, where she spent the rest of the morning going through her statement. When it was typed up (on Wesley's computer) she signed it, and then went through what to expect in the next few days and discussed the probable consequences. She was talking to Dennis when she paused.

Zood. Men come from big water. Men with big box. Want see Zood. More men by horse house. In tree behind. Go to small water, with flowers.

Show me.

She saw a television crew coming up to the back of the house from the lake. They were creeping along by the yew trees. She projected the picture to Dennis. He had been watching her carefully and saw the picture instantly. She then showed him the other press by the stables, and in the sunken garden by the fish pond. He said nothing, but nodded. The secretary with him, realising the conversation had stopped abruptly, looked at both of them rather strangely, and they waited while Dennis rushed downstairs and came back with a radio. They listened while all the intruders were rounded up and taken away. The cameras were confiscated, and film removed.

"What do you want us to do with them? They haven't really committed a crime, but we have detained them for being likely to provoke a breach of the peace. We have the papers the journalists were from, and the TV station I can get our press office to call the editors and give them a really nasty fright."

"Yes, but if they come back, I would like their details. Give them to Wes, he will compile a list."

Judith pictured the press being thrown into the lake and diving for the camera. She projected the image to Dennis, who laughed and tentatively projected another image of the same people, standing soaking on the jetty with pond weed in their hair. They both laughed. The secretary looked at them as if they were mad. Nora came up, and told them that their meal was ready in the library, and the three of them followed her downstairs. The curtains were drawn. They had a pleasant lunch and made arrangements for the following day.

Dennis left after lunch, leaving an inspector in charge. Judith retreated to her bedroom and watched afternoon television. She dozed off, and woke when the inspector knocked on the door to say the main force of officers were leaving. Those remaining would be doing security, and Dawn and Bert would be arriving soon. He thanked Judith for her help and then left.

Nora came upstairs and told her that they had postponed the staff meeting. Liam had threatened a press reporter with a punch on the nose, if he got in the way of the mower once again, and Bill had threatened two with a hoe. Stuart and Sam were doing hourly rounds of the house and stables.

Nora then produced a huge key and suggested Dawn and Bert lock the main gates by the lodges. Judith did not know they could lock. When the night officers arrived, the gates were locked, and Judith participated in a Chinese take away with them. They watched the news and saw that Judith was still critical, but stable. Judith went to bed early and slept fitfully through the night.

In the morning she made herself scarce, while a large party went off in a minibus for the trip to the police headquarters. Mary went with them, and June and Lucy. Dawn and Bert stayed for the day, and Sam and Stuart insisted on checking the grounds for press. They only found one, a bumptious little man, who got very angry when Stuart threatened to throw him on the compost heap. The police took him away when he tried to return. Judith sat writing letters and watching television. She watched the news and was startled to learn that one man had been detained following a further attempt on her life in the hospital. Dennis rang shortly afterwards to tell her that someone had tried to stab the decoy in the hospital but had not injured the officer. He said he would be out some time in the morning and that he was interviewing.

The children arrived with Sharon and the rest of the party, well after six. They been given a wonderful day, and were packed off to their respective homes. Two officers arrived to cover the night security, and watched the television between security checks. Sharon and Judith chatted until quite late, and then went to bed.

Zood sleep. Need sleep. Zood tired. All well. Many men make Zood safe.

Goodnight Garr. I am sorry I have neglected you today.

Dennis rang in the morning to say he would be out in the afternoon to see them, and that officers would be there all day. Judith explained that there would be no meal available as it was Mary's day off. Dennis said they would bring packed lunches.

Judith stayed in the house and Sharon answered the door to let the police in. The administration inspector asked to use the drawing room, ballroom and conservatory.

Judith told Sharon what she could about her adventures, and then they went down to the basement to look at some of the paintings that Judith had found. Sharon had studied art at college, before going into modelling. There were many pictures, and examining them took sometime. When they had made a list, and thought they had finished, they found a lot more. They cleared the cases away, and behind them, discovered a door which led into a wine cellar where they began to count bottles. They gave up after a while. Sharon suggested that some of the wines were very rare and could be valuable. She was sure the pictures were. They were all rather grimy, and she suggested Judith get an expert in to clean, restore and value them, and then they went up to the kitchen. The inspector came and found them, and asked if the officers could eat in the conservatory and if he could boil a kettle.

Dennis turned up about three, and invited Judith and Sharon to the debrief he gave the officers in the ball room. He explained that they had obtained sufficient evidence to charge everyone arrested with offences, and Judith could now make a miraculous recovery. He thanked her for her help, bravery and hospitality, and to her acute embarrassment, everyone applauded. He explained that they had uncovered drug smuggling, currency and diamond smuggling, in addition to solving the murder of a security guard, several robberies, fraud and false accounting, drug dealing, and conspiracy to murder, attempted murder, and numerous other offences. He thanked all the officers for their hard work and then asked Judith if she wanted to say anything. She was taken by surprise but got to her feet.

"Yes, thank you, there is. I would like to thank everyone for their dedication and hard work, and for protecting me and my staff, not to mention my house and grounds. I know it is early days yet, and we still have to nail these bastards in court, but I would ask for a list of every officer involved, including those who never made it here, and the civilian staff as well, so when the gang are convicted, we can throw the biggest party this place has ever seen. I can't say how pleasant everyone has been, and I appreciate it. Thank you, everybody."

She sat down, rather flustered, and directed her thought to Dennis, while the inspector took over.

You bugger, you might have warned me! Putting me on the spot like that!

Dennis winked at her, and thought back,

I know, you would have refused to come in. Sorry. Will you come for a meal with me tomorrow evening?

Sharon joined in.

Go on, have a break. You two old fossils need to lighten up. Do you both good.

Dennis and Judith combined wills, and thought.

We'll show her a thing or two! Cheeky lass! Sharon, you just have no respect for your elders and betters.

I know, she thought smugly, *it is just so sad.*

The meeting broke up and Sharon went off to make tea while Dennis talked to Judith. When Sharon came in with a tea tray, Dennis looked at her and said,

"Young lady, you do not seem to be showing the proper respect for your senior officer!" He smiled at her.

"I know, but I never said a word, did I? This 'think talk' has its uses. I didn't mean any disrespect, you two enjoy yourselves. Judy, would you be terribly offended if I went back tonight? I would like to get ready for tomorrow, you know, uniform to press, shoes to polish."

"Of course not, Sharon, just come back soon. I'll run you back whenever you say. Thanks for giving up most of your weekend. Your room is always here for you."

"I can give you a lift back, Sharon, I'm going back to HQ this evening, anyway. Judy, can you keep in until tomorrow? I'll ring you in the morning. I may need you to help me with a press conference. It might stop them swarming all over here, but you will have a guard here for several more days."

They finished their tea, and Sharon packed a small case, and they left together. Judith went and luxuriated in a hot bath, and then put some food down in the pantry, and cooked herself a pasta dish. She wrote letters in the library, and then let in Dawn and Bert, when they relieved the two day shift officers. They checked the house, and she wrote some more letters, and then the three of them played cards for a while. Bert and Dawn played chess, and Judith finished her letters. She went to bed and read for a while, before sleeping heavily and deeply, through the night.

Much refreshed, she rose early and made coffee for all three of them, and they all prepared breakfast and managed to clear it away, before Mary and Nora arrived. Wesley came soon afterwards and Bert and Dawn left. Judith asked that all four of them have a chat, and suggested to Mary that she was cooking far beyond the original meals anticipated, and asked if she could do with an assistant. Mary agreed that extra help would be useful. Mary suggested one of Mr Sandell's daughters, who had just finished catering college and was a pleasant girl with whom she could happily work. Judith asked Nora to fix it and see if the girl was interested.

She then asked Wesley if he needed an assistant, as he too was taking on more than they had anticipated. Wesley agreed and said he knew just the person, who lived nearby. He said he would enquire. Nora had moved in to the South Lodge, and asked if Sam could come and fix a dripping tap. Stuart and Sam turned up with the rest of the staff, and Judith then asked all the staff if the press had bothered any of them over the weekend. Bill explained just what he had said to a nosy reporter and they all laughed. Judith took Sam on one side, with Stuart, and said,

"Sam, I am more than happy with what you are doing, but I think you are doing too much. I need your carpentry skills more than your driving skills, and the recent events have proved that we also need someone else as well, to share in the driving and to help with general jobs around the place. Stuart, what do you think?"

Stuart agreed, and asked if they could also be garden friendly, and able to help out with things like packing, fruit picking, and vehicle maintenance. He also asked for a small van to move things with. Judith agreed and they discussed what to get. They went to find Wesley and Judith made some calls.

Jake called about an hour later and Judith gave him tea, and thanked him for coming.

"Jake, I wonder if you could help me. From what you were saying the other day, you are pretty close to retirement. You will know others who are, too. I am looking for a driver, handyman, security advisor, and general helper. Do you know anyone about to retire, who might be interested?"

Jake replied, "Would there be a house with the job? What sort of pay would you be offering?"

Judith said, "The accommodation offered would be the North Lodge, two bedrooms, medium garden." She named a salary, and what benefits went with the job.

"When would you want them to start?"

"As soon as possible, when we find the right person."

"I would be interested, very interested, if you would consider me. I have over thirty years in, and a load of leave owing. I was just waiting for a job with a house to turn up. Could you consider me?"

"Jake, I was rather hoping you would say that. Can you work under Stuart and with Sam? If you can, the job is yours."

Jake left, promising to be in touch. Dennis rang and asked her to be ready in an hour and she would be picked up. She went to sort some things with Wesley, and asked Liam to post a load of letters for her. She put some quite smart clothes on, and mentally thanked Ingrid for making her buy them. Whatever else Ingrid was, she had excellent taste in clothes. She wondered how Ingrid was coping, with finding out about Francis. They would be in desperate trouble, and she considered helping them, but wondered how any gesture on her part would be received.

She put on make–up, brushed her hair and went down to see Wesley, who gave a wolf whistle as she came in.

"Judy, you have legs! You look good, very smart. I've got hold of that person and she is interested in the job when do you think you will be available to interview? Nora says any time this week, for Mr Sandell's daughter, Rachel, who she says is really keen. Do you want me to take notes at the interviews? It might be easier if we do them on the same afternoon."

"Actually, Wesley, I would like you to do the interviews. I'll sit in, if you don't mind, but you know what we want, especially so far as your own assistant is concerned. Could we put her in the room next to the dining room, as the general estate office? If she is suitable, let her choose the colour scheme, but you choose the furniture. I'll leave you to get the office equipped. She could have the switchboard in there I am also taking on Jake Falls, the policeman, when he retires next month, to help Sam, and be in charge of security. He will have the North Lodge, unless you want it to live in? No, I didn't think you did. Wes, you already know there are a lot more properties than just this estate. The pub and seventeen houses in the village to start with, not to mention properties in Leeds, and all over Britain. I cannot expect you to deal with all of them, as well as this estate. Cummings had his dirty paws on them, but I have to find someone to handle them. I wondered, could you deal with the pub and the houses in the village if you take an assistant on? The other properties will need some thought. I don't know enough about that kind of thing. If only Cummings had been honest. Any suggestions?"

Wesley sucked on his pencil, and then sat back. He looked at her, and commented,

"I'll think on it, and see you tomorrow. Can we do the interviews on Wednesday?"

"Yes, that is fine with me. Find out if we need bigger cookers, or better kitchen equipment, will you? Could you find me an art expert, mainly oils, and a few water colours, who can clean and restore pictures. I'll need a valuation on quite a lot. Also, I need a wine expert."

"The art expert, I'll work on, the wine expert is simple. Talk to Mr McDuff. I believe he is the man for round about. I'll give him a ring. He rang earlier, most concerned about you, and I said there was no news. He was quite distressed, and I said I'd let him know. Can I ring him and tell him, and ask him to come over, maybe on Wednesday as well? OK, tell me where you are off to, and will you be out all day? I am dying to know. I take it you are no longer dead, and will be resurrected?"

"I am going into town for a press conference, and then I am being taken out for dinner. I have no idea when I will be back. I shall be in safe hands, I assure you. Which reminds me, did you get the digital camera?"

"Yes, do you want to take it with you?"

"No, I want a photo of everyone who works here, and lives here, in the general office. Farm staff too, except of course, Brian Hall, and a 'rogues gallery' of us all put up in the Lost It Room, which we will now call the staff room, and everyone should have an ID badge, who visits. We need everyone working here knowing who should, and shouldn't, be in the grounds. Can you keep a photo of everyone on the files, please? Could you ask poor Reg Hall, and his wife, if she wants to come, to come and see me tomorrow morning? They must be wondering what I expect them to do. They may even hate my guts. I want you and Jim in on that too, please, Wes. Can you fix it? Best through Jim, I think"

Judith just had time to grab her bag before a nice young policeman picked her up in a plain car, and drove her to town, to the headquarters, to meet Dennis. Over coffee, Dennis explained that the conference was not for another hour and asked a favour. He wanted Judith to confront Brian Hall in a corridor. Brian believed her to be dead, or near dead, as all the prisoners did. Dennis thought that seeing her in the flesh, might unnerve him sufficiently to make him tell them everything. He was, he explained, trying to bargain with them for information, but he, Dennis, was in no mood to be bargained with.

"Neither am I. Can I say nothing to the poisonous little snake? I won't threaten or intimidate him, I promise. I don't want him getting away with anything. Has he had a bath yet, or does he still stink?"

"He'll get one when he gets remanded. He has been offered several. His dad wouldn't come near him, washed his hands of him, and won't have him back. We have obtained a secure placement, and the court will not let him back within fifty miles of you. Mrs Hall is here, but she isn't much help to him or us. Social Services are here, and he has his own brief. The video evidence we have, plus the mike tapes, are pretty damning. We have charged him, and are holding him on burglary, drug possession, and conspiracy to murder, at the moment, but we want to hit him with attempted murder after you confront him. It might shake him enough for him to say more."

"Let's do it then, I am going to enjoy this, quite a lot. Is his solicitor there?"

"Yes. All we have ever said to him is that you are injured, which is, of course, true. Hall hasn't seen the video or heard the tapes yet, but his brief has. Hall is convinced you will never be able to give evidence. His brief has just been in with him, and may talk some sense into him. Hall is an arrogant lad and thinks we cannot prove anything without you. The video, even with infra red, is dark, and the tapes middling, but with you to prove them, they are dynamite. Without you, we would have no more than a good case. The brief only knows that we believe you will live. Are you ready?"

They went down to the cell block, and waited silently outside an interview room. Before long, the door opened further on, and they were just 'walking by', as a constable waiting outside the room walked down the corridor towards them with Brian, the solicitor, and a social worker. They had to stand aside, as Dennis and two other officers ushered Judith past. She stopped and looked Brian in the face. She saw him go white and start to shake. He screamed, covered his face and shrank back. The solicitor looked at Dennis, who quietly said,

"As you see, Mrs Swallow will make a full recovery and remembers everything. Put him back in the detention room, please, officer!"

They walked on and went into another room, where Dennis shut the door. Judith sat down, and said,

"I really enjoyed that, I mean **really** did. There is a God! Thank you! I hope it has the desired effect."

They could hear Brian gibbering as he was taken away. They then went upstairs to an office, where she was offered a light lunch and coffee, which she declined. Soon Dennis took her to the conference room where the press were waiting. The flashing of lights went on for some time. Judith sat down and Dennis made a statement, which he read from a sheet of paper. Then it was her turn and she read from her paper.

"I would like to thank the police for protecting me, and my staff and property. As you can see, my injuries are not as bad as was first suspected. I am delighted to have been able to play a part in the arrest of those suspected of such serious crimes. I can say no more about the circumstances as the case is sub judice, but I will be giving evidence if required. I would ask the ladies and gentlemen of the press to respect my privacy. I have been through a traumatic time, and will say no more about the case at this time. Thank you."

"Mrs Swallow, is it true that you inherited a vast fortune from a distant relation, which brought you to Yorkshire?"

What do I say?

Tell them what you want. Just don't talk about the case.

"Yes. I inherited the estate, and live there now. I wouldn't class myself as poor."

"Is it true that your brother-in-law is involved?"

"I have no idea."

"What are your plans for Porthwaite Hall? Is it true you are employing a lot of staff? Are you going to turn it into a conference centre, or a hotel?"

"I have not yet decided what to do with it. I have employed staff who I have found to be very loyal. It will not, in the foreseeable future, be either."

"What are your injuries?"

Don't be specific, just say chest and back injuries, which is true.

"Mainly chest and back injuries."

"Are you in much pain?"

"I'm not very comfortable."

"Do you have a partner?"

"No. I am a widow."

"How much are you worth?"

"I have no idea at this time. Are you trying to chat me up? It's not a very good line."

Everybody laughed, and the man sat down. Dennis interrupted,

"That is the end of this conference. Thank you ladies, gentlemen, and the person who just sat down."

There was more laughter. Dennis got up and helped Judith out of the room. As they left, the cameras continued to flash. Once in another room, Judith could feel his anger. He turned to one of the officers and said,

"Get me the editor of that offensive little jerk's paper! I want words. Judy, that was brilliant. Are you all right? Can I leave you in this officer's hands while I sort a few things out? I'll be tied up for at least a couple of hours. Is there anything you want?"

"Yes, I'd like to go shopping for a few things. I haven't been to a town for ages. I need some clothes. Am I safe to go out? I doubt if anyone will recognise me this quick."

"Yes, I can lend you Dawn and a driver. Where do you want to go?"

"A sports shop, an outdoor clothes shop, a department store and a computer shop, just for starters. Sorry, but there are things I need. I would have got them last week but I was dead!"

"If the press spot you, come back, just stay out of trouble!" *That pays me back. Just be discreet. No winding people up! This think talk is quite useful. How far does it reach?*

I have no idea. Just trust me.

That's what worries me. See you later.

They lent her a different jacket, and Dawn went with her to the shops. She bought underwear, wellington boots, waterproof leggings, tee shirts, a crash helmet, warm socks, some trainers, a new stick, some knitting wool and needles and pattern, a selection of balls from the sports shop, and then went to a music shop, where she purchased the best clarinet she could buy, which she was assured was concert quality. When she presented her platinum credit card, the manageress asked her to come into an office. Dawn went in with her. The manageress explained that she knew the holder of the card was critically ill in hospital, and they would have to wait for the police. Dawn explained that she was the police, but it took a telephone call to the control room before she was believed. Dennis spoke to the manageress, who apologised, but Judith thanked her for her vigilance. As they left, Dawn and Judith laughed, and they headed back to the headquarters.

They went up to the canteen to wait for Dennis. Judith invited Dawn to the house, any time she wanted to come out. Dawn was fun and they laughed a lot. Judith heard Dennis coming before he came in.

I knew you'd get into trouble somehow! You're quite incorrigible. Fancy trying to buy a clarinet, when you are meant to be dead! You don't play one, do you?

Dennis came into the room and Dawn made a quick getaway. He looked at Judith and laughed and then asked where all her shopping was. She indicated a large pile in the corner of the canteen and he said he would have it delivered that night. He asked if she still wanted to go out, and she asked if that was how he normally treated the victims of crime.

"No, not at all. I do need to talk to you, and tell you what has transpired, but more essentially, I find you good fun, and would enjoy an evening in your company. Please don't turn me down, I'd be devastated!"

"Have you not got a wife to go home to?"

"No. We got divorced years ago. Don't send me home to an empty house. I shall feel obliged to do some gardening. Come on, I have a table booked at a good restaurant. After we get there, I'll tell you how things have gone. Have you got what you need? Then let's go. There is a taxi waiting out the back. Let's go and eat."

The taxi took them way out of town to a pleasant village, and a

222

large pub. It was quite crowded, and they were shown into a posh restaurant. The food was excellent and the wine better. Dennis told Judith that Brian had gone quite to pieces and had told everything he knew, which had been most helpful. Cummings had been charged, and had also come clean about the whole matter, and had admitted trying to falsely implicate Judith. Cummings' wife had been very uncooperative, and had tried to rely on her wealthy father to bail her out, and was shocked when he couldn't, or wouldn't. The man who had shot at her from the cave had initially said nothing, but when presented with evidence, admitted everything. The Dutchman with him had also admitted his involvement, and had turned round and provided a great deal of information about currency, diamonds and drugs. Two other members of the gang had been connected to, and charged with, the murder of the security guard. He added that Customs and Excise had seized a lot of drugs, and were working, as he was, with Interpol. Numerous further arrests had been made, and he admitted it was the biggest case he had ever dealt with. Several guns had been seized and had been sent for forensic tests.

Dennis went on,

"The diamonds were from a heist at Hatton Garden three months ago. There are about six missing from the set, the six best ones. They were all clear brilliant diamonds, several carats, but someone must have taken them out en route. There is a considerable reward for that, and it should be coming to you, after all, you recovered it. What are you going to spend it on?

"I would like half of it to go to the security guard's family, and the other half to go to the Police Dependants' Trust Fund. I don't want it. Can you arrange that for me?"

"That's generous of you. How are you feeling? Really? Because you took a hell of a kicking. Judy, I do want to thank you, you were so brave. I should never have asked you to do what you did. Mr Elgar has almost roasted me alive over it. I told him you were special, and the only reason he hasn't had my guts for garters is because you are all right and the whole thing is likely to make us look very, very good. Mr Elgar wants to meet you and thank you personally. I loved the way you dealt with that reporter today. I spoke with his editor and he is back to reporting the auction prices at the Cattle and Sheep Marts. Remind me not to cross swords with you too often."

They moved from the soup to the fish course. Judith went for whitebait, and Dennis for salmon.

"Dennis, please tell me, what is the score with Cummings? How did he get involved? Do you think I'll get my money back? What about his other clients? Tell me."

"Right, I will. He is pathetic. He reckons his wife, who is a first class bitch, by the way, introduced him to cocaine about nine years ago, up at the Country Club. He got hooked, and his supplier blackmailed him into getting involved. They needed him, and your place. Miss Holt was very old, and there were a lot of empty and unvisited properties there. His problem was that he couldn't keep his habit under control and they overstretched themselves with their house. She sent the kids to expensive schools, and he couldn't pay for the house, the schools, their expensive hobbies, and the mortgage, and their habits, so he started 'borrowing' from a few of his clients. Miss Holt was an obvious choice, as were a few others. He invested very unwisely with Francis Heldman, who he had been at school, and then at University, with. Heldman was the one who targeted Cummings, and I believe is behind the whole thing. Of course, Heldman didn't really invest it unwisely, he just said he had, to keep Cummings in line and put the pressure on him."

"It all went well until Miss Holt died and you and your husband inherited. Cummings knew better than to muck with the inheritance tax assessors, but you may find some valuable things secreted, he admits to hiding some pictures, which he intended to steal from the house. He says your husband, Clive? was pretty astute and suspected something, so he paid up the outstanding amounts by borrowing and being pulled into the currency scam, and the diamonds. By this time he was in up to his neck. He and Heldman tried to put you off, and hoped to buy the estate cheap, and then sell it off at a massive profit, once they had finished their business there. Then the unexpected happened, you were involved in the crash. Because you had inherited jointly, the estate reverted to you. They didn't know Clive was so rich, they had no idea of his foreign holdings. They also did some research on you, found out you had been in the police, and assumed you didn't know anything about business and that you could be put off. More fool them. When did you first smell a rat?"

"I'm not sure. Clive said there was something strange and he didn't think everything was quite right, and he took a dislike to Cummings. He was going to sort it out when we got up here. He dealt with all the finances, I just knew he was well off, not how rich he was. I had no idea! When I went down for Clive's funeral, I was warned there was something up by Jack Gough, Clive's uncle. Heldman was so charmingly concerned, and it didn't ring true. I always thought he was a creep. I don't like his wife, Ingrid, much, either. She was just greedy and grasping. You can tell a lot from people's children, I think. Their kids are so grasping as to be obnoxious. Everyone seemed to be so keen on my **not** coming up here, it made it important that I did. At the time, I had to find something to hang on to, an aim. I had lost not only Clive, but our baby. I needed to find out for myself. Then Cummings didn't keep in touch when I asked him to, and I started getting cross."

Dennis poured some wine when the main course arrived. It gave Judith time to get her sorrow under control. She knew he could read it, and had to be careful. They ate in silence, and then he said,

"Go on, you started getting cross."

"Yes, at first I thought I was just confused, and I didn't understand how things should work, so I did a bit of homework. I was a bit emotionally fragile at the time. Chatterton's visit unnerved me a lot, but I never connected it. I even thought I might be getting a bit paranoid. I had time to think and decided to come up here. I wanted Cummings to provide an explanation, and wanted to believe him. I'd had a tough time, and hoped I had got it wrong. When I got here and saw the state of the place, I started to get angry. By this time, I knew I had more than enough money to do what I wanted, and I admit I did want to rattle Cummings' cage. I had planned to keep my cool. I had no idea what I was getting into. I saw, just too late, that he was on something. He was such a lying, patronising lump of lard, and he had the best clothes, on what I assumed was **my** money, that I did go a bit OTT. I got him to lose control, and when he belted me, I thought that was the end of the matter."

She paused, drank some more wine, and he refilled her glass. She ate a little more steak, and then continued,

"From then on, things were rather taken out of my hands. You know the rest. What has been fuelling me isn't bravery, it is sheer anger. I don't like being taken for a ride. The money is no longer important to me, but life is. I have made good friends here already and I think I can make a difference. I will bring the estate up to scratch, and I have plans for it. I just want to be left alone to do it. I'm not stupid, just determined. I never asked for all this money, it is a hell of a responsibility. I could give it all away, but I would never know how much good I could do with it, unless I tried. A lot of people depend on me now. I won't let them down. If I fall to pieces, then they will suffer. I have learned, much too late, that anger can fuel you, but it doesn't help much in some situations, like that reporter today. I hope I didn't go too far, but he got up my nose, yours too. Can I have a pudding? I don't know why I am so hungry, but I am."

Dennis laughed, and asked the waiter for the sweet menu.

"Judy, you can have a dozen sweets if you like. You have explained a lot, but not quite everything. There are several things I do not understand. I know you don't want to talk about it, but how the hell did you find out about some of the things you knew? It was almost as if you could see things, when you were not there. I had no idea that I was telepathic, but you knew. How? I've tried to find out a bit in the last few days, and you can do things others cannot. So apparently, can I, and Sharon. I believe it, only because I have to. I'll never admit to it, except to you and Sharon. I have often wondered why I could hear what some people were thinking, and it did give me an edge sometimes. I never knew what it was, but now I do. You, however, can do more than that. This telekinesis thing is amazing, but you made a mistake. There was no opportunity for you to swap the bullets back. When we checked the gun, the original bullets were back in the packet. The cartridge we found was one of our blanks all right, and the others in the rifle, but the spares were original. Oh, don't worry, I have covered it, but it would help if I could have the remaining blanks back."

Judith, choosing between a pavlova and a creme brulee, replied,

"But I did have time, you gave it to me, remember? After you asked me to lie back down. That's why I was so knackered in the ambulance, it wasn't all acting. You shall have your blanks back. I'll get them tomorrow. Can I have both sweets?"

"Of course. You wouldn't like to tell me where they are, I suppose?"

"You suppose right! I'll go for the creme brulee first. I cannot tell you any more Dennis and I never will. You just have to accept, Lothario, that there are more things in heaven and earth, than are dreamed of in your philosophy! Now I have something to ask you."

"Go ahead."

"Two things, actually. First, I've offered Jake Falls a job. Partly security, and general driving, and general handyman. He is going to move in to the North Lodge. He is due to retire. Could you ease it for him?"

"Yes, we served together several times, and you've made a good choice. It might solve a problem for me, too. You will need some security from us for a while, I could get him in for us, first, and then you can take over as his employer. What's the other question?"

"Are you ever going to tell anyone about the 'think talk'?"

"No. They would think I was nuts. How could I explain?"

"Exactly, so don't ask me to. I shall deny it, and if you are sensible, so will you."

"You realise this case will go on for ever? You will give evidence, won't you? I am afraid the press will now be fascinated by you. We'll do our best to help."

"Yes, I know. You will keep in touch, let me know the twists and turns?"

"Judy, I hope we will always be in touch, even when the case is over. Can I come and see you, just to be sociable, and to invite you out

226

occasionally? Anyway, I need to raid your garden and I want to help with your rose garden."

Judith laughed, "Just remember, I shall see everything you do, I see everything round there! You can't surprise me."

"No, but it won't stop me trying. Would you like a liqueur?"

Judith and Dennis spent the rest of the evening talking and laughing. He sent her home in a traffic car with her shopping, a lovely bunch of roses, and an orchid plant for the conservatory.

Chapter Fifteen

Goy, Garr can we talk? I have lots to tell you, and I need your help again.

Garr always hear. You are happy. More warm in heart. Niss make you happy. We hear you on box that speak and flicker. Men in house talk. Garr listen.

I can relax a bit. I think the worst is over. Yes, I enjoyed myself last night. Niss is good to be with. Zood miss Garr.

Garr here for Zood. How Garr help Zood?

You remember the bullets that you took to the cave, and took back after man fire stick that bang? I need them back, all that are left.

Niss take some. Others Niss man take with stick that bang, Zood want others? Garr give Zood under. Soon. Zood open wood.

Zood be there soon. I have gift for Garr young.

Judith took the bag of balls down to the cellar, unlocked the trap door, opened it, lit a candle, and put out the light. She waited and soon several Garr came into the basement, including far more young than she had ever seen before. She emptied the balls and some other toys onto the floor and for half an hour the young Garr romped round with the balls. Several of the older Garr were examining a Rubic cube and other such toys. Goy approached Judith and touched her.

Goy thank Zood. Zood give pleasure to Garr. Zood want this?

Goy passed a leather pouch, containing the blank bullets to Judith. They were clean and dry. She tipped them into a carrier bag, without touching them and handed the pouch back to Goy.

Thank you Garr. Zood grateful. People will come to basement to take pictures and wine and other things. Niss may come, be careful, he is beginning to hear quite well. Also Zaron. I will have to lock the wood, as people will be arriving soon.

She detached a small Garr from around her neck and handed it to one of the older warrior Garr. The baby was dark grey, with silver fur. It looked like a little dragon. She stroked it and it stirred.

Garr put round things in net, or take them with you?

The small Garr took about half the balls and went down the well with them. The others were put in the net, which was hidden in an old wardrobe. Goy and another kept the cubes.

Goy keep box? Garr keep box?

Zood bring for Garr. Keep it, Zood get more. Garr like?

Garr like. Speak later.

They disappeared and Judith locked the trap door and covered it with an old carpet. She had enjoyed the time spent with the Garr. She took the bullets and locked them in her safe. She met Nora as she came in and they had a coffee together. Stuart arrived, and Judith asked him how to care for the orchid. They took it to the conservatory, and he planted it for her, and said he would care for it. He told her it was rare, and very precious, and asked her if she would like some others. He was dying to know where she had acquired it, but he forgot it when he saw the roses she had been given. He almost drooled over them. She asked Haley to arrange them in her bedroom.

Liam was quite excited and hugged her warmly when he came in. Bill told her about his brush with the press, and Dot and Betty asked her what she wanted them to do in the new estate office. Wesley went with them, and soon everyone was busy.

Jim came in with Reg, and they sat, in Judith's sitting room with Wesley and Nora. Reg looked drawn and old and very uncomfortable. He stared at the floor and said,

"Mrs Swallow, I just don't know what to say. I am horrified at what Brian has done, and I can't see what I can do to put it right. Me missus has gone to be with him, but she don't like him much. I had no idea he was in with them folk. All I ask is that you give me time to find a new place before I leave. I told Mr Morpeth here I was handing in me notice yesterday, but he said I should come and see you personal. Will you accept my resignation? I just can't stand the shame."

"Reg, Jim speaks highly of you, and your skills. You have worked here for some years, well and faithfully. Any parent can have a child go wrong. It is true, I have no love for Brian, I think he is a very unpleasant young man. He also tried to help kill me. I wouldn't, even if I could, withdraw charges, but I do see that drugs is part of his problem. I have asked you to come in and see me, for several reasons. The main one is to say I do not blame you, as I know you to be honest and hard working, and good at your job. I do not want you to leave and you could help me more by staying on. The second reason is that I have, as you know, offered private health care to staff and their families. This includes Brian. When he has been released from custody, whenever that is, if he agrees to it, and if it helps, I will pay for him to go to a clinic to treat his addiction. When he spoke to me last week, I know it was a ruse to get me down to the lake, but a lot of what he said had a ring of sincerity to it. I do not, however, want him back on this estate. Another reason is, you must be going through hell, and your wife. Can I help in any way? You need some leave, have a break for a while. Jim, can you find someone else to take on Reg's duties for a while, a temporary worker, perhaps?"

Reg sat looking in his lap. His head came up and he looked at her. He said,

"It might help, but Brian has bled us dry. He has stolen from us, and we just can't afford to go anywhere, but I would accept the time off. Just a few days. To come to terms with the whole thing. We could go to my sister's, over in Lancashire, or maybe my brother, in Dumfries."

Jim said,

"Reg, I think you need a decent break, this has really knocked you up. You haven't had one in four years. I'll lend you some money to go away for a fortnight, if you like. Go to the seaside, or something. Get away, while you can. We can sort the money out after. Mrs Swallow will give you holiday pay, I'm sure."

Judith nodded,

"I'll do more than that. My staff, all of you, have been there for me, and have helped me when I was in trouble. The very least I can do is return the compliment. All I ask is that you don't leave me in the lurch. Reg, I need you, but not feeling guilty and depressed. Can you talk with Jim and pick a decent holiday, somewhere away from here, from all this mess. The estate will pay because we value you and want you back here. You have stuck with the estate for years, and Jim says you have put in many extra hours. I feel it is time we paid you back. Let's call it a stress break. The press will be hanging around, which won't help, so why don't you go to Majorca, or somewhere like that, get away? Brian will be on remand for a while, and if you take the mobile, you can keep in touch."

Jim added,

"Yes, it's a good idea. You enjoyed it when you went to Greece five years ago, why not go somewhere like that?"

Reg shifted uncomfortably in his seat.

"My son tries to kill you, and you give me a holiday? It don't seem quite right to me. How could I ever repay you? You have already put up my wages, and the house is being redecorated. I was beginning to think that we could be all right, if we could solve the problem of Brian. I don't want no charity, mind."

"It isn't charity, Reg, it is being part of the team. Mrs Swallow actually values her good workers, and looks after them. If you want, you can repay her by coming back, and working as hard as you usually do, and maybe a bit extra. You can help out in the gardens sometimes, you could do some of your wood carvings for her to sell when we start the farm shop, things like that. Things have changed since Mrs Swallow took over. Let her help," Jim pleaded.

"Jim, can you sort this out with Reg? Just tell Wesley what you come up with, and he will arrange it. Reg, I am so sorry you have had this problem, but together we can try to make the best of it. You are always welcome at the house, thank you for coming to see me. Have a break, and when you come back, this will no longer be in the news, and we can try to help Brian."

Judith and Wesley left and Jim talked for a while to Reg. They went back to the farm. Wesley said he had contacted the art expert, who would be sending someone out that afternoon to look at the paintings. He asked where they were, and Judith said could he find Sam and Liam, to get them up into the ball room. Wesley zoomed off in his chair to do so, and Judith went down to the cellar. Soon, Haley, Dot and Betty came down and were joined by Stuart, Sam and Liam, and then Lucy and June. Nora came down too, and they carefully took all the pictures, in their boxes, up in the lift from the basement, and put them in the ball room. There were dozens of boxes, and many more loose pictures. Dot dusted those she could and Haley gave a shriek when a small spider ran out of one of the boxes. Judith picked up the offending arachnid, and put it out of the door, onto the terrace and told it not to come back.

"Do you know, that is the first spider I have seen since I got here? I haven't even seen a cobweb, which is very surprising. I wonder why?"

Garr eat. Tasty.

You eat spiders? What else do you eat?

She was shown earwigs, cockroaches, grass hoppers, dragon flies, blue bottles and maggots. She shivered.

They arranged the pictures on chairs and left the room. Wesley asked to talk to Judith and she went to his office. He gave her a sheaf of messages, and they went through them. Several were from the press, asking for interviews, and there were messages from Clive's mother, two from Ingrid, and one from Ruth. Mike and Uncle Jack had asked her to ring, and so had Tom Barker. Celia had said she was visiting and Dr Tippett had said he was calling that afternoon. Mr Wynn wanted an appointment and the vicar had called. They wrote out the diary. He said,

"I have given the matter of the management of the properties some thought and wondered if I could run a zany idea by you. Until Cummings mucked up, the firm had a good reputation. Mr Wynn is devastated, and I hear the firm is going under. He is going to retire. The other partner, Simon Porter, is going to try and set up on his own. He will get tainted by the whole thing, and will find it difficult to get business. I wondered, if you talked to him, if you couldn't use him. I don't think he would let you down. I can understand if you don't want to, but it could work."

"Wesley, you are a genius! Can you make an appointment with Mr Wynn and Mr Porter, as soon as they can come? I wondered if we couldn't start our own company, and they might be interested. Invite them to lunch, and fix it with Nora. Better invite Tom, and Celia too.

I'll need to write some business letters soon if this woman you're thinking of taking on is suitable, I could do it with her. Any luck with Stuart's van yet? Is the Landrover arriving soon? When we have them, they can all go to the signwriters. Can we book a morning together some time soon, so I can sign things, and you can bring me up to date? I think I have neglected you a bit, and you have been coping so well. Are you still enjoying yourself?"

"Yes, I love it. You said it was on a two–month trial, but I want to make it permanent. Once it is, I want to ask Sonia to marry me, if she'll have me. She is a nurse, and with our combined wages we can get a mortgage, especially if we live together in my flat. I thought I would tell you first, but I wondered, could I bring her out here, to ask her? It is the loveliest place I know, and I want it to be right"

"Of course you can, tell me when, and I'll make myself scarce. I'll leave you a bottle of champagne, so if she says yes, you can celebrate! Stay over if you want to. I think, if you want to stay, we will make it permanent now. I certainly cannot cope without you. You have proved yourself to me. Tell me, what is your ultimate ambition? Do you want your own company, or a managerial role?"

"A month ago, all I wanted was a job. Now I want to be good at it, and my ambition? I want to run this place, and see it become a thriving business, with a shop, nursery, and open to the public. Personally, I want my own place, and to be with Sonia and start a family. You have made it seem more than a dream. Given a choice, I'll be around a long time. Can you stand it?"

"Yes, but all I have done is open a door. You are the one who can make the dream come true. You can also help me realise mine. Enough of this, it must be nearly lunch time. I will need you to do an inventory of the pictures, so let's have a break. Thank you, Wes, I have been through the mill recently, and you have thrown me a lifeline, keeping things running for me."

"Judy, what are you going to do, once things are running smoothly? Have you a special project in mind ? Something you have always wanted to do, but never had the time or money? You will need something, you know. I have my music, Sonia likes embroidery. Nora has the Parish Council, Sally her music. Stuart his roses, Sam likes tinkering with cars, I could go on. What do you want?"

"Wes, I don't know. I'll think about it. You're quite right, I was thinking about it the other day. I'll have to talk to Jim."

They reached the kitchen, just as the dinner gong went. After the meal, Judith went round the house, looking at all the pictures that were already hanging. There were only a few she actually liked and very few she felt she could live with. She hoped that some in store were more to her taste. The doorbell went and Betty showed in a middle–aged, very thin, grey–haired, short woman, who was wearing very 'arty' clothes. She had a bubbly personality, and asked where the pictures were. She accepted a cup of tea, with a tiny bit of milk and four sugars, and then Wesley and Judith took her to the ballroom. Sam and Liam helped to unpack the pictures. The woman, Tanya Harbottle, began to get very excited very soon, and as more pictures were unpacked, she said,

"I think these are incredibly valuable. If they are genuine, then we need someone more expert than me. Some of these were believed to have been lost decades ago. Do you have any provenance for them, are there records as to how they were brought here? I will need some help cataloguing them, I'd like to ring someone in London, if I may?"

She went with Wesley to his office, made a call, and came back, and together they looked at more of the paintings. She was making copious notes, and so Judith went to the library, and started looking, for the first time, through a set of shelves where she saw old ledgers. After an hour or so, she found a file of receipts and letters relating to the paintings. They were addressed to Miss Elsie I Garreton. They documented many of the pictures. At the back of the file, she found more, addressed to Agatha Eccles. There were a few more recent ones naming Susan Holt. She took them to Tanya, who examined them carefully.

"Mrs Swallow, this seems to be what we need. You have a priceless collection here, if they are really what I believe them to be. Are you looking to sell? Whatever you do, they should be in a gallery, and in safe keeping at least. Yes, they need cleaning and restoring, but this has to be the find of the century. There are a few modern ones, like the two Lowry ones over there, but most of them are before the turn of the century. There is a good Picasso there, and several Van Dykes, if I am not mistaken. There are three Cezannes, and that is as far as I have got. I'll get a couple of experts to come and look at them. It will take some weeks, is there anywhere near here that they could stay. A local Inn?"

"Yes indeed, the Gargoyle, in the village."

"Could we shut them away until the experts arrive? I feel quite nervous around them. You should put an armed guard on them."

She was quivering with excitement. They carefully packed the paintings up under her direction, and they were placed back in the basement. Tanya was very worried about their security, and asked if there was an alarm, but Judith assured her they were quite safe. Judith asked for her opinion of the pictures hanging in the house, and they went round looking at them. Tanya said some of them were quite valuable, one or two were very valuable, but the rest were modest copies. They looked at the big picture of a view of the Dales on the wall in the drawing room. Judith said,

"To be honest, I don't care much for it. Is it at all valuable?"

Tanya looked closely at it, and then looked at it from the other side of the room. As Judith waited she looked at the picture, properly, for the first time. Something didn't ring true with the picture. Tanya said,

"There is something wrong with this. I think this picture has been painted over another, much older one. It might be a lost master. It is very large. We ought to get it X-rayed. How interesting."

Picture of Garr. Garr show Zood.

She saw the picture through Garr eyes, and it was a very accurate scene of all the different types of Garr, in moonlight by the lake, with the Folly in the background. There were two types of Garr Judith did not recognise.

Do you know how old it is?

Made when Charles king. Guardian paint. Elders remember. Guardian killed by men. In battle. Garr sing. Garr honour.

I have not met all of you yet, have I?

Zood not know mother Garr or Garr who make metal.

Will I meet them?

Zood will.

Judith turned to Tanya

"This painting will never be sold, or lent out. I want it restored back to its original, and hung upstairs in my bedroom. It is a fantasy, I think. I don't want anyone but you to do it. I don't want it seen by any experts. Could you do it?"

"Yes, it will take a while, and might be a bit expensive. Could I have a room to work in here?"

"Yes. There are many to choose from."

Are there any other paintings of the Garr?

Four. Garr show Zood.

Judith was shown two smaller pictures, both rural scenes, in the dining room, and another large one, in the old master bedroom on the first floor, which was painted over as a hunting scene. The last was a small still life on the landing.

"There are four others I want you to look at especially. I think they are painted over too. Come and see."

She took Tanya to see all four pictures. Each of them looked 'wrong' when they were examined. As they walked round, Judith grew to like this talented, flamboyant woman. She was funny and very perceptive. Judith asked her to stay for a light tea and they discussed all the pictures. Tanya told her that if they were genuine, they would be worth millions, and asked what she would do with them.

"I haven't a clue. To be honest, I'm not that keen on most of the ones I have seen, and I don't have the facilities to display them properly here. I might sell quite a few, and lend the others to galleries and exhibitions. I want to keep those five for my own rooms, and I would like the Lowry ones on display in the public part of the house. If I sold some, could I buy a Jackson Pollock or a Hockney, do you think? I will keep some, but I hate to think of all of them stuck away where no one can see them. I will select the ones I want to keep and sell some. Would any of the local galleries be interested in exhibiting some of them, do you think?"

"I should say. Some of the smaller galleries would get put on the map, and would pay you a good hiring fee for old masters. Can the experts come up this week? When I rang, they were all set to fly up from London to Leeds/Bradford today. They would need three or four rooms to work in. I will be quite honest, and tell you I would get a hefty finder's fee, if they sell some. I would also charge you for restoring the five you have picked out so far. I won't touch water colours, I would have to send them away, and above all, sell them one at a time, not all together."

"How long will you take to restore the five?"

"About three months, give or take a month, working four days a week, every morning, and some afternoons. I'd quote you per picture, not by the hour."

"If, for example, there was a very unusual subject revealed, could you keep it to yourself?"

"I think, somehow, you saw what was under that one in the drawing room. I saw your face change. It was like you were listening to something far away. You saw something I didn't. Yes, of course I will keep it quiet, you would be paying me to restore and clean them, not talk about them. You know, I've been longing to meet you. You're all over the papers, quite a heroine, in fact. You've been having an exciting time, haven't you?"

"Yes, a bit too exciting! I must look at the papers. When could you start, if you want the job?"

"Want it? I should say! I'd love it. I could start this week if you like. I'll give you an estimate tomorrow. Could I look at some of the rooms, see where the best light is? I hate to say, but some of the pictures you have around need re-framing. I could do that, if you want."

"Yes, that is why I wanted your advice. The staff here all have lunch during the day. Do you live locally? You would be welcome to join us. Just let Wesley or Nora know when you will be here. We have to be a bit security conscious, and I like the place to myself in the evenings. What tools and equipment will you need, and what furniture? Let Wes know, and he will order it for you."

"Mrs Swallow, there is one thing. I would want the work rooms locked when I'm not here. I would do the cleaning and would be responsible for them. Obviously you would need a key, but I don't want anyone touching anything. Would that be acceptable?"

"Good idea. Have a look around, at the bedrooms. Could your experts use the attic rooms? You might like to look at the rooms above the library. Tell me which ones you want, and what you want done. We have a few house rules for everyone here. If you go out in the grounds, which you are welcome to do, you take a radio or mobile with you. No one goes out alone after dark. No one swims or goes on the lake alone. We need a photo of you, so the staff know you. You comply with Health and Safety, and while here, you repeat nothing you hear, unless I say. Any problems with that? OK. Do you want to call those experts and get them up? I am interviewing tomorrow afternoon, and the Operatic Society meets in the house tomorrow evening. If you want help, Sam (and Jake, soon) will lift anything for you. Choose your room and I'll get a phone plugged in. You will want a music system I expect, or a radio. Do you want Wes to get one for you?"

"I'll bring my own, if you don't mind. I can only work in natural light, and I would love to visit the grounds. I will need to take frequent breaks, and I am happy with your conditions. I have studied art for years, this kind of break is what everyone dreams of. I am just so thrilled. May I make that call now? I know the Gargoyle. I'll suggest they book in there. Then if I may, I'll pick my room. Where shall I find you?"

"In the kitchen or library. If you get lost, just yell."

Dr Tippett arrived as Tanya was going up the stairs. He asked to speak to Judith alone, and they went to her sitting room. He asked to see the bruises and then manipulated her leg. He took her pulse and her blood pressure.

"The Garr have been helping again, I see. Your leg is no better, you must give it time. You are using it too much. If I am to look after your health, then you must listen to me. I nearly had forty fits when I thought you were nearly dead. I rang the hospital and was a bit puzzled when they refused to let me visit, or discuss your case. I know why now. Have you any idea how worried everyone was in the village? They said prayers for you in church. This community has been turned upside down since you got here. I, for one, can do without this much excitement. You can too. Why you are as fit as you are, I have no idea, but you seem less stressed today than I have seen you yet. You are forty–four years old, and you don't want to be fighting on a daily basis.

If you don't rest the leg, I'll plaster it up again, and that will cramp your style, either that or I'll put you in a nursing home. I mean it Judy, you have to take things a bit easy. Relax a bit more, go out, meet someone you like. Why are you blushing?"

"I'm not, I'm just hot!"

"Yes, you are. I see, you have been out, and there is someone you like. Good. Oh, don't worry, I won't say anything. Just don't get hurt. A bit more looking after yourself, and a little less worrying about everyone else, is what you need. You should take a break, go away for a week, I would suggest a cruise, not a boxing tour of the prisons of England! Someone has got to tell you, and I'm the one. How are you sleeping?"

"Not very well, actually. I have been a bit on edge. I seem to wake so early. I try and spend time with the Garr, before everyone else arrives. I am discovering such exciting things about the house. I have had a lot of visitors. Wesley has been great, as has everyone."

"Talking of which, I had a reply from the States. Wesley would be a suitable candidate, and they would be prepared to treat him. Estimated cost, about one hundred thousand dollars, plus expenses. Do you want me to put it to him?"

"Will it make a lot of difference to him?"

"It could do. He could walk better, and do a lot more physically. With good aftercare, and regular exercise, he could be a lot more active. It would take about a six–week stay there, and then it would be up to him."

"Yes, go ahead. We are taking on an assistant soon, so I could cope (just) without him for a while. I'll pay all the costs, and for a holiday after. Whereabouts in the States will he be going?"

"Probably Seattle. I'm seeing him this evening. I know he has dreamed of being able to go."

"Funnily enough, we were talking of dreams this afternoon. Can you let me know?"

"Yes. Now tell me, who is the person that you like?"

"I don't know what you are talking about!"

"I'll find out, in due course! See you soon. You seem to have a visitor, so I'll go."

Judith walked to the front door with him and met Dennis coming up the steps. She introduced them and as Dr Tippett opened his car door, she saw him watching her carefully, and smiling, as she went into the house.

Dennis asked,

"Did you get them? I can't stop, but everything is going very well. Will you come to the opera with me on Thursday night? It's La

Traviata, I've got two tickets. I'll bring you back, or send you back in a taxi, if you would rather."

"Dennis, I'd love to. Don't come all the way back. You live in Skipton, I'll get a taxi from there. I'll meet you in Leeds. I can go by train. I want some shopping. Where shall we meet? At Opera North, what time, seven? Yes, I've got them, come with me. They are in the safe. Thank you for the orchid, and the roses. Stuart is dying to know where I got them from. I wouldn't tell him."

Dennis went to her sitting room and she handed over the blank bullets. He got into his car and drove away.

Niss like Zood. Zood like Niss.

I know. I'm not sure what to do about it.

Do what Zood want. Zood not hurt Garr. Zood hurt too long for mate. Have new mate, Niss. Niss would like. Zood would like. Garr would like. Zood do.

Having had her love life arranged for her, she went to find Tanya, who was talking to Nora in the hall. Tanya said she had found the perfect room, and had organised with Nora what furniture she would need. She had a key and Nora gave the other key to Judith. Tanya then said she would return in the morning with the expert team from London. She gambolled like a lamb down the steps to her estate car. It seemed very dull, when she had gone.

Nora looked at her and said, "Are you all right, you look a bit flushed?"

Judith said, "Yes, I'm fine, just a bit hot, that's all."

A marked police car drove up and Jake got out. He came over to Judith and said,

"That job, can I accept it now? I have just been posted for an indefinite period to security here. They have suggested I stay in the North Lodge. You obviously have friends in high places. Before I put my ticket in, I thought I'd check it was still open. When can I move in?"

"Jake. I hope you didn't mind. I didn't mean to go over your head. I can get it changed back, if you want?"

"I'm delighted. Thank you. My job, until I retire, is to protect you and the estate here and the staff. I am to be in plain clothes and blend in as part of the estate. I'm not officially yours for a month, but I'm here and I start on Thursday. Tomorrow is my rest day. Today I clear my paper work. Can I move in, in the morning? The lads from the shift are coming up to help, and we can use the paddy wagon. Could I have the keys, to measure up for carpets, and see if my old ones will fit, until I can get new ones."

Nora said, "Jake, I'm Nora. I live in the South Lodge. Before you go ripping up your carpets, I think you had better come and look. New carpets have been fitted throughout, and the place is equipped with all kitchen furniture. All you have to choose is the curtain fabric, and what furniture you want. You can either bring your own, or use the spare stuff in store here. Now give me a lift in that swanky police car of yours, and I'll show you. Lucy will make the curtains for you, and I will be around to help, during the morning. You and your helpers can eat here for lunch. Sam and Liam can help as well. I'll just get the keys."

She darted back into the house and returned with the keys. Jake was grinning foolishly, and they got into the car and went down the drive. Judith decided it was a day for surprises.

She made a lot of phone calls that evening. Jim came and told her that Reg had finally come round, and would be off to Greece with his wife by the weekend. Jim said he had arranged temporary cover and wanted to thank Judith.

"I think he is very close to the edge. He's been very faithful over the years, and has helped us out a lot. That boy has fleeced them for years. He doesn't understand why you are being so forgiving, and quite frankly, neither do I. Why would you want to help that nasty, murdering little, well I won't say it? If Brian ever comes near you, or me again, I'll rearrange his face in a serious way. I feel very sorry for Reg. This holiday will help him. He told me that he has had to use all his savings to make good what Brian has been taking. Wes has booked the holiday, and says you have given some spending money too. Thank you. Wes asked me if I could sit in on an interview for an assistant for him tomorrow. Yes, I can. What I want to know is, what has come over mother? She introduced me to Jake, who I knew anyway, and she is positively skittish. Have you any idea what the matter is?"

"I don't think anything is the matter, Jim. Far from it, do you mind?"

"Oh. I see. No, I don't mind. Dad's been dead a long time. He would never have wanted her to be lonely. She has given everything to help us, since before the twins were born. Wes said something about you having to talk to me about something, but he didn't know what it was. Have you time now? Mary is cooking, and wants me out from under her feet."

"Jim, there are several things I want to talk through with you. Would you like a drink? I'm going to have one. Come through to the conservatory."

They got their drinks, and went and sat down. Jim lit his pipe, and got settled.

"I'll start. Thank you for the salary rise and the back pay and the bonus. Wes explained it, and it is very fair of you. I never expected it. I think you are overpaying me. Can you explain how you came to that sum?"

"Yes. You will be taking on two farms, effectively. As a farm manager, for that acreage, you should receive what you are getting. Maybe a bit more. I am not overpaying you. I contacted the NFU to find the average for your responsibilities. You also have, or will have, seven or eight staff. I am paying what is right. Not top whack, but a bit above the average. The back pay is for the work you did over lambing, and what overtime you put in since I inherited. The bonus is for all the extra work you have done here. I need to keep you, Jim, I don't want someone tempting you away with a better offer. It is not a gift, it is your right. Anyone is worthy of his hire. You have earned it. I cannot ever pay for your friendship and support, or that of your family. That I value beyond all else. I know how worried you have been, and how hard you have worked to save this place, even when you thought I was going to take it away from you. Now, it's payback time. I won't insult you by offering you money, but I would like you to consider a partnership in the farming business with me, on a profit sharing basis. Think about it."

"I have also paid Mary what she has been owed since I inherited the estate. I have had to estimate the hours she put in, but I think I have been fair. Also your mum. She has been paid her redundancy, as she should have been, and she is now getting a proper salary. That's between her and me. Which brings me to Sally. She is a gem. Wesley tells me she is very talented, especially on the clarinet. She won't ask you, because she knows you cannot afford it, but she needs, so Wesley tells me, a decent instrument. I would like to encourage her talent, so I have got one, which I think is the one she needs. I don't want to offend you, so I offer it to you, for as long as she wants it. If she gives it up, or it isn't what she wants, the orchestra can have it. I have also paid her for the lambing she did. It isn't much, and I paid her at minimum rate. Will you take it?"

Jim smoked his pipe, and had one of his thinking sessions. "It's a gift?"

"Yes. No strings attached. For you to give to Sally. So she can develop her considerable talent. Are you offended?"

"No. I didn't realise she was that good. She is saving to go on this tour of the States next summer. We have been putting a bit aside, to help her. Even now, we cannot get her both. I accept your gift, on condition you will accept ours. It hasn't arrived yet, but it will be here in a few days. No, I won't tell you. I want it to be a surprise."

Judith fetched the clarinet and handed it to Jim, who took it. He smiled as he looked at it. His smile, she knew, was a rare event, and it lit up his face.

"What else do you want to talk about, Judy? I know there is

something. Mum told me you had something in mind. What is it?"

"Yes, it has been rattling round in my head for a while. If you take on this partnership, there are a few strings attached. For a long time, long before I came up here, I have been interested in organic farming, and also rare breeds. I would like to keep rare breeds, especially sheep, and would like to take the second farm into an organic scheme. It cannot be done overnight, and I know it probably won't be very profitable, unless we market it right. I want to breed the best tups and ewes, in several breeds. You can run your farm as a commercial enterprise, and I will finance the second one. Have you had any response to the advert for a shepherd? It's early days yet. We need the right person, and an assistant. Some of the grounds can be used. I have a fancy for Castlemilk Moorit sheep, in the meadow by the lake. In addition, I think we should get the best Suffolk sheep we can find, and breed tup lambs. When we have a farm shop running, we can market our own meat and vegetables. I believe in it and will undertake to cover any losses."

"You are talking a lot of money, lass. Are you good for it?"

"Jim, I have more money than we could ever sink into this. There is another string, and you won't like it much. I want to learn how to work on a farm. I want to help at lambing, to clip sheep, drive a tractor, feed the beasts, and even move shit. I need to have something physical to do. I have the staff to do the running of everything else. I need you to teach me what I need to do to be useful around the place. When I am learning, you will be boss, and you can swear at me, shout at me, and give me all the shitty jobs you like. If I get it wrong, you tell me straight. There will be times when I have to do things here, so it will take me a time to learn, but I want to know I can do what I ask my staff to do. All right, shoot me down in flames! Let me have another drink, before you do. Say what you think. I'm tougher than I look!"

She sat, looking suitably penitent, and apprehensive, waiting for him to go ballistic at her. After what seemed an eternity, he smiled at her and then began to laugh. Her heart sank. She knew he would be against it, but she didn't think he would ridicule her. She began to feel a little hurt, as he roared with laughter.

Man like Zood. Man want what Zood want. Man make noise of relief. Not make fun.

Judith smiled and then began to laugh too. Jim spilled his drink over himself, and sprang up, and swore emphatically and some length. He looked at her and blushed. She laughed, and it was his turn to look bashful.

"Judy Swallow, you are amazing! I think you can reach into someone's soul, and extract their inner most secrets. This plan you talk about, of organic farming and rare breeds, has always been a dream of mine, and now is the time to get into it. It needs a big capital investment, but can be profitable. You have been doing your homework, I can see that. I would love to do this, but it means a lot of work. I'll take your partnership, lass, and I'll train you to help. When you work for me, you'll get the harsh side of my tongue if you muck up. We be grand enough friends to accept harsh words from each other. You will have incentive to work, and with your disciplined background, you can take instruction. I'm a hard task master, mind!

"Tell me, did you ever do anything conventional in your life? I bet your senior officers lived in terror of you! There is no doubt we will have some real spats. You can give as good as you get. So can I. You are infinitely tougher than anyone I know. I do need to know that we will not be up to our ears in international criminals every few days, and that you are not going to be murdered every other day, and that the police are not going to take us all into protective custody every other night, but I think we can work together. Next we'll be having a major art smuggling racket based here, or illegal immigrants living in the cellar. What have I said? You've gone white! Judy, what have you done now?"

"Well, we have found some very valuable works of art in the basement, actually. I don't think they are smuggled. The experts are arriving here tomorrow. I didn't tell you, because I didn't want to worry you. Jim, don't be angry, it isn't my fault!"

"I have never, never, met the like of you in my life! You are the most troublesome, exasperating, artful female I have ever met. You sail through life, causing mayhem, chaos, and panic, wherever you go, and try to cope with the fallout on your own, never thinking that your friends are worried sick about you, and you won't let them help! Will you share some of this, or are you so selfish that you want to keep all this worry to yourself! Don't look so innocent, you know exactly what I'm talking about!"

After this, the whole exchange degenerated into a shouting match and nearly ended in blows, until Judith started laughing. Jim stood looking at her and then said,

"Witch! You provoked me! It is only because we have been so worried, and you are not good at sharing troubles, you know. I shouldn't have said what I did. Forgive me!"

Judith retorted,

"Yes, I know. I'm glad we had it out. I thought you didn't approve of me, and you have always kept your distance. God help us, if we ever really have a fight!"

She flung a cushion at him, and he threw it back. She then hit him with another cushion, and they had an enthusiastic cushion fight, until one rather old cushion burst, spreading feathers all over the place. They stood looking at the mess in guilty horror and then laughed. Jim cleared his throat, and said,

"Er, we're behaving like the twins, worse, in fact! Can I have another drink, and then I'll help clear this up? We'll get shot if anyone finds this mess. Come on, you get the bin bag, and the hoover, I'll get the brush."

It took some time to clear up, and several drinks. They left the conservatory reasonably tidy. When he walked off to the farm, he was a bit unsteady on his feet but hung onto the clarinet case under his arm.

Judith, feeling very relaxed, made a strong coffee and sat in the kitchen. She thought the day through, and then heard a small voice in her mind. It sounded very sad.

Zood. Meet Gode. Under, Soon?

Judith went to the cellar, lit a candle and waited. The smallest gatherer Garr appeared, transmitting sadness. It climbed onto her lap, and thought,

Round thing flat. Gode break. Zood angry?

It produced a rubber ball that had totally deflated. Gode was very upset, she could sense it.

Zood not angry. Zood understand. Gode want another one? Ball go flat when Gode bite ball. Gode not bad. Gode choose another ball, just for Gode.

She carried Gode to the old cupboard and got out the bag of balls.

Gode want ball ? Gode take new ball? Gode choose.

She gently put Gode on the ground and tipped out the balls. Gode moved around the balls and picked a shocking pink plastic one.

Gode take?

Gode take. Gode ball. Gode not bite ball.

The little creature put its ball aside, and Judith put the others back in the bag and put them away.

Gode crept back onto her lap, and had its tummy scratched, and then snuggled into her arm.

Gode ride Zood?

She carried the little Garr around, scratching its tummy and stroking its scales. It began to croon happily. It was crooning the tune of 'The Soldiers of our Queen'. She kissed it fondly between the eyes and received a toothy, wet kiss back, on the forehead.

Gode go. Zood kind.

Taking its ball, it went down the well, much happier.

She locked the trapdoor, replaced the rug, and went to bed.

Chapter Sixteen

Judith got up early and checked the diary for the day. Wesley had arranged her desk in her sitting room, and had even installed her personal computer for her. She saw that her day began early, and she had appointments all day. She knew the only time to herself would be before breakfast, and grabbing a radio, she walked down to the back gate, and on the way back, went into the conifer wood, behind the stable block. She came out onto a huge meadow, leading down to a stream. This had been recently cut and the horses had been put onto it. The foal was growing and came over to her, whinnying with pleasure.

She saw the moor rising up from the far side of the valley, beyond several more fields, some of which had cows in them. It was not a warm day, autumn had come in with a vengeance. She walked back past the stables but was called by Lucy, and was invited in for a cup of tea and some breakfast. Lucy and Sam had made the flat very nice, and it had been redecorated with taste. She was shown the nursery, and as she sat at the kitchen table, the cat rubbed against her legs and jumped on her lap. Lucy looked well and told Judith how happy she was. She asked to move her sewing machine to an attic room at the house, to use as a sewing room. Judith warned her of the imminent arrival of the art team, and said to use two rooms, one as a sewing room, and the other as a nursery, once the baby was old enough to be taken to the house. Sam asked if he could decorate it and make a second crib to put in there.

Sam went to fetch the minibus to collect the team, and Stuart and Lucy joined Judith as they walked to the house. Judith told Stuart about the book on plants in the library, and as soon as they arrived at the house, she went with him to find it. She asked him if he could find an Orientalis Tibetensis for Dennis, and he said he would do so.

Wesley arrived early, and gave Judith a bunch of flowers and a big kiss. She asked him what it was for.

"I saw Dr Tippett yesterday evening. He told me about the chance of the trip to the centre in Seattle, and of your offer. I don't know what to say. I never thought I'd be able to do it. Can I go? It will be very expensive. I have some savings. Sonia has some too, so she could come out and visit me. I would love to be more active, and this gives me the chance. Thank you, I'll pay it back over the years, I promise."

Judith said, "Wes, I had sort of assumed Sonia would go with you. I have had a bit of a windfall with the paintings, so we can afford for her to go. Why don't you use your savings for your house? Let me do this for you. When did you plan to go?"

"After the new year, if that is all right. We can train up my assistant, and Sonia can take leave then. My Mum has got all emotional over it, and she and Dad want to come and thank you. Can you stand her crying all over you?"

"I expect so, bring them out one weekend, and they can see where you work, talking of which, we had better get on. We have a full day."

"Dr Tippett said I must not overwork you, and you need more rest. I had no idea just how badly injured you had been. Shall I cancel some of your appointments? I didn't realise, I'm sorry."

"No. Let's get as much done as we can. I can rest over the weekend. Are you stopping for the Operatic Society this evening?"

"Yes, I forgot to tell you, they have offered to pay me to play, as accompanist, at least until the regular one comes back. I understand she is very ill. Mr Wynn and Mr Porter are coming this morning, and Celia. Tom is in court again. Mr McDuff is coming out for lunch. I have warned Mary, it's all right. Then at two, Rachel Sandell is coming, and at three, Karen Cooper, who I think will be a good assistant. Jim says he will be there, and Nora, who I haven't seen yet. Did you know there are people in the North Lodge?"

"Yes, that is Jake moving in, I expect Nora is helping him. His friends will be here for lunch too, and Sam and Liam are helping. It's all right, Mary knows. We also have the two art experts arriving, to take up several attic rooms, and Tanya, who has a room on the first floor, to which she and I have the only keys. She is going to restore some pictures for me. With kids around, we don't want them playing with her chemicals. Could you sign everyone in, and take their photos for the gallery?"

"Yes, and I want yours as well. I think we might have pictures of regular visitors, so we know who is meant to be here."

"Lucy wants a couple of rooms in the attic, one as a sewing room, the other as a day nursery. Sam will sort it out for her. Wes, sometime, can you find out how I can get the lake restocked with fish? I also want the garden pond stocked, not with exotic fish, just whatever is common, and will survive in there. I see no point in feeding herons with expensive koi carp."

"I didn't know you were into fishing"

"I'm not. I'm rather scared of fish when they are alive, but I think they are important to the ecostructure. I don't mind swimming with them or eating them. How's the new chair, by the way?"

"It's great. Very comfy. I'm going to get a coffee from the kitchen, do you want one?"

"Yes, I'll come with you."

Wes and Judith went to the kitchen, where Stuart was discussing the orangery with Sam. Judith pointed out that she had yet to see this

245

place, and asked him what state of repair it was in.

"Not bad. Judy, I need to talk to you about orchids. Both the orangery and the conservatory would be suitable for growing them. There is a lot of money in rare orchids, and we could even grow our own organic vanilla. I need to know where you got that orchid. It is beautiful and rare. I looked it up. Whoever gave it to you is someone I need to talk to. Please tell me?"

"Superintendent Carlton gave it to me. He grew it."

"You must have made a hit there, it is a precious gift. Why have you gone red?"

"I'm just hot, I'll ask him to talk to you. I am borrowing Sam and Liam, if I may, this morning, to help Jake move into the North Lodge, then to move some pictures for me. Have I mucked up your plans?"

"Not at all. I want to clear the sunken garden soon, there are some shrubs in there I want to prune. June asks if she can help me, and loves the place. What do you want done with the old tennis court? We took a great hay crop off it. Shall I restore it to a tennis court? Or we could turn it into a croquet green, have a think, and let me know. Can you come and look at it soon. I have several ideas for it. How about tomorrow evening?"

"I can't tomorrow, Stuart, I'm being taken to the opera in Leeds. How about the weekend, if you have time? Can I borrow Sam to take me to the station tomorrow morning?"

"Do you want me to pick you up in the evening? I was going to take the kids to the cinema. I'd rather pick you up, than risk you getting kidnapped by a stranger."

Remembering Jim's anger at her refusal to let anyone help, she accepted, and said she would ring him when she got to Skipton, and accepted his offer. He asked how she was getting to Skipton from Leeds and she told him that was organised. The doorbell went, just in time, and she went to answer it. Betty beat her to it, and Dot asked her if she had been plucking chickens in the conservatory. Dot smiled when she explained that she had burst a cushion in there.

"That would explain the missing cushion then, where did you put it? I'll get Lucy to make a new one and restuff it."

Judith produced the bin bag with the remains of the cushion, and handed it to Dot, who said,

"There is another cushion rather torn there, I'll get her to do that too."

Dot walked off, smiling to herself.

Mr Wynn, and Simon Porter were in the library with Celia and Wesley. Mr Wynn looked old and ill and Simon Porter just looked tired. He was an athletic man, with brown eyes set wide apart, and a goatee beard. Mr Wynn got up and introduced him to Judith. His handshake was firm and his gaze direct.

"Thank you so much for coming to see me. I have a proposition to put to you, which I would like you to consider. Mr Wynn, is it true that you are retiring? Yes, I had heard. Mr Porter, you are hoping to start on your own? How are the matters relating to my estates?"

They told her that they had located the money, or most of it, owing to her and the other clients, but there was a considerable amount missing. They had applied to the courts and had unfrozen the money and would pay her what they could. They would have a certain amount of insurance money to pay to all the clients. Judith asked Wesley to outline her proposal, and then asked Mr Porter if he wanted to take on her other properties. She suggested that he pay all the other defrauded clients, in full, and that the amount outstanding to her be considered as her investment to the new company he intended to form. They argued and discussed it, and finally he agreed to consider it. They discussed the proposals at some length, and Celia took notes to take to Tom. Over a coffee break, Judith suggested they meet again in a few days and they agreed to do so.

"Now we've thrashed that out, can someone tell me what to do with these horses? Who do they actually belong to, and what do I do now? One of the mares, at least, is pregnant. Can you find out for me, as a matter of urgency? They will have to come in soon and need looking after."

Mr Wynn said,

"Yes, I went to see Gerry the other day. He bought them as an investment, and they are quite valuable. He signed them over to me, so I will have to sell them. The mares were all covered with a top stallion, and I have all the papers. They are show jumpers and three day eventers. One of them, the grey, is, I believe, a potential dressage horse. If I sell them, we can repay you quite a lot. The foal should be a good buy for someone. I will pay you for their stabling, of course."

Judith asked,

"Do you have a valuation on them? Can you get one? I wondered if it might be a good investment for me to keep them. I'd have to get someone to look after them, but there is no rush to move them. I said I'd take them in lieu of money owed. We have plenty of grazing and hay and the stables. Would that help you, Mr Wynn? Or would it make it more complicated?"

Mr Wynn replied,

"It would be a good investment, and it would help. I suggest you sell the mare and foal and two of the others. I even have a couple of buyers. A famous show jumper wants them, but not the three who are not so good. Can I enquire and get back to you?"

They then talked more about the proposed business, and Judith felt quite redundant. She excused herself, and said she would see them at lunch. She assured them Wesley would speak for her and went to the kitchen. Mary was busy, with Haley, putting things in the oven. She asked if she could help.

"Yes, Judy, you can. Could you whip up that cream in the bowl for me?"

Judith did so, and then helped with chopping some carrots, and preparing and washing some broccoli. When they had time, they paused for breath and Mary said,

"I've got a bone to pick with you. What do you mean by sending my husband home half–cut, covered in feathers? He went all silly on me, and said you two had had a row. He was babbling on about having lost his temper, and having a go at you. Then he said something about a partnership, and ended by showing me the clarinet, which is beautiful. I couldn't make sense of what he said, and he had such a head this morning, I couldn't speak to him. Can you please tell me what happened? He hasn't been like that in years. Getting him drunk, I don't know!"

Judith told her what had happened, and admitted to the cushion fight, and begged Mary not to tell Dot. Haley was laughing with them and promised not to tell.

"I hope you had a hangover too, Judy. I haven't seen Jim that silly in a long time, but whatever you said, made him very happy. Thanks for the clarinet, we we're going to give it to Sally after school today. She has been studying hard, and has been worried, as we all have, about you. She is sensitive and it will be nice to give her a treat."

Betty came in, and said she had shown Mr McDuff to the Chinese Drawing Room, Tanya wanted a word and there were two men getting out of a taxi and where should she put them?

Judith went to see Gregory and asked him to join the others in the library, and then met Tanya in the hall, She was wearing a vivid pink outfit and sandals, instead of the blue one of the day before. The art experts were introduced and Tanya suggested they use the Drawing Room, before going to the basement. Judith showed them in and rang through to the lodge, to get Sam and Liam back to move the pictures up to the attics. The house was full of people and Wesley came out and asked everyone to sign in. He took them to his office, took their pictures and explained the house rules. They then dispersed and Judith helped lay the table in the dining room, and then the kitchen table.

As lunch was being dished up, she rang through to Nora and told them to come down to the house, and they arrived, in the 'paddy' wagon. John Arrowsmith asked after Sharon, but seemed to know more about her movements than Judith did. The population in the house divided for lunch. Stuart, Wesley, Judith and Tanya were in the dining room with the art experts and Mr Wynn, Celia, Gregory and Simon. Everyone else was in the kitchen. Mary had found some good wine which Gregory dealt with. The lunch was excellent and everyone was chatting happily, mainly about art, except Judith and Celia, who admitted to each other that their knowledge of the subject was limited. They talked about what Judith should wear to the opera. Hot water was served for coffee from the samovar, and everyone went to the drawing room, before dispersing around the house. Wesley, Celia and Gregory joined Judith in the library. Mr Wynn and Simon came in to take their leave, and thanked Judith.

They had about ten minutes before they expected Rachel, and Mary was fetched in, to be on the interview. Celia suggested she didn't need to be there, and asked if she could look round the house, and she would come down for the next interview if they wanted her to. She went off and they sat down and Judith told Gregory about the wine in the basement. He agreed to look at it. Betty showed in Rachel and Mr Sandell on the dot of two. He asked if he could wait somewhere while his daughter was interviewed. Judith got him to go with Betty, to sit somewhere and be given a drink.

In the interview, which Wesley started, she sat quietly, and he explained about the job, the hours, the rates of pay, and the conditions of employment. Mary took over and asked about her experience, and Gregory put the girl at her ease, by saying that her qualifications and CV were very good. Rachel was very nervous and rather overawed, but seemed a pleasant, cheerful girl. Judith offered to show her the kitchen, and the lower floor of the house, and they went off together. Rachel seemed terrified of her, but she soon relaxed, and confided that this was her first interview for a proper job. She said she was glad to help her parents by getting a job, and didn't mind working over the weekends if needed. She spoke of her younger brother's recent bar mitzvah, and of her family. Judith left her with her father in the Chinese Drawing Room and returned to the library where they all agreed she would be suitable. Wesley and Mary went to offer her the job, and Gregory then ran through the employment contract with them. Mr Sandell was most pleased, and thanked Judith profusely. It was arranged Rachel should start on the Monday and would be picked up in the minibus with the rest of the staff.

A terrible thunder storm broke as she left in her father's van, and the next visitor arrived. Jim rushed in, took off his coat and sat in the library, dripping onto the carpet. He grinned at Judith and shook hands with Gregory.

Karen was a chubby, short woman in her twenties. She had short ginger hair and thick glasses. She came in to the library, and knew Wesley, Jim and Celia. She produced her references and CV. She was married to a lorry driver, and lived in Applebeck. She had her own transport and was knowledgeable about farm matters. Judith left the questions to Wes, Jim and Celia. Gregory listened and Judith assessed Karen. She saw nothing to dislike and wondered if the woman had any character. She pushed gently against Karen's mind and felt a barrier of fear.

What is she frightened off? Can you see?

Mate. Mate hit, many time. Woman want escape Mate. Need work. Zood help.

Judith thought about it. Karen went with Wesley, to see the general office. Gregory said she had a good background, and Jim seemed happy with her farm knowledge. Celia said her secretarial skills were excellent. Judith said nothing, and Wesley came in, having left Karen in Mary's hands. The others agreed that she was suitable, and turned to Judith. Celia looked at Judith, and said,

"What's wrong, Judy? You don't seem convinced. Is there something we have missed?"

"I agree, she is ideal for the job, and has the skills we need. Offer her the job."

"You are pretty astute about people. Something is worrying you about her. What is it?"

"No, I just have the feeling something is worrying her, nothing to do with the job. I can't explain. How much do you know about her husband, Wes?"

"Not a lot. Seems nice enough, but basic. She is a farmer's daughter, and willing to help where she can. I like her. I could work with her. She could start straight away."

"Yes, I agree, give it to her. I'm just being silly. Whatever she is worried about, it is at home, not here, and none of my business."

Wesley went out to talk to Karen, and Celia asked Judith,

"What did you see, Judy? You saw something. Tell me."

"I think her husband is knocking her around, and she wants to escape him. Maybe we can help her, if it comes to it."

"Oh, yes, I see your problem. I don't know how you know, but it would account for the high neckline of her top, and the heavy make-up."

"Never mind, if she wants help, she'll soon know us well enough to ask for it."

Judith welcomed Karen to the staff, and left her with Wesley, while she went up to the attics to see the art experts. They didn't actually appear to belong to the human race, at least not the ones Judith understood, and she found them hard going, but managed to discover they had everything they needed. They were poring over three paintings, none of which Judith liked, and asked her what she intended for the pictures. She asked if the artist was known and they were shocked that she didn't know. She said she would probably sell them. All the paintings had been fetched from the basement and were stored in two adjoining rooms. She asked them to keep her informed, and left them to it, and went downstairs to find Gregory, who was watching the removal of the picture in the drawing room. It was taken carefully upstairs by Liam and Sam under Tanya's direction.

As soon as the lift was free, she took Gregory down to the basement, and showed him the wine racks and cases of bottles. He asked for a notepad and a decent light. He fetched a chair and began reverently brushing the dust off some bottles. She went upstairs, and found Karen and Wesley, who informed her that Karen had offered to start immediately. She smiled at Karen and asked if she could assist in the basement by listing bottles with Gregory. Karen fetched a pad and pen and followed Judith downstairs. Judith found chairs, a small table and some decent torches, and sent Sam down to join them, and left them listing wines.

She spoke to Wesley about the day's events, and told him she would be out the next day and he was in charge. He wanted to show her the estate office, and she saw it was a pleasant room, once the junk had been cleared, and he said the decorators would be in to do it in the morning. He wanted to get on with some calls, so she went to the kitchen and talked to Mary. Jim was sitting at the table and Mary ordered them both out, as they were in the way. Jim smiled, and said he was in the doghouse, and it was all Judy's fault. She agreed, and they ended up in the Chinese Drawing Room, while he spoke to her about the rare breeds he envisaged on the farm.

She answered the door to Dr Tippett, who came in and said he couldn't stop. He declined tea and acknowledged Jim. He then turned to Judith, and said,

"Have you had any rest today? I bet you haven't. Has she, Jim? No, I didn't think so. I mean it, you must slow down a bit! I've brought you something that should do the trick. Take one at night with a drink, and one at lunch time. Can you make her slow down, Jim? She will never get that leg right, if she doesn't."

Dr Tippett dashed off. Jim looked down at Judith and said,

"He is a good doctor, and if he says rest, then you must do so. How long has he been saying that?"

"Almost since I got here. I am all right, he's just fussing. The leg is heaps better than it was. I exercise it like he said. I do rest when I am tired, and if it aches too much. I'll have a good rest at the weekend, I promise."

Jim was looking at her, very thoughtfully. He had a very unnerving stare, with his bright blue eyes. He picked up the tablets and stalked into the kitchen, telling her to come with him. He put the tablets firmly on the table and called Mary over.

"Dr Tippett has just brought these for Judy. She is to take one at night with a drink, and one with lunch. She is supposed to be resting her leg, and the rest of her, and she isn't doing it. She should have been, since she got here. Judy, we cannot afford for anything to happen to you, as I said yesterday, and if you won't look after you, then we will. Can I leave it with you, Mary? I'm going to talk to Wesley, and you are going to sit down, Judy, now, before I get cross."

"You'll be locking me in my room next. All right, I'll sit down."

"Don't tempt me! Mary watch her, she is to sit down for a while, at least until tea. Give her some spuds to peel, or something."

He strode off, and Judy burst into laughter, and reached for the bottle. Mary grabbed it and said,

"You asked for that. Don't push him, he means it. So do I. He's probably raking Wes down, and telling him to cut down on your appointments. You **will** have a rest in the afternoons, and I will see you get these at the right time. Spuds it is, then. We need some for tea tonight."

"Remind me not to get Jim drunk again, is he always this masterful?"

"Only when he cares. Did you say you are going out tomorrow? Good, you need a break. Stuart says he is picking you up in the evening. Opera is it? Who are you going with?"

"A friend, I'll be quite safe, I took Jim's advice, and accepted Stuart's offer to bring me back. I want to do some shopping in Leeds, before the opera. I'll have tea, and a break at a nice hotel."

Gregory, Sam and Karen arrived and begged a cup of tea. Judith got up to make it, but was pushed back down by a firm hand, and saw Jim had followed them in. Sam made the tea, and Gregory sat down, and told them all,

"In the basement, you have some of the finest wines I have ever seen, also some of the oldest. You also have fine cognacs, whiskeys, ports, and champagne. Some of them would fetch a great deal of money. They have been well laid down, and are a considerable investment. I would suggest you sell some, they are so rare, that they would only be of interest to collectors. Young Karen here has kindly offered to list them all. I think you should keep a lot, for consumption and as an investment, but I have indicated which. Have you any other interesting secrets lurking around the house? This establishment is turning into a veritable treasure trove."

Jim's hand squeezed her shoulder, and he said, "Judy won't be entering any more adventures just yet. She is going to get some rest, even if we have to make her."

"Gregory, can you stay for tea? Before my keepers lock me away in the Folly, to be fed on bread and water until I behave?"

"Thank you, I would love to. Can I stay to hear the singing tonight too? Wesley has offered me a lift back. Don't look to me for sympathy, young woman. If you need to rest, you should do so."

Jim chuckled and sat down. When Judith had finished the vegetables, she asked for another task, and was given some beans to string.

Later, she got up and went up to her room, and relaxed in a bath, and changed into fresh clothes for the evening, and went down to the ball room, to see the chairs were out, but Sam came in and told her it was all done, and tea was nearly ready in the kitchen. Celia and Gregory had stayed on with Bill and Dot, and the boys and Charlotte, Sally and June and Stuart. Lucy and Jake were sitting with Nora. After they had eaten, Jim gave Sally the box containing the clarinet. She opened it and gasped. She took it out of the case, and handled it as if it were made of gossamer. She looked at her parents in wonder, and then round the table at everyone else. Jim said,

"Judy and Wes tell me you need this, and Judy wants you to do well with it."

Sally sat down and said, "Oh thank you, thank you! It is the best thing I could have had, thank you everyone." She carefully replaced it in its case, and hugged Judy and her parents, and then Wesley. "Can I try it now?" She rushed off to the music room. Wesley followed her, with Charlotte and June.

Judith got up to help clear away the meal but no one would let her. Gregory and Celia suggested sitting in the drawing room, where a fire had been lit. Judith sat, telling them all about the previous week and they had a pleasant hour, chatting. Soon, the operatic members turned up and Wesley could be heard playing. Judith went through and was soon greeted by dozens of people all dying to find out about her recent adventures. Jim came to her rescue and firmly told everyone that she was still recovering from her injuries and was supposed to be resting, and he made her sit down, and Nora sat on one side of her, and Celia on the other, in the back row of the altos. Behind her was a solid row of Bill, Jim and Jake. She went to get a score, but was handed one by Jake.

The rehearsal began, with Margaret getting them to sing through several choruses, for which they needed to stand. They learned the harmonies and tried again. At halftime, tea was produced by Mary, and several of the women helpers from the society. Judith got up to fetch a cup, and Tim and Chris appeared with one and a plate of biscuits. She thanked them, and then turned to leave the room. Jim, who was standing talking to two of the tenors, politely excused himself from them and caught up with her by the door. She hissed,

"Jim, I will go to the loo unaccompanied! I know you are trying to protect me, but this is necessary!"

Jim backed off and she went up to her room, and used the loo in her bathroom. She did feel very tired and wanted to get to her bed, and when she returned to the ballroom, she sat meekly in her chair, until everyone was settled. Jim, Stuart and Sam regarded her suspiciously, and Jake hovered around her until the singing restarted. She could sense the Garr enjoying the music, but they didn't join in. At nine thirty, the rehearsal was over and she went to help clear the chairs. Sam had taken a large group back to the village in the minibus, and Mary, Nora, Lucy and June were tidying up. As she picked up a chair to move it, Stuart took it from her hands, and wouldn't let her move anything for the rest of the evening. Nora walked down the drive with Jake, Sam returned from the village, and took Stuart, Lucy and Stuart's family back to the stable block. When Wesley had gone, with Celia and Gregory, Judith went into the kitchen. The Morpeth family were just preparing to go. Mary handed her a cup of chocolate and a tablet.

"Thanks, Mary, I must admit I'm ready for bed. I'll take this upstairs with me, and drink it up there."

"No. You drink it now, and take the pill. Jim doesn't think you will take it, just do it."

Judith took the pill and drank the cocoa, and looked menacingly at Jim, who she knew was laughing at her. As they left she locked the door, and thought after him, *Bully*.

It really shook her when she heard him reply.

Next time, do as you're told. Good night Judy. Sleep well.

Chapter Seventeen

Judith finally woke, to hear people moving round the house. She got up, showered, dressed, and went downstairs, and was horrified to find it was well after nine. She was given a breakfast tray and told to eat. Mary asked how she had slept, and told her she should lie in more often. Judy felt rather woolly–headed, and said so. She ate her breakfast, and went to the estate office to see Karen.

Karen was busy typing a letter on the computer, and said she had everything she wanted. She handed Judith a list of the wines, and told her Gregory was calling for it later in the day. Judith went in to Wesley, and asked if he needed anything from Leeds. He said he would give her a list before she left. Nora already had one, which she gave to Judith. Jake came in and said he would be driving Judith to the station, not Stuart, but that Stuart would be fetching her. She sat in her sitting room, and compiled a list of her own. She collected her bag from the bedroom, and a front door key, and Jake drove her to the station, in time for the 10.32. She purchased a ticket, from a large, genial, and helpful station master.

The station was immaculate, with pots of flowers on the platforms, and the waiting room, which included the ticket office, had a real coal fire going in the hearth. Everything was painted in Midland colours, and was a showpiece. Jake waited until the train came in and handed her bag to her. The station master handed up her stick. She made herself comfy, and looked out of the window for a while, until her ticket was checked by the conductor. He recognised her from the television, and told her if anyone bothered her, he would throw them off!

It took an hour to get to Leeds where the station was huge, and being renovated. She limped down the platform and was offered assistance by a nice young woman in a turquoise uniform jacket.

Once out of the station, she walked to the shopping centre and, armed with her lists, purchased most of the items required. In a sports shop, she bought another bag of balls, and laden with her purchases, she went to the posh department store in the shopping centre. Her first visit was to a hairdresser there, and then she tried on dresses, shoes, and jackets. She finally found an outfit that was suitable for the evening. and purchased it and some other clothes as well. She arranged for the delivery of her shopping and went to an old–fashioned hotel for lunch. She took a room for the day, and then walked to an art gallery and spent a happy afternoon there, returning to the hotel, where she showered, changed and had tea.

She settled up and just before seven, walked round the corner to the theatre and waited in the lobby. It was rather crowded and she had to stand. Someone took a photograph of her, and she was annoyed to find it was a press photographer. A reporter was soon pestering her, and she was about to ask the assistance of the foyer staff, when Dennis, looking very smart in a dinner jacket, appeared as if by magic, and taking her arm in a firm grip, ushered her through the crowd and upstairs to a box. He complimented her on her appearance, and offered her a drink. She nodded. He produced champagne, and asked her about the day and just how much trouble she had got into!

She was annoyed at the reporter and he picked it up. He told her not to worry. After a visit to the Ladies, she settled down in the box and he fetched a programme and told her how the case was progressing. He picked up her hand and looked carefully at the ring she was wearing.

"That's a fine diamond, it's an unusual ring. It goes with your pendant. Black diamonds are very rare, I believe. Wherever did you get this jewellery? It is worth a fortune, you should be careful, wearing it in a place like Leeds."

"It came with the house. It is very old. I like them." *You look very dashing!*

Judy, you look fabulous, very sexy. I wish I could get you a ring like that. I have to work on Saturday, can I take you out for Sunday lunch?

No. I will take you. If this is going anywhere, I must have my independence. It is not yet a year since Clive was killed. Don't rush me, Dennis.

I'm falling in love with you.

I know. I am feeling the same way, but I must keep my independence. If we do get together, and it is only if, I don't want to be tied down.

You'd only bloody escape! I couldn't offer you much, I'm always at work.

Is that why your first marriage broke up?

Sort of. She went off with my best mate. I was never there for her.

Let's take things slow, talk about it Sunday?

The lights went down, and the overture began. She had a wonderful evening, and Dennis was a knowledgeable and comfortable companion. They had more champagne in the interval, and when the performance ended, they left together, and got into a taxi, but not before they had to evade a posse of press. They went to a restaurant for a light supper, and then a car picked them up, and they were driven to Skipton. Judith rang Stuart en route, and told him where she could be picked up.

Dennis managed to steal a kiss, or two, before Stuart arrived at Dennis' house, and was asked in for a drink. Over a coffee, they talked about orchids, and then she left, thanking him for a wonderful evening, and he kissed her goodnight.

I know I love you. I cannot stop thinking about you.

That's fine, when I even think about you, I blush! I spend the whole day saying I'm hot!

Goodnight, sweetheart! Take care of yourself.

I am able to look after myself.

Not from what I have seen. You dice with death, without even thinking about it.

That's not fair. That hurt!

I know, it might make you more careful. I need you to stay alive, if only to prove the case!

Of course, that is all? I'll consider trying to stay alive, just for the case!

Stuart drove some distance, before he said something.

"That's how the wind blows, is it? It's all right, I won't tell a soul."

"Like hell you won't! Everyone will know by breakfast. Don't read too much into it, we are just friends. He's coming out Sunday, and we're going out for lunch. You can talk to him about orchids then, if you want to. How was the cinema?"

Stuart smiled and then told her about the film. He dropped her off at the front door, and she let herself in.

Garr, is everything all right, do you need anything?

Garr good. Zood happy, Zood sleep.

By her bed was a glass of milk, a tablet, and a note, which said 'Take Me'.

She took the tablet, and put her clothes away. She unpacked her bag, took off the ring and put it in her wall safe.

She was confused. She still grieved deeply for Clive, but also wanted Dennis. She felt guilty. Being as rich as she was, how could she ever know who wanted her for her money? No decent bloke would propose to her, because they would know she would never know.

It was all very worrying.

She lay on the bed and tried to make sense of it. She slept, eventually, and woke quite early, and went down to the basement with some left over food and a bag of sugar. For an hour, she played with the young Garr, Gode wanting to be carried. Gode brought her its ball to throw several times, and then she said she must go.

Zood worry. Zood live life for now. Mate gone, Niss here.

They took the food and she went up to face the staff at breakfast. She checked the post and then went up to the art rooms, and looked at the pictures they were examining. She picked one Matisse to keep, and the rest she put on the 'for sale' list. Tanya was much more interesting, as she explained the process she was using. She had revealed a small corner, but nothing could be seen of the actual picture.

Judith walked down to the horses, taking some apples and carrots, and some sugar lumps. She was called on the radio, asking her to return to the house. Gregory had arrived, and said he had arranged for some of the wine to go in to a high class sale in London. He wanted a decision. She walked back along the drive, thinking about the problem.

As she reached the front door she met Jim, who asked her if she had walked down to see the horses. She nodded. She talked to Gregory and negotiated a deal with him for the sale of the wine he advised disposing of. She invited him for lunch, and they had a sherry before they went in to the meal. Over lunch, talk was mainly about the Landrover and the van, both of which had arrived. The signwriter was doing all the estate vehicles, except the Astra, the next week.

Jim asked, "Did you enjoy the opera last night, Judy?"

"Yes, very much. It is one of my favourites. I had a good day. Wes, there should be some deliveries for me. I did some shopping while I was in Leeds. Then I went to an art gallery for the afternoon. Very restful. The only unpleasant thing was the press at the opera house. The opera was wonderful. I really enjoyed it, and Stuart very kindly picked me up afterwards. I got a lift to Skipton."

"I am glad you enjoyed it. I'm quite sure you walked miles in town, and from what I know of art galleries, you walked miles there too. I thought you were supposed to be resting. How are you today?" She sensed his disapproval.

"I'm fine, yesterday did me good. I plan to have a quiet afternoon, we have the staff meeting, and I have to do some reports with Wes."

Liar, you're tired.

I'm not too bad. Stop bullying me.

No. I won't. Something is worrying you, do you want to talk about it?

It's personal. I've got to sort it out myself.

I'm here if you need me.

How long have you been able to think talk?

Since you came, and I started to hear you.

Does it scare you?

No. It could be useful.

Yes, but don't eavesdrop too much. You might hear something you didn't want to!

Fine, but I **do** *know when you are tired, You are, go to bed after the meeting.*

I might.

Over coffee, Mary presented her with her tablet, which she sneaked into her pocket, not wanting to fall asleep in the middle of the meeting.

She caught up with paper work during the next hour and they held the meeting in the staff room. She welcomed Karen, and they discussed a number of things, and Jake gave some advice on security and how to deal with the press, who were still hanging round the village.

As Wesley wound the meeting up, he handed over to Jim, who said he had an announcement to make.

"Judith has been with us for a month now, and she has given all of us hope, and a very well–paid job. She has been good to every one of us, and through all of this and the danger she has been in, she has coped on her own and has been more worried about our safety than her own. Since she has been here, our lives have been turned upside down, inside out and backwards. She has become a friend to everyone."

Jim, you're embarrassing me.

Shut up, and sit down. I haven't finished.

"We realise how lonely you have been, for a long time, Judy. The other day we made a bargain, you gave us a present, you have given us all presents, in many ways. We got together, last week, when you were going through all that hell, and everyone chipped in, and I mean everyone, and we got you a present. You promised to accept it, so, Stuart, would you bring it in?"

Sam and Stuart went out, and were gone some time. Sam came and put two huge bin bags on the floor, full of things, including something that clanked, and held the door open. Judith watched a little, woolly, liver–brown head peer round the door, and in waddled an Irish Water Spaniel puppy. Judith had had a Water Spaniel before and knew what it was. She knelt on the floor and called it and it came lolloping over to her. She picked it up and it licked her chin. She looked at it and saw it was a bitch. She held it in her arms and cuddled it. It lovingly peed down her front. She turned to the staff and said,

"I accept your gift, with all my heart, and I thank you for her. Yes, I have been lonely, and yes, this is my chosen breed. I shall love her and she will be happy here. I am. In the past month, I have found the place I want to be, and a reason, no several reasons, for living here, indeed for living at all. I shall call this wonderful creature Zan. I will no longer be alone. Now before I burst into tears, let me take her out for another wee."

She went out to the rough area just off the lawn, near the shrubbery, and Jim went with her.

"She has had all her jabs, she is chipped, vetted, and insured. We had more than enough, so we have dog beds, bowls, food, and collar and leads. Her ID disk has the Hall emblem on it. Are you really happy with her?"

Jim, she is wonderful. You must have talked to Sharon.

"She is, according to her breeder, house trained. I doubt it, but she is a healthy wee pup." *Have fun with her.*

Jim, I love her. She is just what I need. Thank you.

Judith spent twenty minutes playing with Zan, before the happy puppy fell asleep in her sitting room, and she crashed out beside it on the settee.

She woke a little later when Zan yelped to go out. Judith went out in the garden and the puppy gambolled along beside her until it had done what it wanted. She praised it and came back in. Wesley said Dennis was on the phone and Judith took the phone from him. As he handed it over, Wesley winked. She blushed. Dennis wanted to warn her that the papers were carrying the picture of her at the opera, and worse, of him. She told him about the puppy, and he said he already knew about it. He told her he would be out on Sunday and they could go to the Ugly Imp where Toby would allow the pup in.

Everyone was leaving and Mary asked Judith to lunch on the Saturday. She looked at Zan, who was quietly chewing Jim's shoelaces, and said she could come too.

That evening Judith took Zan down to the basement. She unlocked the cellar door and waited for the Garr.

I have a puppy with me. Please be kind to it. I want it to know you. I have called it Zan.

Garr know. Zan good name. Garr young will play with Zan. Other Zan have dogs. All good friend with Garr.

They came to the basement and Zan was curious but not aggressive. Soon the Garr and Zan were playing happily together in an enthusiastic romp over Gode's ball.

Zood worry over Niss. Why Zood worry?

If we get close, I am worried I will betray you to him. Zan say you only have female guardian. I need you more than Niss. I have a duty to you.

Zood not worry. Guardian can be male. Painter of pictures male. Niss not threat. When ready, Garr show to Niss. Niss and Zood can be mates. He love Zood. Wants spend life with Zood. Niss special.

Judith looked on her lap, to find Zan and Gode fast asleep in each other's paws. Goy came close, and touched Judith.

Goy want Gode. Zood want small Zan. Young sleep.

Thank you, Goy. You will look after Zan, and the animals on the estate, as well as me?

Garr guard, Zood guard. Niss guard. Zood sleep.

Judith took Zan upstairs and after a short dispute, which she won, Zan lay beside the bed, and not on it, on an old blanket.

Chapter Eighteen

Porthwaite Hall

January

My dear Jack,

Thank you so much for your Christmas card and gift. Zan loves her new bed. I thought I would bring you up–to–date with life here.

⠀⠀. The estate is now running quite smoothly. I have an excellent, loyal staff, and recently we have employed a new shepherd. She has moved in with four dogs to the other farmhouse. I went with Jim to some auctions, and we now have some splendid stock. We sold four of the horses and the foal, and the other two are worked daily by me or the groom, a nice woman. I use the horses, most days, to get round the estate. Her husband is an agricultural mechanic, and very handy around the farms.

The gardens are beginning to take shape, and Stuart is doing wonders. He is breeding orchids by the dozen, the best of which are in the conservatory. The lawns are neat and tidy, and the cricket pitch is taking shape, as is the croquet lawn. The vegetable garden is now Bill's domain, and Stuart has started on the best rose garden in the world! The lake is restocked with fish, much to the heron's delight. Zan insists on swimming in it most days. There are Castlemilk Moorit sheep in the meadow, on the other side of the lake.

I have my own bit of garden, one of the walled ones, where I train Zan. When I am in there, I am left alone, unless I invite anyone in.

My staff get on well. Nora and Jake have announced they will be getting married in the spring. Liam, much to everyone's surprise, has fallen for Rachel, our assistant cook, who is very protective of him. She seems taken with him. Wesley is engaged to his girlfriend Sonia, and he is going for his operation in the States next week. Karen, our secretary, has had a lot of problems. Her husband was knocking her around, and she eventually confided in me. She stayed here for a while and was divorcing him. He came here and tried to get at her, but Zan held him and Liam and Jim threw him out. He came back later that night, and something spooked him, and he was found, a mile or so down the road, after having been involved in a hit and run accident. He was horribly mutilated. He must have been dragged by a vehicle. They never found it though. She was pretty upset, but has moved back into the village, and is now coping well.

Lucy's baby is due any day now, and all seems to be going well. Jim and Mary are also due to have another baby in the summer. I have been asked to be godmother to both. Betty, Haley and Dot are happy, and look after me very well. Sharon has got her posting, she is going to Skipton, not far from here. She is going out with our local bobby, John Arrowsmith. We had a great weekend when her course came to stay here. She is very happy and very popular. She is buying a house in Applebeck. Sally has won a scholarship to study music. I gave her Susan's oboe for Christmas. Charlotte is studying hard, hoping to be a doctor. Tim and Chris are firm friends with Julian, and all three are always in some scrape or other.

Reg Hall has come back to work a new man, and his wife seems to be looking after him. His son, Brian, is in a secure unit. The trial should be around Easter, I'm not looking forward to it. I understand Francis is being investigated for lots of other things, I had no idea Ingrid was so involved. It is good of Peter and Jane to take on the children. I have made a contribution to their school fees. I cannot forgive Francis, he plotted to murder me, and when I heard Ingrid knew, I didn't feel too happy with her either.

Cummings has named names, and is talking to the police and customs. A lot of the money has been repaid. What I can never forgive him for, is the destruction of Albert Wynn. The poor man died just before Christmas, of a stroke. I know he had been ill, but this finished him. I went to the funeral. It was a sad affair. Simon Porter was really cut up. Simon has taken on the job of land agent for me, and is doing a good job. I am a sleeping partner in his business. The farm is now a partnership, between me and Jim. We have formed a company to set up the farm shop and marketing.

I sold some of the wine found in the house, don't worry, I can still provide a good cellar! Gregory is a frequent visitor, and a good friend, and he sends his regards. The sale of some of the paintings found in the house has made a lot of space in the basement. They fetched a fabulous price, most of which I have put into a trust to keep the estate intact. I paid for a new church hall, and the repairs to the church roof, and the new scout hut, with just some of the money from the Reubens. I think the vicar likes me! I kept a few paintings I liked, portraits of a few previous occupants, and some special favourites, all of which are still being restored. Tanya has become a good friend, as has Celia, and we sometimes go out for the day together.

I took all the staff and their families for a day out just before Christmas. The children had a day at a theme park, and the adults went to a show. We all had a good time. We had a Christmas party here, too. I got caterers in, and asked all the villagers and staff. Jake dressed up as Father Christmas and actually made it down the chimney! All my friends came, even Albert Wynn. He died two days later. He gave me a lovely gift, of a silver dog whistle, which I shall treasure. Tom sends his regards, he says he is making a lot of money out of me, but he has been a real friend.

Jim and Mary and Nora are firm friends. Jim bullies me a bit, he watches over me. If he thinks I am tired, or doing too much, he gives me a hard time. Dr Tippett too. They guard me like a dog with a favourite bone. I am trying to learn some farming skills, and work there when I can. It is only recently that Dr Tippett has let me. The leg will never be right, but it is stronger, and I can do most things, but in moderation.

The carol service in the church was lovely. I was asked to read one of the lessons. Tim sang a solo, and Chris and Julian did a duet.

There is much to do yet, things are far from running perfectly, but we start a residential course here in February. The art experts have left now, and most evenings I have the house to myself. The house and I go together. I am happy here. I think I always will be. I feel very safe. Hopefully, my exciting adventures are over! Please, come and stay soon.

Could you give the enclosed letter to Clive's mother for me, and stay with her while she reads it? I feel she should be the first to know, and I would appreciate knowing how she feels about it.

Toby and Dee from the Ugly Imp have told me they want to retire soon. They have a house in Devon to which they will go. I have offered the management to Mike and Marion, if they are interested. It is a profitable pub, and I await their reply

As I write, the snow is falling, and this place is so stunningly beautiful it quite takes my breath away. Zan wants to go and play in it, and I must post the letters, before we get snowed in.

Your grateful friend,
Judy Swallow.

****

Porthwaite Hall

January

Dearest Mum,

Thank you for your letters. It has been lovely to keep in touch with you. I'm so glad you enjoyed the cruise. I hope it did you good. I am so sorry about Ingrid and Francis. It must be a great worry for you. I feel that I was the catalyst in bringing their involvement to light. I can never forget that they wished to kill me, but in time I may forgive them.

As you know, I loved Clive very much. I wanted to spend the rest of my life with him. When he was killed, I felt there was nothing left to make me happy. You were kind to me, and I thank you. I never meant to bring trouble on you. I moved to Yorkshire to remember him, not forget him, and I never could forget what we had. Please, don't think me disloyal.

I have met another man, who cares for me. In many ways he is like Clive. I care deeply for him. His name is Dennis Carlton. He asked me to marry him yesterday, and I accepted. He knows he will never take Clive away, but we have a bond so strong, that I believe it cannot be broken. Dennis insists on a pre-nuptial agreement, as he says he never wants my money. I have a way of knowing that is true. He needs to work away a lot, and I will still have the house to myself most of the time. You will always be welcome here, as a loved relative. We will be married in the spring, after the court case is over, and live here. He has a good career, and has just been promoted. He loves gardening and music and he wants to share the rest of his life with me. It is important to me that you understand. I will never forget Clive, he will always be a part of me. If anything should happen to me, Sharon will inherit this house.

Please forgive me,
Judith.

****

Hinton House
Blewett Lane,
Somerset,

My dearest Judith,

Thank you for your letter, I read it when my brother Jack gave it to me. I knew that this could happen, and, indeed, hoped it would do so. Clive loved you, because he saw something special in you, and because you were brave and true, and you loved life, as he did. He would never have wanted you to give up, or to grieve for him for ever. He always said that life must go on, and I know he would approve. If you love this Dennis, then love him for Clive too. I want you to be happy, as Clive would have. If you don't mind, I would rather not come to the wedding, but I wish you every happiness in the world. I don't just understand, I approve! Please, Judith, keep in touch. Nothing that has happened is your fault. Ingrid has always been greedy, and Francis has made my life hell, and I do not intend to help him.

Just be happy, and give all that love you have to this man. I hope he deserves you.

Esther Swallow.